IN THE HOUSE OF FIVE DRAGONS

ERICA LINDQUIST & ARON CHRISTENSEN

LOOSE LEAF
STORIES

This is a work of fiction.
All characters, organizations, places and events portrayed in this book
are either the product of the authors' imagination or are used fictitiously.

Find more of our books at LLStories.com

*For Kristin Lindquist
and Evan Christensen*

1

THE ROAD

"There are terrible beasts that lurk inside us all. Dragons, if you will, that consume and corrupt from within: greed, lust, rage, pride and fear. The Terran soul is home to monsters far worse than those of any story."

— UTORA MAESUS

Ssssh.

Ssssh.

Ssssh.

His uneven steps whispered through the dry grass like a mother shushing her child. The long summer had turned the grass into brittle blades that snapped and crumbled at the slightest touch. Hot wind rippled the hillside and stirred the grass into dry yellow waves. A few droning bees and bright butterflies fluttered through the heat in search of the last late-season blossoms.

The man who could not remember his name crushed them all under steel-shod boots. Long, wild black hair tickled at his sweaty, windburnt neck.

Ssssh.

Ssssh.

Clank.

He stopped. The new sound dragged his gaze down in weary wonderment. The yellowing grass gave way suddenly, sliced as though by the blade of a knife to reveal the bones beneath – worn and dusty stones each cut and fitted together. They were cracked and chipped with wear.

He crouched down and trailed his hand over the hard, alien thing winding through the grass. Was it real? Whose idea was this? A scarred metal cap on his forefinger scraped unpleasantly against broken stones.

What...?

Men could lift and cut rocks, he remembered. With their hands. And lay them together to make trails that led between important things. These rock-rivers had... names. The certainty of it weighed solidly in the palm of his mind. They had names, titles that didn't change from one moment to the next, depending upon the song and who was winning.

Real names.

Terran names.

Roads! I remember now. Terrans have to take the long way between places. They travel on roads that stretch like a great spider's web across their land.

But where did *this* road lead?

The blazing summer sun pried at his sore red skin with tiny, burning fingers. With an effort, he lifted his eyes again and they stung in the bright daylight. A pale, angular smear shone on the horizon. It glittered like desire. A city, sprawling over two sloping hills and covering them like jeweled turtles' shells. To the east, the Mazren River flowed in a slow pewter arc around the city.

A city.

Dormaen.

Home.

My home.

The nameless man braced himself against the sharp pain that he knew was coming, the searing and screaming attack that was the Shatter's always-answer to thoughts of home. He armored his memories in bristling blades of howling rage. They would not take the last shreds of him!

But the sharp, tearing despair never came. All remained still. He felt pain, but it was only a distant, disconnected sort. It seemed no more real than the sun that burned the back of his neck or the sticky blood oozing from gashes in his numb, wooden flesh.

He lowered his streaming eyes again and staggered along the cracked road toward Dormaen.

Clank.

Clank.

Home.

Clank.

Time marched on far more evenly than the wounded man. His chin – dark with a week of stubble – sagged down to his chest, following the sun as it sank toward the horizon. His body was trembling, weak. Even fear would not rouse it. Want and longing did nothing to banish the uncomfortable gnawing sensation deep inside his skin.

What was wrong with him? He craved something. His body begged for it in an alien voice, grumbling loudly. There was something familiar about it all. He had known this feeling once, long ago, and known it very well.

Before, in ice and stone, while fire howled down on us.

His knees went suddenly soft as indecision. Finally unable to bear his weight, they buckled and he collapsed onto the road with a clatter of steel. His eyes were sticky and swollen. They fell to angry, glowering slits, and then closed completely.

Am I finally dying?

Not content with his vision, the darkness surged up from the depths and swallowed his thoughts.

The tree-tower called the Uprising tossed and creaked in an imaginary wind. It rose majestically – smooth, rough and multi-form – from the arched back of a great hill that rose from glassy nothing. Great leaves, bleak-browned by age and disuse, fell and swirled like smoke rising the wrong way.

But the air of the Uprising remained still, taut with anticipation. Watching.

Waiting.

The Shatter. The Shatter. They shatter.

A serpent made of cloudy rain and stars coiled in the branches of the leaning old tree-tower, listening. The malachite nightingale perched beside it coughed sickly, shuddering loose a green fragment of stone from under his wing. It fell and bounced off another branch. It twisted into an oversized blue snowflake, then scrawled inky to the distant ground. The serpent glittered comfortingly at the nightingale.

Where's he going, Flickerdim? asked the malachite bird.

A city. He'll be there in a few days, thought the snake-shape.

Which city?

Home, Flickerdim decided in a flash of starlight. *He's finally going home, Stumble. To his birthplace. It's the center of his world, even after all these years. After all he's done. All we've done to him. He's going back to the place where he left his life.*

What's he looking for there? His life? It's old *now,* griped the little curiosity, Stumble, with the sulky certainty of the young.

Home never gets old, Flickerdim said.

Empty wind rattled the great forest tower again. The sky high above twisted in on itself and silent thunder boomed all through the Uprising. Under the hill, the sky remained placid, colorless. For now, the Shatter waited. They had time. Stumble flexed his stripy green wings restlessly.

Wait, wait! What's he doing now? he asked suddenly. *He fell down!*

He's sleeping, said Flickerdim. *His kind does it with some frequency. It is a strange thing, a little death every night, and then rebirth when the sun rises.*

When will he be done? We need him. Make him hurry!

We cannot rush him, Stumble. We must give him time.

But there isn't time! Not for us.

All the more reason we must give him what little we have left.

2

HATCHLING

"The veil between Terra and Alterra is more like skin than stone. If you hold your hand up to a bright lamp, you can quite clearly see the shape of the bones and even the blood that runs beneath. We know what lies beyond our world, Huron. We know that they can see our blood, too, even better than we can."

— LIAM IO

ORTHO'S LUNGS were on fire. His eyes filled with tears. The smoke choked him and raised sour acid at the back of his throat. He coughed and spat, but burning smoke clung to his breath like a horribly inverted winter chill. Ortho wiped his nose and mouth on his sleeve, almost dropping the pipe.

Beside him, Jaesun chuckled and leaned back against the wall. The older VEIL knight was convinced that he could not handle the tobacco, but Ortho was determined to prove him wrong. Ortho braced himself and sucked down another mouthful of stinging, bitter smoke. How did anyone enjoy this stuff? He coughed and Jaesun laughed again.

"Ah, shut it," Ortho rasped. At least the pipe gave his voice a properly rough, growling quality.

"Little boys need little toys," Jaesun said with the world-weary air of a lecturn with his most troublesome students. "Give it here."

"I'm not done yet!"

"You'll be done breathing, boy, if you drool all over my pipe anymore."

Ortho licked his burning lips. He didn't dignify Jaesun with a response, but handed back the shiny hywood pipe. Jaesun smirked and wiped the stem on the black sleeve of his saela, then held it up as if to toast the younger knight's failure. Jaesun put it in his mouth, puffed a few times and then blew a long stream of gray smoke into the clear blue sky. Ortho rolled his eyes and turned his attention back to the city.

Mazrem Square was busy today. It was always busy, even on worship days. Most everyone in Dormaen passed through the plaza at some point during their week. Visitors came from all over the fifty provinces to pay their respects to the memory of the Carcaen Empire's greatest hero. Outside the imperial palace and the wealthy Everstone district, Mazrem Square was the most important place in all of Dormaen. And here in the capital city of Carce and center of the largest empire in history, that was saying something.

Mazrem Square was not an actual square, but a circular agora where the four main roads of the city crossed one another. On the north face was the popular Vaestra Amphitheater, surrounded by green grass and golden-leaved aspen trees. A plaza stretched out beyond them, paved all in marble and dotted with sculptures and carved benches under the tall hedges.

Visitors rested, shared gossip and news in the fragrant company of jasmine and lilies. Across the wide white road that encircled the plaza, Mazrem Square kept good company: the best of Dormaen's universities, high-rent and high-priced stores, laweries and even a few small, outrageously expensive homes.

Ortho surveyed the crowd that filled Mazrem Square. Like him, most were native to the old kingdom of Carce – tall and dusky-skinned, with dark eyes and straight black hair. But there were hundreds, perhaps thousands, from the rest of Carce's fifty provinces: pale Lynceans, thick-limbed men from Erastrasus and slender, veiled women from Caspin, Nianese in their gray wool cloaks despite the heat, midnight-skinned Jumaari, even Suvestri decorated in flashing gold jewelry.

In the center of it all rose Ortho's charge: a statue of the hero himself: Captain Rikard Mazrem. The monument was carved ten times life size in pristine alabaster and girded in titanic armor. Standing guard over his statue was one of VEIL's least exciting duties, but Ortho never turned down the chance, even if it meant working with Jaesun for the day.

Captain Mazrem's face always captivated Ortho. The dark jasper eyes were wise and kind the way no living man's could ever be. The statue's expression was properly grave, heavy with the worries of an infant empire and his dying army. But there always seemed to be a small, secretive smile playing about his stone lips, as if Captain Mazrem knew that his sacrifice would someday be immortalized in the very heart of the nation he died for. A fluted marble pedestal bore a simple, elegant bronze plaque:

IN REVERENT MEMORY OF LORD-CAPTAIN RIKARD CAELIS MAZREM

MAY ALL OF CARCE PROVE WORTHY OF HIS SACRIFICE

A short fence surrounded Mazrem's statue, almost completely obscured by piles of offerings left over from festivals the week before in celebration of the thirtieth anniversary of Lord-Captain Mazrem's astonishing victory and tragic death in Njorn Pass. There were flowers, wilting and drying in the late summer heat. Even now, the delicate blossoms clung to their color and gentle scents. There were effigies and incense, colorful stones and candles, ribbons and even several sealed jars containing secret, personal gifts to Captain Mazrem. Prayers written on scraps of paper stuck out from between the offerings like pale imploring hands, reaching up toward Rikard Mazrem.

After a few puffs, Jaesun offered his pipe to Ortho with another mocking warning. Ortho scowled and wiped the stem on his shirt until it was reasonably clean. The carved hywood was hard, slippery and seemed intent on escaping his mouth. The smooth golden cap on his finger made just *holding* the pipe tricky. How did Jaesun make smoking look so easy?

A girl separated herself from the crowd. At first, Ortho paid little attention to her and concentrated on the not inconsiderable task of smoking Jaesun's pipe. But she was moving toward them, Ortho realized, not the statue or its collection of offerings. The girl was younger than Ortho, maybe in her late teenage years, though it was difficult to say for certain. Her skin was pulled drum-taut over her bones with no fat and little muscle to soften the sharp lines. Her angled eyes were the same shape as any Carcaen, but that white skin and tangled hair the color of fire... The girl had to be Fiori.

What did she want? Money, probably. Or food.

There were rumors of some kind of mold or blight in the grain fields of Erastrasus. The poor were almost as panicked as the wheat sellers and their investors. Maybe the girl was coming over to beg. She must have been very bold – or very desperate – to approach VEIL knights.

"There's a Fiori coming this way," Ortho said.

He elbowed Jaesun in the ribs and repeated the warning.

"Hae," the girl hissed when she was close enough. She tugged on Ortho's sleeve. Her shoulders were hunched into a tight, frightened bow. "Hae, sirs."

"What do you want?" Ortho asked.

He slurred a little around the pipe still in his mouth. A gob of saliva gathered on the stalk and dribbled down onto his chest.

Ortho flushed and tried to scrub it away, but Jaesun had already noticed.

"Looks like she's got you drooling. I'll just leave you two pigeons alone," he said, then laughed and paced around the far side of Captain Mazrem's statue.

Ortho blushed harder and quickly tucked Jaesun's pipe into his belt. He wiped at the blotch on his saela again, but succeeded only in smearing the wetness around.

"Gods, girl, this had better be important," he said. "What do you want, Fiori?"

"Not *all* Fiori! My father's a fine Carceman, sir, just like you. Can't help the rest of my blood, can I?"

"No... I suppose not."

The defeat of the barbarian tribes was thirty years past, by the blood of Captain Mazrem himself. Now Fiore was just another province of the Carcaen Empire. The Fiori people paid the same taxes as anyone else. For a half-starved, dirty little foreigner, the girl was almost pretty. Pretty enough, at least. Ortho found himself smiling at her.

"What's your name, girl?" he asked.

"Senna, sir."

Ortho nodded and wiped his sleeve across his face. The day was hot, so he only wore the black saela of the Star Court, without the traditional steel-banded leather VEIL armor over it. Of all the people in Carce, only the knights of VEIL wore pants and buttoned-up saelae. Everyone else, men and women alike, wore wrapped tabbae pinned at one or both shoulders and belted around the waist. Senna's tabba was so dirty and patched that its original color was only a memory.

After a furtive glance around the crowded plaza, Senna reached under a fold of the threadbare cloth and looked up at Ortho.

"I got something nice for a knight like you, sir," she said. "Something special."

"What is it?"

Ortho leaned in. He had a good guess what it was that Senna wanted. It was not the first time his uniform had won Ortho a girl's attention, but was one of few enough occasions that he didn't want to pass it up. Perhaps Jaesun would let him go off with the girl for a few minutes...

But Senna surprised him. From her dirty tabba, she withdrew something folded in a piece of canvas, something that sat heavily in her hand. When she unwrapped the cloth and held out the contents for his inspection, Ortho gaped.

It was a medal, a flat bronze disk etched in careful detail with the Carcaen lion-and-laurel crest. There was a date printed at the bottom: 1248, the same year marked at the base of Rikard Mazrem's statue. The year of his legendary sacrifice.

"What the bloody hell is this?" Ortho hissed under his breath. "Where did you get it?"

"From... from a trader just out of Fiore. Said he came through Njorn Pass and found it when he pulled off to sleep for a night."

"Njorn Pass? Are you sure?"

"Hae. That's what he said. You know what it is, sir?"

"Yes," said Ortho. "Do you?"

Senna squirmed under Ortho's scrutiny and looked away, turning her eyes up to Rikard Mazrem's benevolent face instead. Ortho followed her gaze.

"This medal is the Emperor's Favor," he told the Fiori girl. "It's only given to the greatest heroes of Carce."

Senna looked at Ortho again, her eyes wide. "The Emperor's Favor? But who would throw away something like that?"

"No one. But maybe someone dropped it."

"Sir?"

"Well, it's marked the year of the conquest, but the army didn't enter Fiore by Njorn Pass," Ortho said with growing excitement. "The battle of Njorn Pass was at the *end* of the war, when Captain

Mazrem began retreating back to Carce. By then, the generals of the Star and Moon Courts had all been killed by the Fiori. Don't you see? Everyone of consequence was already dead by the time the army got there!"

With an effort, Ortho snapped his mouth shut. Senna shook her head in slow stupidity. She didn't understand. Not yet.

The knight fumbled under his saela for his wallet and pulled out a few gold-rimmed coins, each stamped with a smaller version of the same lion and laurel tree on the medal. Senna's eyes widened at the sight of the money, probably more than she had ever seen in her short, dirty little life. Ortho took the medal from her boneless fingers and replaced it with the coins.

"You shouldn't have this, girl. Take these instead and walk on," he told her.

"Four laurels for a piece of bronze? But that's too much, even for the Emperor's Favor! Why, sir?"

Ortho could no longer keep the grin from his face.

"This must have belonged to Captain Mazrem himself," he said. "Rikard Mazrem was the only man important enough to carry an award like this into Njorn Pass. There were only a few thousand VEIL left and none of the common soldiers would have been given a medal like this. It *must* have been his."

"Rikard Mazrem?"

Senna lunged for the bronze disk, but Ortho curled his thick fingers around it and backhanded the Fiori girl. She sprawled on the ground, clutching one hand to her jaw. A few heads turned and a murmur rippled through Mazrem Square.

"This is robbery!" she cried. Senna looked as though she might leap at Ortho again. "I could buy an entire district for what that medal's worth!"

The crowd filling Mazrem Square looked on, frozen in fear. What if the girl stood up and hit the knight?

Gods, what if he *bled*?

Even in her fury, Senna would never risk it. Her face turned purple with rage and tears trembled in her coppery lashes, but she didn't dare fight back. Ortho dropped a few smaller willow- and oak-stamped coins to the ground.

"This medal isn't for the likes of you, Fiori," he said. "It should be in the VEIL archouse, not in some dirty urchin's pocket. Go on, get out of here."

Ortho gave Senna a parting kick in the ribs and the girl scrambled away, fingers pressed to her bruising jaw. Jaesun was hurrying back toward Ortho with a curious tilt to his head and a smirk on his lips. If the Fiori brat wanted a good beating, Jaesun had no intention of missing out on the fun.

Ortho grinned at the older VEIL knight. Jaesun would never laugh at him again for how he smoked, not once he had shown off his new-won prize. Ortho would surely be promoted over him within a month for returning such a prize to VEIL... Let Jaesun put *that* in his pipe and smoke it.

Senna fled into Dormaen, already forgotten.

3

FIREBRAND

"In the early days of the kingdom – predating the empire – Carce was a nation of scholars. Before creating VEIL, Carce first created science. It was Carcaen science that reached forth and discovered the strange truth of our worlds."

— OUR RED HISTORY, BY AVILLA SALLUSI

THE YOUNGER VEIL knight excitedly showed off his new purchase to his superior, the one with the tobacco-stained teeth and breath that stank like an entire field of the stuff. Ortho held out the medal, full of pride. The gold cap on his first finger gleamed even brighter than the polished bronze.

Thainna Vahn scooped up the coins Ortho had thrown at her and tucked them away into a fold of her tabba. No one was paying any attention to the girl who had called herself Senna now. Though briefly alarming, nothing strange had happened. A VEIL knight abusing some dirty street urchin? The knights of Verita et Illumina Lansinos were among the most powerful men in the city, in the whole empire. They had conquered the entire world, after all, and unified it under Emperor Tychon.

Who would dare interfere with men like that?

Still, it wasn't a good idea to linger. If the older knight was any smarter than Ortho, he might realize that the medal was a forgery. Thainna would get much more than a slap and a kick for that.

She hurried away from Mazrem Square. When she was safely out of sight behind one of the black and white striped columns of a nearby lawery, Thainna stopped to rub her aching jaw. That was going to bruise, if it hadn't already.

A lecturn and his students were gathered in the shade of the deep colonnade. The teacher's long tabba was edged in deep emerald green and pinned at the shoulders with silver clasps shaped like laurel leaves. The crowd of children in plain white tabbae clustered around him like a flock of ducklings. Some used writing sticks to take notes on wax-covered boards, but most of them just giggled and chased each other, fighting miniature battles with the sharpened reeds. With a great deal of clapping and whistling, the lecturn finally managed to shush the children.

"Quiet! Quietly now!" the teacher said. He was not an old man, but he tugged at a long, graying beard as he spoke. "Now, who can tell me why last week was so special?"

"Because there were no classes!" answered a young Carcaen boy. Several of his classmates agreed enthusiastically.

Their teacher sighed and clapped until the children fell silent once more. "Hae, but do you know *why* there were no classes?"

"The Mazrem Festival?" This came quietly from a shy Nianese girl.

"Very good, Ellin. Yesterday was the thirtieth anniversary of the battle of Njorn Pass, where Captain Rikard Mazrem traded his life to the Alterra in return for those of his men."

The children cheered and waved their sticks at that.

"Now, at that time, there was no empire," the lecturn went on. "Only a scattering of kingdoms, all warring over borders, land, water and anything else. His Imperial Majesty, Emperor Tychon – King Tychon, in those days – had just taken the throne. He wanted to end the constant fighting, to unify the kingdoms into a single great empire. He sent his knights, the *Verita et Illumina Lansinos*, to do precisely that."

"The knights have magic blood," said a boy. He swished his reed through the air. It whistled sharply. "That's why they have lids on their fingers, so they can bleed without cutting themselves up all the time."

"VEIL knights *do* have gold cannulas on their right forefinger, put there by special surgical fosters, so they can bleed as required in their pacts. But it's not their blood that's magical. The gods made all things in pairs, in twins. Day and night, life and death, the sun and the moon. And that includes our own world, Terra. We have a twin world."

"Alterra!" chimed the children in unison.

"Hae, that's right. But there's a barrier between our worlds, a sort of veil. Only blood shows through. It glows in Alterra like flame and attracts the attention of the strange creatures that live there. The knights of the Verita et Illumina Lansinos make powerful pacts with the Alterra and write out their terms in blood."

A Mor woman, older than Thainna by several years but still young and quite pretty, stopped beside a striped column to listen to the lesson. She interrupted the lecturn with a question, something about the politics after the war. He answered her in a rush, quickly before his students lost interest and decided to reenact the battle of Njorn Pass with their sharp writing sticks. Children were never careful enough about blood...

Thainna loved stories of the heroic Rikard Mazrem, but the politics bored her. What did it matter to someone like her? Money was much more important. Let the Lyceum consuls argue about the rest. When the Mor woman thanked the lecturn and turned back toward the busy street, Thainna followed. She held out her hands and put on her saddest expression.

"Spare an acorn?" Thainna asked in a voice she hoped was pitiful. "My brother's sick and–"

The other woman shrugged apologetically and shook her head. "Sorry."

"Is something wrong?" The lecturn scowled at Thainna.

"No, everything's fine," the woman answered. She gave Thainna a small smile and then turned away.

The old Carcaen teacher was still glaring at Thainna, so she ducked her head and hurried off down the street. He was hardly a large man – about as imposing as a plucked chicken – but Thainna didn't want to make trouble. Rikard Mazrem's statue and its attendant knights were just across the street. If the lecturn raised a fuss, they might come to investigate. Thainna's face still stung from their last encounter.

The road circling Mazrem Square bustled with activity. Goats and horses drew small two-wheeled chariots that carried important people to important places. The most heavily gilded chariots were lashed to kajjas, huge birds from the deep jungles of Jumaar, with long legs, beady eyes and brilliant feathers that shone like exotic gems. Human bearers carried sedan chairs suspended on poles across their muscled shoulders while their passengers remained gently shaded by parasols under the late summer sun.

The long walk back home to the Rows was going to take most of the afternoon. Thainna set a brisk pace up along North Tychon Road. Ortho's slap was a small price to pay for the profit she had just made. She would stop by the shop, Thainna decided, and deposit the money. If she were lucky, maybe Pata wouldn't be there yet. The last thing Thainna felt like doing with her bruised jaw was argue with her father. Again.

The chariots and sedans became fewer as Thainna made her way through Dormaen, though the road became no less crowded.

Wagons rolled by, heading toward the city center with their heavy loads of wood, flax and wool. Donkeys brayed sullenly at their drovers and chafed under the barrels and boxes lashed to their backs. Pedestrians walked and ran alongside – and sometimes right in front of – the drovers and wagoneers.

Many were foreigners visiting or living in the empire's capital city. Some still wore the clothes of their homelands, but most had exchanged them for the traditional Carcaen tabbae. There was no official rule of dress in Dormaen, only practical considerations. The Kaelos Valley that made up most of Carce was a vast, grassy strath bordered on the east by the Mazren River and the ocean on the west. The Carcaen summers were long and hot, making the heavy clothes of places like Nian and Lyncea extremely uncomfortable. All but the proudest provincials were quick to adopt the local dress.

Thainna's feet hurt. Not for the first time, she wished for one of the chariots or wagons or just the sandals worn by the other pedestrians who shared Tychon Road. The interlocking stones of the road used to be as perfect as snake scales, but after decades of heavy traffic and little care, the roads of Dormaen were cracked and rough... and so were Thainna's feet.

Earlier that morning, she had wrapped her feet in rags, but the seven-mile walk to Mazrem Square was too much for the tattered old cloth. There was little left now but shredded tangles around her ankles and threads stuck between her blistered toes.

The sun began its slow westward tumble before Thainna passed into the temple district. Enormous temples to the elder Carcaen gods lined the Tychon Road, looming in judgment over the crowds below. It wasn't Oraday yet, but most of the shrine doors stood open. The sounds of prayers and smell of incense drifted out into the streets.

The temples were as lavish as any Everstone manor, adorned in traditional tall columns and intricately carved friezes. The largest and grandest temples were a pair painted in the same blue as the midday sky – the house of Surma, goddess of life – and the red and black temple of her twin brother, Saerus, the god of death.

Beggars crowded the steps to Surma's azure temple, their hands outstretched. There were more of them today than the last time Thainna had passed. With the wheat shortage in Erastrasus, there was less food and more fear to go around.

But the beggars left Thainna alone. A skinny Fiori girl clearly had nothing to give. They were wrong, of course, but Thainna didn't tell them so. Ortho's gold-edged laurel coins were heavy in her tabba.

When she passed the silver-scrolled temple of the sea goddess, Thainna turned down River Road. Her toes swelled like tiny red sausages. It should have been revolting, but every glance downward only made Thainna unsettlingly hungry. She hurried on.

Smaller avenues split off like the branches of a tree, leading further into the temple district. Some led to the shrines of the lesser gods – Suzukarri, Eru and a hundred others, deities imported from the outlying provinces like exotic fruit. But as Thainna passed a narrow and nameless cross-street, she kept her head down and hurried past. If she was lucky, she would never have to go *that* way.

From River Road, Thainna followed ever smaller and narrower streets, winding further through Dormaen. The buildings out here were smaller and narrower, too, until they were little more than blocky refuse piles, broken mockeries of real houses. Out here in the Rows, the people were just as worn as their homes. Thainna returned a limp wave from Senna, whose name she had borrowed for the day. Senna resumed sweeping at her pitted gray stoop with a ragged broom that wasn't much more than a handful of twigs tied to the end of a longer stick. Dust puffed into the air and then fell right back down where it had started.

In a better part of Dormaen, Senna would still be young enough to wear a bright, summer-thin tabba and make eyes at the men. But life in the Rows left lines across her skin and gray in her black hair.

A racking cough made Senna shudder and she spat a gob of dark, seedy-looking phlegm into the gutter.

How long until I'm just like Senna? Thainna wondered. *Until I'm too sick and too tired to even leave the Rows anymore?*

Not long, she suspected. Thainna's feet throbbed with every step like a painful second heartbeat. Her jaw ached and was starting to feel stiff.

Which means I have to work even harder now, while I can. Besides, I don't have years until the Auction. Worrying about anything after that is a waste of time.

This district wasn't that old – older than Thainna, certainly, but she wasn't even twenty yet, so that wasn't saying much. Everything in Dormaen was older than her. The Rows were the poorest part of the city, run down by hard use and infrequent repairs. No one knew where the name came from anymore – certainly not from any kind of orderly city planning. The rutted, shadowed streets twisted and wound together like a nest of filthy snakes.

No, the people who made their homes in the Rows were the *real* snakes. They were poor, hungry and dirty. Difficult, scrabbling lives made them suspicious, close-mouthed and poisonously dangerous. Most of them would do anything for a meal, for a warm place to sleep. For a pair of shoes.

And among the vipers, live the dragons...

The House of Five Dragons. Anyone who didn't work for the House lived in fear of it. Or so it had been in her father's day.

Now even those of us who do work for the House are afraid.

Things were getting worse throughout the Rows, even for agents of the House of Five Dragons. A living in the Rows wasn't much, but even that was getting hard to scrape together, like trying to carve meat from a carcass long since stripped to bones.

Thainna turned down another narrowing road and again onto a twisting dirt road. A hunch-shouldered man herded some thin, bleating goats through the dust, cursing the beasts wearily and smacking at their bony hindquarters with a long switch. Thainna watched her step around the mangy animals and crossed the street.

One of the few intact buildings of the Rows was a small shop with no sign over the door. Thainna shouldered open the door. A cracked bronze bell clunked tonelessly against the wood.

Just like any other shop in the Rows, this one was lined with empty, dusty shelves. A handful of unraveling reed baskets held hard loaves of rye bread and balls of cheese covered in cracking wax. A middle-aged Carcaen man sat on a stool in the corner. Thin limbs stuck out from under his threadbare tabba like the twigs of Senna's broom. He dozed in the slanting amber light of the shop's single window. Thainna sighed in exasperation.

"Pata!" she snapped.

Aelos Vahn startled suddenly awake and jolted upright on his stool, raising his arms as though to ward off a blow. It wasn't an entirely unreasonable fear. Thainna scowled at her father and put her hands on her hips like she imagined a woman might to properly scold a foolish old man.

"Wake up, Pata! What are you doing here? You're supposed to be with Thain today!"

Aelos grunted and rubbed at his eyes. Like everyone who lived in the Rows, he looked much older than the thirty-nine years of life he had endured. His dusky Carcaen skin was leathery enough to make boots out of and deeply lined. Aelos' hair had been dark in his youth, a deep brown-black like mahogany, but now it was thin at the top and gone quite gray. Aelos' eyes had the reddened, drooping look of a man who drank more than he should, but less than he wanted to.

He coughed and then squinted at Thainna as though hoping his daughter was just a fading dream.

"You're back," Aelos said with a grunt. He lowered his hands and slouched against the wall again. "They sent Hadrian an ash-mark this morning, so I'm stuck here for the rest of the day."

"There are plenty of coin counters! Any one of them could cover for Hadrian. What about Thain?"

"Thain?" Aelos thought about that for a moment, then shook his head. "I'll see him tomorrow."

"That's what you said yesterday!" Thainna cried. Fury made her skin feel too tight and seemed to push at the back of her eyes until she was sure they were actually bulging from their sockets.

Aelos shrugged. "Thain's not going anywhere. He'll be in that bed all day tomorrow, won't he?"

"You can't say things like that, Pata! Thain is sick and he needs his father!"

How could Aelos be so heartless? Thainna's twin had been so sick for so long, and the occasional visits from his father and sister were the only things he ever had to look forward to. Now Aelos didn't even want to do that! Not that this sullen resistance was anything new...

"Thain's been sick since the day he was born," Aelos said in a flat voice. "If he died tomorrow, I'd have nothing new to tell him."

Thainna opened her mouth to scream again, but could think of nothing to say. Instead, she kicked the stool where Aelos sat, intent on knocking the spiteful drunkard over. But without shoes, she succeeded only in cracking her blistered toes against the leg of the stool. Thainna howled in pain and jumped away.

"Bloody hell!" she screeched.

After what felt like an eternity of agony, Thainna's foot could bear her weight again. She finished hopping in clumsy circles and inspected the damage. Her nail was torn and oozing drops of blood. Thainna rubbed at the wound and flicked the tiny red beads at her father.

Aelos leapt back, pale-faced and shaking. Thainna's blood spattered on the plank floor and quickly soaked away into the cracked wood.

"Thainna!"

It was Aelos' turn to be angry, though his cry was sharp-edged with fear. Thainna stuck out her tongue. Let him be angry with her. He deserved it, didn't he?

Father and daughter glared balefully at one another for a long moment.

"I... brought some more money," Thainna said at last.

"You could have bought some food with it," Aelos grumbled.

But he withdrew a thick book from behind a stack of baskets. Aelos laid it open on a shelf with a resounding thump and searched for something to write with.

"Idiot girl. Fine. How much do you have today?" he asked.

"Four laurels, seventeen willows and twenty-seven oaks."

Her father raised an eyebrow. He found a splintering reed and dipped it into an inkwell. Thainna took the coins from the folds of her tabba and dropped them at Aelos' elbow. He dutifully counted and recorded the money, then scooped it up into a leather pouch that was worn shiny by use. He cinched the bag tightly shut and tucked it into the bottom of another half-empty basket.

"How much do I have now?" asked Thainna. "All together."

Aelos sighed. He had been about to put the register away, but opened it again. He traced a long column of numbers and muttered to himself as he added them up.

Years ago, when Thainna first started making her regular deposits, Aelos would ask his daughter if she wanted to do the math herself, but she never did. Thainna didn't share Aelos' head for sums. Thain did, of course, but that never seemed to make their father proud. If anything, it only annoyed the old man even more.

"Six hundred and twenty-two laurels, forty-eight willows," Aelos announced at last.

"How much do the others have?"

"More than that," Aelos answered shortly. "A lot more."

He thumped the book closed and beetled his brow at Thainna. "This is pointless. You've been saving every acorn for years now and you don't have a fraction of what anyone else will be bidding this winter. You won't win the Auction, child."

She *would* win. 'Pointless' was arguing with her father.

"Just make sure it gets into the vault, hae?"

Thainna's father ignored her. He wasn't stupid enough to keep any of the money for himself. Not that Aelos Vahn was somehow above thievery, but the money he accepted and recorded belonged to the House of Five Dragons and few were foolish enough to steal from them.

"Tragos wants reports from all the Talons," Aelos said. "How did your job go last week?"

Thainna bristled, but icy fear swiftly cooled her anger. Tragos was an Eye for the House of Five Dragons, one of the ten who answered directly to the Crest, who watched over the Flames and lowliest Talons.

"I left that vase exactly where I was supposed to," Thainna said, probably a little too quickly. "It's not my fault if Caelin hasn't picked it up yet!"

"They're asking after all of the Talons, not only you. It's just routine."

"I... I know," Thainna said.

She did, but that didn't make the fear any less. The Crest of the House was a mysterious and dangerous man. Thainna didn't want *any* bad news reaching his ears that had her name connected to it.

"I'm sure Caelin did his job, Thainna. And if he didn't, that's not on your head."

Was Aelos trying to comfort his daughter? He must have been worried, too. It was almost enough to make Thainna forgive him, but then she thought of Thain, all alone in the fostral and waiting for his father to come visit. Her teeth ground together.

The last tatters of daylight barely lit the empty store. Thainna turned to leave, then glanced back at her father. Aelos had dropped himself back onto his stool under the window. She frowned.

"Aren't you coming home?" Thainna asked.

Aelos leaned against the wall and shut his eyes again.

"Why would I?" he asked. "It's warmer here and it's not as if there's dinner at home. I'll stay."

"But..." Thainna could think of no real objections. He was right. "Fine. You'll go see Thain tomorrow, hae?"

Her father grunted wordlessly and didn't open his eyes. He did not invite Thainna to remain, either. She waited in the doorway, chewing her swollen lip, but Aelos was already asleep once more. With a sigh, Thainna stepped back out into the streets.

4

UNDER THE SKY

"There has never been an enemy like the barbarians of Fiore. Emperor Tychon's emissaries returned with little more than ghost stories, when they returned at all. When the emperor sent VEIL into the mountains to conquer the Fiori, they had no idea what awaited them in the snow and ice."

—ACCOUNTS OF NJORN PASS, BY ALEXANDER FERRO

Voices. He heard voices in the darkness.

"Is he dead?"

"Don't think so. Just sleeping."

Sleep. Hae, I remember sleep. Death took his twin, Life, as his bride. Their children were Sleep and Dream.

I was sleeping. Did I dream?

"He's injured," said one of the voices. A foot prodded roughly at his shoulder.

"Passed out, then."

"But look at the armor! That's the VEIL crest. Star Court."

"Look at the *blood*, you jackass!" said the second voice. "Come on, let's get out of here!"

"Wait. If he's a knight, he's got to have money."

"Are you out of your mind? He'll kill you! Or feed you to the soul-eaters!"

"Just give me one minute."

Rough hands worked their way under his shoulders and rolled him onto his back. His eyes flew open. A man with a sun-creased brow stared down at him. Not at his face, but at the empty scabbard on his belt.

"This armor is thrashed pretty bad and he doesn't even have a sword! It must have been one hell of a fight... Juniper, hand me your knife."

A gauntleted fist smashed up into the man's face, cutting off the words. His would-be thief fell, spitting curses and broken teeth. With a ragged howl of fury, the nameless knight lurched to his feet and grabbed the second man's throat and squeezed as hard as he could. Bones popped and then the man was no longer a man – just an empty sack of flesh.

He dropped the body and whirled on Juniper. The man had pulled a knife from his belt, but now clutched it in nerveless fingers and groveled in the worn road.

"No! Stop! Didn't mean anything by it, I swear! Please, please don't kill me!"

Juniper's voice went shrill and sorrow-sharp as the man in the old VEIL armor slammed his heavy boot down on his head. Once, twice and then a third time. There was a terrible crunch and bright blood pooled on the cracked paving stones. It glimmered with otherworldly light, a burning ember ruby radiance, but nothing more. Juniper had no pact with the Alterra.

The man in the broken black armor wiped the blood from his skin with a handful of grass.

So he wasn't dead just yet. But how much time had passed since he... fell asleep? He couldn't remember how to tell.

He spurred his limp muscles into movement once more. It was time to move on, time to go home.

Dormaen.

Home.

A raven landed on the sprawled corpses littering the road and squawked happily at the unexpected feast.

He killed those men, didn't he? Stumble asked.

In his astonishment, the curiosity opened his beak too wide and his stone head cracked with a small, sharp retort. Green dust sifted down through the great boughs of the Uprising.

All he did was touch *them! He didn't even hate them.*

Hae. Terrans die strangely, easily, when their body breaks. But ours is a strong one, even for a Terran, Flickerdim said. *He will fight. War is his craft, in his world and ours.*

Dormaen. Jewel of the empire. The heart of Carce.

Home.

So beautiful.

The sun was falling out of the sky again. Lights kindled across the distant city, glowing like low golden stars. He was weeping again, blurring his vision with sea-salty water that stung his raw skin, but he didn't need to see the city to know it.

Home.

But curiosity pried his eyes open again and his hands dropped to his sides again. They closed into fists like the curling legs of a dead spider.

The city was so much bigger than he remembered! Even in the dying daylight, he could make out the silver-edged green of gated hunting parks to the east... Where were all of the farms that had surrounded Dormaen like the fertile bridal veil of Surma herself? The mill-houses on the shores of the Mazren River? Where was the white-walled fortress and training grounds of the Verita et Illumina Lansinos?

Where were they? Were they hiding from... from the stars?

Everything had changed, but he knew it all the same – the sharp tang of the distant sea in the air, the scents of smoke and cooking food, the muted roar of humanity audible even from this distance. This was still Dormaen. He was almost home.

Dormaen.

Home.

He is a warrior.

The idea was dark with misery and bright with blood. Stumble guessed there was no worse curse or higher calling in the worlds. Of course, a battle or bitter might not share the sentiment...

He made sacrifices to win his war, said Flickerdim. *He'll make even more to win ours. That was our pact.*

Would you make the same deal? Stumble asked.

Never.

5

THE HOUSE

"The men of Carce have never loved war, but how they adore order! The lands beyond our borders were wild and dangerous. When diplomacy failed to order them, Carcemen turned to blood and the sword. And so it is out of our desire for that perfect peace that Carce has produced the greatest soldiers in history."

— OUR RED HISTORY, BY AVILLA SALLUSI

THE CIRCULAR STONE room was dark. It was always dark. There were rich, shining things secreted away in the endless shadows, but those were only for the Eyes. And for their master, of course: the Crest of the House of Five Dragons.

The only light came from a single lamp that dangled on a long chain at an unnatural angle to the floor. Nothing in the room seemed real. In the wavering circle of yellowed light loomed the Jade Throne – a huge, polished gem in the otherwise empty room. The antique throne was wide enough to seat two men side-by-side and carved with the lion and laurel of Carce. Heaps of overstuffed velvet cushions filled the massive throne like the bloated bodies of dead things.

The Jade Throne was a stark and heavy thing, the stone fossil of decades past. From before Tychon's empire, from the days when Carce had been a simple scholar-state, not home to the greatest warriors the world had ever known. Not long after the founding of the Carcaen Empire, a new throne – one made of jewel-encrusted gold, brought as tribute from the first provinces – had replaced the hereditary seat of the Carcaen kings and stood even now in the center of the Lyceum.

It was said that the Jade Throne had been destroyed decades before, ground to dust. But its massive presence, brooding here in the darkness, testified to that untruth. Exactly how the House of Five Dragons had come to possess the throne, Caelin had no idea.

He staggered along the slanted floor and prostrated himself before the Jade Throne. It was empty, of course. The Crest was the leader of the House and had far better things to do than hand down orders to an unimportant Talon.

Instead, one of his Eyes stood just beside the throne. She was a tall, regal woman of obviously noble Carcaen birth. Her smooth golden skin had the papery look of well-preserved age. The lamp-light glittered on delicate crystal beads that sprinkled her black tabba like stars. She held her hands delicately crossed at her waist. They were as smooth and perfect as porcelain – the hands of a woman who had never done an honest day's work.

But then again, the work of the House of Five Dragons isn't precisely honest.

Caelin did not even know this Eye's name. In over twenty years of service to the House of Five Dragons, he had never received a bloodmark before. What did the House's elite want of him now? Caelin's orders always came from the Talons or Flames above him. Simple things: small thefts, pick-ups and lockbreaks.

He bowed his head in respect. Servitude. The Eyes served the Crest of the House directly. Her words were his words.

"Rise, Talon." Her voice was as delicate as her skin.

Caelin stood, making his knees pop and his spine creaked in protest. A grunt of discomfort escaped his lips and one of the Eye's brows arched into a delicately sculpted ebony bow.

"Let's hope that you can carry out the Crest's orders," she said.

"Still fit enough to serve, lady," Caelin answered quickly.

"We will see. You have a reputation among the other Talons, Caelin. They like you. They say you're charming and funny."

Did they? Caelin knew how to tell a joke, but charming? Maybe the bloodmark, summons to receive the Crest's orders, was better luck than Caelin first supposed.

He smiled at the Eye. *Charming.*

"I do try my best," Caelin said. "Most of us live out in the Rows. Life is stark tough out there."

"Hae." The Eye waved a hand dismissively. She obviously had far more important concerns than the suffering of the lower ranks. "The Crest is sending you to Gaius Mazrem."

Caelin's smile faded and he gaped. "Gaius Mazrem...? Captain Mazrem's son?"

That was a mistake. The Eye frowned.

"Gaius Mazrem is the youngest consul of the Lyceum and everyone expects him to succeed Emperor Tychon," she said. "He's an important man."

"Hae, my lady! How am I supposed to see him at all?"

"Arliss will take care of it. She has recommended you to the Mazrem's steward, Bastil."

"Arliss? Isn't she a cook? I don't know a biscuit from my backside! I can't work in a kitchen!"

"You don't need to feed Gaius Mazrem, Talon. You will serve him in a manner befitting your status. When you have his trust, give him some of this as a gift honoring his father."

She held out a thick envelope in her delicately spider-like hand. Caelin opened it and inspected the powdered scarlet contents. The scent inside was spicy and made his head spin even more than the crooked, slanting room.

"Ophellion?" he asked. "But this is far too much for a shrine offering."

"Gaius Mazrem has a taste for fine things. He will be curious enough to try it."

Caelin frowned, confused. "I'm sorry, I still don't understand, my lady. Forgive my saying, but this seems like a great lot of work to give Master Mazrem some drams. Can't we just have Arliss sell them to him? Seems you could make a tidy profit that way."

"You're even less clever than you appear, Talon," the Eye informed him icily. "Encourage Gaius to try the ophellion. You're not to charge him an acorn for it. It is a gift. Come to us when he wants more. You will be provided with as much as he needs. Ensure his addiction."

Caelin gulped. His mouth was suddenly so dry.

Splitting Gaius Mazrem on ophellion? It didn't feel right. Not at all. Young Lord Mazrem was the only son of a great man. Of the *greatest* man.

"What... what about his mother?" Caelin asked. "I don't see that she'll sit aside while her son gets split."

"Lady Mazrem is a formidable and ambitious woman," the Eye agreed. Her respect was grudging but genuine. "She knows as well as we do that her son is the route to power. She's protective of him."

"Then... what should I do?"

"We understand the delicacy of your task," the regal House Eye went on, as though Caelin had not spoken. She inspected her perfectly clean nails. "You will be busy. The Crest doesn't want you distracted by... family concerns."

Caelin forgot all about Gaius Mazrem.

"What?" he asked.

"Your wife is quite ill, I understand. The Crest has generously brought her to the tower. The Crest, in his kindness, will ensure her safety until you complete your task."

A Fiore winter was warmer than the smile she leveled at Caelin. He fell to his knees. He clawed imploringly at the hem of the Eye's expensive tabba. She stepped back out of reach. Caelin pressed his forehead to the floor. Tears ran down his cheeks and rolled away down the slanted floor.

"Please, my lady! No, you can't! Milla doesn't even know that I belong to the House! Please," Caelin begged. "She's my wife. She's all I've got!"

"Do as you've been told, Talon, and she has nothing to fear. The Crest is an honorable man. Finish the job and then you and your wife can crawl back to the Rows to rot with the rest of the trash."

Caelin scrambled to his feet and staggered from the room.

6

ROAR

"No greater ally has been known to men as our shadow-twins, the Alterra. No greater friend and no greater mystery. We have put forth our best and boldest to take advantage of the bond between our two worlds and our two peoples. These are the Verita et Illumina Lansinos, the Knights of Truth and Light. VEIL, as they are commonly known. But as the sacrifice of Rikard Mazrem demonstrated, we may never know a more frightening enemy than the Alterra. Any knight who makes a pact with these strange spirits does so at the risk of his very life and soul."

— OUR RED HISTORY, BY AVILLA SALLUSI

THAINNA SAT beside her brother's bed for a long time. She brushed the sweat-damp red hair back from his pale face and wanted to cry, but the noise would only wake Thain. He needed his rest. Thain was so thin, like a skeleton covered in a sheet of wax. Weren't they taking care of him at all?

They were priests of Surma, the fosters uniformed in flowing blue. They bustled through the fostral with arms full of bandages and poultice pots and the shining steel implements of their trade. But none of the fosters' duties seemed to bring them anywhere near Thain's bed. Perhaps out of respect for the sick boy, or – more likely, Thainna thought – a desire to avoid his perpetually angry twin. She had a bad reputation among the priests.

The fostral was full of curtained beds that took up the entire eastern wing of Surma's vast temple. Thain's cell was one of the smallest, with a single plain white wall and no windows. How long had he been trapped here in this tiny, stuffy cubicle? It was no better than a tomb. No, it was worse – Thain was still alive to realize the horror of his confinement.

Not that Thain looked very alive. The boy's nails were yellowed like those of a much older man. Years ago, his hair was the same bright red as Thainna's, but years of sickness had leeched the color and left it as stiff as the bristles of a cheap brush, broken and irregular. Thainna wished she had thought to bring a knife or scissors to even it out.

She combed trembling fingers through Thain's hair and her fingers came back coated in fine white dust. Plaster from the white walls? The urge to cry returned, tidal in its stinging weight, but her eyes already felt like peeled grapes. Tears would only make it worse. Why didn't the priests take better care of Thain?

Nothing had been right for five years. Thain had always been sickly, since their mother died giving birth to her twin son and daughter. How many sleepless nights had Thainna spent sitting in the dark, listening to her brother struggle for breath? How many nightmares about one of the fosters coming to tell her that Thain was dead, that he had left her alone...?

Blue tabba stained black by night, the clothes of a foster turning into the uniform of Saerus' death-priests. The ash-god always came, reaching with claws like scythes, reaping and cutting...

Someone had set Thain up on a pole, like a splinter man strung up in a wheat field to scare the birds away. Saerus flowed across the ground toward him like blood from a wound. All Thainna could see of the god was a boiling cloud of smoky darkness and the lighting-strike flashes of great metal talons. Thainna screamed and reached for her twin, but something held her back, as easily as a child holding a squirming worm just before he spears it on a barbed hook...

A light touch on her arm made Thainna jerk upright. Her eyes were sticky and blurry. Thainna blinked and rubbed at them until she could see again. Thain was sitting up in his bed.

"You're awake!" said Thainna.

A smile spread across her brother's thin, pale lips.

"You're not," he said.

"I was sleeping?" Thainna asked, ashamed. After shouting at Aelos for his inattention, she'd gone and fallen asleep when she was supposed to be visiting her brother.

"A little, but it didn't seem very restful. What's wrong?"

Thainna just shrugged. She didn't want to share her nightmares with Thain. His life was hard enough. Instead, Thainna enfolded him in a gentle hug. Even the careful embrace made her brother wince and cough. Thainna released Thain and let him sag back into his blankets. He wiped his mouth with the back of his hand. His veins were stark blue lines under the papery white skin.

"Did Pata come to see you?" Thainna asked and immediately regretted it.

A shadow crossed Thain's thin face.

"No. Was he supposed to?"

"Um..."

Thainna fell silent again. What else could she say? Nothing new, nothing true. *Don't worry, Pata loves you. He's just... busy.* She had said it so many times that the words were becoming mushy nonsense inside her own head.

Love. Busy. Lousy.

Perhaps she should have told Thain about her nightmare instead. At least he could just dismiss it as nothing important.

Thain toyed with a corner of his rough blanket. "Did you sell the medal?"

Thainna seized on the new topic. "Hae! And got four laurels for it! But it was pretty close. I actually sold it to a VEIL knight."

Her brother's eyes widened, suitably impressed at her daring.

"A knight? You minx!" Thain exclaimed and then coughed.

"He hit me at the end, but then he dropped some more money," Thainna said when Thain could breathe again. "Lucky that he was so thick. Illius put the wrong date on the medal."

"It was fake, though, not a replica. There isn't really a *right* date."

"Hae, maybe," Thainna agreed, but she was still annoyed. "But there was a wrong one! Illius put 1248."

"Hae, Captain Mazrem was trapped in Njorn Pass most of that winter," Thain said. He frowned, but Thainna sensed that the twist in his lips was for Illius, not her. "There wasn't anyone around to give out medals. Certainly not the Emperor's Favor. Illius should have used an earlier date, before Rikard Mazrem left Carce."

Thainna rarely had to explain things to her brother, and never more than once. He was the clever one between them, with a quick, deft mind that belied his frail body. Thainna was so proud of her twin. But why couldn't Thain's body be as strong as his mind?

"What about the other job, the one with the vase?" he asked in a wheezing voice.

"Nothing worth talking about," said Thainna. She rubbed her brother's bony back. "Maybe you should go back to sleep. Are you hungry? I can get you some food."

"No, I'll eat later. It doesn't matter, anyway. I'll just throw up. Please tell me about the job, Thainna. I never get to leave the fostral anymore."

"There's not much to tell," Thainna admitted. "I got an ashmark with orders to sneak into the Everstones and take a vase. Some expensive antique, I guess. Someone had knocked into it during one of the Mazrem Festival parties and so it was on its way out for repairs. I took it from a servant while he was fixing his sandals and left it in a drop-spot for Caelin."

"Did the man chase you?" asked Thain. He grinned with excitement at his twin's adventure. There was even a faint flush in his pale cheeks. Thainna wished her story were really that thrilling.

"Hae, but not very far. He was a great big man," said Thainna. "Like a walrus with legs! He was panting and sweating in no time at all. I guess all the good food in the Everstones weighed him down."

Thain laughed a little at her description and took one of Thainna's hands. He gave it a weak squeeze.

"You do good work," he told her. "Someone will notice it someday. You won't be a Talon forever."

Now it was Thainna's turn to blush. Her cheeks stung, scrubbed raw by tears and now prickled with the rising blush.

"Neither will you, Thain."

"I haven't been a real Talon in years, not since I've been stuck in the fostral. I wasn't even much of one before. I was so young. Fourteen years old when I came here..." He gestured at the curtained cell with an impatient flick of his stick-thin fingers.

"When I win the Auction, everything will be so much better," Thainna promised.

Thain smiled at her. She lingered for a while in hopes of filling her brother's monotonous time, but before long, Thain was asleep again. She kissed his cheek and left.

Thainna passed a priest dressed in dark blue on her way out of the fostral wing. She caught the man by the arm and was greeted by a familiarly contemptuous sneer. The priest was a tall man, probably about the same age as Thainna's father, but had weathered the years far better than Aelos Vahn. His monastically close-cut hair was still dark and lustrous.

"Hae?" he asked. "What do you want?"

"My brother's resting in that cell over there. Number seventeen," Thainna said, pointing back the direction she had come. "He's not...

I mean, he doesn't look very good. He's too thin. Can you take him something to eat?"

"I don't work the dram halls," said the priest.

He brushed past Thainna, but she grabbed the corner of his tabba. Frowning, he jerked the cloth free of her grasp.

"So? Can't you help?" Thainna fought to remain calm, but her voice was rising, just like it always did.

"Ask one of the fosters. That's *their* job."

With that, the priest strode off down the hall.

"They never do anything, either!" Thainna shouted after him.

She stood fuming in the hallway. A young acolyte stood before a tall statue of beautiful, buxom Surma with an ewer of scented oil upturned in her hands, filling and quickly overflowing a marble bowl carved into the shape a seashell. She stared in shock until Thainna turned away and stormed out of the temple.

Thainna didn't slow until she had run down the blue-and-white steps of the temple and back out into the street. Her heart raced, thumping out a quick, furious drumbeat. Why didn't *anyone* care? Surma was supposed to be the goddess of life, of healing... Why didn't her priests and fosters take better care of a sick boy? It was a sacred duty, wasn't it?

A Suvestri man pushed past Thainna, wearing a belt of beaten gold over his Carcaen linen tabba. He nodded a curt apology with a bob of his shaven head. Thainna turned to flip him a rude gesture and saw the crowd of beggars filling the colonnade of the temple, ragged ghosts that haunted the blue shadows. They were just as hungry as her or Thain. But they didn't have the shelter of the fostral or the debatable blessings of employment by the House of Five Dragons.

Thainna turned away. Ignoring them.

Just like the priests ignore Thain.

It wasn't the same. Right? Thainna had nothing to give the beggars, after all. Surma's priests and fosters had more, didn't they?

More than enough to share. That was *their* job... Thainna had her own to worry about.

The sun was still bright gold as a laurel coin. It was high in the sky and cast short, dark shadows across Dormaen. Thainna found a dial and counted the hours. It was still early, not even noon yet. She would have liked to have the afternoon to herself, or at least to work for herself.

Someday, I'll have something worth giving.

But how long would that take? Whether or not Thainna wanted to admit it, her father was right. After four years of work, she had collected only a few hundred laurels for the Auction. Come winter, she would be bidding all of her money against that of much richer, much more powerful members of the House of Five Dragons. She had only a few months left to earn, wheedle and steal a whole lot more money.

Reluctantly, Thainna decided that her own pursuits would have to wait. Both Aelos and Thain had asked her about the vase job. If Caelin had failed to retrieve the vase, then Thainna could claim success on her half of the job and wash her hands of the rest. If he *had* made the pickup, it would be nice to know instead of keep wondering.

Either way, she needed to report back to the House. The older Talons and Flames ranked above Thainna probably had some annoyingly menial, time-consuming task for her by now. If the Erastrasus blight was as bad as everyone said, she would be stealing bread for them before long.

It took most of the afternoon to cross the increasingly cramped and filthy miles from the temple district to the Rows. The air was full of too many sounds and smells, few of them pleasant. Close-leaning houses and shops funneled the summer heat into a poisonous miasma. An emaciated mother cradled her screaming baby in an open window and waved with resignation at a buzzing cloud of black flies.

Thainna stopped in front of a building with fishnets hung in the windows and that stank acridly of unfiltered alcohol. A gaunt Karabosi man lounged in the door, watching the road. His real name was unpronounceable, so he had long ago adopted the name *Dorros* after the Carcaen lecturn who had first proposed the existence of the Alterran world. This Dorros was no scholar, though. He was a Flame in the House of Five Dragons – a full rank above Talons like Thainna.

Dorros caught sight of Thainna and beckoned her over. Obediently, she followed him through the tangle of nets and into the murky half-dark beyond. The inside of the cheap taphouse was dim and smoky. Things skittered underfoot, leggy things that didn't invite closer inspection. Dorros ordered a clay cup of something that could probably cure leather. The scarred old bartender looked down at Thainna, but she shook her head. She didn't want to do this with a muddy head, even if she had any money to throw away on a drink.

Dorros dropped himself onto a bench against one of the soot-blackened walls. Thainna sat beside him, close enough to hear over the shouts, gurgles and snores of other patrons.

"I finished the last job. A vase from the Soveus manor house, out in the Everstones," she said. Dorros hadn't given her the job, but the Flame was doubtlessly aware of what the lower ranked Talons were up to. "Did Caelin get it?"

"Caelin?" Dorros snorted and took a long pull off his drink. "I doubt it."

Panic and bile rose in the back of Thainna's throat. Did something happen to Caelin? If he hadn't done his job, no one could blame Thainna for that... right?

Or would the Crest punish Thainna for the failure?

"What happened?" she asked.

Dorros dropped his cup down onto the bench. It bounced once and then tipped over. Dorros swiped the cup away and it rolled off across the floor. Thainna chewed her lip. Dorros was *not* in a good mood today.

"Caelin has a new job," he said, voice dropping to a hiss. "The Eyes sent him to Gaius Mazrem with a pocket full of ophellion."

The words were quiet, but Thainna couldn't help staring suspiciously around the room. What in the worlds was a Flame doing talking to a Talon like this, much less in a public place? Though Dorros had finished his cup, the reek of alcohol remained strong on his breath. He had been drinking for some time, Thainna realized.

And he was still talking.

"This Crest... He's going to kill us all," Dorros said. "Takes our money, our families. He has turned us into assassins and murderers. It wasn't always like this! You're too young to remember, child, but your father does."

"What does that mean?"

Thainna was curious in spite of herself. It was dangerous to sit with Dorros when his tongue was wagging – what if another House agent overheard? – but she could not make herself leave. Thainna had never heard a Flame speaking so openly. Or so bitterly.

"The House, Dormaen... It was better than this. Before I joined, I was just a merchant. I carted wool from Liefport. Aelos kept books for the army. We moved money for people, kept it for those who didn't want the empire to know how much they had. We shaved our fair share of laurels, too."

Dorros sighed and rubbed his sunken cheek.

"But we weren't killers," he insisted. "Not assassins and bonebreakers. Not until *this* Crest. Gods, we don't even know his name! What kind of man won't even show his face to his own folk?"

"Hae, he's changed the business," Thainna answered carefully. "What about Caelin?"

"Caelin got a bloodmark, with orders to split Gaius Mazrem on ophellion. Poor bastard. Caelin, not Lord Mazrem. They took his wife, you know."

"Milla? But... but isn't she sick?"

Thainna felt sick, too. The Crest had turned Dormaen into a treacherous place even for the members of his own House. It was not the first time the Crest and his Eyes had taken friends and family to ensure complicity with dubious orders. But things were going to get better soon, Thainna reminded herself.

"It's the wheat blight in Erastrasus. It's ruining the investors. All the money-counters are in a panic. And the Crest is taking advantage of it, snatching up everything he can as others loosen their grasp. He's gambling big and we're all on the table. It's all burning away, Aelos."

"Thainna," she corrected. "It's not over yet. The Auction is this winter, and then we'll have a new Crest. A better one, I promise."

Dorros leaned back. His head thumped against the wall. The Flame's eyes closed to red-shot crescents. "Hae, the Auction... You're young. They've never sent you a bloodmark. You've never worked for the Crest. Don't hope too hard, Thainna. I don't think the Crest will give up the Jade Throne when his time comes."

"He has to, unless he can outbid everyone else for another term. But that will never happen! Everyone in the House hates him."

"We've never had a Crest like this," Dorros sighed. "But I would bet laurels that he's the only kind we'll ever have again."

7

MERCY CRIED

"When Captain Errain of the Sun Court died in battle with the Fiori, leadership of the remaining forces fell to the commander of the Star Court Ninth Wing, Lord-Captain Rikard Mazrem. Under his orders, the last of the Carcaen army began their withdrawal from the Fiore mountains. Captain Mazrem led the VEIL knights south, which would have led them out of Fiore and into Erastrasus. But the Fiori cut off the retreating army and trapped them in the infamous Njorn Pass."

— ACCOUNTS OF NJORN PASS, BY ALEXANDER FERRO

THE BRANCHES of the tower were as bare as those of a Terran tree in winter. Stumble was changing bodies again, trading his comfortable malachite nightingale to a more watchful jasper owl. He was weaving the last strands of attention and wakefulness into shape when Flickerdim nudged him with one dark coil.

Look.

I can't, Stumble grumbled. *I'm not done with my eyes yet. What's going on?*

He's at the city gate, on the road of the highest house. He is close.

Stumble hummed a sound midway between a nightingale's song and the swish-and-silence of his new owl body. He craned his head this way and that, listening.

I can't see yet. Show me, Flickerdim! Stumble thought excitedly.

Flickerdim let out a whisper-taste of sigh, but then did as the younger Alterran asked. He encircled Stumble in the deep, dusky-sweet sense of *home*, of a place so long loved that the sense of it was pressed and rich as sweet wine. There it was, the so-Terran fire of passion, so hot and so vivid that it surely warmed even Flickerdim's coldest scorn!

But at the center of that heart was the Terran rage, *his* rage, the blossom of blood that belonged to no other creature, not of either world. Stumble's feathers puffed out in every direction as though to push it away.

Take it back, Flicker. Age has sharpened your eyes and you can see things I can't. Take it back.

Flickerdim's cool touch retreated like a frost in spring. *Hurry with those eyes, young one. You must see what is to come.*

A needling pain bit at his guts and grew worse with every passing hour. Something inside him growled and he shook so badly now that the steel bands on his armor clattered like a sack of seashells. The strange blackness had come and gone again, full of misty memories of things that never happened.

Home. I'm home! I...

He stood at last at the edge of Dormaen, queen of cities and the marble heart of civilization! But where were the north gates, the huge iron doors twice the height of the tallest man and inscribed with the Carcaen laurel? The pointed stone arch that should have held them stood open and empty, unguarded. The broad whiteness of Tychon Road lay gap-toothed and broken.

The poets called it the great ivory river of Dormaen, twin to the silver-run Mazren.

An old woman, riding a bow-legged gray mule and half hidden by the heaped sacks of corn she held steady, ducked her head at him as she passed out of the city. He stared after her. Where was she bound? Did no one ask? Where were the VEIL knights that stood vigil at all hours of day and night in the name of the holy Carcaen Empire?

I'm home. All is changed, everything is new. But I am home.

He stepped through the arch.

What's that? It glows with life, Stumble asked.

But the shadows run deep with death. That's the city, Dormaen. He's passing through the gates now.

They don't recognize him.

Why should they?

He's a hero. Their hero.

No, he's not their hero anymore. No one is what they once were.

The next day, Thain was too tired for company and a long-faced priest turned Thainna away at the fostral door. Disappointed and sore, she was determined not to waste the trip all the way up from the Rows. Thainna returned to the taphouse, wondering if Dorros had anything else interesting to share, but the Flame was nowhere to be found. A different man behind the plank bar told her that Dorros had not been seen since yesterday. Thainna thanked him and did not linger. It was getting late, too late for much else. The whole day wasted...

It was time to go home. The road was full of people finished with a long day of underpaid work. Thainna joined the dirty tide of humanity flowing into the Rows. The night was darkening quickly, turning the sky from pink to purple to a blue so deep it seemed to have been pulled up from the distant depths of the sea. Even that dim light was sinking rapidly into inky black and stars bloomed one by one, all silvery, cold and distant as the eyes of the gods.

Thainna lived deeper in the Rows than most of the crowd. By the time she had reached her own neighborhood, the crush of humanity thinned to a trudging trickle. Thainna's steps became slow and heavy, too, though it wasn't the pain of her still-raw feet. She just didn't want to go home. What was the point? There was nothing to go home *to*. Her brother was in the fostral. Her father was probably at the shop again, collecting money from more successful members of the House and tucking it away for safekeeping. There was no one at home waiting for her, no meal or even a warm bed.

But even the slowest feet eventually reached their destination. Thainna stopped between two lopsided shanties, rough-split planks and spars of wood strung with taut-laced pieces of cloth. One of them looked like it might have been some rich woman's sheet once, but now it was torn and filthy beyond any hope of cleaning. It was all just trash now.

Thainna was jealous of the shabby little lean-tos. Hole-riddled and flea-ridden though they were, those homes still had walls. It would be warmer inside. Summer was coming to an end and the nights were growing colder. Flickering light from small cooking fires – few in the Rows could afford stoves – silhouetted faceless and shadowy occupants.

Thainna squeezed between the walls and through a narrow gap in the crumbling mortar. The alleyway beyond was cramped and irregular, squashed between two of the slanting hovels and backing on a third.

Home. This is my home.

Years before, Aelos covered the narrowest places overhead with thick mats, woven from rushes that young Thain and Thainna carried from the shore of the Mazren River, but those were long since gone. As soon as the twins were old enough to enter the service of the House of Five Dragons, there was no time to mend or replace the makeshift roof anymore.

A rotten old barrel squatted in one crooked corner, many times patched but still leaky. Thainna leaned over the rim and had to reach deep to scoop up a handful of water. It hadn't rained for weeks. Her fingernails scraped the tar-coated bottom long before Thainna had enough to drink. When she was done, she coughed and spat out a slimy clot of something she could not identify and didn't really want to.

The water wouldn't hold out much longer. Nothing would.

Despair crashed over Thainna, pressing down on her stomach like a physical thing, crudely fashioned of heavy lead. Everything was falling apart.

It wasn't a sudden thing. It wasn't violent. This was a thousand times worse. It was plodding and inexorable, inevitable. It was the decay that turned even great men into putrid shreds of meat, that ground mountains down into sand. The Rows were rotten and Thainna was just another maggot wriggling through them. The best she could hope for was to grow up into a fly, buzzing and eating and soiling carrion. How could she ever be so stupid, to think that she could make any of it better? She lived in filth and drank water that tasted like mud.

Stupid, stupid, stupid!

And trying to steal and save enough money to bid in the coming Auction? Stupid. Thainna was competing with Flames and Eyes, many of whom had been rich even before joining the House of Five Dragons.

It's not for me, Thainna reminded herself, but it did not help. Selfless or selfish, it was all a pointless waste of time.

Thainna could run. She could take Thain away from Dormaen. Maybe out to Lorrus or Myra – one of the smaller cities in the southern parts of the Kaelos Valley. All the money she had saved would be enough to start a new life. A real life.

But no one walks away from the House. And what would I do in a new life, anyway? I don't know a trade. I'm just a thief. I steal what I need. I don't make bread or mill it or bake it. All I know how to do is take it.

Thainna threw herself down on a chaff-filled sack that served as her bed and cried until there was nothing left to cry. It changed nothing.

Her despair was exhausting, but Thainna couldn't sleep yet. It wasn't that cold yet, but her weeping had started a bone-deep shiver that would not abate. Thainna pulled herself back to her feet. Despite the pain in her feet, she needed to walk, to get her blood moving again. Thainna squeezed back out the way she had come, sideways like a crab evading a fisherman's trap.

The streets were all but empty now. She had been crying longer than she thought. In other parts of Dormaen, lanterns filled the streets with a friendly glow that guided late-night travelers, but not out here. Once, hae... The iron lamp hooks bolted to the sagging, failing walls had stood empty and cold for as long as Thainna could remember, only good for streaking the stones with rust every time it rained.

Still, there was light enough to see by. The moon and the stars all shone pearly white, making even the shabby, ugly Rows appear embroidered in silver on perfectly black velvet. It was almost pretty.

Thainna walked. She had no destination in mind, but she knew the streets of her home. She wouldn't get lost. Too bad, she thought.

It wasn't a completely unpleasant thought, to vanish mysteriously into the night. Like Rikard Mazrem in Njorn Pass. Let everyone wonder where she had gone.

Of course, he didn't just vanish... He died. Rikard Mazrem traded his life for those of his men, to save them from the Fiori.

The wild Fiori were as much her own kind as the Carcaens, but Thainna didn't feel much pride or sympathy for her mother's race. It was said that the Fiori even ate their own dead. But now, because of Captain Mazrem's sacrifice, the surviving Fiori were as much a part of the great empire as the Carcaens who had founded it.

Thainna turned down another narrow alleyway, only slightly broader than the one she lived in and barely wide enough to walk through. But unfettered by such pedestrian confines, her thoughts whirled wildly like leaves on the wind.

If she *did* disappear, would anyone even notice or care? Her father? Probably not. He rarely came home anymore and it wasn't like Thainna brought any money into their pathetic excuse for a home. Everything she earned went either into the hands of the Talons and Flames who gave her orders or else into the vaults to be saved for the Auction. As far as her father was concerned, Thainna was just another mouth to feed and one that spent entirely too much time talking.

No one from the House of Five Dragons would miss Thainna. She was one of hundreds of Talons. The Crest probably wouldn't even notice the loss. Maybe when some of the others finally had to do their own petty thievery... Even then, they would only find some other young, unimportant Talon. Thainna was replaceable. Easily replaceable.

But Thain would miss her. That was enough to banish even idle daydreams of leaving. Thainna's twin would be broken without her. Thain loved her. He needed her.

Cheered up, Thainna turned back at the closed and darkened bread shop, ready to make her way home. There was still no new work from the House. Tomorrow, she could have a word with Illius. For a cut of the take, he might be willing to pour a few more of the fake medals. She could tell him to change the mold, put the right year on the damned things. It wouldn't be hard to sell some more of them before someone finally caught on. Every laurel brought her one closer to winning the Auction.

8

MIDNIGHT

"By the time scouts spotted the Fiori horde, the slaughter had already begun. Njorn Pass ran with Carcaen blood and rang with the Fiori victory cries. It was then, in the midst of the slaughter, that Captain Mazrem cast a circle of blood in the snow. He called across the veil to the Alterra and begged them to save his dying men. In return, he would give them anything. They could take from him any price that they wished. Such an open pact had been discussed since the scholarly days of VEIL, but never attempted."

— ACCOUNTS OF NJORN PASS, BY ALEXANDER FERRO

IRRITATION FANNED into fury did nothing to rekindle the failing sun. Pinpricks of light filled the sky, but they shed only a little light on the road beneath his feet. There were iron hooks in the walls that, after a moment's concentration, he remembered should have been hung with cages of fire.

The dark streets were close and cramped. They stank of fear and decay. He didn't remember this part of the city. He should have been on the banks of the Mazren River. Was this place new...? No, it couldn't be. Everything here was run down, tottering on the verge of collapse. Many of the shadows that he passed weren't true buildings at all, but the spaces between broken walls hastily boarded up to make cheap shelters.

Scabs over a wound. One misstep and they'll tear open again, filling the city with blood.

Thainna heard the footsteps long before she saw the man. The sounds of his footsteps were heavy and rang like iron bells in the midnight silence. A lifetime of thief's instincts stopped Thainna dead in her tracks and she slipped silently back into the deeper shadows.

That was the sound of armored boots, something with metal. Not the leather shoes of soldiers or guards. That meant a VEIL knight. Out here in the Rows? There was no way his business was good for anyone else. Women? Drink? Thainna doubted it. There were much better brothels and taphouses in other parts of the city, ones that offered huge discounts and better fare to the knights of VEIL.

What if the knight out there was hunting down the House of Five Dragons? The Crest was overreaching, Dorros said, trying to control Gaius Mazrem. If VEIL ever found out, they would never let that pass, would they? There were spies among the knights, of course, but who they were was a closely guarded secret even within the House.

Even if VEIL *had* embarked on a crusade against the House of Five Dragons, surely they would send more than a single man. Was it really only one set of footsteps? Maybe there were more. Thainna strained to listen. It was hard to hear anything over the pounding of her own heart.

She leaned out just enough to see past the wall, out into the street. It was a man – and only one, Thainna noted with relief – but something about him looked... wrong.

Thainna squinted. Details were difficult to make out in the colorless moonlight, but he looked somehow familiar. The man wore a full suit of armor, banded steel riveted to molded leather and emblazoned with the Carcaen laurel tree and lion. But something about it looked strange. The design was different, with wider steel strips and leather that looked a shade lighter. It was plain brown, not dyed black, blue or red like modern armor.

Modern armor?

Thainna *knew* that style of armor. The statue towering over Mazrem Square wore the same kind. Thainna leaned out a little further as the man neared. He limped slowly in a crooked, staggering path. The old-fashioned armor was dented, the leather torn and cut. It was streaked with something unpleasantly thick and dark. Mud, maybe? But Thainna doubted it.

He walked like a corpse might if the gods wrenched him up from his grave and set him restlessly wandering. The man's steel-shod boots scraped across the paving stones, one after another in a raw cacophony that made Thainna's skin crawl. His head hung forward, chin resting in the gorget of his armor.

Was he even looking where he was going? He moved as though sleepwalking. The man's long, dark hair had been pulled back into a tail at some point past, but most of it had fallen free and now hung in front of his face in a dirty curtain.

Was he drunk? Mad?

Thainna was so caught up in her curiosity that she failed to notice how close the knight had come. His head snapped up and he saw her watching. He lunged, closing the last yards between them as fast as a diving hawk.

Thainna startled and leapt back, but not nearly quickly enough. He snarled and grabbed her by the throat, lifting her until her feet kicked at empty air. Thainna clawed at the strange man's hand and writhed, turning her body this way and that to wriggle free, but his grip was like stone. Something between her eyes seared with pain. Thainna screamed in agony.

"Fiori!" the man howled, tightening steel fingers around her neck. "Will you animals never die? Let us go!"

Face to face with him, Thainna's eyes widened. Even through the hazy red starbursts of pain, she recognized him. It wasn't just his strange old armor.

Thainna knew that face. Everyone in Carce did.

That's Rikard Mazrem.

The little barbarian squirmed in his grasp, as slippery as a writhing snake. Rikard tightened his gauntleted fist around her throat with cruel slowness, delighting in the wet grating of bones under his fingers.

Fiori in Dormaen? Never, never! Monsters, animals...!

The girl's face darkened as she choked. His hate and fury bored into her, making her eyes widen and roll in their sockets with agony. The pain was terrible, he knew all too well.

"Half!" she gasped. "Only half... Fiori...! I'm Carcaen!"

Rikard jerked in surprise, minutely relaxing his deadly grip. He yanked the girl closer until their faces almost touched. She was right. She had the slender build, the sharp foxy face and fiery red hair of a Fiori, but the huge, frightened eyes that stared back at him were the wrong shape and color. The mountain tribe all had round, ice-blue eyes. This girl's were the same angled shape as his own and a Carcaen dark green.

Mixed Carcaen and Fiori blood? What horror of war had bred such a creature? Rikard's shocked inspection dulled the edge of his rage, replacing agony with a hot discomfort. The girl quieted a bit, but she was still watching him intently, gasping for breath and dark purple in the face.

"Please, let me go, Lord Mazrem," she wheezed.

Rikard instinctively tensed himself. He tightened his fingers around her neck again. "You won't take my name!"

Whatever response the half-Fiori girl expected, this wasn't it. Her all-too-Carcaen eyes were still huge with terror and she gasped. Her mind squirmed under Rikard's touch, curling and twitching like a hook-skewered worm, but his hold was too strong.

Gods! It's Rikard Mazrem... But he's dead! Oh, gods, he's a ghost and he's come to kill me for the fake medals... It can't be Rikard. He looks just like the statue, but... but it's been thirty years! Surma and Saerus, what's going on?

But there was no deception in the girl's thoughts. Only her fear, searingly painful to the touch. Rikard hissed and retreated from her mind.

"Thirty years?" he repeated.

It couldn't have been thirty years. Rikard searched for confirmation, but the half-Fiori whelp would not be still, in body or mind.

"Please! Please, let me go," she gasped.

Rikard wasn't listening. Thirty years? Three decades? But there was sense to it. The changes in the city, the smoky tang to the air that never used to be there, the worn and cracked road. All of it.

He dropped the girl to the ground and stared at his hands. They were scarred and roughened by years of rigorous VEIL training, but were firm and unlined. The hands of a young man.

Thirty years since they took me. Thirty years I've been gone from the world, from my wife and my son. Thirty years! The world has changed, but I haven't...

Rikard Mazrem wrenched his gaze up from his hands and back to the dark, dirty street. He would get answers from the Fiori girl and then he would have her heart out!

But she was gone.

Thainna ran until her feet bled, leaving spots of red on the broken cobbles behind her. Her lungs pressed too hard inside her ribs. She did not even feel the pain that she knew should be there. Everything except her hammering heart was numb and seemed strangely light, as though she floated on the swirling midnight air instead of running for her life.

When she had put half a mile between her and the wild war-hero, Thainna finally slowed and stopped. She slumped against a crumbling wall, wheezing and feeling suddenly drained. The blind shock of her strange meeting pulled back like a curtain.

Rikard Mazrem.

But how can Rikard Mazrem be alive? He gave his life to kill the Fiori in Njorn Pass!

She had just met Lord-Captain Rikard Caelis Mazrem, the most famous hero in the worlds. It sounded mad. It *felt* mad just to think about, but who else could it be? How certain was anyone that Captain Mazrem had actually died in Njorn Pass?

The question seemed profane, even in the jumbled turmoil of her own mind. Rikard Mazrem was a great man, a near-mythical hero whose renown rivaled even Emperor Tychon. All of that fame, all of that reverence was for a martyr, for Captain Mazrem's historic sacrifice. If he hadn't actually died, what did that mean? Anything? Everything?

The man she had just escaped certainly didn't seem like much of a hero. He was dirty and bloody and tried to choke the life out of her for being even part Fiori. All of that snarling and screaming... Was that really the hero of Carce? But his armor, his face! It had to be Rikard Mazrem. There was simply no other answer.

Not for me, at least. But then, I'm not clever like Thain.

Thainna's toes hurt now, almost unbearably. She cursed and sat down on the edge of the road. One at a time, she pulled her feet as close to her face as she could manage. But by moonlight, blood and dirt looked too much alike. It was impossible to tell the extent of the damage. Her feet smelled awful, but that was nothing new.

Thainna gritted her teeth and stretched her legs out in front of her. Some rest first, then... then what? Go home? It seemed like she should tell someone what happened. But who? No one would ever believe her.

I'll bang on the gates of the imperial palace. How about that? You've been wrong all along! Rikard Mazrem's still alive! And he's in a bad mood! They'll just throw me back out into the street and shake their heads at the crazy girl. If they don't whip me.

It really wasn't very funny, but Thainna laughed anyway. The sound had a sharp, hysterical edge. What if someone found out that she had *not* said anything? Wasn't that just as likely to get her punished? What about VEIL? Shouldn't they be told that Captain Mazrem was still alive? But the guards that always stood outside the Verita et Illumina Lansinos archouses were no more likely to listen to Thainna than those of the imperial palace.

What about the House of Five Dragons? A shiver turned quickly into a full-body shudder that made Thainna's teeth rattle. No. If they thought she was making up stories for attention or some kind of profit, the Crest would probably have Thainna beaten to death and then dropped behind someone's house in a puddle of her own blood.

But what if she didn't say anything and then the Crest found out anyway? What if he knew that Thainna was keeping such valuable secrets? She couldn't begin to guess.

Thainna hugged her arms around herself and wondered what to do.

9

STAND

"Who are the Alterra? What are they? These are questions that we have asked since their discovery a century ago and for which we have few answers. All we know for certain is how truly little we know about these strange, alien creatures."

—A HISTORY OF OUR WORLDS, BY CARNUS ORPHAEM

THE HORIZON TIPPED up on its side, like the joint of two vast walls in the immeasurable distance. But with every passing verse, it drew closer as the Shatter consumed the dreamlands between. Sizzling tears shot sideways with lethal despair. A lanky Alterran sang them on, an antlered form somewhere between rebellion and a leaping stag. He raised his long-fingered hands and the tears caught a color-less curl of smoke in their whipping rain.

The ashy smear writhed silently, trying to escape. But before the rain scoured it away, the blank-bodied Shatter coiled into a tight, invisible ball and then exploded outward in a boom of blindness.

The stag-headed Alterran's resolution was no match for the blast and he fluttered to the ground in tatters.

A moment later, even those faded and there was nothing left to mark his passage.

Stumble sparked his bright new owl-eyes unhappily and flew back to Flickerdim. The other Alterran had uncoiled from around the silver-slick tower branch and hung like a thick vine, weaving sinuously from side to side. Stumble spread his wings and glided to a lower limb, closer to the serpent's head.

Did you see that? Stumble asked.

I see many things, Flickerdim thought. *And know more.*

He surged a short sound of unhappiness in a rapid-fire succession of snow and stone as the sky burned with loss and unfounded resolution.

But Jingleblack... They just killed Jingleblack! Stumble cried.

Flickerdim looked back to the upended horizon. Of Jingleblack, there was no sign. His tear-rain spiraled and spun, but that would be gone soon, too. The ground beneath the battlefield twisted and thinned. Colors cracked as it stretched, peeling away like layers of cheap paint. Flickerdim turned away from the encroaching Shatter with a flick of his tail.

They will not reach us here, he said. *Not yet.*

Not yet? Where was Firelight? Stumble asked. *She was supposed to help Jingleblack!*

Firelight is dead, too.

Stumble clawed at the air until he found a stable memory and held tight. Flickerdim stretched his coils until the younger Alterran could see quite clearly through the stars and storms of his body. The thin, tenebrous form reminded him disconcertingly of the fragile, failing Uprising. Flickerdim touched his thoughts against Stumble's lightly, comfortingly.

They aren't here yet, he said again. *There is still some time.*

Rikard's struggle with the Fiori girl had unexpectedly wearied him. *Half Fiori,* he reminded himself. It seemed like an important distinction.

He tripped over a broken paving stone and nearly fell. Everything hurt. The acid growling in his gut was gnawing away at him until it seemed that his armor was the only thing holding him up. His eyes were lumps of drying glue. Every time the sticky things closed, it grew harder to open them again. The little night-death was coming back for him soon.

Home. I want to go home.

Rikard was impatient. Who knew how long the colorful blackness, the twins Sleep and Dream, would take him again? He wanted to move, to keep going. Get home. But how? The streets here were dark and narrow and twisted.

The last time Rikard had been in Dormaen – *thirty years ago!* – all of this was different. Farms. Farms on the bank of the Mazren River. Rikard raised his eyes to the rotting husk of a house. No, not a house, but a barn with an arched roof that had tumbled in some time ago. But why? Where were the farms? The vineyards?

Thirty years. What happened? Did we... win? Is the war over? How big is the empire now?

Rikard jerked upright, his very bones protesting the movement. He had to keep moving. Everything was so heavy, so empty. As long as he kept moving forward, toward the center of the city, he would eventually reach something he knew. He was so close.

But so far along the time-road. Thirty years. Thirty...

The road had widened again, gently smoothing in course and texture. Proper houses and shops replaced the ramshackle shanties. And people. Real people, not like the unnerving half-Fiori girl. Carcaens, with golden skin and angled eyes. But the girl's eyes had been familiar, too. Everything was the same but different.

A bilious surge of resentment flared inside Rikard, but smothered under the oppressive weariness in his body.

How strange to feel his body again after so long. Other bodies, too. Rikard had forgotten how easily they betrayed the thoughts shielded behind mere layers of flesh and bone. Or had he ever known? It was so hard to remember anything from before the broken-glass war of Alterra.

Even that's hard to hold on to. The war... What happened?

There were few others in the street during the dark hours. *Night.* Most were at home, safe and warm with wives and husbands and children. But there were some midnight travelers, maybe lost like Rikard or with duties that demanded their late-night attention.

A fat Carcaen lounged in a sedan chair with a young woman in his lap. The pair giggled and wrestled in a manner that belonged in a bedroom, not the open street. They were utterly oblivious to the discomfort of the four porters that struggled to keep their gilded chair upright. The woman's dress would have been embarrassingly revealing even if she was still wearing the whole thing. She sat up in the man's embrace, pointing at Rikard plodding past and laughing at his disarray.

He kept walking.

Most of the other evening travelers were not so lucky as the couple, or at least not so rich. Like Rikard, they traveled on their own feet, many reeling drunkenly in pairs or groups. Others looked more like the half-Fiori girl – dirty and pathetic, with a subtle, dangerous ferocity that Rikard could not place. There was nothing like it on the battlefield. Some eyes tracked him, but most remained fixed on their destinations, as though they could see their homes even through the distance and obstacles.

Just like me.

Everyone is going home.

But Rikard was slowing down. Even his momentary consideration of the other Carcaens was chipping away at his fading energy.

How long had it been since he had last... what? Rikard still couldn't remember what he needed, but it was something he had been a long time without.

Even his thoughts began to fray and it was difficult to focus. Sleep was coming for him again, inescapable and treacherous as bad luck. Darkness welled up from some hidden place inside his own body and Rikard fell.

Marus Gallard sighed and shook the sleeping knight. The man on the ground was little more than a faintly glistening lump in the long dawn shadows, like the rolled-up ball-bugs Marus had played with in his mother's garden when he was a boy.

He shook the other VEIL knight again. Another one too drunk to make it home or to the archouse. This was the fifth this week.

"Come now, get up," Marus told him. "If you're still down here when the captain makes his rounds, we'll both get in trouble. Let's get you back to the archouse."

The knight on the ground grunted and uncurled from his fetal coil, though he did not stand or even sit. Marus sat back on his heels, frowning. Something was not at all right here. Though the other man looked about ten years younger than Marus – who did not consider himself anything like an old man just yet – he was in a stupor that rivaled the oldest, most besotted drunkards. It must have been a fun night.

Or a rough one... It wasn't very often that a VEIL knight lost the fight that he picked, but it was known to happen from time to time. There were several deep rents in the fallen man's armor, but most of the blood streaked around them was flaky and brown, long since dried.

His features were classically Carcaen, handsome and fine, but sunken and unhealthy-looking. Not sick, but as if the young man had not eaten in days. Weeks, perhaps. He wasn't dead, but not far from it. His chest rose and fell shallowly.

Marus shook the other knight again, harder this time.

"Get yourself up," he said. "You can have a better sleep back in your bunk. I'll send a foster and something to eat. Come along."

"Home," mumbled the man on the ground.

Marus sighed. It was clear that he was not going to get a speck of help. With an effort, Marus hauled the young man to his feet, where he crumpled promptly again in a great clatter of armor. Marus grabbed again, groaning and heaving, and folded the limp knight over his shoulder like a sack of potatoes.

The two miles back to the Moon Court might as well have been the distance to the actual moon. By the time he hauled his burden back to the white-columned archouse, Marus' saela was soaked in sweat and clung to his skin. With his hands full, he kicked the doors open. They cracked loudly against the walls and the noise brought a pair of white-tabbaed templars hurrying into the entry hall.

"Long night?" asked the older of the two, a matronly woman named Ephria.

Neither templar looked even slightly surprised to see a knight carrying one of his unconscious fellows into the archouse.

"Don't know," Marus huffed. "Tes Luan, go get the foster. I think he's hurt."

The younger woman bobbed a quick bow and hurried off to do as she'd been asked. Ephria rolled her eyes.

"Really, Sir Gallard, I don't think we need a foster to deal with one drunken knight."

"Damn you with blood, woman!" Marus wheezed. "Stop talking and help me get him to a bed. He weighs like a boulder!"

Muttering to herself, Ephria helped Marus heave the unconscious knight up the stairs and into one of the empty barracks rooms. Together, they pulled him through the door and dropped him heavily onto the bed.

Marus collapsed onto a stool while Ephria – who had taken much less of the burden – arranged the young man on the bed. Her gray-streaked hair was in disarray, like a wispy steel crown. She was no longer smiling.

"You're right, Sir Gallard," she said after a moment's inspection. "He's been doing a lot more than drinking."

Marus nodded. He could not keep enough breath in his body to speak, so he waved a sweaty hand at the damaged armor. Ephria followed his gesture and covered her mouth, stifling a gasp.

"He's been bleeding. Surely no one would dare! Gods, where did you find him?"

"On the street. Not far," Marus panted.

Ephria shook out a pair of oiled leather gloves from a pocket of her tabba and pulled them on. The templar unbuckled and began peeling back the broken armor. She stopped, frowning.

"What?" Marus asked her.

"This isn't the usual armor."

"What?" With an effort, Marus stood and went to the bedside. "Are you telling me I just hauled some *other* soldier halfway across the bloody city?"

"No," Ephria answered. Her voice was unexpectedly soft, almost reverent. "No, I remember suits like this. From the campaign days, when I was younger. I was at Njorn Pass, hae."

Marus knew. The entire Moon Court knew. Ephria reminded them often, but now it suddenly actually seemed interesting.

"This is old armor, the kind they wore during the war," Marus said. "What's this fellow doing with it?"

"I'm not sure," Ephria answered. "None of the smiths have made it in years. It's just too heavy."

In short order, Ephria had the man carefully stripped down to his torn, dusty saela. Star Court black, Marus noted. Luan knocked politely at the door frame before entering, a fat blue-robed foster in tow.

Marus stepped back to make room at the bedside and smiled at Luan. She returned it shyly, bobbed her head and left again. When Marus returned his attention to the sleeping knight, the foster had pulled up a stool beside the bed and unlaced the young knight's torn saela. Like Ephria, he put on a pair of gloves before beginning his examination.

"The cuts are bloody, but superficial," he announced. "Badly malnourished and dehydrated, but otherwise, I would say that he just needs sleep."

The foster brushed back the young knight's long black hair and peeled back his eyelids. Ephria let out a shriek and jumped back from the bed. Marus started, dropping his hand to his sword. The golden cap on his forefinger clacked against the hilt with startling volume.

The stout foster looked up at the other two in annoyance. "I need quiet to work."

"That... that's him!" Ephria cried, pointing to the man's face with a shaking finger. "It's Captain Mazrem!"

The subject of her alarm twitched at the noise. His eyes fluttered beneath blood-flecked lids. Marus pulled the foster away by a handful of cerulean tabba and stared. There was no way Ephria could be right. She must be mad to think this poor, beaten boy was Rikard Mazrem. It was impossible, of course... but the man on the bed *did* look familiar. He looked just like that statue in the middle of Dormaen.

"Calm down, both of you," the foster huffed, straightening his tabba. "Tes Ephria, you're quite mistaken."

"No, I'm not!" said Ephria, her eyes still riveted to the sleeping knight. "That's him. You boys are too young to remember, but not me! That's Rikard Mazrem. Gods, he looks exactly the same."

She did not seem to be speaking to them anymore, or even to the man she claimed was Carce's greatest hero, but to her own long-lost youth. She reverently touched the star emblem, embossed in leather and affixed to the left shoulder of his discarded armor. Rikard Mazrem *had* been from the Star Court... Marus was only a toddling little boy during the Fiori campaign.

"Ephria, are you sure?" he asked the templar. "It's been thirty years."

"I'm sure. I swear it, Sir Gallard. This is Captain Mazrem."

The foster seemed to be reconsidering his objections. He waved Marus away again and bent to examine the strange knight's injuries. With gloved fingers, he prodded and probed the cuts and a couple of deeper stab wounds in the man's chest.

"These injuries *could* have been inflicted by spears," the foster said slowly. "Fiori spears."

"That's hardly definitive," Marus protested. This was madness. Rikard Mazrem was thirty years dead!

"Why don't you believe me?" Ephria asked.

"Because it's impossible!"

She was quiet for a long moment as she visibly struggled to regain her composure. Marus and the foster waited. Even though it could not be true, Marus couldn't shake the feeling that history was waiting to happen.

"You don't believe me, but you'll have to believe his wife," said Ephria at last. "Foster, give this great man milk and water. When he wakes, we'll take him to Laurael Mazrem. I'll take care of the arrangements."

In a stiff of white robes, the old templar swept from the room. Marus rubbed his eyes. It was still early in the morning, but it felt like years had passed. Time enough to turn the whole world upside down.

"Do you believe her?" Marus asked.

"If she's wrong, then I'm not going to be the one to say so. But if Tes Ephria is correct..."

They looked down at the knight on the bed. The ramifications were too great for words.

10

NORTHERN WIND

"The ever-changing realm of the Alterra is one of water and fire, the very same ephemeral humours of our own blood. Is it any wonder, then, that blood calls to them?"

—A HISTORY OF OUR WORLDS, BY CARNUS ORPHAEM

THE BRIGHT LIGHT of the sun woke Thainna not long after dawn. She rolled over and pressed her face into the burlap bag of her bed, but sleep would not be so easily recaptured. Flaky old wheat chaff scratched her cheeks and made her nose itch. Thainna sneezed and sat up. She rubbed her eyes and crawled to the rain barrel. Looking over the rim and down into the brackish puddle at the bottom, Thainna decided that she wasn't really that thirsty.

Thainna rarely had such vivid dreams. Meeting Rikard Mazrem in the Rows? It had seemed so real... But in the early morning light, the whole thing seemed ridiculous. Thainna sat on her sack-bed to examine her toes. They were even worse than the day before, with cracks scabbed over and bruises on her heels.

Like I was running.

So it wasn't a dream, after all. But that did not make it real. How long since her last real meal, since a drink of clean water? Thainna had lived all her life in the Rows. People starved and died of thirst every day, and it was not just the lack of food and water that killed. Desperation sometimes drove the hungry to make meals of poison.

Thainna considered the rain barrel again. It looked unappetizing, but didn't seem toxic. Did it? She was not a physic or a foster or anyone who could tell such things. Maybe the midnight vision of Captain Mazrem simply meant she was sick. Some people believed that such delusions and hallucinations were visions from the gods. Maybe it was some sort of prediction.

Hae, but of what? That Rikard Mazrem's going to come back?

The whole argument seemed circular. Trying to make sense of it all only made Thainna's head ache. She was no one. The gods didn't waste time with dirty little thieves from the Rows. No, it was probably just an addle-brained delusion from some bad water. Nothing more.

At least it made for a good story. Thain would love it. Thainna stood gingerly. Her feet hurt worse than ever. She searched around the narrow alleyway until she found the moth-eaten burlap that used to be her father's bed, until he'd started sleeping at the storefront. Thainna tore the cloth into wide strips, folded two of them into pads and used the rest to tie them to the bottom of her feet. It didn't take away the pain, but it was considerable improvement over bare feet.

On her way to the fostral, Thainna detoured to visit Aelos. He was awake and counting a pile of shaved silver willows under the surly supervision of another Talon – a short, bald Karabosi named Bannon. Both looked up at Thainna's entrance, but recognized the interloper as just another House member and quickly returned to their work.

"Thirty-seven," Aelos said.

Bannon made a displeased noise, somewhere between a grunt and cough. "That's all?"

"That's all."

The stout Talon grunted again and then left the store. Aelos dropped his money into a bowl of other coins. The silver willows clanked and rang against each other.

"You didn't put them away," Thainna said. "Is someone coming to pick it up soon? Is mine in here?"

There were several gold-edged laurels inside the bowl. Thainna reached out to touch one – it had taken so much work to collect them – but Aelos clapped his hand over hers and pushed it away.

"Leave it, Thainna. Hae, your money's in here. One of the Eyes will be by this afternoon to take it out to the temples."

"Don't they trust you to do it?" Thainna asked.

After a lifetime of service to the House of Five Dragons, Aelos Vahn had very little to show for it. No money, few responsibilities, and not an ounce of trust. Of course, if the House could trust their counters, old Kir would still have all of his fingers.

"I'm just a Talon," Aelos said. He shrugged, but the limpness in his shoulders betrayed his own unhappiness, deeper than he would ever admit. "The Crest is... selective in his trust."

"Hae," Thainna agreed dispiritedly.

The two of them stood together in awkward silence for a long moment before Aelos cleared his throat and spoke again. "Do you have more to deposit?"

"No, I just..." Why *had* she come? To tell her father about last night? He would never believe a word of it, even if she did. "I just wanted to say good morning and ask if you'd come home tonight."

"What for? It's an alleyway, Thainna," said Aelos. He had been fidgeting pointlessly with some of the coins, but now he looked up at his daughter. There was something pitiful and heavy in his dark green eyes. "It's not a home. It's just a dirty patch of ground. I'm sorry, Thainna."

She didn't want apologies. He was right, but whose fault was it? Her mother was long since dead, too weakened by the twins to survive their birth. Thain was a sick boy in a distant white fostral bed. Thainna worked all day, every day to make life into something! What did Pata do? What did apologizing ever do? It never changed anything or made it any better.

Thainna left the shop without another word to her father.

"Rikard Mazrem? You *saw* Rikard Mazrem?"

Thainna rested her head against the edge of Thain's bed. The new sheets were clean, but her twin's hair still looked ragged and brittle. Had the fosters done anything about it?

"No," Thainna corrected. "No. I couldn't have, could I? Captain Mazrem's dead."

"But you said that you saw him!" Thain was excited, practically bouncing in his narrow fostral bed as he grinned at his sister. "You have good eyes, Thainna. You said he looked just like the statue in Mazrem Square."

She put her chin in her palm and shook her head. "That doesn't mean anything. There are millions of men in the empire. I'm sure at least one of them looks like Rikard Mazrem. If I really even saw anything! Last time I ate, it was moldy bread. Who knows what really happened?"

Thain touched the top of her head and Thainna looked up. With his thin, sunken face, her twin looked like an old man.

"Why are you so sure it wasn't him?" Thain asked. "You were certain last night. You never trust anyone, not even yourself."

"Forget it."

Thainna lifted her face out of her hands and looked down at them. They were small and very dirty. They didn't look capable of very much.

"I trust you," Thain said. He smiled and took one of her pale hands in his. "I'm not blind, Thainna. You work every day to get the money for the Auction so you can make sure the next Crest isn't like this one. Anyone else would put themselves on the Jade Throne, but not you."

"You'll be a better Crest than I ever could, Thain."

She meant it. For all his sickness, Thain was brilliant, sweet and kind. Not slow and stubborn like his sister. He didn't need physical strength to be Crest, if she could just buy him the position. Thain would have every Eye, Flame and Talon to serve as his able hands. All he needed was his mind, his spirit. Everything would be better once Thain became Crest.

"I know that you think I can do it, and I trust you," Thain said, squeezing her fingers weakly. "If you think I'm clever enough to become Crest this winter, then you have to listen to me, hae? And I'm telling you to have a bit more faith."

Thainna giggled helplessly. It was impossible to argue with her twin. He always won. Thain laughed, too, a thin and breathy sound.

"Tell me more about him," Thain said.

"About... Captain Mazrem?"

"Hae. There are so many legends. What was he like? Grand? Commanding and brave as in all the stories?"

"He wasn't at all like the stories... if it was him at all," Thainna hastened to add. "He was so angry. No, not just angry. Crazed. He was like an animal, Thain. He grabbed me and started screaming and choking me just because I'm Fiori."

"And he seemed young?"

"Not fifty or sixty years old, at least, and he looked younger than Pata. Five years older than us. Maybe ten."

"Was he handsome, like his statues?" Thain asked slyly.

Thainna blushed. "I don't know."

"But you recognized him! You said he looked just like the statues," Thain accused.

"He did! But he looked crazy, wild. Sick, too, or like he hadn't eaten in a long time."

"Hae, and you can talk!"

"And he was injured," Thainna continued, ignoring her brother's jibe. "I don't know how. Who would attack him? Especially the way he was acting. You'd have to be crazy, too!"

"Rikard Mazrem was injured during the Njorn Pass battle," Thain reminded her. "If he hasn't gotten any older, maybe he hasn't healed, either."

"But it's been thirty years!"

"So? If you saw him last night, then Rikard Mazrem didn't die in Njorn Pass. He didn't leave a body, only his sword. He made an open deal with the Alterra. No one knows what they asked for. Maybe thirty years of his life? His mind?"

"His mind...?" Thainna had no idea what her twin was talking about. There were stories about the deals struck between VEIL and their Alterran counterparts, but few details of what the knights traded away.

"Nothing physical can pass between the Terran and Alterran worlds," said Thain. "Blood shows through, but it doesn't actually *cross* the veil. Just thoughts and memories, hae?"

"I... don't really know," Thainna admitted.

She liked the stories about Captain Mazrem. He had been a hero, whatever else her strange midnight encounter might suggest. His sacrifice was noble and his defeat of the Fiori was legend. It was exciting! But the complicated and arcane pacts between VEIL and the Alterra did not make for very good stories. Thain patted Thainna's hand. Even from his bed in the fostral, her twin knew more about the world than she could learn in a thousand years.

"No one has been to Alterra. We don't know anything about it except what the Alterra tell VEIL. And we don't know much about the Alterrans themselves. Mazrem didn't dictate the term of his pact. They could have taken absolutely anything."

"And they took his life. Captain Mazrem traded his life for all of his men's," said Thainna. "Everyone knows that."

"Do we? What exactly does that mean? Maybe the Alterra didn't have to kill him to claim his life. Nobody knows for certain. Except Rikard Mazrem, of course. Aren't you curious?"

Thainna thought back to the howling, screaming man choking her in the dark and shivered. She preferred the legends.

"No. I don't want to know."

11
EVERSTONES

"His own wife barely knew him. Captain Mazrem was the hero of all Carce, the legendary martyr who gave his life to save those under his command, to save the fledgling empire from the Fiori. Can anyone truly say they knew the man behind the legend?"

— HONORING OUR HEROES, BY PERSUS RAVINE

RIKARD WASN'T ALONE when he woke up. He could smell other people, the scents of skin and sun-warmed cloth. Their voices were soft, whispering like old things. How long had Rikard been gone this time? The stiff feeling in his joints suggested that it had been a while.

Where am I?

Something beneath him was much softer than the road Rikard had fallen asleep on. He felt light, too, as though a part of him was missing. But he was still alive, wasn't he?

Curious, Rikard opened his eyes. The sky was gone. Instead, a smooth white something stretched overhead, blank as a sheet of paper. It didn't seem to be the source of the voices, however.

Rikard sat up slowly. His body protested painfully. Every inch of him was stiff and sore, but he could move more easily than before.

It was his armor that was missing. Someone had dressed him in a new black saela and pants. Without his husk of leather and steel, Rikard felt very naked. He pulled the blanket up tight around his shoulders.

On the tip of his right forefinger, someone had carefully cleaned and polished the gold bloodcap. Rikard pressed the metal against the blanket weave until he felt his pulse in the cannula. It tingled down the length of his finger. Reassured by the living throb of his own blood, Rikard turned his attention to the rest of the room.

A pair of old women huddled to one side, whispering to a man in a collared blue saela. He was a handsome gentleman, younger than the women, but not by much. Despite his silvered hair and age-lined face, Rikard recognized him.

Nikas. Nikas Hern of the Moon Court.

One of the women in white – templars, servants and helpers to the VEIL knights, Rikard remembered suddenly – noticed him sitting and hurried to his side, motioning to the other two.

"General Hern, sir," she said. "He's awake."

He turned to look at Rikard, brows raised. Though his face had aged gracefully, Hern's eyes were tired. Rikard reached for a better feel, pushing past the old knight's curious gaze. More than tired. Stretched out thin. Pulled taut like the head of a drum until every poke and prod quivered through his entire being.

His only thought is to push away the beating hands. His every word is civil, softened until it can move nothing at all.

"Blood and bond, Rik," said Hern. He sat beside the bed and laced his fingers together. "You've been asleep for a day. Is it really you sitting there?"

Was it? Rikard wasn't sure. He stared blankly at Hern. In Fiore, Nikas had been a young man, but still older than Rikard by several years and much more experienced.

Thirty years... Was this the same man who gave the too-young Star Court captain his first drink of mulso?

Captain Errain died of his wounds, screaming away his last breath as he cursed the Fiori. When the noise finally stopped, you brought me a cup of hot mulso, so strong it made my eyes water. "The captain's dead," you told me. "You're in command now, Rik. Drink deep."

Hern seemed disappointed at the lack of immediate reaction. He leaned closer, furrowing his lined brow. "Rik? Say something."

"Where... is this?" Rikard asked. His voice sounded so strange, flat and uninflected. How did Terrans manage to communicate anything this way? It was so slow. Clumsy. But at least it didn't hurt.

"We built new archouses in the city twenty years ago. You're in the one that belongs to the Moon Court. One of my knights, Marus Gallard, found you in the street and brought you here. A templar identified you. Gods, it's really you, Rik!"

"Why are there Fiori in Dormaen?"

Hern clasped Rikard's shoulder through the blanket and gave the sore muscles beneath a light squeeze.

"We won the war, Rik," he said. "It's over. You wiped out the entire Fiori army. There weren't enough of them left to fight after that. Everyone else is a citizen of Carce now."

"What of Crast? Po'Mar? Nian and Lyncea?"

"All provinces of the empire. Every one of them," said Hern. "All fifty nations have joined the empire."

All? Even secretive Nian and bold Lyncea, whose rivalry and hatred of one another was legend across the worlds? How? How many wars did Emperor Tychon wage to build his empire?

"How?" Rikard asked. "I don't..."

"It was you, Rik. After word spread about what you did, how one man devastated an entire army, no one wanted to fight Carce anymore," said Hern. His thoughts shuddered, lurching away from something unpleasant, but none of it showed in his face or voice. Nikas Hern smiled steadily at Rikard. "You saved us all, you know.

There hasn't been a single war since Njorn Pass. You're a hero. The biggest damned hero in the world."

All of Terra spun. Rikard closed his eyes. No more wars? But the Alterra fought every day. Didn't the Terrans know about that? The fighting that ravaged the other world, turning the sky to ashes and water into gray nothing? A single glimpse into Hern's tumbling thoughts gave Rikard his answer.

No. They don't know. Or else they don't think about it.

But Rikard himself had not remembered the Alterran war until just that moment. Everything was still so confusing, so overwhelming. A broken jumble. What did it all mean? It was too much. Rikard pulled the blanket up over his head, blotting out the sounds of Hern's breathing and the rustling of the templar's tabbae.

"Captain Mazrem?" Hern asked. His interest would not be so easily quieted, it seemed. His voice was all too audible through the blanket. "Rik, what's wrong?"

"I want to go home," Rikard mumbled petulantly.

"We'll get you home, sir. We need Lady Mazrem to make the final identification, anyway. My vote's got as much weight as anyone else's in the Lyceum – except your son, of course, and the emperor – but they're not going to believe your return until she confirms it," Hern said. He tugged the blanket away and the resurgence of light made Rikard squint.

"The Lyceum... My son?"

Gaius... We named him after Laurael's father. He was just a baby when I left. Tiny and fragile and screaming and pink.

"Hae. Your son, Rik. He's a captain in the Star Court, just like you." Hern clapped on Rikard's shoulder. "Let's get you home."

"He's still injured, general," one of the templars reminded him. "Please, be careful!"

Hern stood. "Captain Mazrem is made of bricks and brambles. Tell the men to step quick. Rik says he wants to go home and we're going to take him there."

The women bowed and scurried from the room. When they were gone, Hern helped Rikard to his feet. He couldn't remember the words to tell the other man about his gratitude.

"Blue sky," he fumbled.

Hern gave him an odd look. "I'm sure. Now let's get you back to your wife and boy. We're not far from the Everstones. Nothing puts the world right at the end of a long day like going home."

Nikas Hern led Rikard through the halls of the archouse, down the stairs and out into the sunlight. Rikard squinted until the blindness passed. The archouse was well named. It was a tall and starkly beautiful building. The outer walls were tiled all in marble and granite, arched like a drawn bow. The archouse bordered on acres of training grounds, fenced off on the northern face by a tall iron gate. A large, circular courtyard was resplendent with its own statue of Lord-Captain Rikard Mazrem.

The yard was full of people, all staring up at Rikard: two thousand VEIL knights girded in freshly polished banded blue armor. Every shoulder was emblazoned with the crescent moon of their court. There were others, too: Moon Court templars and groundskeepers, blacksmiths and a hundred more that worked in service to the knights. The gate that separated the archouse from the rest of Dormaen was thick with spectators from the city, hanging from the iron posts and crowding behind.

Hern led Rikard out onto a raised terrace. The crowd roared. VEIL knights pounded their fists against their armor and held swords upraised like sharp steel blades of grass. The rest shouted and cheered, laughed and cried and pointed. Their exultation rose, crashing over Rikard, threatening to deafen him, drown him. He recoiled, but Hern was standing right behind him.

"So much for awaiting a confirmation, hae? We tried to keep it all quiet, but this place is leaky as an old roof when it comes to secrets," Hern said into Rikard's ear. "All of Dormaen will hear about your return before long, Rik."

Hern gently but firmly propelled Rikard to the raised stone rail. The roar of voices surged deafeningly. What was he supposed to do? Speak to them? Even if Rikard could make himself heard over the tempest howl of voices, what could he say? There was too much to tell them, or else too little. Rikard wasn't sure which.

He raised his right hand and thumbed open the cap on his forefinger. Beneath, tiny gold prongs held open a small circular wound, little bigger than a pinprick, and funneled the blood to a point, like a pen. Uncovered, the puncture began to ooze with bright red blood. Rikard brought his finger to his brow and drew a circle there, the mark of the bond he and all VEIL knights shared with the Alterra, a mark visible and bright in both worlds.

The closest knights and templars fell suddenly silent. Whispers rippled through the crowd – *Wind through the brown grass. He's bleeding!* – and told those further back what was too distant to see. Hern grabbed Rikard and pulled him into an ostensibly brotherly embrace. The Moon Court general wiped the blood off Rikard's forehead with his sleeve.

"No one does that anymore, Rik," he whispered.

"Why?"

"It risks Alterran attention and no one wants that," said Hern. "We use more... casual gestures these days."

Rikard didn't understand. The circle of blood had served VEIL knights as a sign of respect and good will for more than a century. Nikas' words made no sense at all. Risk Alterran attention? But that was the very purpose of the bloody salute, to show Terra and Alterra that their bond remained strong. Without their Alterran allies, VEIL knights were no more than common soldiers.

He reached deeper, hoping for some kind of understanding, but Hern's thoughts were slippery and elusive, as difficult to grasp as raindrops.

Bewildered, Rikard followed the aging VEIL general down the stairs and toward a group of knights arranged in neat rows on either side of a moon-emblazoned chariot. They banged their fists against their breastplates once at the officers' approach and then spread out to encircle Rikard and Hern.

"Hae! Close ranks!" called a man with scarred cheeks. "March!"

The knights formed up as Hern and Rikard climbed into the chariot. The general flicked the reins and urged the pair of black horses into a quick canter. All around them, the knightly escort cut their way through the crowded Moon Court yard. The crowd had overcome their astonishment enough to resume the riotous cheers. They parted and pulled open the iron gates for Rikard and his entourage.

While the knights and templars reluctantly returned to their duties in the archouse, the Dormaen citizens were caught up in the moment. They followed the chariot into the city streets, fanning out behind them like a bridal train and chanting his name.

"Mazrem! Mazrem! Mazrem!"

"For the love of all the gods, Mother, you look fine," Gaius snapped. "Stop fussing!"

Laurael Mazrem gave her son a withering look.

"You heard the templars," she told him. "Your father is coming home."

"I heard nothing of the sort, Mother. I heard a couple of hysterical girls screeching about some drunkard who *looks* like my father. Exactly as he looked the day he died. It's ridiculous, Mother! The man died thirty years ago!"

"No one has ever been quite sure of that, Gaius," Laurael told her son primly. "VEIL knew your father better than I ever did. If the Moon Court templars are correct, the whole empire will soon be celebrating. We can't afford to appear hesitant. We must be at the forefront of this."

"They're dragging some poor, stupid man here for your identification! Can you even do that? You're getting on, after all. Would you even remember him without all the statues and paintings?"

"Watch your tongue. I am your mother. Show some respect."

Lady Mazrem gestured impatiently to a pair of her slender Jumaari servants. The women bobbed their heads obediently and hurried forward, hands overflowing with bottles of exotic perfume, cakes of powder and rouge for their mistress' skin, soft black sticks of wax and charcoal to line her eyes and lips. Laurael sat stiffly on her lushly overstuffed divan, curling her fingers into the upholstery.

The years had been kind to Laurael Mazrem, or the expensive physics and their cases of costly preservative extracts had been. Even after almost fifty years of life, her beauty still rivaled the youngest women of Carce. A strict daily regimen of pungent herbal creams and oils kept her flesh firm, her skin unlined. Her complexion had picked up a certain translucent quality in the last decade, but the nobility of Carce agreed that the moonstone cast only added to the revered Mazrem widow's loveliness.

Her decadent life, however, had somewhat widened Laurael's hips and waist. One of the young islander girls strained red-faced with the laces of a leather corset until she could finally tie them off. Still puffing, she draped her mistress in a glittering, gauzy tabba that was fashionable this season.

Gaius crossed his arms and leaned in the doorway of the ornate dressing room. Gaius Mazrem was the very image of his father. His mother made sure of that. He was tall, broad-shouldered and wore his long hair pulled back from his square jaw and sharp, hawkish nose. As a boy, Gaius' hair had been a shade or two lighter, taking more after his mother than his father. But a glossy black dye purchased each month by Lady Mazrem ensured that Gaius remained a fitting homage to his sire.

"You're more worried about your makeup than this impostor!" Gaius said. "Damn it all, Mother! This is going to ruin *everything*."

"And why should I worry?" Laurael asked. She paused as her maids smoothed the edges of her black lip paint. She prodded the dark makeup with her tongue and made a distasteful face. "This tastes horrid. Have some pride, Gaius. You're a knight of VEIL, just like your father."

Her son's jaw clenched. Urged by his mother and easily promoted by the family name, he was already a captain in the VEIL Star Court. The prestige of his bloodline could have carried him to a higher rank, but it was poetic – as Lady Mazrem had pointed out in terms that brooked no argument – that Gaius aspire to his father's rank and no higher. Not within VEIL, at least.

"It can't be him!" Gaius said, slapping the wall hard enough to make a nearby urn jump. "My father's been dead... gone... my entire life. And now he appears on the streets of Dormaen, not looking a day older than he did in Njorn Pass? Just like that?"

"No one knows for certain what the Alterra demanded of him, Gaius. And you know no one's ever asked," Laurael said. She gave her son a pointed look before continuing. "Most of Carce assumed your father dead, but there have always been fringe elements that questioned his disappearance."

"That just makes it worse! Those are the same bloody people who hate me. What do you think his reappearance is going to do to my standing? Who wants Rikard Mazrem's son when they have the great hero himself? And if the reports are true, he hasn't aged a day. He's *younger* than I am! I won't even outlive him, Mother. He'll ruin me!"

Laurael rose gracefully, scattering servants in all directions. Her dark, kohl-lined eyes were dangerously cold.

"I said to watch your tongue," Laurael said. "Your father was a great man, and neither you nor anyone else will say otherwise."

She placed her hands against her corseted midsection and sat again, wincing as though the outburst had physically pained her. Perhaps it had.

"Be the wise, respectful son you've always been," she said more softly. "Even if this man is not your father, we must seem hopeful that he is. Who would not welcome Rikard Mazrem's return?"

A brisk knock on the door interrupted his response. Laurael waved one of her maids over to admit the newcomer. An aged man-servant bowed deeply from the doorway.

"They have arrived, my lady," he announced.

Laurael nodded and brushed a curl of brown hair back from her face. Her expression was one of suitably excited anticipation.

"Come along, Gaius. Let us welcome your father home."

By the time they reached the Mazrem estate, nestled deep in the Everstones, Rikard's train of spectators filled the road. Charioteers and drovers cursed until they learned the crowd's purpose, then joined the ever-swelling throng. At a well-guarded gate, most of the VEIL knights broke off to redirect the crowd while General Nikas Hern drove Rikard up the long avenue paved in fine white stone.

Rikard twisted and turned in the chariot to stare. Was *this* his home? All of this? It was in the right place, but it looked nothing like the place he remembered. Before the war, Rikard was just a young VEIL knight, only recently promoted to captain and full of worry about his new duties. Rikard certainly had no time to tend the rocky ground or plain house his father had left him. Laurael's dowry was enough to buy food and clothes, but not for the servants she wanted, nor nights at the theater or expensive books. When young Rikard Mazrem had left for the brewing war in Fiore, he wasn't sorry to leave the place behind. His family, certainly, but not his house.

It had grown like a flower garden in his absence. Surely even the imperial palace was not half so lovely... or vast. The grounds were sprawling and lush, as perfectly sculpted and painstakingly colored as a lady's face. Beds of bright-blooming flowers, arches twined with roses, copses of slender birches and willows, even silvery streams artfully crisscrossed by tiny wooden bridges. No rocks. At least, none that weren't prettily arranged into mossy hillocks skirted in soft purple heather.

His old house was gone, too. Two manors crowned the smooth green hill, with expensive red-tiled roofs and deep colonnades that shone gold in the afternoon sun. A half-dozen other buildings encircled them, all carefully placed as the flowerbeds. Rikard didn't recognize any of it and had no idea where to go.

It was dizzying, like some kind of twisting maze, even worse than the ones children drew in the sand. Those ones had walls and corridors that pushed the hapless wanderer one way or another. This one was impossible, a lovely and sweet-smelling blur where home was supposed to be.

Home. Where's my home?

The knights escorting Rikard shared none of his confusion. They guided the chariot unerringly toward the northern house. A golden star dominated the central frieze, carved in stone above the rows of columns, a star with eight points and cardinal tips half again longer than their neighbors – the mark of the VEIL Star Court, Rikard's company.

"Almost there," Hern said.

"Home," Rikard repeated. "I want to go home."

"And your family wants you to come home to them, too, Rik. Look there."

As the chariot rumbled to a stop, Hern pointed to the broad, carved steps of the great house. A dozen servants in colorful tabbae stood in the shadows of the gold-fluted columns, whispering and wondering. Every eye was on Rikard, but he saw only the tall, beautiful woman standing on the steps – Laurael, his wife. Older now, but still lovely as the moon-goddess for whom she was named. Perfect.

So beautiful.

Home. I'm home.

And the man at her side, so handsome and proud, dressed in the black saela of a Star Court knight. A little heavy, but not yet gone to fat. Hair the color of pitch and eyes the same dark brown as Rikard's own, but with his mother's fine-boned face. Gaius, his son.

My son. My son is grown. And a knight!

Rikard's eyes filled with hot, stinging water. It tasted like the sea when it fell down his cheeks and onto his lips. How fitting – it felt like an entire ocean filled his heart to bursting.

The knights surrounding him pulled hastily aside as Rikard leapt from the chariot and ran to his wife and son, pulling them into his arms. His wounds protested, but the entire sky could have crashed down on Rikard in that moment and he would not have cared. He clung to his family and swore that he would never let go.

"I'm home," he wept. "I came home to you."

12

CLUTCH

"What awaits us in the ultimate beyond? We have devoted lifetimes to pondering the meaning of the question. The Alterra have told us more, but deciphering their answers only poses more questions."

— BEYOND THE VEIL, BY AELUS KAR

It's not going very well, is it? Stumble asked forlornly. *Why hasn't he told the Terran knights yet?*

He doesn't remember. Alterra isn't his world. His time here and the journey back through the veil have cost him much, answered Flickerdim. *He is lost and needs more time, Stumble.*

Can we help him?

Not with this.

Stumble hopped across the branch. His soft owl feathers stirred and blurred, shifting through myriad colors and textures. Fluffy white clouds twisted as they circled the empty gaps in the sky like soapsuds circling a drain. The Uprising shivered.

General Hern waited at a respectful distance while Rikard embraced his family. Lady Mazrem kissed her husband's cheek. Her lips were cool and hardened by dark paint.

"We've missed you so much, Father. Gods, we all thought you were dead!" Gaius announced.

"All of Carce has honored you in your absence, my lord," said Laurael.

Did she think he cared about that? Honors, homage... All that mattered was finally being home. Rikard couldn't answer. All he could do was sob into their shoulders and hold them close. They were so solid, so very and beautifully real. Not dreams that led him this way or that, not torn memories like war-hooks through him, pulled tight and then ripped away to leave him bleeding tears. Real.

Hern reluctantly cleared his throat until he caught Laurael's attention.

"I don't think the Lyceum will need very much, Lady Mazrem," he said, "But it would avoid complications if you'll confirm Captain Mazrem's identity yourself. Emperor Tychon's called a session tonight. Will you present your testimony?"

"I've not seen my husband in thirty years, General Hern," said Laurael firmly. "I will be with him tonight."

"Understood, Lady Mazrem," replied Hern diffidently, inclining his head. "But the emperor will be awaiting your word on Captain Mazrem's return. This is an important time."

Laurael glanced past the Moon Court escort and down to the distant crowd gathered outside her gate. Their cheers and applause were only a soft rumble from this distance, like the purring of some vast but contented cat.

"My son will speak for me tonight," she said.

"Hae, Mother," Gaius agreed. "I'll be there. Is that all, General Hern?"

Hern raised his eyes at the impatience in Gaius' voice, but made no comment.

"A minor detail," he said with a small, polite nod. "Lord-Captain Mazrem is still wounded. They appear to be the same injuries he sustained at Njorn Pass. They've been cleaned and dressed, but we would like to send a foster from the temple of Surma tomorrow to continue his care."

"Thank you, General Hern," Lady Mazrem answered smoothly, with none of her son's irritation. "The Moon Court has always shown the utmost reverence and respect to our family."

"We're all in your husband's debt. Captain Mazrem, I need to meet with the other generals before the Lyceum session tonight. I'll come to see you again soon."

Rikard had listened to the whole conversation in occasionally sob-punctuated silence, afloat in a warm, sweet sense of return that made everything else feel so unimportant, so very far away. It was like listening to Jingleblack tumble-ramble on about the Ravel Scree, a place Rikard had never seen and never would. It was gone, all Shattered.

But now Hern was actually speaking to Rikard, not just about him. Captain – *no, General* – Hern was a good friend who deserved his attention. Rikard did not remove his arms from around Laurael and Gaius, but craned his neck so he could look at the man.

"Soon as the blooming moon," Rikard told him.

"Ah... Emperor Tychon will want to see you, too," Hern said with a slightly faltering smile. "I'd expect summons to the imperial palace before long."

Summoned by the emperor? Castum Tychon, who sent Rikard and his men to die in the mountains of Fiore? *He took me from my home the first time, sent me away into ice and stone. Tychon will never take me again! Never!*

Rikard flung his wife and son protectively behind him, ignoring their shocked cries of protest, and lunged at General Hern. He threw all of his weight into the much older Veil knight, bowling them both over to the ground. Hern landed hard against the stones.

"What are you doing?" Laurael cried. She reached for Rikard, but Gaius pulled her back.

"He won't take me away again!" Rikard screamed. He grabbed the general by the front of his blue saela heaved him up until the two men were face to face. "I'm home! I'm not leaving! Never, never leaving!"

A pair of Moon Court knights seized Rikard by the elbows and hauled him back. They wanted to take him! Rikard struggled, howling in fury and terror. They were trying to take him away from his home, his family again!

He twisted and bit into one of the men holding him, forcing his teeth through cloth until he tasted blood. The knight grunted in pain and let go, clapping a hand over the wound. Two others leapt in to replace him. One wrapped both of his arms around Rikard's and the other hooked his elbow around the screaming hero's throat, pulling him backward, off balance. Together, all four toppled to the ground in a writhing heap.

Laurael freed herself from Gaius' restraining grasp. "Rikard, stop this at once!"

"They'll take me!" he screamed.

"No, they won't. These knights are leaving you with us," she said firmly. "Aren't you?"

Hern picked himself up and dusted off the seat of his pants. "Hae, my lady. Let him go," he instructed.

Reluctantly, the knights released Rikard and stepped hurriedly back. He rose to his knees, shaking his head back and forth like a beaten dog. Laurael said they were not trying to take him. But that's what Hern had said, wasn't it? That he would be summoned?

Summoned. The Alterra summoned me, called my name across the veil and I had no choice but to go. Through glass winds and across black fields of stars, they took me away and led me until I bled out every wish in unending battle. Summons left only sand. Dry and blowing on mute winds.

Rikard sat back on his heels and looked up at Hern. The other man rubbed his head and grimaced. He did not *look* like he meant to rip Rikard away from his family. Rikard reached past Hern's deep, pained frown, but found no such intent, only a firm desire to avoid further quarrels.

You just want to get away from me. You think I'm... different. No, that's not your word. Wild. Crazy. Dangerous. But you don't want to be the one to say anything. All you want is quiet.

General Hern lightly kissed Lady Mazrem's hand and saluted Gaius before turning back to Rikard. He bowed deeply, as though to a prince.

"Take care, Rik. I'll find you later."

He was lying. Rikard could taste it, like bitter slip. Hern had no intention of returning unless he had to. As far as he was concerned, Rikard Mazrem was still dead. This wild animal that came back wearing his old friend's skin was something best caged and locked away.

Rikard felt sick. His guts hurt again, as they had before, during the long trek into Dormaen, but this aching throb seemed to push out instead of in. He vomited onto Hern's boots, something frothy and white. Rikard stared in wonder. What was it? Had someone put that stuff inside him? How?

Hern sighed. "Goodbye, Captain Mazrem."

He pulled himself back up into his chariot and motioned to the knights, who fell into step behind him. Together, they marched back the way they had come, down the grassy hill and then out into the Everstones.

When the Moon Court knights were gone, Gaius let out the breath he had been holding.

"Hae, *that* went well," he said.

"Enough," Laurael said. She brushed back her mahogany hair and went to Rikard, kneeling beside him. "You must tell us the details of your return, my lord. What happened?"

"I don't know," he mumbled. The sick, sticky mess drying on the ground still fascinated him. It used to be something else, he knew that much.

Laurael pursed her dark lips and then snapped her fingers at a servant boy.

"Get Lord Mazrem something to eat," she said. "He must be famished. And clean this up."

Eat. Hae, that was it! The stuff on the ground had been in his stomach first. Milk, maybe. Rikard dimly recalled bladders of goats' milk for knights and soldiers knocked unconscious in battle. Someone had fed Rikard while he slept, cared for his body while he was not in it. The thought was oddly touching.

"Is it really him, Mother?" asked Gaius.

"Yes, it's him."

Rikard stood. His wife rose gracefully beside him and offered her arm to steady him, but Rikard took her hand and led her toward the house, toward their son.

"We should..." He struggled with the words, so long unused. "We should sit. And trade talkings."

"We have a great deal to discuss," Laurael agreed.

Gaius gestured for Rikard to follow. He took them through the colonnade striped in shadows and into a large atrium. Sunlight streamed through the open roof and sparkled on a burbling fountain. The atrium was full of lush, leafy green things from Jumaar and Zurest, many in bloom and filling the air with a lively, floral perfume. It was all beautiful, lovely and rich. Just as Laurael always wanted but he had never been able to provide on a VEIL captain's wage.

Servants brought out chairs and a low table. The boy Laurael had sent off before returned with a plate of fruit, bread and cheese. He set it on the table near Rikard, bowed deeply and retreated. A nervous woman poured and served him pale wine from a crystal decanter. Rikard snatched the glass away before she could drop it.

She flinched and then hurried away as quickly as decorum allowed. Laurael watched the interaction without comment.

"We have been lost in your absence, my lord," she said.

"Lost? You left Dormaen? Where were you lost?" Rikard asked. He almost dropped the glass.

"Only in spirit," Laurael corrected herself. She took a long sip of wine. "Please, eat. Perhaps a meal will ease you."

Rikard was not quite sure what his wife was talking about, but the food *did* look good. His recently emptied stomach ached. How to get the food into it? Well, Laurael and Gaius were putting wine in their mouths.

He tried the same thing with a wedge of apple, but it was too big to swallow. It took Rikard long moments to recall that his teeth were more than weapons. Chewing proved easy enough to master. At first, he gagged and threatened to be sick again, but Rikard spat and ate only a little at a time.

It was delicious, sweet and substantial and real. When the apple was gone, he licked and sucked his fingers. But still his stomach grumbled, so Rikard took a slice of cheese and repeated the process.

"Will someone please clean him up?" Gaius asked. He slumped into his chair and half-covered his face with his hands. "That's truly disgusting. Where have you been? Stuck in the Fiore mountains? You're certainly acting like one of those little savages."

"Be kind, Gaius. Your father has suffered much," Laurael said.

An old man with spotted knuckles brought a basin of water and a folded square of soft cloth. He gently took Rikard's hand, but the VEIL captain pulled away and snarled until the servant slunk off once more.

"What exactly *have* you suffered, Father?" asked Gaius. "So far, we've only been able to guess."

"I asked the Alterra for help," Rikard answered slowly.

They knew that part already, it was obvious. Bits and pieces of it floated at the front of their thoughts like foam pushed before a breaking wave. But he wanted them to understand better than that, these ones he loved most.

"They agreed to help," Rikard told them. "Slitherstream promised to... to remove the Fiori."

"They all vanished without a mark and have never returned," Laurael said. "Yours was the greatest victory in history."

"We know that part. What happened after that?" Gaius was impatient, but he had uncovered his face and sat forward now, frankly curious.

"The Alterra took my life," Rikard answered shortly. It hurt to say. The words stuck in his throat and made it difficult to swallow or even to breathe. "My Terran lifetime. They took me away to pay my debt."

"That was their price? You? Where did they take you?"

"Alterra."

"They took you *into* Alterra? Through the veil?" Gaius asked incredulously.

Laurael nodded like she had expected just such an answer from her husband.

"A world of thought and dreams, not one of body and substance like Terra," she said. "Is that why you've remained of such a handsome age, my lord, and why you are still suffering from the wounds of Njorn Pass?"

"I... don't know," Rikard admitted.

It made some sense, but none of the Alterrans ever mentioned such an effect. But then, he was the first Terran ever to enter their world. Perhaps they didn't know, either.

Or they did, and told me, but I don't remember. There are holes in my thoughts.

"So they took you away to Alterra. Hae, then. For what?" asked Gaius.

"To fight."

"To fight? To fight whom?"

Rikard finished off a fifth apple, piled with cheese, and followed it up with a handful of bread. It was thick and dark and filled his stomach comfortably.

"Each other," he said between bites. "The Alterrans are fighting one another."

"An Alterran civil war," Gaius repeated, shaking his head in dumbfounded wonderment. "Imagine that! What are they fighting over?"

"Us."

"What?"

Rikard stopped to collect his thoughts. This was all so terribly complicated... and tiring. He hadn't used his voice so much in thirty years and it was growing rough around the edges. Laurael sensed his discomfort and made a slicing motion with one slim hand.

"That's enough, Gaius. Your father's been away for such a long time and he's weary."

"He's already slept for half the day!" said Gaius. "Surely he can answer a couple of questions."

Rikard sat back in his chair. It was made of woven reeds and deeply padded. His shifting weight made it creak and puff a few tiny motes of golden dust into the close, secretive air of the atrium. He wanted to answer his son's questions, but Laurael was right. He was tired.

I need sleep. The dark-full dreaming.

But he was afraid to sleep. What if everything was gone when he woke? The very thought made Rikard's vision swim with tears. After everything he had endured – surviving the war with the Fiore and then the Alterran schism, the long journey home – the gods could not be so cruel to take it all away again, could they?

"If I go dark... sleep, will you still be here?" Rikard asked. His question was small and frightened.

"You're home now, my lord," answered Laurael. Gaius rolled his eyes and she pinched his arm. "There's nothing to fear anymore."

"Hae, home."

Rikard let himself fall back into sleep. When the dreams were gone, his wife and son would find him again.

Home.

"Is he asleep?" Gaius asked, finally breaking the tense silence.

"He's snoring," Lady Mazrem answered dismissively. "Hae, he's asleep. The man always did snore like a choked smokestack. You two, get him to bed."

The indicated servants lifted Rikard, chair and all. Carefully and quietly, they carried him from the atrium. Gaius reached for the plate his father had failed to finish and sandwiched several slices of mango and blue-veined cheese between some of the bread. Lady Mazrem arched one of her dark, finely shaped eyebrows at her son.

"If you didn't eat so much, your uniform would fit better," she remarked.

"What's the point of Father's little sacrifice if we can't enjoy the advantages?" Gaius said and then bit into his second helping of lunch. Through a mouth full of crumbs, he continued. "I'm starting to wonder if killing him might have been better than what the Alterra *did* take."

Lady Mazrem gazed out across the atrium. A pair of red and gold butterflies chased each other between the flowering jasmine vines.

"And what is that?" she asked.

"You saw him, Mother! He attacked General Hern for what? Because the emperor might want to meet with the war hero who all but built his empire? Father's gone completely mad, hasn't he? The Alterra didn't just take a memory or borrow a joke. They took his whole mind."

"He is… different, hae," Lady Mazrem agreed.

Gaius threw the crusts of his bread onto the mosaicked atrium floor and jumped to his feet.

"Doesn't anything ever bother you, Mother?" Gaius asked.

"So you often ask. Why should this bother me, my son? I never met Rikard Mazrem before my father promised me to him. Our wedding was the first time I ever laid eyes on the man. We were only married two years when he went to war with the Fiori. I barely knew my husband when he died. Why should it bother me at all that I do not know him now?"

Gaius flinched a little at his mother's chilly, matter-of-fact tone.

"Even if you don't care, don't you think the rest of Carce will? What about Emperor Tychon? Since you've so kindly volunteered me to represent our family to the rest of the Lyceum, I'm going to have to be the one to tell them – to tell Castum Tychon himself – that Lord-Captain Rikard Mazrem is well and truly insane."

"You will tell them no such thing!" Lady Mazrem snapped.

She seemed to be truly paying attention for the first time in the entire conversation. Gaius scowled.

"I don't particularly want to, Mother," he said. "I'm not stupid. I know how it's going to make us look. Everything we have is built on Father's good name, but what do you think General Hern is going to tell them? You saw him when he left. He knows as well as we do what's become of Father."

Laurael had calmed herself, now as hard and cold as a Fiori glacier.

"Nikas Hern will say nothing," she told Gaius. "He has benefited from your father's sacrifice, too. He could never have led VEIL to victory in Fiore and he knows it. But because of Rikard, he returned to Dormaen a victor. He will hold his tongue."

"Because he's honorable, you're saying?" Gaius asked. "Because he owes Father some kind of debt?"

Laurael shook her head. "No."

"Why, then?"

"Because unless someone else substantiates his claim – which you will not – Hern will only seem jealous. At best. At worst, the people will believe he wants to destroy a much more popular rival to his own authority."

Gaius frowned. "What makes you so certain of that, Mother?"

"It's the same reason he's never challenged you."

13

THE JADE THRONE

"Breathe a word of our secrets and it will be with your last breath."

—A HOUSE OF FIVE DRAGONS AXIOM

"Rikard Mazrem? Are you sure?" Narissa asked.

The Crest sat forward on the throne, his lips pressed into a thin, tight white line like the string of a crossbow.

"Are you questioning me?" he asked in a deadly quiet voice.

"No," Narissa answered quickly. "I'm simply... surprised. We've known Captain Mazrem to be dead for a long time."

"He's not dead. Did you hear about the procession to the Everstones this afternoon?"

"Certainly," Narissa said. "But there have been men claiming to be Rikard Mazrem before."

"None that VEIL has ever taken the time to confirm."

That was true, as far as Narissa knew... And her knowledge was considerable. Besides her position as an Eye of the House, Narissa served as the senior priestess in the temple of Surma. Four hundred fosters worked – and gossiped – under her watchful eye.

"I want him," the Crest said.

"Want him?"

"Hae. What good is control over Gaius Mazrem when his father has returned? Rikard Mazrem's popularity will eclipse his son's. Rikard is the more important target now."

Narissa circled the room slowly, as necessitated by the slanted floor and the deep, inky darkness that the Crest preferred. She was full of nervous energy. How the younger fosters would gape to see their temple matron pace like this.

It was the Crest. Something about him made Narissa feel as though snakes squirmed in her stomach. She wished some of the other Eyes were about, but it was late and most were tending to their own business or else on their way to the evening's unscheduled Lyceum session. There were Talons, of course, lurking in the dark, with weapons never far from their gloved hands. But thinking of the Crest's guard did nothing to settle Narissa.

"You heard something else," said the Crest. "You rarely pace, my lovely priestess. Tell me."

"I don't want to waste your time."

"You hear a great deal, Narissa. It's for your ears that I elevated you to my Eye." He laughed thinly at his own little joke. "I would regret having to force your tongue. Speak."

Narissa swallowed hard. Her mouth was suddenly very dry.

"It was the Moon Court general," she said. "Nikas Hern. He has commissioned a foster. Captain Mazrem's injured, they say. General Hern wants a foster to make sure he recovers."

"How useful."

The Crest's smile glinted in the dark tower room like a sharp crescent moon.

"There's more," Narissa said. "General Hern's letter also warned the temple to select a foster very carefully. He says that Captain Mazrem's been deeply affected by his time away and to send someone... gentle."

The Crest sat forward on the Jade Throne, emerging from the cushions like a viper lifting its head from bloated coils. "Interesting. Did Hern explain any further?"

"No," Narissa said. "That was all."

"Who's supposed to arrange a foster for Captain Mazrem?"

"Orria's been tasked with the choice, though I outrank her. Do you want me to handle it?"

More soft laughter from the Crest. "Ah, you understand me very well. Hae, I do."

"I'll place one of our fosters with Captain Mazrem, then."

"No, I think not," said the Crest. The humor suddenly vanished from his voice, replaced by icy intensity. "We're playing for Rikard Mazrem himself. This is a delicate matter. I want Thainna Vahn."

"Thainna? But she's just a common thief. She doesn't know the first thing about fosterage or building influence."

"Are you challenging my choice?"

Narissa swallowed her objections. "No. Of course not. But don't you think that–?"

"Good. Arrange it," he interrupted, and then paused thoughtfully. "I trust that Thainna can handle Captain Mazrem, but she can be terribly unfocused. She's been working on her own little side project for the last four years, after all. I'll need to convince her that this is far more important."

"I will make those arrangements with the fostral staff, as well," Narissa said.

"Good. We can't have Thainna worrying about her brother at a time like this, can we?"

"No, my Crest."

"Send Thainna a bloodmark before dawn tomorrow. She'll need to start work early."

"Hae. It will be done," Narissa promised.

14

THE GOLDEN THRONE

"King Castum Tychon ascended his father's throne at the age of twenty-eight and ruled Carce for only four years before word of another war between Nian and Lyncea spurred him to action. He vowed to build an empire of the fifty nations and to put an end to the ceaseless bickering and bloodshed."

— ACCOUNTS OF NJORN PASS, BY ALEXANDER FERRO

"All rise!" boomed the herald. He was a small man with very little hair left – on his head, at least, though his arms would have made a bear jealous – but his voice was rich and filled the Lyceum chamber. "All rise for his highest and exalted Imperial Majesty, Emperor Castum Orastus Tychon."

Preceded and followed by an armed procession of VEIL knights in star-branded black armor, the master of the known world strode across the domed Lyceum chamber. He was wrapped in a longer and more extensively draped tabba than the common folk he ruled or even the Lyceum consuls that shared some part of his power.

Emperor Tychon wore his silvery white hair short and oiled smooth in the style of older Carcaen gentlemen. A large blue sapphire – mined from deep under the mountains of Fiore – glittered in a circlet of gleaming platinum. The emperor's face was as folded as his tabba, lined by years and the weight of his golden throne.

But what could a man like Castum Tychon have to worry about? Gaius wondered.

But he rose along with the other consuls and applauded. The emperor did not often emerge from his palace. When he did, it was always cause for attention.

Emperor Tychon climbed the stairs of the alabaster dais and seated himself in his tall golden throne. The dark-armored guards took up positions behind him – two rows of stern faces, sharp swords and shining fingercaps. The imperial herald stumped along behind, clearing his throat, but had no other announcements for the moment. The consuls sat once more, but the air of the Lyceum remained restless. Emperor Tychon waited for silence.

"All Dormaen is afire with curiosity," he said when the noise subsided. The emperor's voice lacked the resonance of his herald, but it was still strong. "They say that Rikard Mazrem has returned, untouched by the years and still bearing the wounds of his battle in Njorn Pass. We must know the truth of this. Has Carce's most beloved son come home? Who can speak to this strange and startling news?"

Gaius sat with the other VEIL consuls, all of them the highest ranked members of their order, generals of the three courts. On Gaius' left, General Hern sat still and silent on the hard marble bench, just as Lady Mazrem said he would.

Though his rank was the greater between the two, Hern was general only of the smallest of the three VEIL courts. The Moon Court held the middle rank once, below Sun but above Star, but since Rikard Mazrem's heroic sacrifice, the Star Court had risen to prominence. Hern was only here because he was a VEIL general.

Gaius Mazrem, on the other hand, held his seat at the express appointment of Emperor Tychon.

Thin, long-nosed Cadmus Castor of the Sun Court narrowed his eyes. General Castor was too canny and observant a man not to have heard the rumors of Captain Mazrem's return. But he was stubborn, too, and proud. Before the pronouncement of victory in Fiore, the Sun Court ruled over the other two and served as the emperor's own guard. Now, that honor belonged to the Star Court.

Gaius' own commander, General Darius, turned to look back over his shoulder. Saul Darius was a round man, twelve years older than Gaius. He was not a talented leader or a skilled fighter, but had served under Captain Mazrem as the great hero's squire. Every one of the VEIL court generals owed their success or decline to Rikard Mazrem.

How many others, Gaius wondered? How many of the civilian consuls had earned their seats by friendship to the Mazrem family, real or pretended?

"Gaius, this is for you to say," General Darius whispered.

Gaius glanced around the tiered marble expanse of the Lyceum. Darius was right, though probably not for the reason he thought. All eyes, including those of Emperor Tychon, were on him. Gaius suppressed an immodest smirk, but it felt good. It felt *right*.

A son should succeed his father, shouldn't he?

Rikard Mazrem had done his duty in the war with Fiore thirty years ago. He was a legend, and now it was time for Gaius, his only son, to rise and to shine like a new star. All of the most important men in the Carcaen Empire were staring at him in rapt, attentive silence.

Rising son... rising sun. A star in the Star Court. It can't be a coincidence, can it?

But they were all waiting for information about his father. They didn't care about Gaius anymore, not when they had the great Lord-Captain Rikard Mazrem to worship. It was a depressing reminder.

Gaius stood and raised his hands, motioning for a silence that had already fallen. Still, he liked to imagine that the gesture looked quite grand.

"I tell you now that the rumors are true. My father, the revered Lord-Captain Rikard Caelis Mazrem, has returned! My mother, his wife, has confirmed his identity," he announced.

"Lady Mazrem recognizes him?" asked another consul, a pale Cellestrian with a necklace of thick silver links around his neck. "What about you, Captain Mazrem?"

"I was only a baby when he left, less than a year old. But like every one of you, I've seen my father's face on the monuments we've raised to him all over the city, all over the empire," Gaius answered. "It's him."

The Cellestrian consul nodded and sat. Another man stood, thin and wearing a gray cloak over his tabba despite the heat. Gaius recognized him as Liam Io, the senior Nianese consul.

"We all believed that Captain Mazrem was dead, Gaius," he said. "For thirty years, we've honored his sacrifice. How can he be alive? Has he told you what happened?"

Murmurs of agreement echoed through the Lyceum and the emperor waited for Gaius' answer.

"My father told us that Alterrans removed him from Terra. He joined them in their own world. That's where he's been, why only his sword remained in the Fiore ice. They took him away to spend a lifetime in the service of the Alterra."

The muttering took on a darker note, angry and afraid.

"The Alterrans *took* Captain Mazrem?" asked Liam. "I thought VEIL maintained amicable relations with the Alterra. Why would they steal a VEIL captain?"

"Do they tell a different story in Nian?"

It was not Gaius who answered, but Saul Darius who was on his feet with a bright flush in his cheek. General Castor gave the other knight a pinched frown, but Darius ignored him.

"You know as well as any man here that Rikard made an open pact with the Alterra!" Darius said. "He didn't dictate the terms. He offered them anything they wanted."

Liam was taken aback by the vehemence of Darius' response. "It's our right to ask questions here, general. And our duty. I meant no offense."

"I took none," Darius huffed.

It was not offense, Gaius knew. After Njorn Pass, no one trusted the Alterra. VEIL least of all.

Gaius raised his hands once more to regain the attention of the Lyceum.

"My father's said nothing about theft or even being a prisoner," he said. "He was taken to fight a war in Alterra that he says rages even now."

Emperor Tychon did not have to stand to speak. "An Alterran war? Generals, I've not heard of this. Are we to be worried?"

Darius and Hern looked as surprised as anyone else. General Castor only scowled again.

"This is the first we've heard," Darius said.

"A civil war," Gaius said, feeling a hot thrill at the words. These were things that only *he* knew, of all the powerful men in the chamber. "My father said that it's a civil war being waged. Alterran pitted against Alterran."

Emperor Tychon sat forward in his throne. "And it's still being fought?"

"I think so, hae," Gaius answered.

A hundred consuls murmured again.

"Then why is Captain Mazrem back?" the emperor asked. "Like all men, I celebrate his return, but he is a great warrior and a great man. I mourned his loss at Njorn Pass. Why did the Alterra send such a warrior back to us with their war yet unwon?"

"Perhaps as a kindness to us," Gaius suggested.

Maybe he was too crazy to be useful anymore, he thought. But he could never say such a thing. His mother would tear his eyes out.

"Have you asked the Alterrans?"

"I have been with my family all day," Gaius answered. "Until summoned here, of course. No, Your Majesty, I have not."

He looked to the VEIL generals. One by one, they each shook their heads. They hadn't asked, either. No one wanted to talk to the Alterrans. An embarrassed silence lingered in the vast marble chamber until Liam, still standing, spoke again.

"There are the other rumors, as our emperor has stated. That Captain Mazrem still bears the wounds of Njorn Pass, but is untouched by the passage of these thirty years. Can you confirm or deny this?"

"I can," Gaius told him. "Hae, my father appears to be unaged since he was taken from us. He is still injured, but whether or not they're the injuries he sustained against the Fiori, I can't say. That question is better put to General Darius."

"General?" asked Liam.

The commander of the Star Court stood. "I've spoken a bit to General Hern about it. I haven't had the chance to see Rikard myself, but by all accounts, these are the same wounds. A spear to his ribs on the left side, a cut on that side to his throat and a few other grazing wounds."

"Is Captain Mazrem healing?"

"Hae," General Hern answered. "He doesn't seem to be in any immediate danger. He walked into Dormaen without bleeding to death. Captain Mazrem is not well, but he will live. I've sent for a foster to ensure that, after all of this, we don't lose Captain Mazrem again."

Hern was trying to look loyal. Darius seemed annoyed and rolled his eyes. Castor watched the other two generals in contemplative silence. They were so busy politicking amongst themselves, Gaius thought, that they didn't even see the real problem: Rikard.

With the legendary Captain Mazrem back, how long until even the generals were working for him? All of the power plays between the courts would amount to nothing now that Rikard Mazrem was back in Dormaen.

"Will Captain Mazrem recover soon?" asked the emperor from his throne.

"Hard to tell, Majesty," said Gaius. "My father is a strong man, but he needs rest."

General Hern kept his eyes on the emperor and did not look at Gaius. Emperor Tychon stood and nodded to the Lyceum consuls.

"Then we will adjourn for the evening," Tychon announced. "The hour has grown late and the day's events have been exciting. Please give our respects to Lady Mazrem, Consul Gaius, and to your honored father. We look forward to speaking with him."

The imperial guard escorted Tychon from the Lyceum to the drumbeat rapport of heavy boots. A palpable tension followed him from the building. When the emperor was gone, the Lyceum immediately erupted into shouts and whispers, cheers and hisses. While Darius and Hern argued loudly over which one of them should have dispatched the foster, sharp-faced General Castor touched Gaius' shoulder to get his attention.

"Thank you for keeping us all informed, Captain Mazrem," he said dryly.

"I'm certain that this wasn't your first report on the matter," Gaius shot back. "I don't serve the Sun Court. If you don't like when and how I give my reports, I suggest you take it up with General Darius."

Castor's mouth twisted in a small, thin smile that did not reach his olive-colored eyes. "The responsibilities of the Star Court are numerous these days and General Darius is a very busy man."

"Hern knows as much as I do and the Moon Court hasn't been quite so challenged for time," Gaius answered. "Maybe you and he can talk."

"We have," Castor said without pause. "General Hern seems to have other things on his mind. He's proved reluctant to discuss the matter of Rikard Mazrem in much depth."

Gaius figured as much. General Castor was a bad man to have as an enemy, but no one could really claim friendship with the proud, surly old stick. Even after thirty years out of favor, the Sun Court general never adjusted to being the low man, the last to receive information.

Gaius offered Castor a careful smile, the one Lady Mazrem made him practice so many times in the mirror. "When my father's recovered, I invite you to visit him yourself. Maybe he'll be able to tell you more about all of this strangeness. I'm certain he'll be overjoyed to see an old friend."

General Castor's face went blank like a waxboard passed over a flame and melting back into smooth, unmarked flatness. Charged in the early days of the Carcaen Empire with the protection of the new emperor, much of the Sun Court had remained behind under Castor's command while the rest of VEIL marched into Fiore. What might have been an enviable stay of execution at the points of Fiori spears had become an embarrassing absence from the most important battle in history.

Hern and Darius had apparently finished their argument and now returned their attention to the other knights. Darius nodded to Gaius.

"I'm sure we can handle things here. It's just going to be a bunch of excited old men with excited questions," Darius said. "Why don't you go home to your mother and father? Please give them our respects."

"Thank you, sir," Gaius answered demurely.

He snapped a salute and picked his way down the aisles, toward the Lyceum floor and the door. Before the rising voices drowned out their conversation, Gaius overheard Hern talking again.

"Rikard's return is going to muddy the waters."

"Which waters are those?" Castor asked.

"The succession. Tychon's always had his eye on Lady Mazrem, but they both knew better. The emperor's never going to marry," Hern said. "He was going to choose Gaius to succeed him, but do you really think Tychon is going to go through with it now that Rikard's back?"

Neither of the other generals answered that.

"I need a word with Consul Liam," Castor said after a moment. "He asked many questions and I'm curious why. I didn't even expect him to be here tonight, not with his investors screaming for blood over the wheat blight."

Gaius wondered what Darius and Hern might say once Castor was gone, but the red-clothed Sun general was coming his way. Unless he wanted to get caught eavesdropping, Gaius would have to move on. He turned away just in time to avoid catching the attention of an old Korenthian consul with a concerned expression. Gaius nodded to another knot of consuls near the door and then slipped out into the dark Dormaen streets. A row of guards – ordinary soldiers, not VEIL knights – stood vigil before the Lyceum.

"Evening, sir," said the closest. "It's getting late. Do you need an escort home?"

"No, I'm fine." Gaius waved off the soldier. What menace could lurk out in the city that a simple man with a sword could handle that a VEIL captain could not?

The guard nodded and bowed. "Hae, sir. Good night."

Gaius circled the Lyceum rotunda until he reached the stables. A girl held the blue and copper kajja steady while he climbed into his chariot. When he had wound the reins around his fist, she handed a short whip up to Gaius and lightly swatted the tall bird's colorful flank. The chariot rattled over the cobbles and then out onto the smooth, well-worn Tychon Road, toward the Everstones.

Lady Laurael Mazrem stood beside her bed. It was wide and lavish, canopied in velvet that hung from ornately carved mahogany posts. The bedroom in which it sat was no less extravagant... Nothing like the one she and Rikard had shared on their wedding night.

She leaned over the coverlets. The stiff leather corset held her tightly – like a giant's fist and about as comfortable – and perfectly concealed the softening, aging body beneath. Many of the older women of Carce wore them and joked that they wished someone clever would invent one that did the same for their decaying minds.

But Lady Laurael Mazrem never wished for that. Her mind remained sharp as the day she learned of her husband's death and put an end to her affair with the young Emperor Tychon. He had asked Laurael why, of course. He pleaded with her, but she would not be dissuaded. Men were so simple, so predictable. They would risk everything – a career, a life, even an empire – for love.

Or at least a nice pair of breasts.

Women took a much longer view of things. Lady Mazrem was the honored widow of a war hero. To remarry or even take another lover would be seen as a slight or failure to properly remember her martyred husband. His apparent death made Rikard the most powerful man in the empire. Of what further use was its emperor to her?

In death, Rikard Mazrem had become a legend. What would he be now, alive but so obviously deranged and damaged by his experiences in Alterra? A god? A mad god? There were certainly plenty of those in the Carcaen pantheon. There were people who already revered Rikard, prayed to him for protection and favor. Would it be so different now?

Perhaps. Perhaps now he would answer those prayers.

Laurael looked down on her slumbering husband. He didn't stir. How long would the man sleep? Rikard had always been a heavy sleeper, which suited his wife just fine. He was an amorous man, to be certain, but theirs was an arranged marriage and Rikard never could keep Laurael's attention for long. Once he was asleep, she had always done whatever she liked.

Not that Rikard was an unattractive or unskilled lover. Laurael pushed his long hair back from his face. He was thin and needed a shave, but Rikard was still a handsome man. A beautiful hero was better than an ugly one, Laurael supposed. Maybe that was why there were so many statues of the man, to give lonely women and men something nice to look at while they shopped.

Laurael had grown used to an empty bed. There were braziers of scented wood and quilts of fine sendal to keep her warm, and the knowledge that her son would one day rule all of Carce.

What would warm her late nights now?

15

BLOODMARK

> "You can't catch a shadow. Try and you will find yourself bitten by the slithering things that home in the dark."

> — UTORA MAESUS

"Thainna Vahn."

The voice was firm, and so was the foot prodding at her ribs. Thainna groaned and rolled away. It was still dark, but close enough to dawn that the sky shone with dim, colorless light. She turned reluctantly back, opened her eyes and sat up to look at the source of the disturbance. Her visitor was a tall Carcaen man, slender and athletically built. His short tabba was simple, but made of much finer – and cleaner – weave than anything Thainna owned.

He held out a folded piece of paper and Thainna took it with a sigh. Probably an ashmark, orders from someone in the House with more rank than her. With any luck, it would be an easy job.

When it's finished, I can get back to working for myself, getting the money for Thain, for the Auction. Then I'll be the sister of the Crest. I won't get these bloody jobs anymore.

Inside the fold of paper wasn't ash, but a spot of dark rust red. Thainna gasped and dropped it. A bloodmark – summons from the Crest of the House of Five Dragons, or at least orders from him.

Gods, why...? Had the Crest somehow heard about her strange encounter with Captain Mazrem? Was she going to be punished for being quiet, after all?

Thainna looked around to ask the messenger, but he had gone as silently as he had come. She picked up the paper again. There was more, written in gray ash like the notes she was accustomed to receiving.

Narissa

Temple of Surma

Now

A moment or two of scrubbing with the heel of her hand erased the message. Thainna folded up the blood-spotted square of paper and tucked it into her tabba. She might need it later to prove her identity or legitimacy.

The temple of Surma? Well, Thainna was at least familiar with the place. She spent enough time there visiting Thain in the fostral wing.

It was a long walk to the temple district and her summons said *now*. Thainna wrapped her feet and hurried out onto the street, bolting down a hard piece of bread she found the afternoon prior. It was amazing what some people threw away.

The early morning was clammy and dark with thick gray fog from the Mazren River. Lights glowed in a few windows, but most of the Rows was still asleep at this hour. Mist-blurred silhouettes passed Thainna along the road, the occasional early riser up before the sun on business or just restlessly wandering. They were as distant and silent as ghosts. Thainna felt strangely alone in the vast city – just another faceless specter.

Is this what Alterrans are like? Everyone says they live in a world that's made of thoughts instead of... stuff. Whatever the world is made of. Terra, I guess. Is this what they're like? Unformed things just sort of... floating around?

The fog burned off long before Thainna reached the temple. So had the chill. By the time she passed the first outlying temples mixed in among the shops and houses, Thainna was sweating and panting. Her feet hurt, too, but that was getting old and easy to ignore. She reached the blue-painted steps of the temple of Surma and took them two at a time.

Inside, a priestess recognized her and asked if she wanted to go back to the fostral. Thainna reluctantly declined and asked for Narissa instead. She was led back through the temple. The temple to the goddess of life was full of dancing golden light – tiered walls covered in rows upon rows of candles, each one representing a prayer to Surma. The temple kept the nearby chandler's shops in good business. It was beautiful, but made the air sizzle with hot, sweet scents.

The priestess took Thainna to the western wing of the temple, opposite the fostral, and left her to wait in a large room with a blue rug in the center. Thainna's toes sank deeply into the softness as though into dark water. These walls, too, were lined with flickering candles. The priestess excused herself and left Thainna alone.

There were voices coming from outside, barely audible through a small window. Curious – and happy to distract herself from the bloodmark business – Thainna leaned close to the glass to listen. A pair of Suvestri women leaned against the wall outside and shared a breakfast of caked rice.

"...to the Moon archouse. But it can't be him," said one, shaking her head. Her thick, dark hair rippled down her back like perpetually spilling ink.

"Why not?" asked the other one. "Captain Mazrem may well be a god now. Who knows what he could do?"

What? Rikard Mazrem was back in Dormaen…? Thainna's heart beat fast. But it had all been a dream…

Another voice came from the doorway. "Thainna?"

Thainna jumped. She looked up to see a new priestess enter and pull the door closed behind her. Thainna had seen the woman before, giving orders to the other priests, but had never spoken to her. She was tall, with dark hair and skin. Pure-blooded Carcaen, of course. All of the important people were, even in the House of Five Dragons. She had to be Narissa. Thainna held out the folded bloodmark. She was embarrassed to see the paper flutter in her trembling hand.

"You're late," Narissa said.

She took the bloodmark from Thainna, but did not open or check it. She held it over a candle until the paper caught flame and within seconds, it burned away into ash.

"I came as quickly as I could, lady," Thainna said. "I'm sorry, I had to walk."

"No matter," Narissa answered. She dismissed the excuse and barely spared a glance for the dirty girl. "You're here now and I have your orders. You will go to the Mazrem estate and present yourself as a foster of this temple. Captain Rikard Mazrem requires care and you will administer it."

"What?" Thainna was dumbfounded. Pretend to be a foster? Work for Rikard Mazrem? This had to be another dream or a joke or… or something. "But I don't know anything about fosterage!"

"I'm aware, but Captain Mazrem's injuries are superficial. He walked all the way across Dormaen with them, if not further. He suffers much more from dehydration, malnutrition and exhaustion. Change his bandages daily. I will give you a salve to apply directly to the wounds to prevent infections. If you need more, come ask any of the fosters for it or send a message. Make sure Captain Mazrem eats and drinks, but slowly at first, or he will make himself sick. Do you understand?"

"Hae, lady," Thainna said, but then shook her head. "Wait, no! Please, I don't understand. Why does the Crest want me to take care of Captain Mazrem? Why not send a real foster?"

"Rikard Mazrem is the single most powerful man in Carcaen history. The Crest wants you to find a way to control him."

The bottom dropped out of Thainna's stomach like a gallows trap, leaving her dangling and choking. She certainly did not feel like her feet were touching the ground.

"What? Control Rikard Mazrem?"

"Use whatever means are required," Narissa said. "The House will make available to you any dram you wish, if you think you can get Lord-Captain Mazrem split on one – or more – of them. Watch him carefully for any illicit activities we can hold over him. Seduce him, if you must."

Thainna's head spun. It made *some* sense. Narissa was right – Rikard Mazrem was a popular historical figure and probably more powerful than even Emperor Tychon. Of course the Crest wanted him. The House of Five Dragons had sent Caelin to get Rikard's son addicted to ophellion, Dorros said.

They would work ten times as hard to get to Rikard Mazrem himself.

"Please, lady, I think this is some kind of mistake," Thainna said. "I'm just... just a thief!"

"These orders come down from the Crest himself," Narissa told her. "You may not refuse them."

"No," Thainna said. "I don't mean the orders. It makes sense, hae, but surely this is for someone else! I'm a thief, not a... a seductress. I've never even sold a dram. I have no idea how to get Captain Mazrem split on them!"

"The Crest is confident that you will adapt to your new duties. You've met Rikard Mazrem before. The Crest believes this may give you additional insight."

"How... how do you know about that?"

"Don't be naïve. You spoke to your brother about it within these very walls. The Crest knows a great deal. You have been selected for a singular duty, Thainna. Be grateful."

"I can't do it. Please! Ask the Crest to send someone else."

"We all follow the Crest's command, my girl. I have my orders, too," said Narissa. "And the Crest wants you focused on the task at hand."

Angry, frustrated tears welled up in Thainna's eyes. She blinked them away and hoped Narissa did not notice. It was all so stupid! What did the Crest think she could possibly have learned about Rikard Mazrem while he was strangling her?

"The House knows that your twin brother is quite ill and commands much of your attention. So the Crest has taken Thain into his keeping," Narissa said. "He will be well cared for so long as you are carrying out your orders."

"What? No!" Thainna cried. The tide of tears surged razor-sharp against her eyes and streaked her cheeks. "Please, don't take him! I swear I would never refuse the Crest's orders. You don't need to do this! I'm loyal. I've always done my job. Please!"

"It's already been done," Narissa told her. Her tone was terribly final.

Thain. They took my brother. The Crest will hurt him... or kill him if I can't manage this insanity!

This couldn't be real. The worlds weren't that unfair... Thainna squeezed her eyes shut and pressed her fingers to the lids until the darkness exploded into red splotches. But when she opened them, Narissa remained stubbornly before her, looking down at Thainna without remorse.

"Can I see him?" Thainna asked. "Please, can I just see Thain before I have to go?"

"No. Time is already short. You must be at the Mazrem house before noon. Come with me. You need a bath and proper clothes if you're to represent the temple of Surma."

Narissa led Thainna down a narrow hallway to an otherwise empty bath room. The priestess took a simple blue tabba and a pair of silver shell-shaped shoulder pins from a cabinet, placing them on a stool. Narissa pointed to the sunken tub. Steam rose from the surface, warmed by fires burning beneath the tiled floor. Thainna felt the heat of them under her feet.

"There's little time to linger, but make sure to wash thoroughly," Narissa instructed.

Thainna sniffled and wiped her nose on the back of her hand. She nodded and sat down to unwind the rags from around her feet.

"*Very* thoroughly." Narissa looked down at the tattered and stained cloth. "I'll bring you a belt and some sandals."

Thainna could not bring herself to thank the woman.

Narissa left her alone to bathe. Thainna disrobed quickly and slid down into the hot water. It stung her many scrapes and the places where her dry skin had cracked, but the prickling sensation passed quickly. She could almost enjoy the water, so deep and warm. It came all the way up to her neck when she stood in the deep center of the pool, where the water was the hottest.

Thain's a prisoner... and I'm taking a bath.

But what other choice did she have?

Thainna collected a scratchy brown sponge from a basket at the edge of the tub, and sniffed a slippery, pale yellow ball. It smelled like jasmine, but underneath was the sharp scent of lye. Thainna lathered the soap over her skin, into her long, lank red hair and scrubbed the worst of the dirt with the sponge.

She was still working gingerly at her stained toes when Narissa returned. As promised, the priestess brought with her a belt-sash in a blue a few shades darker than the tabba and stiffened by fine silvery wire. Narissa also deposited a pair of long-laced sandals on the floor under the stool that held the rest of Thainna's costume.

"You will be impersonating a priestess of some status – since we would never send a junior foster to care for Captain Mazrem – and you must conduct yourself as such," Narissa explained from the steps of the bathing pool. She held out a towel and gestured for Thainna to climb out. "However, I don't have time to teach you all of the proper Surmaen prayers, so you will be demur. You will leave the proper homages to Lady Mazrem. Do you understand?"

"Hae."

Narissa clearly had no intention of leaving her alone anytime soon, so Thainna quickly climbed out of the bath and snatched the towel to cover her nakedness, blushing furiously. Narissa furrowed her brow and frowned at Thainna.

"Priests of the mother-goddess have no shame of their bodies. We are proud of the feminine form... skinny and bony though yours may be. Don't blush and don't balk if you are instructed to bathe with the other women of the Mazrem house."

"Hae... fine," Thainna mumbled.

Reluctantly, she used the towel to dry off instead of covering herself, and then wrapped herself in the priestly blue tabba. When Thainna had pinned the shoulders in place and tied the belt around her waist, Narissa held out a comb and gestured for the girl to sit.

"Do you have any other questions?" Narissa asked.

Thainna gritted her teeth as she yanked the comb through her wet, tangled hair. She picked out the worst of the mats and tried to think. "What if... ow... if something goes wrong? What if Captain Mazrem gets worse or someone discovers me?"

"There are other Talons already in place in the household. Do you know Arliss and Caelin?"

Thainna nodded.

"Good. Speak to either of them if you need to send word back. If Captain Mazrem's condition worsens, tell me and I will send you further instructions. If you're discovered, notify Arliss or Caelin and then leave. Do not return to the temple. Go back to the Rows. No one must trace you back to the House of Five Dragons."

"But they can connect me to Caelin and Arliss?" Thainna asked. "Isn't that dangerous for them?"

"They know and accept the risks."

Dorros said the Crest has Caelin's wife, just like he has Thain now. Does the Crest have something on Arliss, too, to ensure her loyalty? Probably. Even if he doesn't need it.

Thainna's remaining hair was in order. The other half seemed to be caught in Narissa's comb. The priestess braided the damp red strands into a long plait and tied it off with a piece of cord. When Thainna had laced up her sandals and smoothed her new tabba, Narissa handed her a satchel. Thainna looked inside. There were bundles of bandages and a large whaleskin cylinder sealed in wax, stamped with the curvy mother-form of Surma.

"The salve," Narissa informed Thainna. "Apply this to Captain Mazrem's wounds daily. If you need anything else – ophellion, cardak or maephos – send word and I will provide it."

Narissa escorted Thainna to the front door of the temple. The morning was ripe now, clear of mist and quite warm. The sun hung huge and golden in the sky. Narissa gave the young Talon a final inspection and nodded.

"I suppose that's the best I can do on short notice," the priestess said. "You look enough like a foster. Be sure you act it. Thain will be counting on your success. Do you know the way to the Mazrems' estate?"

"Hae. I've worked in the Everstones before," Thainna answered more sharply than she intended. "I know where it is."

"Go, then. They're expecting you." Narissa pulled a few silver willows from a wallet on her belt and gave them to Thainna. "You're already late. Rent a ride."

Thainna trotted down the stairs and into the street. The world felt strangely soft and springy through the soles of her new sandals. She wanted to save the money Narissa had given her, to add it to her Auction bid. But if she arrived late to the Mazrem house, they might request another foster. And then where would Thainna be?

Where would Thain be? He'll never have the chance to become Crest if I ruin things now.

Thainna waved down a small chariot and climbed in beside the driver. His eyes widened when she told him their destination, but he accepted Narissa's money and clucked at his horse. The man tried to strike up conversation, gossiping about Rikard Mazrem's return and the blight in Erastrasus, but Thainna could not concentrate on the conversation.

She was going to the doorstep of a man who had already tried to kill her once. What if Captain Mazrem discovered who she worked for? What if he recognized her? Thainna probably wouldn't even have time to tell anyone, let alone run. Rikard Mazrem would kill her just for her Fiori red hair, or maybe feed her every memory and thought to his Alterran allies until she went as mad as him. And then the Crest would kill Thain for her failure.

Every bump in the road, every swerve her driver made around some other chariot or pedestrian threatened to make Thainna sick. How could the day get any worse?

At least I'll die in clean clothes, Thainna thought. *That's something, isn't it?*

16

SHATTER

"Emperor Tychon's decision to send most of the Verita et Illumina Lansinos into Fiore has been a subject of much debate, but not one the emperor himself has ever addressed. At that time, the nations who joined his new empire had done so by diplomacy, but it was agreed that war would eventually prove necessary. Was Fiore a bold show of force by a young emperor or his desperate gamble?"

— ACCOUNTS OF NJORN PASS, BY ALEXANDER FERRO

Rikard dreamed.

He stood on a field of glass. Long tales before, Yearn Valley had been a lush paradise. Colorful streaks of favorites and daydreams once cut across the southern reach like smears of paint. Bright, soft and spring.

But now the Yearn Valley was a battlefield that only barely held its form. Gilded green grass became skeletal and as colorless as ash. The ground was stretched out thin as a drumhead, frail and utterly transparent. Glass. Great cracks and fissures snapped and slithered through the Yearn Valley, as wide as the greatest Terran roads and bleak as old age. But through the ever-moving tears, Rikard felt... nothing. No cold, no trace. Nothing. The Shatter were nearly done with their work here.

Shards of old wounds – Yearn Valley's brittle, broken bones – cut painfully at his soul. The tenuousness tugged at him, threatening to unravel his very being. Rikard tensed his own form reflexively, bracing it with name and rank. Beside him, Flickerdim and Jingleblack coiled and uncoiled restlessly.

Are you certain about this place? Jingleblack asked with jittering, nervous thoughts that bounced about like fleas.

Rikard bled reassurance for the young Alterran soldier. *Hae, this is it.*

But there's not enough dream left here to hide anything, much less a plan, said Flickerdim, then gave Rikard a sly sidelong insight. *But that's your very idea, isn't it? If we stretch it out thin enough, we can hide it here and they will never even think to look.*

Exactly. It's a desperate measure, but we're running out of ideas.

What if you can't find it later, when it's time? Jingleblack worried. *What if you don't remember what to do?*

I will forget, Rikard thought. *Remember what it was like when I first came here? The journey nearly Shattered me, too. It will be even worse when I return home to Terra. Hiding the plan here is only buying ourselves time. And maybe not enough.*

Flickerdim rustled, raven-black fingers sprouting along his back. They flared, reaching for something necessary. Stumble hopped down the branch to nuzzle his friend. The shade-shadow fingers furled and closed like flowers by night, then sank back into his general deepness.

What is it? asked Stumble.

He remembers me in his dreams.

Really? Does he remember me? Stumble was eager, fluffing his stony feathers excitedly until they began to float off, light and soft as clouds. The wound of thinking that Rikard might have forgotten him already actually bled tiny pearls of gold and blue along his feathers. *Does he? Does he remember me, all the things I showed him?*

Flickerdim star-sparkled a short laugh. *Not yet, no. He will, Stumble. But don't worry, he will remember you before the end.*

Stumble wanted to thank Flickerdim for that, but the Alterran general was a proud old memory. The gratitude would have cut him open surely as the fear of being forgotten had bled Stumble.

Something soft moved beneath his fingers. Rikard woke with a start, jerking upright in the bed and instinctively clenching the sensation in his memory. But the softness was not a thought. It was an actual thing. Something in his fingers.

Rikard looked down at his hand. It was the corner of a sheet, nothing like the one Rikard had clutched around himself back in the Moon Court archouse. This was fine and slippery, not the rougher weave of a soldier's gear. Rikard ran his fingers over the cloth, marveling at the feel of it against his skin.

"It's much better than anything we had before, isn't it?"

Laurael stood in the doorway of the bedroom, holding aside a curtain of layered brocade. Her skin was different. No, her clothes, Rikard recalled. Her new tabba was as lovely as the sheets.

She smiled at Rikard – small and prettily, just like she did everything. That slightest upturning of her dark red lips made his heart leap. Rikard had never seen anything so beautiful in his life. He lurched out of the bed and swept Laurael into his arms, tangling the fingers of one hand in the elaborately pinned curls of her hair. Rikard sought Laurael's lips and kissed her, diving into the feel of her. His wife tasted like the clove oil she liked to dab on her teeth in the morning, to clean away the sticky taste of sleep. Wonderful, delicious... Rikard never wanted to taste anything else ever again.

He forgot to breathe and didn't care. Laurael wedged her hands between them, against Rikard's chest and pushed him away.

"I missed you, Laura," he whispered.

"As I missed you, my lord," Laurael told him. "Are you hungry? Breakfast awaits you."

Suddenly, his wife's sweet clove-oil kiss wasn't the only thing that sounded delicious. Rikard sniffed the air and smelled something salty, buttery and rich. The scent itself seemed almost enough to fill his stomach. He bolted past Laurael, following the smell, and burst out onto a porch that looked out over the rolling, landscaped green hill of the Everstones. There were other houses, too, all white marble and red tiled roofs, further down the slope.

Rikard's abrupt appearance startled the pair of servants setting out breakfast. A young boy shrieked and jumped back, dropping a pitcher of chilled tea. It shattered on the ground and tea splashed into an expanding liquid sunburst. A wedge of orange slid to rest against Rikard's bare toes. It was cold and rubbery.

The boy hurried to sweep up the broken shards of his pitcher, mumbling his apologies through a thick Po'Marran accent. Rikard stared down at the fruit at his feet. It was so bright and smelled so good, sharp and sweet. When the boy reached for it, Rikard snarled at him.

"Leave it!"

The boy whimpered as he scurried off. Another servant – the balding old Carceman that Rikard had seen the day before – stared with his mouth hanging open. When he realized that his master was watching, the servant covered his expression with a deep bow. But he could do nothing to stifle the sinking, stinging fear that rippled out from him with every thought. Rikard turned away.

"Please sit, my husband," Laurael said from the door.

She stepped through onto the sunlit porch and seated herself. Rikard picked up the orange wedge and sat beside her in a wicker chair just like the one in the atrium. The servant kept his eyes nervously, uncomfortably downcast and Rikard was relieved when Laurael dismissed him with a wave of her hand. The man bowed and retreated.

"This is better than what we once had, too," said Laurael.

The table standing between their chairs was piled high with food. Cubed fruit and flat cakes of golden-brown wheat, slabs of honeyed ham and – the source of the mouth-watering smell – a bowl of scrambled eggs. Rikard heaped food onto his plate until it threatened to spill over.

"Slowly, my lord," Laurael warned when he began shoveling it into his mouth.

"It smells good. I'm... hungry," he said through a mouthful of egg and half-chewed apple. "Very."

Laurael shrugged. "As you wish. Do you like it?"

It was hard to keep his mouth doing two things at once.

"You talked about before... before now," Rikard said haltingly. "About things before that, before the wars. That things you have now are better. Lacier. Nicer."

Laurael held up a glass of cream sprinkled with cinnamon. "We never could have eaten like this before."

A young woman stepped through another door and out onto the porch. "Lady Mazrem?"

Laurael sipped her spiced cream and set it aside before giving the girl her attention. "Hae?"

"Someone to see you, my lady," she reported, then corrected herself. "Both of you, Lord and Lady Mazrem."

"Who is it?"

"A foster from the temple of Surma. She says she's supposed to look after Lord Mazrem."

Laurael nodded. "General Hern sent her. Bring her here, then."

The maid curtsied and withdrew. Rikard's stomach was beginning to feel stiff and bloated from his sudden gorging. He had trouble following with the conversation. There had been images in the maid's mind, but listening with both ears and mind at the same time was painstaking work. Rikard remembered Nikas saying something about sending a foster, but that seemed like elegies ago.

Why did everyone treat Rikard so carefully, as though he were some... some fragile little hope that might dash away to glass in a moment? He was back home, and if everything the other Terrans said was true, then he was exactly the same as before, when he vanished from Njorn Pass.

It was everyone *else* who was different, who had gotten older and stranger! So why did Nikas Hern think Rikard needed a nursemaid? And why did Laurael agree?

The puddle of iced tea was evaporating quickly in the warm morning. Rikard caught sight of his reflection in the shiny amber pool and stared, distracted and fascinated. Mirrors were supposed to hang on walls, not dribble on the floor and turn into air when they got hot.

Pondering this strangeness, Rikard forgot about the other ones that had seemed so important a moment ago. The man reflected in the shifting puddle had dark, ragged hair on his cheeks. An image came to mind of a blade and soap being dragged over his face, but Rikard could not remember the word.

Sharp steel that does not cut flesh, except by accident. I had to explain it to the Alterra when they came to ask. They thought it all very strange. Why can't Terrans just shape their body by wish? I told them something, an answer. What was it? I can't remember.

Soft footfalls snapped his attention up once more. The maid had returned, leading a smaller girl dressed in blue. She was thin and pale, with hair of a bright, sunset red. It was plaited and still damp at the tips. The newcomer bowed deeply, falteringly. When she stood again, Rikard started.

It's her, the girl from the closed, stinking place. No lights but stars through shrouds of smoke.

The Fiori.

The half-Fiori.

Rikard jumped up from his chair and she recoiled, fear in her eyes and mind. Her terror thrust sharply back at Rikard, as brittle and dangerous as a broken sword. Laurael stood, too, frowning but not trying to restrain her husband.

"What is it?" she asked sharply. "My lord?"

"I know her!" Rikard snarled. His fingers twitched, itching to twine themselves around her throat once more and finish the job begun at their last meeting, but her costume gave him pause. "You… you're a priestess?"

There was a face in the girl's thoughts, one that looked much like her own, but even thinner, more drawn and wan. Through her thorny fear, Rikard could reach no further. Hissing in pain, Rikard pulled his thoughts away as though recoiling from a hot stove.

"Answer my husband, child," Laurael commanded.

"Hae, my lady," the girl said in a quavering voice. "Hae, Captain Mazrem. I work in the temple fostral. Mana Narissa sent me to look after your wounds."

Wounds? The holes in his skin, the bleeding places. Rikard remembered now and it made enough sense. He sat down again and picked up his plate. Laurael gave him a slightly frustrated look and reclaimed her seat, too.

"What's your name, my dear?" she asked the girl.

"Thainna, my lady. Thainna Vahn."

"Welcome to our home, Thainna. How long has your mana instructed you to stay and watch over my husband?"

"Until Lord Mazrem is well, my lady. As long as I'm needed."

"A foster's time is valuable. General Hern and Mana Narissa are very kind."

"Hae, Lady Mazrem."

Laurael stared at the skinny girl for a moment, then smiled and resumed her breakfast.

17

FOSTER TRUST

"We are servants to the gods and their mother, Surma. We strive in the service of life and light, ever against our brothers and enemies, the sons and spawn of Saerus. Yet we must remember always to respect his dominion and those he has claimed."

— THE BOOKS OF SURMA AND SAERUS

THAINNA STOOD awkwardly in front of Lord and Lady Mazrem, not quite sure what she was supposed to do next. Her knees seemed to be made of rapidly melting wax. She wanted to sit and catch her breath, but Rikard Mazrem and his wife occupied the only chairs.

They believed her. It was insanity to even think it, but they actually believed that Thainna was a foster. Rikard didn't ask after any more details of their prior meeting. But why? He obviously hadn't forgotten, and surely Captain Mazrem wondered what an educated priestess of Surma might have been doing in the Rows in the middle of the night, filthy and dressed in rags. But he didn't ask. Instead, the great war hero was stuffing food into his mouth like a starving man.

Which he might well be. Lady Mazrem now ignored Thainna with a noblewoman's easy obliviousness, leaving her free to examine Rikard Mazrem more closely. The VEIL captain was terribly thin, though a career of soldiering had muscled him well enough to hide the worst of it. But Thainna grew up in the slums of Dormaen and she knew starvation when she saw it. Sallow skin, the slight bulge to Rikard's stomach, and the redness in his gums that meant he had not eaten fruit for a long time. He needed a shave, too. Carcaen men just couldn't grow decent beards. They always ended up looking like drowned rats.

Rikard Mazrem was eating too fast. He dropped crumbs and bits of yellow egg on the front of his black saela. His wife watched out of the corner of her eye and did not look pleased. The smell of the food made Thainna's mouth water, but Narissa's advice was still fresh in her mind.

Thainna tried to speak, but little more than a terrified squeak escaped her dry lips. She cleared her throat and tried again.

"Captain Mazrem... sir? You shouldn't eat so fast."

Lady Mazrem gave a pretty, bell-like laugh. "So I've told him, but my husband has a will of iron and refuses to listen."

Thainna chewed her lip and took a step toward Rikard. "Please, Captain Mazrem. You're going to make yourself sick."

He ignored her and kept eating. Things would be messy and unpleasant unless he stopped. Thainna hesitated, and then put her hand on Rikard's wrist. He jerked back as though she had touched him with hot iron instead of nervous-weak fingers.

"You won't take anything from me!" he cried.

He snatched back his plate and food flew into the air. Thainna staggered back and fell to one knee. Lady Mazrem sighed softly but did nothing else about her husband's strange behavior.

Thainna straightened, but kept her distance this time. "I don't want to take anything, Captain Mazrem. Eat all you want, but do it slowly, hae? Stop when it hurts."

"When it hurts?" Rikard asked suspiciously. "No. It hurts when I *don't* eat."

"Because you're hungry, sir. But it hurts if you eat too much, as well."

Why was she explaining this as though to a child? No, even a child understood the difference between hunger and overeating. What was wrong with Captain Mazrem? Thainna was fairly sure she knew most of the stories and none of them ever mentioned him being simple-minded. He was injured... maybe a blow to the head? Or was he truly as unhinged as she had first thought at midnight in the Rows?

"Why?" Rikard asked Thainna. "Why does it hurt?"

Lady Mazrem watched in silence, politely sipping her morning cream.

"You... um... you haven't eaten for a long time, Captain Mazrem. Your stomach is used to being small," Thainna said. She cinched her hand into a fist to demonstrate. "If you put too much in before you're ready, it will cramp and make you sick. You'll throw up and then what's the point of having eaten at all?"

Rikard twirled his fork in his fingers, staring at the piece of meat speared on the pronged tip, glistening with honey. He nodded and bit, chewing much more slowly this time. When he was done, he put the plate down on the table.

"Are you finished, my lord?" asked Laurael.

"Hae," he answered thoughtfully. "For now."

"Then why don't you let Thainna take a look at your dressings?"

"Dressings?" He looked down at his egg-spattered clothes.

"The bandages that Hern's templars applied when you were at the archouse."

"Oh. Hae, then."

In her terror, Thainna had nearly forgotten about the bag of bandages and medicine Narissa had given her. It came back to her in a rush that she could actually hear roaring in her ears. She had no idea how to tie a bandage.

This is insanity. I can't do it, Thainna thought for the thousandth time. *What am I doing here?*

Rikard stood and stared at the buttons down the front of his saela. He prodded one with a questing finger, but could not seem to figure out what else to do with it. Someone else must have dressed him. Lady Mazrem went to her husband, unfastened the shirt for him and helped him shrug out of it. She folded and laid it across his chair.

"Do you want to do this somewhere more private?" Thainna asked nervously.

"My husband's injuries are hardly a source of shame," said Lady Mazrem.

Thainna shrugged. She doubted anyone who wasn't on Mazrem pay could see, anyway. The Mazrem estate was huge. Even with a lens, it would take a sharp-eyed neighbor to catch a glimpse of anything interesting. Of course, there was probably nothing to hide, as far as either Lord or Lady Mazrem were concerned. These were war wounds, honorably won. It wasn't like anything was going to fall out when she removed the bandages...

I hope.

Thainna inspected the swathes of blood-crusted cloth wound all along Rikard's neck and chest. The bandages definitely needed changing. There were other cuts, too, mostly along his arms and shoulders. Most of these had the scaly, pink-edged look of wounds on the mend, but several had recently torn open and darkened with dried blood.

Thainna circled to look at Rikard's back and found much the same. She touched one of the ragged slices as gently as she could. Captain Mazrem tensed under her fingers. The skin was cool, not fevered-hot. That was good, wasn't it?

"What happened? I thought the templars took care of these. How did they start bleeding again?"

"There was an... altercation," Lady Mazrem answered. "My husband was bold in the face of a certain confusion."

"I hit Nikas," Rikard said rather sullenly. "He wanted to take me back."

Thainna had no idea who Nikas was, but she figured that she had better clean Rikard up. Like any sane person, she was nervous around blood, especially that of a VEIL knight.

"I... I need to get some water and a towel to clean these," said Thainna.

Lady Mazrem called for a servant and one appeared in a doorway. "Get the foster hot water and washing cloths."

"I can get them myself, if you can just tell me where," Thainna said.

"A foster's time is much more valuable than that," Lady Mazrem told her as the servant hurried off.

Thainna wasn't at all comfortable with being served. She had two good feet – with brand-new sandals – and hands to do it herself, but couldn't bring herself to say so to the commanding Lady Mazrem.

What would I say, exactly? Hae, it's worth my time? You both scare me badly and I'd really like to get away from all of this...?

But instead, Thainna picked at the knots of Captain Mazrem's bandages. He held perfectly still, rigidly tensed as though ready to grab her. Like a statue about to spring to lethal life. More than a little unnerved, Thainna unwound the bandages until the blood clotted in them made it impossible to keep going. She searched through the supplies Narissa had given her until she found a small knife. Thainna slipped it out of the leather sleeve and bit her lip in concentration as she carefully sliced away the rest of Rikard's red-stained bandages.

Don't cut him!

The servant returned with a bowl of steaming water. Two more followed, one with a stack of towels. The other set out a stand for the basin. Thainna thanked them and began her work. When she had cleaned up the blood and painstakingly picked away the final threads of old bandages, the water was stained red. Rikard's cuts were oozing again.

The nervously waiting servants gathered up the discarded bandages and rushed them off to be burned. Thainna took the canister of salve from her satchel and peeled away the wax seal with her thumbnail.

"Will the Alterra be confused by all of the blood?" she asked.

"No," said Rikard.

"Why not?"

"A ship of stone sails in sorrows."

Thainna waited, but that was all of the information that he offered.

He really is mad.

Thainna found a pair of white lambskin gloves at the bottom of Narissa's supplies and pulled them on before rubbing the sharp-smelling medicine into Captain Mazrem's wounds. She was careful around the one in his side. Someone – probably the templars that Lady Mazrem mentioned – had stitched it tightly shut with fine black thread, but it had been a wide, deep cut and Rikard's skin was pulled taut over it.

Thainna rubbed salve into the angry, reddened skin as much as she dared, then wound it up under bandages again. It wasn't much different than wrapping her feet, she decided.

"Are there any other uh... injuries?" Thainna asked, motioning at Rikard's black pants.

If there were any other injuries, she could not see them and Narissa hadn't exactly given her a catalog of the man's wounds. Lady Mazrem pursed her painted lips a little tighter and Rikard nodded. He rolled up one of his pant legs to display a long, shallow set of scratches in his calf. These hadn't bled recently, so Thainna just rubbed them with the medicine Narissa had given her and then pulled off her gloves, wrapping them in a towel.

"That's all," she announced. "You can dress again."

With his wife's help, Captain Mazrem replaced his saela and buttoned the collar up under his chin. She brushed the remains of his breakfast from his chest and retied his tail of dark, straight hair.

"Do you feel well enough for a walk, my lord?" Lady Mazrem asked.

Rikard seemed to think about that for a moment and nodded

"Good. Things have changed a great deal since you left and I'd like to show you. Thank you for your time, Thainna. Go inside and ask for Bastil. He'll give you a room. Are you hungry? And some breakfast, then. Check over my husband again after dinner."

Thainna offered her very best – but still very clumsy – curtsy. Lady Mazrem took Rikard's arm and led him away across the manicured lawn, toward a large, domed white building. When they were gone, more servants appeared from the porch doors to clear away the remains of Lord and Lady Mazrem's meal. Thainna gathered up her supplies.

"Where can I find Bastil?" she asked one of the girls collecting plates.

"In his office, at the servants' house."

"Where is that?"

"Just across that lawn there. When you get inside, go down the hall until you reach the first crossing, and then turn right. Bastil's office is at the end there. Knock before you go in. Bastil will yell at you if you don't."

"Thank you," said Thainna.

She pulled the strap of the sack over her shoulder and made her way across the indicated lawn. The servants' quarters were in a long, low building with dozens of small round windows. Inside, Thainna made her way down a hall tiled in blue and lined along both sides by doors. Most of these were closed, but those that were not opened on small, neat bedrooms. Some were larger than others, containing more than one bed. In one room, a pair of small children wrestled while an old woman smiled and mended a torn black tabba.

At the first intersection of hallways, Thainna turned right. At the end of the hall stood another door, this one closed tightly. She rapped her knuckles on it and waited.

"Come in," answered a muffled voice.

A serious-looking older Carcaen man sat behind a desk inside, sorting through papers and waxed writing boards. His head jerked up at Thainna with a surprised look, as though he had entirely forgotten that he had just told her to come in.

"Who in hell are you?" he asked.

"Thainna Vahn. I'm a foster."

"I'm not blind, girl. I can see that. What are you doing here? Did someone call for you?"

"General Hern and Mana Narissa sent me to care for Captain Mazrem," Thainna explained in a rush. "I... I'm sure there's a record of it somewhere."

Bastil picked through the half-ordered mess on his desk until he found a folded letter with a dark blue Moon Court seal. He opened it, read over the contents a couple of times, sighed and dropped it back into the heap.

"Thinny, you said?"

"Thainna."

"I'm Bastil, steward of this house. Since you're talking to me, I suppose you need a place to stay. For how long?"

"I'm not really sure. It depends upon how long it takes Captain Mazrem to heal."

"Well then."

Bastil stood and went to a map on the wall that seemed to be of the building they were in. The steward frowned.

"I can't bunk a foster with the other help," he said. "They will never leave you alone. One of the private rooms, then. Liselle left a few weeks back and her room is free. It doesn't have much of a view, but will that suffice?"

Bastil's tone suggested that any other accommodations he might be able to rustle up – at considerable personal sacrifice – would be much worse. Thainna barely kept herself from laughing. Not much of a view? Did he think Thainna cared, that she would make some sort of a fuss? Her own room, with a roof and a real bed!

"That will be fine," she assured the steward.

Bastil nodded and headed for the door, gesturing for Thainna to follow. He led her back the way she had come, then up another corridor lined in rooms. At a small open doorway, Bastil stopped and motioned Thainna inside. The chamber was tiny, only a little larger than Thain's cell at the fostral. But it was clean and for the moment, it was hers.

Thainna plopped down on the edge of the bed. It wasn't lavish, but the pallet was stuffed with something softer than reeds and the blanket had no holes. She set the sack down next to the bed and stood on tiptoes to look out the single window. *Not much of a view* proved to be the back of another building.

"What's that?" she asked, pointing.

"The storehouse. There's a bathhouse next to it that you can use and I suggest that you do so frequently," said Bastil frankly. "Lady Mazrem does not abide dirty servants."

He turned to leave, but Thainna had one more question.

"Lady Mazrem said I should... that I could ask you for something to eat?"

Bastil glanced back to Thainna.

"You haven't eaten? Down the hall and turn two rights," he said. "That's the servants' kitchen. Go there and speak to Arliss. She'll take care of it."

Thainna jumped up and embraced the sour-faced old steward.

A real bed, a real room, real food, real clothes… It was too much to take in at once. Tears filled Thainna's eyes, pure gratitude leaking down her cheeks.

"Thank you!" she cried.

Bastil gingerly extricated himself from Thainna's arms and inspected his tabba for any tearstains. Finding several, he rolled his eyes.

"Hae, you're quite welcome," he sighed.

18

BELOVED

"What is it about us that the Alterra need? Their power here in Terra is profound and strange. They can stop a man's heart or summon lightning from a clear sky. We don't understand why or how, only that it is true. So we must ask – what is our influence in their world?"

— BEYOND THE VEIL, BY AELUS KAR

LAUREL HAD EXPANDED their home hugely over the years. She must have bought a quarter of the Everstones and the tour she gave Rikard was staggering. There were several buildings now, including an entire longhouse for guests, another one for servants, a private shrine, three storehouses and two heated baths. Every one of them was lovely, with carved friezes and painted murals, many depicting various artists' renditions of the battle of Njorn Pass.

When it became apparent that Rikard was tiring, his wife led him back to the largest house.

"Are you hungry again?" she asked.

"Hae," Rikard answered.

Ravenous, in fact. The foster girl was right – he felt ill if he ate too much. But less meant he would be hungry more often.

"Is it too soon?" he asked.

"No, it's just about time for lunch."

She led him to a different patio than the one they had used for breakfast. Wooden arches surrounded this one, all wound in green vines with little white star-shapes that smelled almost overpoweringly sweet. Jasmine. Rikard spent a long time just inhaling their sugary scent, until Laurael called him over to sit beside her on a divan.

A woman in a bright green tabba served them chilled wine and fruit juice with chunks of ice floating in it. There was more fruit and fluffy rolls of freshly baked bread smeared with sweet butter. Laurael ate very little of it. Rikard reminded himself to eat slowly.

"More," he said when he had blunted the edge from his hunger.

"There is plenty of food, my husband," Laurael told him. "Don't worry about that."

"No, not that. Tell me more, Laura. Gods, thirty years fell since I saw you. Since I held Gaius. Tell me, please. Does he have a you?"

"A me?"

Laurael was obviously confused and Rikard cursed the clumsy Terran speech again.

"A… a wife," he said. "Did he make a marriage? Children?"

Laurael raised her chin proudly. She was so very fine, so pristinely beautiful even after the three decades that lay between them. Rikard burned for her in a way words would never describe. He took her hand – so lily-pale that she might have been wearing a pair of the foster's gloves – and kissed it. Laurael smiled at him.

"No, Gaius hasn't married yet. He's been so busy," she answered. She squeezed Rikard's hand gently in hers and then released it so she could pick up her wine again. "I've arranged a wife for him, but he keeps putting off the wedding."

"Why?"

"Gaius is a captain in the Star Court – just like you were – and a consul in the Lyceum, the ruling council. There are a great many demands on him, my lord. Gaius spends time with the emperor, too. They've grown quite close."

Rikard choked on a mouthful of raspberries and clotted cream. He leapt to his feet.

"Emperor Tychon?" he snarled. "My son is a friend to Castum Tychon? Is that where he is now?"

"Perhaps," Laurael said slowly, frowning. "I expect the emperor is curious about you, my lord. Of course, the Lyceum met last night to answer such questions, so perhaps not."

Rikard was on fire again, but this time with fury. His son and Emperor Tychon? He clenched his hands into fists so tightly that his fingernails bit into his palms and drew crescents of blood. Rikard stalked back and forth across the patio like a caged beast. The blood filled his clenched hand and dripped down between his fingers.

"What are you doing, my lord? What's wrong?" Laurael was on her feet now, wine forgotten.

Rikard couldn't hear her. His blood roared far louder than his wife's voice. Rikard opened his hand and flicked his wrist, spattering blood onto one of the flower-wound trellises.

Break, he thought. Commanded. *Fall! A dream on waking. For this, I trade the scent of jasmine. White-blooming stars. For a moon.*

Dark lines shot out from around the bright spots of blood on the wood, crackling and cracking. The wooden trellis twisted and warped, knotting in terrible, unnatural shapes, and then exploded into splinters. Jasmine vines tore and filled the air with a snowfall of drifting white petals, suddenly as scentless to Rikard as snow.

"My gods," whispered Laurael.

Her kohl-lined eyes were round. With her hands pressed to her mouth, she took a small step away from Rikard. There were flowers in her hair.

"What have you done?" she asked.

"My son is a friend to the emperor!"

"Not as close as I would like, but hae," said Laurael, collecting herself. "And it's a blessing upon our family. Emperor Tychon never married, never fathered any blooded children. Gaius is the only heir left to him."

Another thought swam beneath Laurael's words, like a beaked crowfish under deep, still waters, but Rikard couldn't bring himself to reach into his own wife's mind. Furious, he stalked back and forth, crushing fallen leaves and flowers beneath his feet. Laurael sat again, trembling. Spots of bright color shone in her cheeks. She plucked a jasmine flower from her hair and rolled it between her fingers.

"Why such anger, my husband?" she asked in a clipped voice. "You should be proud of our son. He will be the next emperor of Carce."

"Tychon sent us to die in a war that we could *never* win!" Rikard said. His bloody hands stung, but not half as badly as his heart. "We couldn't fight in Fiore. Too much ice, too many spears. It was all death!"

"That's why you rage against our emperor, my husband? A war that ended thirty years ago?"

Laurael, his beautiful Laura, didn't understand. She couldn't reach for his memories, didn't hear the dying moans of soldiers and knights, smell the copper-salt tang of blood on the snow, feel the tearing, biting cold and ice! All Rikard had were the flat Terran words to tell her. Maybe if he said them loudly enough, he could make her *hear*.

"They died, all of them!" he shouted. "They were not curse-mock, not... ready for mountain warfare! It was the... ice-heart... the middle of winter!"

"But you won the war," Laurael told him. She patted the divan beside her until Rikard finally stopped pacing. "Not everyone died.

Survivors returned to Dormaen with tales of your bravery. You destroyed or banished the entire Fiori horde, my lord. It was the war to end all wars."

"Iron as beloved night!" Rikard pulled at his black hair in frustration. He flung himself down on the seat beside his wife. Njorn Pass was casual history to her. "End all wars? Tell me the string-strung, the... stories. What happened?"

"The tale is a short one," Laurael answered with a small shrug that made her filmy outer tabba drift like mist. "The last of your army returned to Carce victorious against the barbarian Fiori. There were no other wars. The other nations quite willingly joined Tychon's new empire."

"Which ones?"

"All of them. Every single nation of the world is now a province of the Carcaen Empire. Word of your victory spread like wildfire, my lord. The Fiori were a fierce people, even more infamous than the Lynceans for their bloody disputes. But they were finally defeated by the glorious deeds of a single man. You, my lord. None dared challenge VEIL after your display of power and no one dared risk not being a part of such a powerful alliance. Even Nian and Lyncea sent envoys to Dormaen."

"All of them," Rikard repeated, shaking his head.

"There has been peace for thirty years, my husband. Emperor Tychon founded the Lyceum twenty-five years ago, an appointed council to give a voice to all of the provinces. And to VEIL, as well. The generals of all three VEIL courts sit on the Lyceum. The Lyceum even voted to allow provincials to join VEIL. Numbers have been low ever since the Fiore war."

"Because they all died!"

"Very few knights returned from Fiore," Laurael agreed in a soft voice. "And many of those who survived left the order shortly thereafter. The cost for the Carcaen Empire was high, my lord, but it's been thirty years paid. And look what it bought us."

She gestured around them, to the houses and gardens of their home. Rikard's eyes followed her sweeping motion. Carce's rise had certainly raised her up, too. Money, land, respect and adoration all lavished upon his widow.

And my son, too. Heir to the throne...?

As though summoned by the thought, Rikard saw Gaius picking his way along the hill toward them, red-faced and sweating with the effort of the climb. He waved as he approached, then paused as he stepped over the remains of the shattered trellis. Gaius pushed a piece of wood out of his way with his foot and went to Laurael. He kissed her powdered cheek.

"Good morning, Mother." He nodded to Rikard. "Father."

"It's afternoon, Gaius," his mother told him.

"Already? It was a late night."

"Was the emperor at the Lyceum last night? Did he speak to you in particular?"

"Hae and then no. I'm sure he'll call me in for a more private talk soon, though. Or you, maybe. What happened here?"

Gaius picked up a splinter of wood. It shone red and wet. Gaius frowned and looked at Rikard, then down at his hands. He threw the bloody wood to the ground as though it had bitten him.

"Is that your blood?" Gaius asked Rikard, then whistled when his father nodded. He examined the broken arch and shredded flowers with new fascination. "Where was the pact? I don't see one."

"I... star-river..." Rikard struggled with the words.

Laurael was already tired of looking at the mess and uninterested in the answers there. She called for someone to clean it away. A tall Jumaari in a sweat-damp work tabba brought a broom and a large sack to do as she asked.

"There's blood in that," Gaius warned before taking a seat and joining his parents' lunch.

The Jumaari swallowed hard as he got to work.

At Laurael's request, dinner was light and simple. When it was finished and Gaius had made his farewells for the evening, Laurael took Rikard's hand, carefully scrubbed clean of blood by nervous servants. She led him through the house, back to her lavish bedroom. It was huge, at least the size of the entire atrium. An entire face stood open to the cool night air, framed by columns carved with vines and flowers, hung between with colorful silk curtains. Dangling strings of shells and glass beads chimed musically in the breeze.

The bedroom was full of soft light from delicate glass oil lamps and flickering candles that burned with a spicy, heady aroma. It smelled just like the pleasantly hot, thick feeling beneath the pit of Rikard's stomach every time he looked at his wife.

Laurael pulled aside the rippling drapes. The night beyond was incomplete, still touched with twilight violet at the edges but already dusted with twinkling diamond stars. A slender crescent moon hung in the sky, a celestial goddess' silver smile.

Rikard followed Laurael and circled his arms around her waist. She felt different against him than he remembered, and he remembered very well. Thoughts of her had protected him for so long, against every cold emptiness that the Shatter hurled at him across the broken battlefields of Alterra. Laurael was softer in some places now, harder in others. Age had changed her body, but not Rikard's desire for her. It burned so sweetly, so bright that he felt certain Laurael could feel it. Had to feel it. Rikard pulled her tightly to him.

"It's beautiful, isn't it?" she said.

"You're beautiful," Rikard murmured. He kissed the side of her neck.

"I spent all day showing you what we've built here, my lord. Do you see any of it?" She looked not at Rikard, but out at the vastness of the world outside. "I showed you what you have done. Not only for Carce, but for us. For your family. You're angry with Emperor Tychon, but I am grateful to him. What did we have before you left for Fiore on his order?"

"I had everything I wanted."

"What did we have?" Laurael asked again, heavily emphasizing the question. "Nothing. You were the only son of a minor family, a junior captain of the smallest and least important VEIL court. I contributed little else to our standing. I was the youngest daughter of a father with a little more money than yours, but never enough. We had nothing to give our son but a life of hard work and a small house on a stony hill."

Laurael turned so she could look up into Rikard's eyes. He kept his hands pressed against the graceful curve of her lower back.

"Are you happy now, Laura?" he asked.

"Even the VEIL generals don't live so well as we do. The Everstone manors sprang up around us simply to be near the memory of you. By your sacrifice, you gave us everything."

"I wasn't trying to. I didn't want to be a hero, Laura."

Rikard slid his hands along his wife's back to caress her neck. The soft, delicate curls of her hair tickled the sensitive skin around his bloodcap. Rikard leaned in to kiss her, but Laurael pulled away and strode over to the huge bed, which was raised up on a steeply stepped dais.

"You never did have any ambition," she said. "But the gods had other plans, praise them. Do you not care about the fortune you've given us? Are you not at all pleased? Grateful that your family has been provided for?"

Rikard could not understand the chilly, sour-tasting displeasure oozing from his wife. She had what she wanted, didn't she? What did it matter what he thought of her riches? He was glad, of course, that his family had lived well in his absence. But it was Laurael and Gaius who had enjoyed that bounty, not Rikard.

I don't know this life. I only met it this morning, and I never sought it.

Laurael watched Rikard, waiting for him to respond. He was searching out words to give her when he was interrupted by a polite rapping at the door. Laurael sighed and went to open it. The little red-haired foster, Thainna, stood outside. Her eyes flickered between Rikard and his wife. A blush darkened her cheeks.

"I'm sorry, my lady. I can come back later. I just thought... Well, it's after dinner," she stammered.

Laurael stood back and ushered her inside. "Come take care of your business."

"Thank you, Lady Mazrem."

Thainna bowed and entered, carrying her satchel over her shoulder. Her eyes wandered through the room as she crossed it, marveling at the beauty and richness of it all. She was impressed, just as Laurael seemed to think that he should have been. Thainna tore her attention from the decadence and returned it to Rikard.

"Captain Mazrem," she greeted him. "How do you feel?"

"Whirlposted," he answered. The argument with his wife, one-sided though it had been, made Rikard's head ache.

"Um, hae. Can I look at your bandages?" Thainna asked.

Rikard nodded wearily. He went to the bed and sat on the edge, laboring to unbutton his saela, as Laurael had done that morning. Thainna watched with a curious expression, but didn't do anything. When Rikard was finally free of the saela, she took a lamp – a pretty little bulb of iridescent glass wrapped in gold wire – from a nearby table and held it up to Rikard's bandaged midsection.

"It doesn't look like you bled through, but I'm going to change the dressings anyway. I don't want you getting an infection."

I wouldn't know what to do if you did. Thainna's thoughts were restless and scattered. Rikard felt her worry like spiders crawling over his skin. *And I don't want to report problems to Narissa this early into the game.*

He clasped his hands behind his head as Thainna unknotted and unwound the bandages. They came off quickly and easily now, without using the knife this time. The foster held the lamp close to check the stitches over Rikard's ribs.

"Does that hurt?" she asked

"No."

It was not Rikard's body that ached.

Thainna covered his injuries with fresh salve and bandages from her satchel. She bowed and left, lighting her way through the room with the lamp. When she was gone, Laurael sat down beside Rikard. The glowering needle-spike of her anger was gone. His wife was cool and smooth and soothing once more. Gratefully, Rikard hooked his arm around her waist.

"Did you see that girl's eyes?" Laurael asked. "She must be from the country. She's never seen anything like this."

Thainna's awe seemed to make up for the lack of his own and Rikard found himself suddenly grateful to the skinny young foster. He pulled his wife into his lap and kissed her. Laurael wrapped her arms around him. Rikard had not replaced his saela and her fingers seared honeyed fire across his bare skin.

"I've been gone so long," he whispered into her ear. "I thought of you every breach. Every day. I love you, Laura. I need you."

Laurael slipped out of his lap and lay across the bed, smiling invitingly. Rikard hesitated. He remembered this scene from their wedding night, but as faintly as a faded painting. Rikard searched frantically. He didn't know what came next, only that he wanted to be close to his wife.

"I... don't remember what to do," he admitted.

Laurael quirked an eyebrow and shrugged sinuously. "Well, there will be time to remember. Come lie in my arms, my husband, and let memory come when it will."

Rikard let Laurael pull him into her arms. Sleep came for him swiftly.

The tower-tree shuddered again, lurching nightmarishly against the stormy sky. Branches snapped and split with the effort, then fell away entirely as the tower aspect eclipsed the tree. Leaves shivered and faded, leaving behind only dark, empty windows. Stumble clung to a flaking sill, digging his talons into the wood-stone-loyalty until he found his balance. He reached wildly until he found Flickerdim, still floating where his perch had been.

What happened? cried Stumble.

He is distracted. Flickerdim pivoted his smooth, star-scaled head toward Stumble. *It's his wife. She wants other things, Terran things. Our bonds with the Terrans are so few and so slender that plucking any one will make the entire Uprising tremble.*

As Rikard drifted into dreams, the tower surged and rippled. Branches bloomed from the great tree once more. Stumble hooted in sudden alarm as his window perch changed, twisted and extended, shooting him outward. The silver-white branch split and fanned out into twigs and leaves, bright with bringing.

Flickerdim settled himself onto the tree with a brittle rasp. He flicked his jet-black tongue at Stumble.

Do you feel her? he asked. *His wife?*

Yes. I don't like her, Stumble thought.

She does not need affection to be, to exist. That is not what makes her real. She is woven from other threads. He loves her, but that is not what she seeks.

Should we tell him? Stumble asked, more worried now than when the Uprising had shifted all around them.

He would not listen, not even to us. He thinks he needs her.

Even in his sleep, Rikard held Laurael tightly. While thirty years apart had apparently robbed her husband of his sanity, it had not made him any less a young man. Though he could not yet recall the intimacies of the bedroom, his sleepy, youthful body nudged at her with an urgency that would not slumber forever.

Eventually, he slipped into deeper sleep and left Laurael in peace, but still she could not follow him into slumber. Rikard's unfocused desire left her still dressed and though her tabba was the height of fashion, it certainly wasn't the height of comfort. The whalebone ribs of her cincher bit uncomfortably into her stomach and the diaphanous outer skirts tangled around her ankles.

Laurael slipped away from Rikard and out of bed. She stretched and felt the stiffness in her joints. There was no way she could get out of this tabba alone. She tugged on a cord beside the door that rang a bell deeper in the house and a moment later, one of the maids knocked softly. Laurael let her in and instructed the girl to undress her.

As the tightness of the corset blessedly released, Laurael took a deep breath and gazed contemplatively out through the curtains. In the distance, Dormaen blazed with lights that filled the valley, like a sea of stars. The soft wind carried snatches of sound, the unintelligible babble of far-off voices. How many of them were talking about the return of the legendary Lord-Captain Rikard Mazrem?

Most of them, if not all. The hero has returned.

When the girl was finished undressing Laurael, she draped a wrap around her mistress' waist. Laurael pulled it up and tied it under her arms.

"Put out the lights," she instructed

The young maid bowed and circled the room, extinguishing the candles and lamps with a copper cone. Laurael climbed the steps to the bed again and lay beside Rikard. Why had he returned at all? Rikard said that the Alterra claimed his life as their price for victory in Njorn Pass.

Rikard was unhinged by his time in Alterra. He was furious with Emperor Tychon and seemed to have no desire or even ability to conceal it. What would happen when Castum Tychon inevitably wanted to see Rikard Mazrem, the man who had single-handedly forged his great empire? If Rikard somehow managed not to make an enemy of the emperor, then he would befriend him. And where would that leave Gaius in the line of succession?

Laurael sat up on one elbow and stroked her husband's cheek with the back of her hand. It was rough with whiskers. Tomorrow, she would make sure someone shaved the man properly. Laurael's fingers moved down his jaw to his throat. Rikard's pulse fluttered under her touch, vital and fragile.

Why did he have to come back? Why couldn't the Alterra just keep him forever?

19

BREAKING DAWN

"Those who survived the slaughter of the Fiori war were so few that most of modern VEIL has never seen war. They have known only this era of peace. Their only battles are of their own making."

—ACCOUNTS OF NJORN PASS, BY ALEXANDER FERRO

THAINNA EAGERLY RETURNED to her room for her first night of sleep in a real bed, but then surprised herself by being unable to get comfortable. The bed was soft, but for a girl of the Rows, it was disconcertingly insubstantial. Every time she fell asleep, Thainna started and dug her nails into the mattress, clinging to it with a terror that didn't match the two-foot drop to the floor.

Or maybe it was her dreams.

Rikard Mazrem chased Thainna up and up through the dark tower of her nightmare. She clutched a little gold and glass lamp to her chest, the one she had stolen from his bedroom the night before. Thain was somewhere at the top of the tower, she knew, and Thainna had to get the lamp to him. Quickly, before the Auction came...

But the stairs were crooked beneath Thainna's feet and she staggered, falling. In a second, Rikard was on top of her. He sank long shadow-fingers into her chest, reaching for her heart...

There was a sharp knock at the door and Thainna jerked once more into wakefulness. Her head and eyes felt stuffed with sand. She sat and scrubbed at her face with her fingers.

"Come in," Thainna called in a sleep-roughened voice.

Bastil opened the door and stood in the frame, gesturing impatiently for Thainna to rise.

"Get up, girl!" he said. "What're you doing still abed?"

"Sorry, I didn't sleep well."

Bastil carried a large package wrapped in paper and sealed in stamped wax. He handed it to Thainna, who took it curiously. In spite of its size, the parcel was quite light.

"It's from the temple of Surma," Bastil said. "A courier brought it this morning. Is it important?"

Thainna had no idea, but she didn't want to open anything sent by Narissa in front of the Mazrem steward. She set it aside and smiled disarmingly at Bastil... at least, she hoped that was what she was doing.

"It's just some extra medicine," said Thainna.

She rose and found her silver shoulder clasps under her pillow, then straightened out her tabba. Was it too rumpled by sleep? Rich people could be terribly fussy about clothes.

"Where are we going?" she asked.

"To see Lord and Lady Mazrem," Bastil answered. "There's a long list of visitors who wish to pay their respects."

Thainna was still annoyed at being awake.

"What do you need me for, then?" she asked.

Bastil was clearly the more experienced hand at irritation. "To tell the lady of the house if Captain Mazrem is well enough to take visitors. His health and well-being are our top priorities, of course, but some of our lord's requestors are important people."

"Hae, then."

Thainna finished tying her sandals, hauled her supplies over her shoulder, and followed Bastil out of the servant's longhouse. They passed other serving staff going to and from the longhouse. Some nodded and waved to Bastil, but most made sure to look busy and avoided the steward's attention.

The morning sun was bright and warm. Colorful birds sang in well-pruned trees. The grass was wet and slippery with dew, but not enough to soak through Thainna's sandals. In the wheat-colored sunlight and clear, clean morning, she couldn't hold on to her foul mood for long. By the time they made it to the Mazrem's main house, Thainna found herself smiling and humming tunelessly. When she was done with Rikard, it would be time for another large breakfast from the servant's kitchen. Yesterday had been full of more food than any day of her entire life.

For a moment, Thainna was almost grateful to the Crest for her new job.

Bastil took her through an atrium and into the main house. A pair of dressers waited at the door to Lord and Lady Mazrem's bedroom. Bastil inspected the clothes they carried and nodded.

"Good. Wait here until you're called," he instructed the other servants.

They stood aside while Bastil opened the door for Thainna and ushered her inside. He followed her quietly.

Inside, layered curtains filtered the morning light into dim, colorful shadows that turned the bedroom into a secretive grotto. But not secret enough to keep Bastil away. The steward pulled open the drapes and tied them back, flooding the lavish bedroom with bright yellow sunlight. Laurael sat up in her bed, yawned and stretched. Rikard groaned and threw an arm over his face.

"I'm sorry for intruding, Lord and Lady Mazrem," Bastil said, bowing deeply. "However, I'm afraid that there are matters which demand your immediate attention."

"What is it?" Laurael asked.

Beside her, Rikard rolled away and resumed his loud snoring.

"There are people lining up at the gates to see Captain Mazrem. VEIL sent additional knights to secure the estate, but the people are eager. There have already been some injuries."

"Injuries?"

"Just minor ones," Bastil assured Laurael quickly. "A few tried to climb the gates and the knights had to pull them down. There are others asking for audiences with Captain Mazrem, as well. General Saul Darius, Consul Liam Io and Alexander Ferro being particularly vocal. There's even been word from General Castor of the Sun Court. The emperor's offices have sent requests, of course."

"Let me see." Laurael snapped her fingers and Bastil handed her a sheaf of papers. "Turn up the lights."

Bastil nodded to Thainna. She had no idea why. Bastil rolled his eyes and pointed impatiently to a lamp, a larger version of the one she had stolen the night before. Thainna hurried to hand it to him. Bastil lit it from a small emberbox, turned up the wick, and held it beside Lady Mazrem. She unfolded the letters and leafed through them, moving her lips as she read. After a moment, she handed them back to Bastil.

"Absolutely not," Laurael said. Her tone was hard and final. She glanced at the snoring young man beside her. "My husband has been home barely a day. He needs rest. Peace and quiet."

"I thought that perhaps the foster could keep us apprised of Lord Mazrem's progress," Bastil suggested delicately.

Laurael sighed. "Very well. Thainna, come here."

Thainna stepped obediently to the bedside.

"Hae, Lady Mazrem?" she asked.

"What do you say to my husband's health? Is he well enough to take visitors?"

Bastil and Lady Mazrem studied her closely. What was Thainna supposed to say? She wasn't really a foster, after all. Still, other than being frothing mad, Captain Mazrem seemed to be in good health. His injuries didn't seem to bother him much and, as Narissa had pointed out, Captain Mazrem walked all the way across Dormaen – perhaps further – with them.

Lady Mazrem knows that, too. She's playing at politics, and Bastil just wants to get down to business.

Thainna didn't know the noblewoman's game, but knew instinctively that one was being played. Why else keep Captain Mazrem secluded? Thainna covered her indecision by circling the bed and pretending to examine Rikard more closely. To her surprise, she found something. There were scabbed-over gouges in the man's palms.

"What happened to his hands?" Thainna asked.

"My husband was distraught yesterday. He used his blood," said Laurael.

Thainna took a deep breath and knelt down. Bastil followed her around the bed, holding the lamp aloft. The blood had all been cleaned away, for the most part, but there was still a little of it under his fingernails. Not daring to touch Captain Mazrem, Thainna traced the line of his finger with her eyes, down to the VEIL knight's bloodcap. It was closed and the gold was still clean.

Why hadn't Rikard used his cannula? He must have already been bleeding from the nail-marks across his palms. Rikard wasn't bleeding with intent – he was simply angry. Mad. Crazy enough to tear his own flesh open instead of using the bloodcap surgically installed there.

Was that what Laurael didn't want anyone to see? If so, Thainna could hardly blame Lady Mazrem. This animal wasn't the hero of Carce. Laurael probably wanted to keep Rikard secluded until he recovered, if he ever did.

And what did that mean for Thainna? The Crest wanted her to control Rikard. Could this help her do that, somehow? Thainna wasn't sure.

But for right now, she would have to agree with someone. Lady Mazrem was powerful, but Bastil could just as easily make Thainna's life here difficult. Was there a way to make them both happy?

"Captain Mazrem is healing well," Thainna answered, looking back and forth between the lady and her steward. "His wounds are healing quickly, but he's been... uh... affected by his trials. I think that Lord Mazrem can see visitors, but only a few and then only for a little while."

Lady Mazrem nodded and smiled at Bastil. The steward sighed as though Thainna had carved her answer into a boulder and asked him to carry it across Dormaen.

"We shall allow my husband audiences, but we will be selective about who he sees," said Laurael.

"Hae, Lady Mazrem," Bastil said stiffly. He bowed and left, back straight and rigid.

Captain Mazrem had slept straight throughout the entire conversation. Thainna stood awkwardly at his bedside and wondered what to do next.

Laurael stood and called for her dressers. Thainna flinched at the sudden loud noise, but Rikard didn't stir. The pair of servants she had seen outside scuttled into the bedroom to help Laurael undress and then wrap her in an elaborate new tabba. Thainna figured that Lady Mazrem had forgotten her entirely until the half-dressed noblewoman called for her.

"Thainna, come here."

Thainna had to stand a few feet back to avoid colliding with the dressers laboring to clothe and paint their mistress. "My lady?"

"You were wise to agree with me, young foster. My husband isn't ready to face with the world. He will be permitted visitors, as you've suggested, but all of Carce is eager to see Lord-Captain Mazrem."

Thainna could think of nothing intelligent to say, so she nodded silently. Lady Mazrem wasn't looking at Thainna, but into the hand mirror she was holding. One of the dressers braided her mistress' hair and pinned it into an intricate spiral while the other powdered her cheeks.

"I want you to attend these visits, my dear," said Lady Mazrem.

Thainna blinked. "What? Why?"

"If any of my husband's visitors believe that their business is more important than his health, I would like you to tell them otherwise. A foster's expert word will ensure that no one overtaxes Lord Mazrem."

"I uh... Hae, my lady."

"I'll speak with Bastil and decide who can see him tomorrow."

Laurael paused as the boy working on her face rubbed a floral-smelling paste into her pale skin. When he was done, Lady Mazrem inspected the results in her mirror once more. She was the palest Carcaen that Thainna had ever seen, almost as white-skinned as a Fiori.

"That's enough for now," said Laurael. "I'm hungry. We'll finish in my sitting room once I've had breakfast. Thainna, bring my husband to me when you've finished with his care."

Thainna and the dressers bowed to Lady Mazrem as she swept out of the room. The other servants wordlessly gathered up her discarded sleeping wrap and makeup, then left Thainna alone in the vast bedroom.

Almost alone. Thainna returned to the bed and the catatonic Rikard Mazrem.

Thank you very much, Lady Mazrem, for leaving me all alone with your mad husband.

As gently as she could, Thainna shook Rikard's shoulder. He grunted, twitched and then ignored her. Weren't soldiers supposed to be light sleepers? She shook him again, harder. Still nothing. Was he catching up on the full thirty years of sleep?

"Captain Mazrem? Captain Mazrem, sir? Please, wake up!"

Thainna gave the sleeping knight a hard shove and jumped back. Finally, Rikard stirred and sat. He blinked for a moment, then jumped from the bed and grabbed Thainna by the shoulders. The metal bloodcap dug hard into her skin.

"Where is Laura? Did they take her?" Rikard shouted.

His dark brown eyes loomed up in front of her like deep holes in the ground, threatening to swallow her. Thainna felt suddenly as though the whole world was spinning like a top. She retched, but there had been no time to eat.

"She... she's just at breakfast," Thainna groaned. "Let go of me!"

Rikard dropped Thainna. She sagged to the floor, shaking her head and wondering what had just happened. Her whole skull ached. Thainna felt as fragile and twisted around as a snail shell. Rikard rubbed at his eyes again and didn't offer to help Thainna up. When the room stopped its dizzying spiral, she stood on her own and steadied herself against a bedpost.

"Laura didn't go far. Not far," Rikard said in a voice like a much younger man. Thainna wasn't sure who he was talking to. "I was in dreams. Back in the bent and twisted, bring and drawn. The water dreamings are rising so bloody slow! Every night, they creep closer to the great tree and yet I can't... I can't..."

"Um," Thainna answered uncertainly. Was that just gibberish or was he actually trying to say something? "Captain Mazrem, I need to check your bandages."

Rikard sat down on the corner of the dais. "Hae."

Other than the gouges in his hands, nothing much had changed since yesterday. Thainna changed Rikard's bandages, applied fresh salve and very carefully cleaned the crusted blood on his hands. The knight was distant and unresponsive throughout the entire process. Thainna might as well have been caring for a doll.

"Captain Mazrem?" she asked.

He seemed so far away, like he was in another world. Maybe he was, for all Thainna knew. Eventually, Rikard looked at her.

"Your wife is waiting for you outside, sir," she told him.

Rikard's face lit up in a broad smile. "Outside of what?"

Thainna blinked.

"Uh, outside the house," she said. "I'm supposed to take you to her. Lady's orders."

The dressers had left new clothes for Captain Mazrem. Thainna held them out and Rikard dressed himself, albeit slowly and with a few pointed reminders from his foster. When he was finished, Rikard followed Thainna from the bedroom, as obedient and eager as a puppy.

A puppy that may bare his teeth and bite me at any moment...

Yesterday, a maid had brought Thainna straight from the front gates to Lord and Lady Mazrem and the house was very, very large. Now Thainna was quickly lost and hesitantly asked directions from a woman balancing a basket of laundry across her shoulders. Stammering and staring at Rikard, the other woman told Thainna that she wasn't far off. Straight through the terrestrium, then right at the next hallway.

Thainna thanked her and escorted Rikard to the terrestrium. It was a large, dim room with no windows, untouched by the dawn sunlight. Just as its name implied, the terrestrium floor was of loose, exposed dirt. There was barely enough light to see by, shed by lanterns hung in each of the distant corners and leaving most of the room shrouded in gray shadow.

They crossed the terrestrium carefully on a path of black basalt tiles. Thainna stepped from one to the next, and then stopped when she abruptly realized that Rikard was no longer following her. She looked back to find the knight wandering through the terrestrium, off the path and sunk up to his bare ankles in the soft, dark soil. Rikard's expressions wavered between confusion and a deep scowl as he stared at the ground.

Thainna's stomach flipped nervously. Now what? Lady Mazrem was expecting her husband for breakfast.

"Captain Mazrem? What are you doing?" she asked, keeping a safe distance away.

"Deep and dominion in a house of Saerus. Taken back into ringing fever and... and closing. The final devastation upon the call of the tree. A... a blight in the golden fields and curdled under sickness' hand. The throne... the throne has been stolen."

Rikard spoke carefully, deliberately. Curious in spite of herself, Thainna followed the black basalt trail back to him. The knight stared not at the ground, as she had first thought, but rather at his own feet, bare in the dirt. She had forgotten to make him put on his shoes.

"What are you talking about?" Thainna asked.

Rikard took a long, deep breath before answering. "Terrestrium, a place that honors the dead who came before. I remember, but I never lived in a house big enough to have one. Honors to Saerus in a house of the living. I was dead, dead to everyone, even me. I was gone so long, but they didn't forget me."

"Where did you go?" Thainna asked.

There were rumors, of course. Were they true? No one had ever listened much to them before, but now everything had changed. Thainna leaned forward on the hexagonal pathstone, pulled by her curiosity.

"Alterra. They took me to fight their war. I asked and I paid. I paid. Died and hated. Feared. Bleeding and blooded..."

So Rikard *had* gone to Alterra after he vanished from Fiore. But what did the rest of it mean?

"I don't understand," said Thainna.

"Alterra isn't like... this."

Rikard fell down to his knees in terrestrium dirt. He grabbed a handful and held it up toward Thainna, then clenched his fingers until soil squeezed from between them.

"Hands there are nothing," Rikard said. "Swords are nothing. They left mine behind, in the snow and stone. I had only my own soul to fight with on the raw battlefields. Gods, how they screamed!

I held and I hoped, but it wasn't enough. To join their war, I needed blades that cut like mourning."

"I'm sorry, Captain Mazrem, I still don't understand." Thainna crouched down on the cool basalt. Rikard did not seem to be in any hurry and she didn't want to risk moving him. Besides, maybe he would say something that could help her in the Crest's impossible task. "I'm trying. Please tell me again?"

Rikard sank his fingers into the terrestrium floor again and shocked Thainna by bursting into tears.

"The words are so fragile!" he said.

Alarmed, Thainna crawled out onto the dirt and gingerly patted the weeping knight's shoulder. Words were... fragile? More likely, they were simply hard to find. Captain Mazrem was mangling the language badly. Of course, maybe that was what he meant. Maybe Terran words just weren't meant to explain Alterran things.

Fragile. Try to use them and they shatter.

"Hae, hae! They break in my hands, in my mouth. Fragile," he repeated. Rikard left streaks of mud across his face as he wiped at his tears with filthy hands. "It's been so long since I used them! There are no voices there, in Alterra."

Thainna nodded, though she still didn't understand. "What did you mean about blades and... and the rest?"

Rikard squeezed his eyes shut, perhaps trying to avoid the distractions of the apparently confounding Terran world.

"I am... I was... Felt. I feel. I am," the knight sighed and started again, a little more steadily. "In Alterra, thought and form are not independent, like they are in here."

"What does that mean?"

"A Terran may think many things," Rikard said. "But they do not change him. If he ponders rabbits, he does not become one. A Terran tree does not think. It does not have to dream in order to... to be. To exist."

"But... Alterrans do? If they think of rabbits, they actually become one?" Thainna asked, trying to wrap her mind around the strange and alien concept. She wasn't quite sure she believed it. Rikard Mazrem did not have to think himself a rabbit to still be quite mad.

"Hae, and... and no..." Rikard answered, struggling with each word. Beads of sweat actually stood out on his muddy brow. "If an Alterran could change his mind, it would make him from one thing into another. A wisdom into a curiosity. But they can't change their minds. A curiosity cannot help himself but to ask questions. It's his nature and he... he can't change it. He is defined by it. Alterran thought is form."

Thainna thought that she could *almost* grasp what Rikard was saying, but it was elusive, strange and he was not explaining it well.

"Blades? Weapons? Do you remember what you were saying about them?" Thainna pressed. Metaphorical weapons were exactly what she needed right now, if she were ever to control Captain Mazrem. If she was ever going to see Thain again.

"Terrans are... are not so bound. They can feel and think so many things without being undone. No Alterran can do that. It is... I was... terrible. Not even Flickerdim won more battles than I did. Gods, why is everything breaking? Fear to undo courage. Suspicion to undo trust. Dawn against dusk! Push against fall! Hail and fail!"

Rikard's voice rose into a scream that made Thainna clap her hands over her ears until he quieted again. But she wasn't the only one who heard Captain Mazrem's shouts – a sandy-haired Lyncean house guard ran into the terrestrium, startling both occupants. He stared around the room with wide eyes and his hand was wrapped around the hilt of a sheathed gladius.

Before Thainna could say a word, Rikard was on his feet and leaping at the guard. The Lyncean gasped and fell back under the onslaught, struggling to free his sword. He brought it up between himself and Rikard, more as a barrier than a weapon.

"Lord Mazrem, sir! I'm so sorry–" he began, but Rikard either did not notice or did not care.

The men crashed together into the ground and tumbled. The guard's sword spun free, skittering across the dirt. Blood gleamed darkly on the stones, but Thainna wasn't sure who it belonged to and did not dare touch it. She jumped up and grabbed Rikard by the elbow, trying to yank him away, but the maddened knight was much larger and stronger than Thainna.

"Lord Mazrem! Stop, please!" she cried. "Captain Mazrem!"

He tore free of her grasp and punched the guard again, driving his fist into the other man's mouth.

"Rikard, stop! He didn't do anything. He's one of your guards. He's here to help you!"

The Lyncean managed to pull his knee up between himself and his madly snarling master. He shoved as Thainna found her grip and yanked Rikard back with all her strength. The guard barely managed to squirm out from under Rikard before he lashed out with claw-hooked fingers. Rikard whirled on Thainna and easily threw her to the ground, pinning her there with one bare, dirty foot.

"Lord Mazrem!" shouted the guard in alarm, but Rikard ignored him.

Thainna coughed and gasped. "Rikard, no! I'm taking you to your wife, remember?"

The crushing weight on her chest vanished. Rikard jumped back and clapped his hands over his ears. She approached warily, holding out her open hands as she would to a hissing alley cat. The blond guard approached cautiously, but Thainna waved him back.

"Captain Mazrem? Rikard? Can you hear me?" she asked. It was a stupid question, even to her own ears, but she could think of nothing better to say.

"Hae," he whimpered. "Thainna. Thain. Talon and foster."

She flinched at the words tumbling out of Rikard like blood from an unstaunched wound. Thainna grabbed his arm and tugged until the knight dropped his hands from his ears. Rikard took her face in his hands and held Thainna's wide-eyed gaze for a moment before releasing her.

"Breakfast, then," he said in a voice like the rustle of dry leaves.

Thainna reluctantly scrubbed the mud off her skin with the corner of her tabba. It was a shame to dirty her nice new clothes. Rikard didn't seem to be injured, but it was hard to tell in the dark terrestrium with so much dirt all over him. Thainna looked back at the house guard.

"Did he hurt you?" she asked.

"Nothing important, ma'am," he answered. He picked up his sword from where it had fallen, shook the dirt off and resheathed the blade.

Thank the gods. Thainna wasn't sure what she would do if the guard asked her to look at his injuries.

"Would you come with us to find Lady Mazrem, then?" Thainna asked.

"Hae, ma'am. I'm sorry, I haven't seen you around before. May I have your name?"

"Thainna. Mana Narissa sent me at General Hern's orders to take care of Captain Mazrem."

"I'm Karl Skaintos," the guard introduced himself. "Thank you for your help with... with Captain Mazrem."

Thainna smiled at Karl and returned her attention to Rikard. "Let's go see your wife, my lord."

Rikard nodded and let Thainna lead him from the terrestrium, Karl following at a respectful distance.

Lady Mazrem was waiting for her husband on the veranda, as promised. The cool morning breeze blew strands of mahogany hair dramatically out behind her and Laurael looked every inch like the moon goddess who shared her name. Karl bowed to his mistress. Rikard put his hand on her shoulder, but Laurael took one look at her mud-smeared husband and pulled away.

"Are you... well?" Laurael asked.

"Hae," he said. "I missed you."

Lady Mazrem gave him a short, careful kiss. "Please eat, my lord. You must restore yourself."

Rikard helped himself to a small breakfast of buttered bread and honey. Despite his disheveled clothes, he looked quite calm, as though he had not just assaulted one of his own guards.

"What happened?" Lady Mazrem asked Thainna, frowning at her husband's filthy clothes and face. She raised a carefully plucked eyebrow at Thainna's equally dirty tabba.

Thainna explained as best she could. Laurael glanced up at Karl when Thainna came to his part of the story, but otherwise listened closely.

"Do you still maintain that my husband can endure visitors?" she asked when Thainna had finished.

"Hae, my lady. But maybe we should be careful to avoid... startling Captain Mazrem or discussing things that might upset him."

Laurael nodded and glanced back at Rikard.

"When you're done eating, we'll visit the bathhouse, my lord," she said. "Karl, have a dresser bring new clothes. Thainna, I'll send for you later to replace his bandages."

Thainna and Karl both bowed, then retreated inside to carry out their orders. Thainna had to jog to keep up with the much taller guardsman. He noticed her struggle and slowed until she could keep pace. The blood on Karl's lip was dry, but his uniform – not the saela of a VEIL knight, but a skirt and vest of steel-studded leather over a knee-length tabba of plain green – was now spattered with red.

"Is something wrong, mana?" Karl asked politely.

"I was going to ask you just that," said Thainna. "You just got attacked."

She couldn't make an accurate estimate of Karl's age. Like most Lynceans, he was huge and muscular. Even Lyncean boys had little of the softness Thainna associated with youth. But the guard's hair was still pale blond, with no sign of gray, and his face was smooth. Thainna guessed he was still a young man.

"I'm fine, but thank you," he said. "I'll clean off and change after I find the dressers."

"You don't seem very upset about what happened."

Karl walked quietly for a moment before answering.

"I'm surprised," he admitted. "I've been in a few brawls and I'm not going to cry over a split lip, but I never thought I'd get into a fight with Rikard Mazrem."

They fell silent again. At a crossing of hallways, Karl stopped and turned to Thainna.

"The wardrobes are this way," he said, gesturing to the hall on his right. "Miss Thainna, may I ask you something?"

"Um... hae," Thainna said, blushing. She was pretty sure she knew what Karl wanted to ask.

She was wrong.

"What do you think is the matter with Captain Mazrem?" Karl asked. "You're a foster. You must know. Is he mad?"

"Oh... Well, I don't know." Thainna thought about the conversation in the terrestrium. "I don't... I mean, I don't think so. I believe his experiences in Alterra have left Lord Mazrem deeply scarred. But given adequate time, I think that he will recover."

That sounded like something a proper foster would say, didn't it? Thainna thought proudly.

"Thank you," Karl said. "I wanted to be a VEIL knight when I grew up, just like Captain Mazrem. Until I was old enough to understand what was involved in their blood pacts... I couldn't do it, so I contented myself with serving his widow. When I saw him this morning, in the terrestrium, and he jumped on me... I hate to think of Rikard Mazrem being reduced to that. I hope he'll recover soon."

The guard smiled, winced as it strained his recently split lip, and put his hand to his mouth. Thainna laughed at his sheepish expression and instantly felt guilty for it as Karl flushed bright pink. He covered his embarrassment with a small bow and retreated in the direction of the wardrobes.

Thainna made her way back up to the servant's longhouse to find some food before Lord and Lady Mazrem finished their bath. The servant's kitchen was smaller than those in the manor houses, but was still a wonder to a street urchin like Thainna. The long, well-worn counters were covered in salt and powdery white flour. A pair of huge brick ovens filled the kitchen with blistering, crackling heat.

Several young children gathered around a taller, rounder shape. Arliss was an enormously fat woman with cheeks baked permanently red by the heat of the ovens. She handed out brown biscuits and butter to each of the children and then waved them out of the kitchen.

"Good morning, Arliss," Thainna greeted the other Talon when the children were gone.

"Morning."

In defiance of her otherwise jolly appearance, Arliss had dark, tired circles under her eyes. She held out a wood plate piled high with more biscuits and Thainna's stomach rumbled. She took two and bolted them down, one after the other. Delicious. Thainna barely suppressed a groan of pleasure.

"I've heard that there was some excitement this morning," Arliss said.

"Some, hae," Thainna answered after she finished swallowing. "Captain Mazrem attacked one of his guards. Can I have some more of these?"

Arliss whistled and handed Thainna more biscuits. The cook went to a large tiled box and poured a cup of cold lemon water from a pitcher inside.

"Want some?" Arliss asked.

"Hae, please!"

Thainna had never eaten so well in her life and fought to follow her own advice to Captain Mazrem to avoid gorging. Arliss gave Thainna a cup and then sat on a stout stool that creaked under her weight. Thainna guzzled down half of her water and finished the rest of her breakfast.

"Why did Lord Mazrem attack one of his own guards?" Arliss asked.

"I'm not really sure there was a reason."

"If he keeps that sort of thing up, it should make your job easy, hae?" said Arliss. "If Lord Mazrem's gone soft in the head, how hard can it be to control him? And then you can get back to your life."

My life.

Thainna looked away. The food was suddenly as heavy as lead in her stomach. She was sitting in a nice, warm kitchen, eating like a rich woman while Thain was a prisoner. Thainna slept in a soft bed while her twin... what? Did the Crest keep him in a dungeon? There were places, unpleasant places that Thainna knew the House of Five Dragons used. Was Thain in one of those? What would happen to him if she did not get results fast enough? Would the Crest torture her brother? Kill him?

The thought was enough to force a sob up into Thainna's throat. She pushed aside the rest of her biscuits and pressed her fingertips to her eyelids, fighting for breath against the painful needling in her breast.

"I... I don't know what to do," Thainna said. "Karl asked me if I thought Rikard was mad. I'm not sure if he is, but his own wife can't seem to rein him in. How am *I* supposed to do it?"

Arliss shook her head. "Sometimes the Crest asks a lot of us."

"Hae."

A tall manservant came into the kitchen then and Arliss stood to find him a pitcher of milk.

"You're covered all over in mud," Arliss said by way of farewell. "Go change."

Thainna nodded, then pinched a final biscuit from the sideboard before heading back to her room. The flat, sick sensation in her guts would not last forever and a girl from the Rows was always hungry.

Thainna closed the door to her room and picked up the package Bastil had given her earlier that morning. The wax seals were the bright cerulean blue of the Surmaen temple, but they weren't marked with the goddess' seashells or curvaceous mother-shape. Instead, someone – Narissa or one of her House-bound priests – had carved a curving shortscribe character into the wax: dragon. Probably to make sure that Thainna didn't open it in front of anyone, she guessed. As if she would be so foolish...

Narissa doesn't have much faith in me, Thainna thought. Still, she could hardly blame the priestess – this whole job was far too much for Thainna.

Inside the parcel were spare clothes: three spare tabbae, a belt and a sash similar to the one Thainna wore now, additional soles for her sandals and an extra pair of shoulder-clasps. The last of these were longer, pinned on either end of fine silver chains. They would let the top of her tabba hang lower, showing off more of her back and shoulders.

Thainna snorted. What did Narissa think that she could do with those? Seduce the great Lord-Captain Rikard Mazrem away from his beautiful and commanding wife? Thainna couldn't even charm one of his guards.

There was more in Narissa's package. Another canister of salve and more bandages, as well as several more sealed jars. One by one, Thainna peeled off the wax and sniffed the contents. She recognized the spicy scent of ophellion and the bitter-burnt smell of cardak, but the others were unfamiliar. None of the containers bore any useful markings or labels that might be incriminating.

Thainna sighed and set aside the ophellion and cardak. The rest she wrapped again and hid under her bed with the stolen lamp.

Not long after she had changed into a fresh tabba and was notching her new belt around her waist, someone knocked at the door.

"A minute!" Thainna called out.

She threw the jars of cardak and ophellion into her satchel, along with the extra salve and bandages, then answered the door. A young page waited outside, fidgeting.

"Hae, what is it?" Thainna asked.

"Lady Mazrem says that they're done in the bathhouse and you should come now."

Thainna threw her bag over her shoulder and followed the boy.

20

STITCHES

"It is said that knowledge is the mother of power. Nowhere in the world is that so clearly demonstrated as in the rise of the Carcaen Empire. A century ago, Carce was a kingdom of scholars, but when their research pierced the veil between the worlds, they rose to become masters of the known world."

— OUR RED HISTORY, BY AVILLA SALLUSI

"MY FATHER IS STILL WOUNDED, TYCHON," Gaius said. "I'm sure you understand."

Emperor Castum Tychon sat forward on an overstuffed couch and drew his white brows together into steep lines. His eyes flashed angrily and he held a glass out to the pretty girl waiting nearby. She refilled it from a golden ewer, then bowed – no simple task in her short tabba – and returned to her seat at the emperor's feet.

"I understand that your lovely mother is very busy these days," Tychon snapped. "And I suppose she can't see me, either?"

"She hasn't seen my father in more than thirty years. Of course she's busy."

The emperor leaned back into his chair and drained his wine. His crown sat askew on his brow. "Laura certainly didn't worry overmuch about Rikard before Njorn Pass. What's she telling him now? That she's been a good wife? That she's kept the flame burning?"

"My mother's been faithful to his memory."

"Only because it suited her purposes," the emperor answered in clipped tones. "I admire Laurael Mazrem as much as anyone else in this pit of vipers, but she's the most poisonous of the lot. Still, she believes in the empire. Gaius, you have to tell me about your father! What's he going to do? What does he say of me?"

The salon in which they sat was not one of the largest in the sprawling imperial palace, but it was private. Emperor Tychon's guards stood vigil outside the thick oak doors and for all her beauty, the serving girl was probably deaf and mute. Exotic Ruan tapestries draped every one of the windowless walls. Ruan stylings ran a little to the abstract for Gaius' taste, but they were chosen more for their thickness than beauty. No one outside the room would be able to hear what was said within.

"My father says very little that makes much sense," Gaius said cautiously. "As I said, he's still recovering."

"Black blood of Saerus, do you take me for a fool? Don't parrot your mother's lines back at me, my boy. I know that Rikard's injury is to his mind, not his body. It will take more than bandages to heal him! How bad is it? You have just as much to lose as I do if your father takes it into his head to denounce me."

The old bastard had a point, but Gaius wasn't ready to give up the fight just yet. "What are you talking about? Even if the great Rikard Mazrem decries you, I'm his son. What do I have to fear?"

"Don't be ignorant, Gaius! And don't think that I am. You're my heir in all but name and that suits us both just fine. But if Rikard speaks against me, the Lyceum will call for me to step down. VEIL will side with their hero, of course, and that won't leave me a stone to stand on!"

"I still don't see where this bites me, Tychon."

"Who do you think the Lyceum – bloody hell, all of Carce – will put on the throne? Not you, my boy, but your legendary father. But Rikard hasn't aged a day since he was plucked out of Njorn Pass. He's younger than you are, Gaius! You'll never succeed him."

"What about my mother?" asked Gaius.

"You're the only thing in this world or the next that Laura gives two acorns about. She would do anything for you, Gaius, but for all her wiles, she can't hold a candle to Rikard's popularity. Don't you understand? No one can challenge him!"

"What if the Lyceum discovers my father's madness?"

"I doubt anyone would believe it who hasn't seen it himself," Tychon sighed regretfully. He swirled his fourth glass of wine contemplatively. "I'm not sure I believe it, in truth. Rikard was a good, solid man before he left for Fiore. Not that I knew him, but General Darius has given me detailed accounts. No, the Lyceum will never believe it unless they are shown, but your pretty mother would not permit that. Her fame – and yours, Gaius – are based entirely on Rikard's impeccable, unassailable nobility."

Gaius almost spat out his own wine. When he did manage to swallow, the taste was biliously sour.

"What the bleeding hell are you suggesting, Tychon?" he asked. "You're not thinking of throwing us under the chariot, are you? Discredit my father and let us fall with him?"

The emperor gave Gaius a wintry smile. "You've always been like a son to me, my boy."

"Hae, because you could never keep your tabba down and settle long enough to spawn a legitimate son. Even if you did, you know that the Lyceum would favor me over them!"

Tychon tipped his glass at Gaius and his smile slid up into a smirk. "Hae, all true. As I said, you're like a son to me and I'm quite happy to pass the empire to you, when the time comes. Until then, I just want to continue on as we have these past thirty years. If the revered Captain Rikard Mazrem doesn't intend to create trouble, then we have no reason to change any of our plans, do we? So I ask you again, Gaius... What does your father intend to do?"

"Nothing," Gaius answered. "He's just happy to be home. All he wants is to remain there."

It wasn't a lie, exactly. Rikard seemed content enough simply to vent his rage at Tychon upon innocent flowers. Would that be enough to satisfy the emperor? Tychon leaned back, stroking the serving girl's blue-black curls. When he looked at Gaius again, his smile was much more pleasant.

"Good. Very good. We want to keep Rikard Mazrem happy, don't we? Well, I'm sure he can't want to stay home forever. He'll need something to occupy his time."

"You could always return him to his previous position," Gaius suggested, eager to prove his helpfulness to the back-stabbing royal old coot.

"No, I don't think so. We can't have the hero of Carce serving as a simple captain, but I can't replace any of the generals. They're all good men, in their own right."

Useful men. Ones that you can control, amended Gaius silently.

"Your father deserves a promotion," Emperor Tychon said. "I think the time's finally come to reunite the VEIL courts, don't you? Who better to do it than Captain... ah, Legens Mazrem? When he's feeling better, of course."

"Hae, Imperial Majesty," Gaius agreed through clenched teeth. "What a *wonderful* idea."

Rikard visited the family shrine before dinner. Laurael declined to join him, citing important business with their house steward. His family was wealthy and important enough to need a steward, Rikard marveled as he picked his way through the twilit gardens.

He passed a pair of guards, dressed much the same as the Lyncean he had attacked that morning.

"I'm sorry, my lord, the gates are closed for the night," one of them told Rikard when he approached.

The guard gestured down the hill. In the deepening dark, it was hard to make out the details of the thick crowd beyond the front gate, just a mass of black blobs holding starlight aloft. Lanterns. He could hear them, though, calling his name like cracks of booming thunder.

"Captain Mazrem! Captain Mazrem! Hae!"

"I'm sorry, my lord," the guard said again.

Rikard shook his head. "No. I'm not raising sails to song tonight. Just the shrine. Wind... where is it?"

"That way, Lord Mazrem," replied the other guard, pointing up the hill behind Rikard. "The rotunda with the blue lights. Do you need an escort, my lord?"

Rikard contemplated that. Did he? The guard... Rikard reached for the man's name. *Deon.*

Deon knew where the shrine was. He could keep it in one place should the shrine decide to hide itself. Rikard almost nodded before he remembered that Terran buildings didn't hide. At least, not once you knew where they were. Rikard followed Deon's finger. There was the shrine, a humped turtle-shape, just as the guard said, ringed in blue light.

"No, I don't need you to hold it," Rikard said.

He started up the hill, leaving the two guards to shrug at one another in shared confusion. The entrance to the shrine was an open arch of polished granite – the bones of the worlds. There was granite even in Alterra. The hard, grainy stone was good for building, though it resisted all but the most basic carvings. Instead, this was smooth-polished and hung with strands of tiny seashells. Stone for Saerus, shells for Surma – father and mother of all life and all worlds.

Lamps sat in alcoves around the outside of the shrine, their flames danced like exotic underwater creatures behind thick blue glass. Everything was so beautiful, so different than Rikard had left it thirty years ago. It was only right that he thank the gods for his family's good fortune.

Rikard stopped in the doorway. The foster was following him. She thought she was being quiet with her feet – and she was – but her curiosity was too loud to be ignored. Rikard turned around just in time to see Thainna vanish around the far side of the shrine.

Why was she hiding from him? The strange Fiori girl's motives were layered and confounding, as difficult to peel apart as sheets of brittle mica. Thainna acted – in part – on Laurael's orders to attend him. But there was more to it. Those thoughts were locked away. Even Thainna didn't want to ponder them. With a shrug, Rikard ducked into the shrine.

Oil lamps lined the walls inside, as well, all shielded in sapphire glass. He brushed his fingers over one of them, but the hot glass burned his hand and Rikard jerked back.

An intricate mosaic of the two interlocking worlds decorated the shrine's floor – Terra and Alterra, blue and white globes edged in shiny bronzed tiles. The shrine's circular walls were vaulted into eight wedge-shaped sections. Rikard stood in the door that filled one of them. Six others each bore altars to the original Carcaen gods, all standing opposite his or her divine twin. Rikard went first to the altars of Surma and Saerus, the gods of life and death. He touched first the white alabaster, then the black basalt.

"Blessed mother, watch over my wife," Rikard said. "Give her long life and good health. Cold father, turn your eyes from my son. He is young and not ready to come to you."

These were familiar words, the prayers he made every night on the long march into Fiore. He went next to the gold- and silver-filigreed altars of Lucaen and Laurael, god of the sun and goddess of the moon.

"Bright lord, grant me strength and honor in the days to come. Gracious lady, give me wisdom to... to understand this new world."

Rikard was not a farmer and had nothing to say at the altar of Haer, the god of the harvest. When he went to Haer's sister-bride, Hanna the storm goddess, he knelt. He struggled to find the right words.

"I fought in snow and stones. I cursed your name when ice buried Kaenus and Haden. Forgive me, Lady of the Snows," Rikard said at last.

He touched his brow to the cold quartz of her altar.

The final wall contained no altar. There stood another arch, identical to the one through which Rikard had entered, except that this door led nowhere and was filled instead by more smooth-polished granite. Rikard closed his eyes and pressed his cheek to the stone. It was not an altar, but a homage to Terra's twin, the dream-world of Alterra.

I remember the doors. I saw them from the other side. Thousands, millions. They filled the city of Mask, on the shore of the Petrichor Sea, where our worlds were closest. Flickerdim took me to Mask once, in the early notes of the war, before the city fell. I could never understand the place, so near to Terra but still so strange.

Flickerdim could never explain, really... Ever the wisdom – full of insight, but no explanations. He gave my questions to the care of a little bird. A curiosity, a young one... Stumble. He showed me doors like this one, made real by the remembrance and reverence of the Terrans who visited them.

And then... then... they were falling to dust even before the Shatter broached the city scales... But how? Why? I can't remember...

Why am I here, Flickerdim? Why did you send me home again before my time?

Rikard trailed his finger over the polished granite. His bloodcap clicked on the stone. What happened? Why was it so hard to remember? How had Mask fallen if not in war?

He felt curiosity behind him again. Stumble? Rikard turned just in time to see bright red hair vanish from the doorway. No, it was the girl.

"I know you," he called.

Rikard realized that wasn't exactly what he meant, but it was close. He waited and then Thainna appeared in the doorway again. In the aquamarine light of the shrine, it was difficult to see clearly, but Rikard thought that the young foster might have been blushing.

"I'm sorry, Captain Mazrem," Thainna said.

"Why?"

"For... for following you, my lord. Isn't that why you called me?"

Rikard shook his head. "No. You were being... loud."

"Loud?" Her curiosity took on a new cast, like water frozen to ice. This was harder, more personal. Thainna looked down at her sandals.

"Not outside your body. Within," Rikard said. "You wondered what I was doing."

"How do you know that?" Thainna asked him. "Maybe I'm just trying to keep an eye on you after what happened this morning."

"No," Rikard answered.

Why did she lie about such a simple thing?

Thainna shrugged and sighed. "Well, Captain Mazrem, what *were* you doing? I've never seen anyone at one of those Alterran doors. I don't even see them in most shrines anymore."

"I was... listening very hard. Remembering. I want to remember the rest, what I'm supposed to do here. But Flickerdim is silent. Stumble is silent. I remember only Mask."

"Mask? You remember a... a mask?"

Thainna looked around the shrine, nervous when she found none. She tensed visibly, ready to bolt. The morning's fight flashed through her mind, all blood and screaming and dirty skin.

"Mask. It's a city, like Dormaen, but out in Alterra. No, not like Dormaen. This is like... like a night of dreams that leaves you weary when the sun rises. Mask was the city of doors and eyes." Rikard reached out to touch the granite again. "It died, but not in battle with the Shatter. Mask is gone. All of those doors are gone. You said that... that you don't know them?"

"Not for years. There was a door like this – but bigger – in the temple of Surma before they expanded it to make room for the fostral. I saw it once before Thain... before I became a foster there."

"And now it's gone?" Rikard asked, surprised.

"That was eight years ago, I think. I was a little girl. This is the first one I've seen since then, but I don't go to a lot of shrines. Other shrines. Since... since I work in a temple."

She was lying again, and not very well, but Rikard thought of Mask again. All gone, all crumbled away to nothing. By the time the war reached the city, Mask was nothing more than sand and sighs.

Is this why? Have the Terrans forgotten...?

Thainna watched Rikard in silence, still full of questions but unwilling to risk the knight's volatile anger. He unclasped the cap of his cannula and drew a circle of blood on the stone, a larger version of the one Nikas had so quickly scrubbed off his forehead in the Moon Court archouse.

"I do not forget," Rikard said quietly.

Behind him, Thainna took an unsteady half-step further into the shrine, reaching as though she might restrain Rikard from his gesture, but then stopped herself. She lingered anxiously in the doorway.

"What are you doing?" she asked. "Why did you do that? Alterrans aren't going to tear it apart, are they?"

"No, it's a... a symbol. A gesture of respect."

Thainna's discomfort was raw and unpleasant. Rikard turned away, swearing silently to visit the shrine again, and soon. But right now, his stomach rumbled. It was time for dinner.

"I need food," Rikard said.

"Hae, my lord. I'll take you up to the house."

He remembers! Stumble exulted, extending his legs to impressive kajja-lengths to dance a tight, jubilant circle. *He remembers me! He remembers the forgotten! It's done, isn't it?*

Not just yet, Flickerdim disagreed. *A step taken, but the march is not over.*

Stumble deflated into golden eyes staring out from a pile of feathers. Flickerdim coiled himself around the younger Alterran until Stumble could summon the interest to fluff his body back into being. But the still wind kicked up, scattering the fallen feathers into the air. Flustered, Stumble pulled his shape into a wheel of soft yellow cheese. He rolled along the branch and bumped gently against Flickerdim's insubstantial length.

What about the girl? asked the cheese. *She burns.*

But she is spiked by lies, Flickerdim thought. The shadow serpent wove his long, sinuous body back and forth, flickering with veins of deeper midnight darkness. *At the center of her lies is love.*

Isn't that good? Terrans like love.

Rikard's wife has love, too. For his son, Flickerdim returned. *The girl's love isn't for him, either. She belongs to someone else.*

I think she might help, Stumble thought.

She may destroy everything.

Flickerdim crackled with violet lightning. Stumble was tired of his non-answers and wobbled off through the Uprising's huge giggle-green leaves to explore his new form. Flickerdim was much older and a powerful Alterran general. What place did a simple curiosity have doubting him?

Still, Stumble wondered about the strangeness of Terrans. Both the false foster and the cold wife wore lies like a VEIL knight wore his armor – a practice that never ceased to mystify Stumble, and about which he never stopped asking – and carried a strong, unshakable love at their core.

Gaius was waiting for them in the house. For Rikard, at least. He dismissed Thainna with a curt nod. The fire-haired girl made polite farewells to her masters and left.

Rikard watched her go. Thainna told so many lies, some of her making, some crafted by others as carefully as a chef prepared a meal. Did she even know the truth? The world of his birth was just as confusing as Alterra.

Gaius followed his father's gaze and leapt to the entirely wrong conclusion.

"A little bony for my taste, but not bad," he said. "Mother would skin you."

"I don't understand."

Did Gaius think that Rikard could ever feel for any woman but Laurael? Though, as he had confessed the night before, even that was a disconcertingly incomplete feeling.

"Of course you don't understand. Worry not, I won't tell Mother," said Gaius with a wink. The sour note in his voice undercut any sort of camaraderie.

Still confused and inexplicably ashamed, Rikard followed his son through a pair of carved oak doors and into the triclinium – the largest dining room reserved only for the final meal of the day. Laurael lay on one of three couches, eating dark purple grapes from a copper bowl and arguing with Bastil. The steward fell silent as Rikard lay down beside his wife.

"I'll discuss the matter with my husband tonight and notify you of our decision."

Bastil bowed. "Hae, great lady. Please enjoy your evening."

"That depends on what's for dinner," Gaius said.

He sat back on another couch and waved up one of the half-dozen servants waiting at the edges of the triclinium. They set out plates of sliced bread and smoked fish covered in clots of jellied berries, a bright-feathered wild pheasant stuffed with mushrooms, butter-yellow gourds steamed in goat's milk and sprinkled with some green herb that Rikard did not remember. Such opulence was still strange and new to Rikard. How could he possibly choose what to eat?

Gaius tore a drumstick off the pheasant, peeled back the feathered skin and took a bite.

"A little dry," he commented, but the critique clearly was not enough to keep him from continuing his meal. Gaius accepted a tall cup of wine from a server and gathered a heaping plate of the evening's bounty.

Laurael sighed and sipped lightly from her own wine.

"Eat lightly," she told Gaius. "You're getting fat."

"I've been *getting* fat for years, Mother, if you're to be believed. As long as I never actually get there, I'm perfectly happy."

"You sound like Tychon," Laurael said. "Speaking of which, you met with the emperor today?"

"Hae."

Rikard had plucked a grape from Laurael's bowl and rolled it across the table. It bobbed unevenly along its path. He didn't like hearing his family bicker, but talk of Emperor Tychon drove even that smaller unhappiness out of his thoughts. The grape fell over the edge of the table and bounced across the floor.

"What did Tychon want?" he asked sharply.

"Just to talk," Gaius said. "He wanted to know if you're well. He's going to promote you, too."

"He does? He is?" Rikard was surprised.

Surely Emperor Tychon knew that Rikard hated him. His fury blazed so huge and so dark that it must have been visible across half the world! *But Terrans can't see such simple things,* Rikard had to remind himself.

"Hae. The emperor wants to make you legens of VEIL. As soon as you're able, Father."

Laurael arched her dark brows. "Really? There hasn't been a legens for a century. Interesting that he would resurrect the office. It was Castum's own great grandfather who separated VEIL into the three courts."

"That was a political move and not a popular one," Gaius said, glancing sidelong at his father. "Reinstating a legens will be much better received."

Laurael seemed about to argue, but simply nodded. Maybe they were weary of quibbling over unimportant matters. Rikard smiled at Laurael as she turned to face him. She seemed pleased at the emperor's decision. Rikard remembered his wife's defense of the man the night before. Maybe she was right about Tychon. Maybe not. A true answer would only come from Emperor Tychon himself. For now, Rikard was simply happy to be home and at peace.

"Legens of VEIL," Laurael said contemplatively. She took a pomegranate from the plate of fruit and pried at the tough red rind. "Very fitting for you, my lord. You will be a good master for VEIL. There will be many congratulations, I'm certain. Which leads me into another topic of importance."

"And what's that, Mother?" Gaius asked.

Rikard took the pomegranate from his wife and broke it in half for her. She took one of the pieces back and pried out a few ruby kernels.

"The foster says you may have visitors, my husband," Laurael said. "A few and only for short audiences."

"Thainna said that?" It was insulting to be treated like a sickly child. "Sever the branches! I don't need to be pampered. I'm a soldier, Laura!"

"A knight," she corrected him. "And the new legens, when you're up to the challenge."

"I'm ready now!"

But is that true? Rikard wondered. *I wasn't very old when I made captain and I made so many mistakes... Like letting Emperor Tychon send my men into Fiore in winter! Am I really ready to serve as legens over all of VEIL?*

So perhaps Rikard wasn't ready to become legens, but seeing a few visitors was hardly a trial! Laurael carefully touched Rikard's shoulder to regain his attention.

"General Darius, in particular, wants to visit his old captain," she said.

"Saul Darius?" Rikard laughed delightedly. His anger melted away like morning frost before this warm, welcome news. "Saul is a general now? Hae!"

"Of the Star Court, no less," Laurael told him.

"I want to see him!"

"Emperor Tychon wants an audience with you, too," Gaius said. Rikard bristled. "No!"

Laurael put her hand over his. "The decision is yours, my lord."

"Mother, don't you think refusing the emperor might be just a little bit stupid?"

"I only want what is best for my family," Laurael said. "There's another request, from a knight named Gallard. He's the one who brought you to the Moon Court archouse. Will you consent to see him?"

Rikard could think of no objections, so he nodded his agreement. Laurael smiled and kissed him softly. Discussion through the rest of dinner was casual and light, carried mostly by Rikard's son and wife. They gossiped about people he did not know and fashions he had never seen. Rikard lay quietly, enjoying his food and listening to his family.

The red-haired foster girl tended Rikard's wounds after dinner and then he tumbled once more into a deep, healing sleep with his head pillowed on Laurael's breast.

When she was certain that her husband wouldn't wake, Laurael slipped out of bed. Donning a pair of doeskin slippers and covering her sleeping wrap in a flowing robe of shimmering white silk, she glided from the bedroom.

Pale and silent as a ghost, Laurael Mazrem moved through the halls of the house, outside and across the moonlit lawn to an only slightly smaller manor. A leather-clad guard bowed and opened the door for her.

"Where is my son?" Laurael demanded of a plump, pretty young maid with tousled curls inside.

The girl covered her surprise with a deep bow.

"He's gone to bed, my lady," she said.

Lady Mazrem raked a frosty gaze over the maid.

"To bed, maybe," Laurael said. "But not to sleep. Go fetch him."

"Hae, my lady."

She scurried quickly away. Laurael found a sitting room decorated with VEIL paraphernalia, including Rikard Mazrem's sword, famously left behind after his disappearance from Njorn Pass. While she waited, Laurael studied the sword closely. It wasn't an artifact she ever thought about except to keep until her son was old enough to receive it.

Rikard's sword was a simple steel thing, with a straight, double-edged blade and an unadorned crosspiece over a hilt wrapped in worn brown leather. Unlike the weapons of nations with a longer tradition of war, like the legendarily quarrelsome Nian and Lyncea or barbaric Fiore, the swords of Carce's VEIL knights were unassuming blades. VEIL's power, after all, was not in strength of arms, but in blood.

But in this time of peace, were the Alterra of any more use than a sword? Even the sword of the famous Captain Mazrem was no more than a display piece. Blades and blood pacts were antiques, either forgotten or feared. Money and favor were the preferred weapons now. And so much more civilized.

"Bloody hell! What do you want, Mother?"

Laurael turned to face her son, who stood in the wide doorway wearing an expression of such boyishly petulant irritation that he managed to look even younger than his father. His black Star Court saela was unbuttoned and draped unflatteringly open around his bulging belly. Gaius raked his fingers through his black-dyed hair.

"What was that at dinner?" Laurael asked him, her voice deceptively soft and quiet.

Gaius knew her too well to think that her question was harmless. He narrowed his brown eyes.

"What was what?" he asked her. "It's far too late to play guessing games, Mother."

"You want your father to see the emperor. Why? You know perfectly well that he hates the emperor. He will make a fuss. What did Tychon say to you?"

"Why are you trying to protect Rikard, Mother?" Gaius asked. "Since the moment he appeared, you haven't spared a moment for me! Is that your plan, to put him on the throne instead of me?"

"How dare you?" Laurael hissed. She took a long step toward Gaius and raised her hand threateningly. "Everything I have ever done has been for you. Don't you dare be ungrateful!"

"How exactly does hiding Father behind your skirts help me? You want to know what Tychon asked about? Rikard, of course. I've spent more time serving VEIL than Father ever did. Yet the emperor is going to promote him right over my head, into a position that's been vacant for a century! I'm sure that suits you just fine, doesn't it, Mother? It's only a short step from legens to emperor, isn't it?"

"I keep your father here because he's mad, because it will ruin us if anyone makes that general knowledge! The great man, the hero of Carce is no better than a rabid dog in the Rows," Laurael fumed. She closed her hand into a fist and, with an effort, pulled it down to her side. "What would the people say to that? What would Emperor Tychon do?"

"*Praise the gods*, probably," Gaius muttered. He wiped his brow with the sleeve of his saela. "Hae, Tychon said you would probably stand with me, but the only thing he really cares about is whether or not Father is going to depose him. He couldn't care less about the rest."

"Then why promote him to legens?"

"To appease Rikard and keep the man busy. It would look strange if Tychon did nothing. Maybe he thinks that it will keep the hero happy and quiet. What else can he do? If Father wanted to take the imperial throne, VEIL would back his claim, regardless of rank. I still don't see how this helps me. Everyone adores Father! He's younger than I am and... and everything! Why *not* abandon me, Mother?"

"Don't you dare say such things. You are my son, my pride and joy. My life. You deserve the throne. All Rikard did to earn his fame was die. You and I have labored our whole lives for this! Gods know we deserve it."

"Very well, Mother," Gaius said with a sigh. "You win. But none of this sounds anything like a plan. We can't keep Emperor Tychon at bay forever, or keep him from promoting Father."

"I will think of something," Laurael said. "We can't risk exposing your father's madness to the world. I will figure out the rest... The foster has said that his audiences must be few and that they must be brief."

"Smart girl," Gaius said, smirking. "How you always manage to get everyone to agree with you, I'll never know."

"I'm keeping Thainna on hand during these meetings, too. She will back me if I call an end to any... problematic audiences. But you're right. We won't be able to keep him here forever. When your father finally rejoins VEIL as their legens, I will no longer be able to shoulder this burden alone. You are a knight of VEIL and it will fall to you to keep him under control."

"How am I supposed to do that?"

"You'll think of a way," Lady Mazrem answered confidently. She gathered up her robes and prepared to leave, but Gaius grabbed her arm.

"Don't be in too much of a hurry to shove Father out the door, Mother."

"You are a grown man, Gaius, and it's time you did your part. You can handle this. It will be good practice for when you rule an entire empire." She paused, sniffing. The air around Gaius was thickly spiced. "And stop smoking that ophellion. It's a disgusting habit. Your father never did anything like that."

"Do you think I care–?"

"You're supposed to be a better man than he was."

"You know, I just noticed something. You never call Rikard by his name," Gaius said, leaning close to whisper into his mother's ear. "Why might that be?"

"It's an ugly name from the barbaric old days. Have you also noticed that you don't share your father's name?"

Laurael pulled her arm from Gaius' grip and stalked away.

Stumble was still exploring, rolling up and down the branches of the Uprising and trying to ignore the blank, broken gray ground far below. At his aimless approach, a snow-white flower opened and filled the air with the scents of breath and honey. Long, slender petals of blink unfurled like scrolls. Stumble rolled closer on his cheese-rind. Where the petals came together in the center, they took on a blushing pink color and darkened to a coy, embarrassed flush deep inside the flower.

In the old days, these blossoms had been common, spawned every time a Terran warmed with the first stirrings of love. But now the worlds were growing apart. Stumble hadn't seen one in years. The curiosity alighted on the branch and twinkled in fascination.

Something went wrong. The flower curled and froze as though caught in a snap frost. A glassy nothing sprouted from nowhere, wound and webbed its way across the twisting petals, consuming the shriveled white with lazy voracity. Where it passed, the hungry frost left only a transparent lattice behind, a quick-fading sketch of what had until a moment before blazed with life.

Stumble fell back, startled. The whole Uprising shuddered and even that colorless tracery shattered, falling away into obscurity.

Flickerdim! Stumble cried. *They're here! The Shatter have reached the Uprising!*

21
WALLS OF JADE

"Why does blood shine through from one world to the next? As far as VEIL can tell us, Alterrans have nothing like blood themselves. Could it be something *in* the blood? Something that our blood holds or represents to them? Or perhaps to us?"

— HURON DURAINNE

THE NEXT MORNING, Thainna ate a hurried breakfast, then jogged across the estate to the main house. The young Talon still marveled that she had a breakfast to rush. Would she ever get used to it?

In the atrium, Karl and another guard that she didn't recognize nodded to her. Thainna paused in the humid green shade of a fan palm.

"I've never seen guards in here," she said. "Is this where Lord Mazrem's going to be having his meetings?"

"I think so. Bastil told us to keep the atrium under watch all day," Karl told her. He gestured to some other servants struggling to carry a heavy gilded divan. "It sure looks like they're setting up for an audience."

"Do you know when we're supposed to start?"

"I'm not sure. Bastil hasn't told us yet."

Karl stifled a yawn. It was still early. His companion shot him a disparaging look. The Lyncean flushed and stood up straighter.

"They're only supposed to be short visits," said Thainna. Karl probably didn't need to know and likely didn't care, but Thainna felt so important. A lowly thief making decisions in the Mazrem house, even small ones... it was impossible not to boast a little. "I told Bastil and Lady Mazrem to keep them that way."

"Hae, Mana Vahn." Karl appeared suitably impressed.

Thainna nodded and swept out of the atrium. Bastil waited outside the closed door of the bedroom and Gaius Mazrem paced not far away. The Mazrem heir looked a little ill. Should she offer to help him? What *could* she do? She was spared any awkwardness by Bastil waving her toward the door.

"Go inside. Take care of Captain Mazrem and then make sure he gets to the atrium," he instructed.

"Hae, sir."

Satisfied, the steward held the door for Thainna. Rikard and Laurael were already awake. Dressers fussed over Lady Mazrem, winding her in a moon-white tabba embroidered with silver and arranging her curly brown hair into artful waves around her shoulders. Unable to turn her face away from the girl who was applying dark color to her lips, Laurael brought only her eyes to bear on Thainna.

"There you are," she said. "Make sure my husband is well and then help him dress."

"Hae, my lady."

Thainna dodged a man laying out a clean saela and went to Rikard. He was still in bed, balancing a half-full plate of eggs and bread and eating in carefully measured bites. She smiled at him and perched on the edge of the blankets. Someone had even shaved his scraggly beard.

Probably not Rikard himself, Thainna guessed. No one in their right mind would let the man near a razor.

"How're you feeling?" Thainna asked.

"Good," Rikard answered. He pointed down to his breakfast and smiled. It lit up his face. "I've been eating slow."

"Keep eating whenever you're hungry," she told him. "You're still far too thin and it's going to take you more than a couple of days to fill out again."

"You're thin, too."

Thainna wasn't sure what to say to that, so she instructed Rikard to stand and set about stripping away the old bandages. She examined the stitches in his side. At some point, they would have to come out, wouldn't they? Not yet, though. Thainna would have to ask Narissa about them later.

"Hae," Rikard said.

"What?" Thainna lifted her eyes to meet his brown ones. "Did I hurt you?"

"No. You have very green hands."

"I don't understand," Thainna said.

"Small, gentle. The stitches... Hae, they should come out when the cut stays closed on its own. This isn't my first time. I can tell you when to cut them," Rikard offered.

"I know my job," Thainna lied. "I don't need–"

"You wondered. You wanted to ask Narissa. But I can tell you when they..."

"I didn't say that!" she hissed quietly.

There were at least a half-dozen other servants in the room and she didn't want any of them listening.

"I heard you," Rikard said.

"You... you heard me?" Thainna asked. "You *heard* me thinking about it?"

"Hae."

"What? Bloody stones!"

Thainna pulled back and her foot came down on nothing. She had forgotten about the stepped dais that held the bed. The world lurched as Thainna tripped and fell. She thumped down on her backside with a grunt.

Clumsy idiot!

"Are you alright?" asked a nearby dresser. He had Rikard's black saela draped over his arm, but offered his other hand to Thainna. "What happened?"

"Hae. I just slipped," she answered hurriedly.

The man stepped back to let Thainna rise again. She looked up at the bed. Rikard Mazrem still stood beside the bed, staring at her with a strangely lost expression. Did he understand her fear? If he could hear her thoughts, he *had* to understand. But that was impossible, of course!

Alterrans live off of our memories and emotions, don't they? Rikard spent thirty years with them. What if he picked up a few tricks after all that time?

Thainna brushed off her tabba and mounted the stairs again. Without meeting Rikard's eyes, she found a new roll of bandages in her satchel and used the knife to cut them to length. She tried not to think, to keep her mind blank, but it was nearly impossible. Gods only knew what would happen if Rikard discovered any one of her lies! She would have to find some excuse to get out of the room, to get away...

Sped by panic, Thainna's blood rushed in her ears, drowning out the noise of the crowded room. She almost screamed and fell again when she felt Rikard's hand on her wrist. Her fingers tightened convulsively around the canister of salve. The knight held her, eyes afire.

"Stop!" he hissed.

Every inch of Thainna's body tensed to run, just like that first night in the Rows. Rikard Mazrem knew she was lying and he was about to tear her apart, to rip her into bloody flinders with a single command to the Alterra. Or make her vanish like the Fiori in Njorn pass...! Or maybe kill her with his own hands, like he had tried to do to Karl! Thainna squeaked in breathless terror.

"Stop," Rikard gasped again, tightening his grip on Thainna's wrist. His expression was not one of anger, but pain. "Stop! You are too sharp... too frightened. Stop, it breaks. It hurts!"

What? Did her fear actually *hurt* Rikard? An idea suddenly took hold, a sort of understanding as tenebrous as smoke. "Was that what you were talking about the other day, in the terrestrium? You said something about weapons in Alterra. Fear undoing bravery or something. Is this what you meant? Fear... hurts you?"

"One of a hundred blades, but among the sharpest."

Rikard sounded half-excited at her understanding, but her earlier dread was obviously still making itself felt... to both of them. The knight rubbed his temple hard enough to leave red marks on the skin, as though his finger had been dipped in paint. He released Thainna's wrist.

"I'm sorry, Captain Mazrem," she said awkwardly. "I didn't mean to... to fear you."

"There was a..."

Rikard didn't seem to know how to put his thoughts – or maybe hers – into words. But before Rikard could try again, his dresser approached the bed and cleared his throat.

"Lord Mazrem, time is running down." He held out the saela. "Foster, are you finished?"

Rikard looked helplessly at Thainna. She nodded to the dresser. "I'm about done here. Just let me tie off this bandage and then we'll get Captain Mazrem ready. Do you have a comb?"

The dresser produced a bone comb from the pocket of his tabba and handed it to Thainna. When she had secured the last bandage, she went to work tugging the night's tangles from Rikard's hair.

Like most Carcaen men, his black hair was perfectly straight and quite rigid. Combing it was an easy task and done in minutes.

Much nicer than her own wavy red mess, Thainna thought. Even clean as it was now, the stuff always seemed as ratted as a bird's nest. She focused on the playful jealousy, hoping that Rikard found it less painful than fear... and that it masked her many lies.

While Rikard's dresser helped him button his saela and pull on his high, polished black leather boots, Thainna slipped the carved ivory comb into a pocket of her tabba. A middle-aged Ruan man came through the door, balancing a crystal goblet of wine on a silver tray. After he had delivered it to Lady Mazrem, Thainna caught his attention.

"Is Bastil still waiting outside?" she asked.

"No, he's gone with Lord Mazrem. Lord Gaius Mazrem, I mean. They went to meet today's first guest."

"Do you know who that is?"

"Master Alexander Ferro, the historian."

Thainna thanked him and turned away. She waited quietly in one corner until the others were done fussing over Lord and Lady Mazrem.

It was too much to think about, too much to take in. Everyone knew that Rikard Mazrem was special. Selfless and honorable. A true hero. Well, a traumatized and intensely scarred hero, Thainna corrected herself. Only with an effort did she keep herself from thinking *crazy*.

Did anyone else know about Rikard's... ability yet? None of the servants, Thainna was certain, or else someone would surely have gossiped that their master could hear thoughts. Rikard's words were hard to make sense of at the best of times. His own family seemed more interested in keeping him quiet than listening to what he had to say or learning what he could do.

She would have to notify the House of Five Dragons. This was exactly the kind of thing that the Crest wanted to know. Thainna wasn't sure how it could be useful in controlling Rikard Mazrem. In fact, it would more than likely make the job impossible.

But if she could manage to do it, Thainna could only imagine the uses of a man who could hear thoughts as plainly as if they had been spoken.

Thainna looked across the bedroom at Rikard. He had finished with his clothes and stood now behind his wife, kissing the back of her graceful neck. Two of the dressers stood to the side, giggling at the display of affection and whispering behind their hands. The man who had been helping Rikard a moment before stood beside Thainna, shaking his head.

"What is it?" she asked him.

"Nothing, mana," he said a little too quickly. After a moment of watching Rikard and his wife, he took a step closer to Thainna and leaned down to speak softly into her ear. "Lady Laurael doesn't look very interested, does she?"

"Interested in what?"

The other servant waggled his brows in a way that Thainna guessed was supposed to be suggestive, but looked so silly that she burst into laughter. He rolled his eyes and found somewhere else to await his dismissal.

He was right, though. Laurael smiled perfunctorily at her husband's attention and then told him to stop so the girls could finish her hair. He did so obediently. Thainna had never considered herself a romantic, but Rikard stared after his wife with such obvious adoration that it made her heart wobble in her chest like a faltering top. And it was a look Laurael Mazrem didn't return. Did Rikard notice? He heard thoughts, just like an Alterran. He had to know. Didn't he?

When the girls finished affixing a pair of mother-of-pearl pins in Lady Mazrem's hair, she stood and took Rikard's arm. They were the picture of regal nobility, poised and perfect.

"We've kept Master Ferro waiting long enough," Laurael announced and gestured to the many servants occupying the large bedroom. "Have a meal ready in three hours."

Lady Mazrem escorted her husband into the atrium. Thainna followed at a respectful distance. A full dozen guards awaited them in the atrium, half VEIL knights in black Star Court armor, the others in the green uniforms of household guards. They all saluted Rikard's entrance. A serious-faced man with gray-peppered hair stood, too, and bowed deeply. Gaius was already in the atrium, slouched in a carved chair and looking bored.

With a tug at Rikard's arm, Lady and Lord Mazrem seated themselves on the divan, surrounded by exotic flowers like bright butterflies pinned in place. Thainna stood uncertainly until Karl broke away from the other guards and came to her rescue.

"Over here," Karl told her, and led Thainna to a wooden chair behind Rikard's.

Thainna smiled her thanks to Karl and sat. He returned to the ranks of his fellows.

"My lord, this is Alexander Ferro," Laurael said, speaking just loud enough to be heard over the creak of leather and the rushing of the atrium's burbling stream. "He's the preeminent scholar and historian on the empire's founding, including your own exploits at Njorn Pass."

"It is truly an honor to meet you, Lord-Captain Mazrem," said the man with the white-streaked hair. Ferro wore it long, much like Rikard himself. It was a young man's style and looked out of place on the aged historian. "Your sacrifice has quite literally crafted the world into its current form."

"You're a scholar?" asked Rikard. "Why do you want to talk to me? I'm a soldier. I didn't even learn to fly the words... to read until I was eight."

Ferro hesitated before answering. "Captain Mazrem, there are a thousand rumors about your epic sacrifice. May I ask after the truth of them?"

Rikard cocked his head and then looked at Laurael. She just raised her brows at him, so he turned to Thainna.

She couldn't think why he might be asking her permission, but she shrugged. Rikard turned back to Ferro.

"Hae, I will try. Time has passed, though, and truths are so brittle," he said.

Ferro was clearly unsure what this meant, but was too polite to say so. He wasn't too polite, however, to bombard the VEIL captain with questions. Perhaps not thousands, but close.

Thainna's interest quickly faded. The historian was obsessed with details, from verifying maps of Njorn Pass to the names of those who had died there, how and when. Rikard struggled to answer as best he could.

As morning turned into afternoon, Ferro's questions became more difficult to answer. He wanted to know the exact details of Rikard's deal with the Alterra. Not only what the open contract entailed, but how he even managed to do it.

"It's been a matter of some interest and debate." Ferro held a waxed board in the crook of his arms. Several others were stacked up beside him, already covered in extensive notes. "I've interviewed a number of VEIL knights and commanders, including your own squire, Saul Darius, but no one has been able to offer much more than speculation."

"I drew a circle of blood in the snow. I stood inside and scored it once to get their snap-finger... their attention. Then I wrote."

"What exactly did you write, Captain Mazrem? DuRainne has postulated that it wasn't actually an open call, that you were simply pressed for time and failed to finish writing out your pact." Ferro's tone made it clear what he thought of his fellow scholar's ridiculous theory.

Rikard sat silently for a long time. "*Save them. Stop the Fiori.* That was what I wrote," he said at last. "I made no contract. There was no time and I didn't care."

"And then the Alterra... took you?" Ferro asked. "It's now known that you didn't die, that they pulled you through the veil into their world in order to fight in some kind of Alterran civil war. What happened? How did they take you? Where in Alterra did you come through? What was it like? What's their war about?"

"It took great mountains... effort to bring me out of Terra. A... a hand. Hardbright, Flickerdim, Crave, Saidmost and Dropheavy. They told me that my men were safe, that the Fiori warriors were gone and that I owed them a lifetime of service in return for the effort they had expended. Lives for lives. They needed me. And so I fought for them."

"A lifetime? What exactly does that mean?" Ferro asked, fascinated. He leaned further forward with every question and was now bent nearly double over his writing board. "How long is a lifetime?"

"How long a life? A Terran time, spindling-span for sixty years... Saidmost called any more ambitious, greedy for a man or meaning to live too long..." Rikard rubbed his jaw as though it pained him.

"Sixty years?" Ferro asked. "It's been a long while since you left us, Captain Mazrem, but only half of that. Why are you back now?"

"It is... They sent me back before my time," Rikard said.

Her position made it hard for Thainna to see his face, but the knight's voice sounded strained.

"The war is painted... it goes badly. We're losing. The Shatter come closer every day. Deepwell, Hardbright and Redling are gone. Crave has fallen to stillness, to flat things with no color. Dropheavy split against an empty door... and... Flickerdim calls to us. They are so many. The Uprising falters...! They will break between us..."

Laurael shot Thainna a warning look. She stepped forward before Ferro could respond to Rikard's rising shout.

"I'm sorry, Master Ferro, but we have to stop. Captain Mazrem is still troubled," Thainna said as calmly as she could. She could almost feel Rikard behind her, blazing like out-of-control fire.

Ferro took in her blue foster's dress and bowed his head. "Of course, mana. I don't want to overtax Captain Mazrem. May I ask one final question?"

Thainna glanced at Laurael once more, who shook her head minutely. Why didn't she just say it herself? Politics, probably. Lady Mazrem didn't want to be the one who had to tell a respected historian to leave. Thainna turned back to Ferro.

"I'm sorry, no. Lord-Captain Mazrem's health must be our first priority," she said with all the authority she could summon. "I'm afraid we're done here."

Ferro didn't look pleased, but he stood, gathered up his writing boards and bowed to his hosts.

"Thank you for entertaining my questions, Captain Mazrem," he said. "Do you think that the Alterra returned you to Terra to spare your life? Or was it something else? You said that the Alterra are losing the war–"

"Damn it, Ferro! I said *no*," Thainna snapped. "Get out!"

Her sudden anger surprised even Thainna, and she was not the only one. The attendant VEIL knights and Mazrem guards dropped hands to their swords. The historian glared at Thainna, but allowed himself to be escorted from the atrium. As soon as Ferro vanished from sight, Lady Mazrem was on her feet and grabbing Thainna by the arm. Her long, painted nails bit into Thainna's bicep.

"You will *never* strike such a tone with a guest in this house again! Do you understand?" she hissed.

Thainna squirmed. "Ouch! Hae! Hae, my lady!"

Laurael released Thainna's arm and snapped her fingers at Karl, who was watching their exchange with a carefully neutral expression on his face.

"Go and catch Master Ferro. Keep him until I can make a proper apology," she commanded.

Karl bowed and ran off after the departing historian. Thainna rubbed her smarting arm while Lady Mazrem spoke with Gaius, who had come when his mother beckoned him over. They spoke together in quiet, urgent voices for a moment, then Laurael looked at Rikard.

"Are you well enough, my lord?" she asked him.

When Rikard nodded, she took Gaius' hand and proceeded from the atrium at a stately pace.

Thainna investigated her wounds. No bruises and even the pink crescents left by Lady Mazrem's nails were fading. Still, it hurt. Her stupid outburst certainly had not been worth the reprisal. Luckily, Lady Mazrem had chosen to correct Thainna instead of dismiss her. Thainna did not want to think about what the Crest might have done if she had lost the job.

What he would have done to Thain. She felt as though she was going to be sick.

"Why didn't you want me to talk to him?"

Thainna turned. Rikard stood right beside her, frowning suspiciously. She had not heard him approach. It was still early afternoon and the day already seemed far too long. Thainna didn't have the patience for this madman or his questions.

"I thought I was following your wife's orders," she said shortly. "Badly, I guess. Sorry."

Thainna turned on her heels and stomped out of the atrium.

22

GIVEN

"Upon his return to Terra, it was learned that Captain Mazrem had been drawn into an Alterran civil war. In this war, he served a central role beside their greatest generals. In our world and theirs, Captain Mazrem seemed fated for legendary deeds."

— AFTER NJORN PASS, BY ALEXANDER FERRO

MARUS TUGGED NERVOUSLY at the buckles of his armor. It still didn't sit right. He had checked it in a mirror a dozen times, but the studded blue leather looked fine. It just didn't *feel* fine. Beside him, Ephria fussed with her long white tabba. The Mazrem's steward – whose name Marus had missed – was speaking.

"Captain Mazrem's still recovering from his wounds and so your audience must be shorter than any of us would like."

"Hae, I understand," Marus said, nodding. He remembered the old armor, crusted in blood. "We won't overstay our welcome."

"Thank you, Sir Gallard."

The steward led them along a curving path, finished in pale stone, to the sprawling white villa that sat on top of the hill like an alabaster crown. He took them to a lush atrium, filled with slender palm trees and sweet-smelling flowers. It was beautiful. Marus was not much of an outdoorsman or even a gardener, but he could still admire the loveliness of the place.

A strikingly beautiful Carcaen woman and a heavyset younger man in the blacks of a Star Court knight greeted them. They could only be Lady Mazrem and her son, Captain Gaius Mazrem. Marus snapped to attention. After Gaius returned the salute, Marus bowed to Lady Mazrem and kissed her hand.

"My lord and lady," Ephria said and curtsied deeply. "Thank you for seeing us."

"We know of Sir Gallard, but I'm afraid you are unfamiliar to us." Lady Mazrem said it so smoothly that it didn't sound the least bit like an insult, but she did give her steward a significant glance.

"This is Tes Ephria, a Moon Court templar," Marus introduced her. "She was the first to recognize Captain Mazrem."

"We're all so grateful, Tes Ephria," said Lady Mazrem. "Thank you for bringing my husband home to us."

She took Ephria's hand in hers and gave it a small squeeze. Both women were probably about the same age, but the difference in their appearance was astonishing. Ephria wore her age like a wrinkled tabba, heavy with dust and folded as though stored away too long. Lady Mazrem defied her years in her every curve, in her tightly drawn porcelain skin and proud, sharp jaw. The result was otherworldly, ageless.

"Oh, hae... Thank you, Lady Mazrem," Ephria stammered.

Marus had known the templar since he was just a raw young squire and had never seen her flustered until now.

"I asked Marus... Sir Gallard, I mean... to let me come with him," Ephria said. "I only wanted to see Captain Mazrem again. I was young, just an acolyte, when we went to Fiore."

"He saved your life," Lady Mazrem finished, sparing her the embarrassment of further babbling.

"Hae, great lady," said Ephria.

Marus supposed he should have been surprised to see the crusty old templar blushing like a schoolgirl, but the past week had seen the return of Captain Mazrem. Nothing in the world seemed steady anymore.

But the more things changed, the more they always remained the same... It had cost Marus a full month's pay in bribes to his captain just to make sure General Hern heard his request to see Captain Mazrem. The exciting new world could be just as corrupt and twisted as the old one, it seemed.

Marus and Ephria followed Lady Mazrem through the lush green atrium, along a path of round black pebbles and over a small, arched wooden bridge. There he was – Captain Rikard Mazrem himself, standing under the green and white mottled drape of a blossoming cherry tree. A thin young woman in a short blue tabba leaned against the trunk, pale arms crossed and looking petulant. Looking young.

Captain Mazrem looked better, healthier than the last time Marus had seen him. He held one of the delicate white flowers in his fingers, pulling off the petals one at a time and letting them flutter to the ground. The girl – a foster, Marus guessed – finally noticed the newcomers and stood up straight. She tapped Captain Mazrem on the arm and pointed.

"My lord, this is Sir Marus Gallard," Lady Mazrem said after she embraced and kissed her husband. "He found you in the streets of Dormaen and brought you back to General Hern."

Captain Mazrem dropped the stem of his flower to the ground and peered at Marus. Then, as if suddenly seeing him for the first time, he saluted. Marus returned it with an involuntary smile. Captain Rikard Mazrem, the legendary hero, was saluting *him*.

"I just wanted to see you, sir," said Marus. "I hope you're feeling better."

"Hae, I am healing. I am... learning."

"Learning?"

"I have been gone for a long time. I have to remember... things. Terran things that are so easy for the forest," Captain Mazrem said, then paused and corrected himself. "Easy for everyone else."

The entire exchange felt like something out of a dream. Marus had heard about Captain Mazrem in Alterra, the first Terran ever to cross over. Did it make him wiser or just stranger? Marus stood uncomfortably, unable to think of anything else to say. Gaius Mazrem looked on with a faintly condescending half-smile while Lady Mazrem pretended not to notice.

What did I expect? Marus asked himself. *I bribed my way into this meeting, hoping to find a good man. A hero. Maybe Captain Mazrem was, once... but now he's broken. He sounds like a child.*

"Captain Mazrem?"

It was Ephria who spoke, but a long moment passed before the knight tore his attention away from Marus.

"Captain Mazrem, sir?" she asked.

"Hae?" Finally, he looked at Ephria and a bright smile lit up his face. "Ephria. I remember you! The pretty woman who brought Nikas coffee and made sure that his armor didn't stick when it got too cold."

To everyone's shock, Captain Mazrem swept Ephria into a tight embrace. The young foster actually looked like she might tackle him, but Captain Mazrem only crowed joyfully and picked Ephria up. He whirled her in an excited circle.

"Ephria! You're alive," he said. "You escaped the pass!"

The old templar's eyes widened in surprise, but she didn't look at all displeased. When Captain Mazrem set her down again, she returned his startlingly affectionate greeting with a formally appropriate bow.

"Hae. I survived, sir, because of your sacrifice. Not a day's gone by that I have not thanked the gods for your nobility."

"Bees and beads, I remember you!"

Captain Mazrem stared at Ephria, grinning like an idiot and apparently utterly content to do so until the sun burned away to a cinder. What was he thinking?

"I am happy to see... life," Captain Mazrem said suddenly, as though he were answering Marus' unasked question. "The war was deep and cold. Sometimes I wondered if it was worth it. I am happy to see that it was."

"Are you well, sir?" asked Ephria. "I worried for your injuries."

"Hae. Nikas sent Thainna to watch over me," he said, pointing to the girl in the blue tabba. "She has been very good."

The foster, Thainna, spoke up. "Captain Mazrem is mending very nicely, Tes Ephria. He'll be fine soon."

The five of them stood awkwardly for a couple more minutes before Thainna politely told them that, in her professional opinion, it was time to call an end to the audience. Marus and Ephria made their final farewells to Captain Mazrem and then green-clad guards led them out of the atrium. As they walked back down toward the gates, Marus raised his eyebrows at Ephria.

"What was all that about back there?" he asked.

"All what?"

"You were jittery with Lady Mazrem and positively girlish on Captain Mazrem!"

"Hae. And what about you? So straight and proper, Sir Gallard," Ephria retorted, coloring. She jabbed Marus in the shoulder, hard enough that he could feel it even through his armor. "I know how much you spent to get this meeting, and for what? You barely said two words to Captain Mazrem."

"I guess..." Marus sighed. "I don't know. I just wanted to see a real hero."

They reached the tall gates of the Mazrem estate. Marus recognized a dozen knights in red, blue and black armor, representing all three VEIL courts. He waved to some of them, but most remained focused on the job at hand.

Outside, a crowd of hundreds, perhaps thousands, jostled one another to get a view. As Marus and Ephria neared, the throng roared together, wondering if the approaching knight was their beloved Captain Mazrem. When Marus drew close enough for the people to see the blue of his armor, their cries died away into disappointed murmurs.

"Thanks," Marus grumbled to himself, but Ephria was close enough to hear.

"We can't all be heroes," she told him. "Ready to do this again, Sir Gallard?"

"They want to see a hero, too," said Marus.

This time, Ephria didn't hear him. Or if she did, she had no answer.

At the bottom of the hill, a Sun Court captain in studded red leather bellowed an order. The guards pulled the heavy iron gates open and the crowd surged forward. A line of knights pushed back and, with an effort, opened a path. Waved on by the VEIL captain, Marus and Ephria passed through the gate, back out into the street.

The lane cleared out by the knights didn't stay open long and Marus was soon surrounded by people. A few of them tugged at his sleeves, asking questions that were quickly swallowed by the din. But moments later, even that attention waned. Marus and Ephria wound their way through the crowd and out onto the streets of the Everstones.

The road was an impromptu fair. No matter how many times the guards turned them away, food sellers parked carts beside the estate and did lucrative business. Even the most devoted worshipers still needed to eat. Men and women stood beside painted wagons and stands, selling flowers and prayer candles, shouting gossip back and forth to one another. The air was one of a festival, heedless and excited.

Ephria thanked Marus for letting her accompany him as they left the Everstones. After a perfunctory but not unfriendly goodbye, she hurried off in the direction of the temple district, probably to say another prayer for Rikard Mazrem. Slowly, Marus made his way back to the archouse, wandering and strangely reluctant to return home to the archouse. Only when the sun began to set did Marus finally flag down a chay and pay the driver to take him back to the Moon Court.

When he stepped through the archouse's gate, Marus found General Hern sitting on the steps overlooking a training field where a few knights and squires fought mock-battles on the grass. They were lit bronze by the orange light of the setting sun, like statues brought to life by the strange day's end.

General Hern held his gladius across his lap and an oiled rag. Marus considered using the back entrance, but stopped instead at the foot of the stairs. The general would corner him sooner or later. Better to get it over and done with. Stifling another heavy sigh, Marus trudged up the steps and saluted the general.

"And how is Captain Mazrem?" General Hern asked without preamble.

"He seems better, sir. His wounds are healing and the foster you sent watches over him."

"What did he have to say?"

"Captain Mazrem didn't speak very much. What he did say was pretty confused. He didn't seem entirely... present," Marus reported unhappily.

General Hern ran the rag along the already shining length of his sword. "He seemed mad, didn't he?"

"I would never say..." Marus stopped. "Hae, he did."

A younger knight appeared up on the landing above them, saluted and then hurried down the stairs. Hern waited until he was gone again before answering. The Moon Court general looked old and tired.

How long until I'm that worn down? Marus thought. *Not long, I suspect.*

"I'm sure you understand the sensitivity of the subject," Hern said at last.

"I'm sorry, sir. I don't take your meaning."

"Captain Mazrem and his family have been through enough without having to endure more questions about Rikard's health and sanity."

"You don't want me to tell anyone what he was like."

"No, I don't."

"General Hern, sir, he's supposed to become legens of VEIL. Don't you think someone ought to know about this? We don't want VEIL in the hands of a madman, no matter what service he's done us before!"

Hern stood and looked down at Marus. "That's enough, Gallard. I won't have any of my knights bringing grief before the Lyceum. You will hold your tongue."

"But... but why did you let me see him at all, sir, if you're just going to order me quiet?" Marus asked.

General Hern turned his attention out across the courtyard. There were only three men remaining in the stretching shadows of the archouse. Two of the larger cornered the junior knight against the side of the armory. The boy was on his knees, arms wrapped around his stomach as he fought to catch his breath. One of the others kicked him again and the smaller knight sprawled on the ground.

Hern gestured at them with his polished gladius. The blade shone in the fading sun, but not half so brightly as the gold of his bloodcap.

"Look at them," he said. "Wolves tearing at the smallest of the pack. Brutal and bestial... yet I can't blame them. We all do what we must to survive. They must show themselves strong or fall prey to the other wolves."

The young knight lunged for his fallen sword, a wooden practice blade. He smashed it as hard as he could into the knee of his nearest opponent. For yard practice, none of them wore armor and the wood cracked loudly, crumpling the joint. The bigger knight fell to the ground, howling in pain.

Marus winced. VEIL had all been so impressive when he was a boy, he thought, but experience had dulled it away to something cheap and tarnished.

"It was never like this when I was young," Hern said softly. "This is a disgrace, a schoolyard of bullies."

"Then why don't you stop them, sir?"

"And become the weakest wolf of the pack? No, I don't think so. This is the way of things now. The world of my youth is long past. No one observes the old ways, practices the old styles."

"I do," Marus protested.

General Hern turned to look at him. There was something sad in his eyes, but hard, too. "Do you?"

"...Hae, sir." Marus suddenly wished he had said nothing. The general turned to face him, swinging his sword in a close, lazy arc.

"Show me."

Reluctantly, Marus drew his own gladius. He held it uncertainly. What did Hern want of him?

"You want me... to fight you, sir?" he asked.

Hern laughed sourly. "I don't fight unnecessary battles, Gallard. No, show me the pact forms. I haven't seen one in years."

Marus nodded and stepped back. There was enough room for a short practice form, but barely. He would have to watch his feet. Marus dropped his sword to his side, parallel to his leg, and then swept it up to a ready position, cocked over his shoulder. He made a quick, controlled thrust to create distance, and then an arcing parry to ward off the imaginary opponent's answering strike. Duck and lunge, pushing ever back. Marus was against the banister, toeing the empty air.

He switched his sword from one hand to the other. Holding his gladius in his left hand now, Marus slashed a protective web of steel as he drew back. With his writing hand freed, he pressed his thumb to the catch of his bloodcap and fell to one knee, scraping the gold over the stones in mimicry of a pact. Marus held his sword in a low guard in his off hand, protective and ready.

Hern nodded. "As I remember it. Enough, Gallard. Get up. You didn't actually bleed, did you?"

"No, sir."

The general sheathed his sword and tucked the polishing rag into his belt.

"When was the last time that you made a pact with the Alterra, Gallard?" Hern asked.

Marus wiped a few drops of sweat from his brow and thought back.

"About five years ago, sir," he answered.

"That's not long at all. You're a braver man than most. What was it?"

"A man out in the Rows barricaded up his shop. There was a little boy in there with him. I made a pact to break through the back wall and get him," Marus said proudly, then sighed. "After that, the shopkeeper brought a suit against the Moon Court for damages."

"What did the Alterra take in trade?"

"A day of memory."

"What was so special about that day?" asked Hern.

"I have no idea, sir. And I couldn't see blue for a week. When the color finally came back, I must have spent an hour just staring at the sky. I'd never realized how beautiful it was."

"Colors, memories. I gave them every nightmare I'd ever had about the sea once, when I was a squire. I cursed the damned spirits when they returned my dreams. What kinds of monsters live by such things?" Hern asked. The general looked out across the courtyard again. It was empty now but for shadows and browning, brittle grass. "You and Rikard are a dying breed, Gallard. I haven't opened my bloodcap in twenty years except to clean it."

Marus wanted to argue with him, to tell the Moon Court general that Captain Mazrem's return would fix everything. But he was thirsty and tired. What was the point of arguing, anyway? Only hours ago, hadn't he reached the same conclusion? Rikard Mazrem was a raving madman and Marus himself was little more than a boy clinging to a lost past and dreams of honor. And for all of General Hern's sad disapproval, he would do nothing.

Hern is like a willow, bending in the wind and always at its mercy. Perhaps that's best... Marus thought of the other court generals. *Saul Darius is more like grass, with everyone always walking over him. And Cadmus Castor... He's an oak, tall and strong. He'll break before he will ever bow. Even if there is something better for VEIL, there's no one to guide us to it.*

Marus looked down at his own hands, at the calluses on both palms, once such points of pride. Even as a squire, he had excelled at the pact forms, but Hern was right. No one practiced them anymore. It was easy to be the best on an empty field, wasn't it?

When General Hern said nothing else, Marus eventually saluted and retreated into the archouse to find some dinner.

23

GAMBIT

"The people love a hero. Be sure to give them one or else they will find their own."

— KING CARSUS TYCHON III

THAINNA WOKE early to visit the kitchen and found Arliss kneading a ball of dough on the sideboard. The fat cook nodded to Thainna and aimed a kick at a potboy's backside.

"Go get some more wood for the stove," she ordered. "Not the flinders in the back. The oak logs from the storehouse."

The boy stuck out his tongue at Arliss, then yelped as she kicked him again. When he had scurried off, Thainna got down to business.

"I need to send some important news to the Crest," she said.

"You need me to run a letter into the city?"

"I don't write very well," Thainna admitted. "And besides, I don't think it's something that should be written down. Can you just tell someone? I can't go myself. I have to stay for Captain Mazrem's visits."

"It can get done, hae. What's so important?" Arliss asked with a nervous frown. "You're not in trouble, are you?"

"No, I'm not in trouble," Thainna said. "Well, maybe a little bit with Lady Mazrem when I yelled at that historian, Ferro. But she didn't dismiss me or anything."

Arliss clicked her tongue. "Don't you go making an enemy of the lady."

"I know that! I didn't mean to and I won't do it again. I can't fail this job. No, I found out something about Captain Mazrem. He... he can hear what people are thinking."

The cook whistled and leaned back against the sideboard. "I knew that he came back strange, but that's a big bite to swallow. Are you sure?"

"Hae," Thainna answered. It *was* a little hard to believe, but she knew it was true. "He can read out what's in your mind and heart like it's written in a book."

"Does anyone else know?"

"I don't think so. But it won't stay a secret forever. Rikard doesn't think about the things he says. It'll slip out sooner or later, but I wanted the Crest to know first."

Arliss cocked her head, listening attentively. "Anything else?"

"Hae, there's more. Rikard said something else, about fighting in Alterra and using things like memories and feelings as weapons. Maybe we can use things like that to... to control him. When Rikard first started seeing into my mind, I was scared and that hurt him. He says that fear was one of the *blades* in Alterra, and it wounds him even now."

Thainna felt guilty even thinking it. Rikard had seemed so... vulnerable in those moments, sharing his weaknesses with the girl pretending to be his nurse.

"What are you going to do now?" Arliss asked in a low voice. "If Captain Mazrem can hear your thoughts, how long until he discovers you?"

Thainna sighed. "I don't know. But it doesn't matter. I can only guess what the Crest will do if I fail in this. What he'll do to my brother. I just have to hide it all from Rikard. As long as I'm frightened of him, I can try to keep him out of my head."

"You're risking a lot," Arliss said, but she shook her head. "I suppose you have to. I'll go to talk to Narissa this afternoon."

"Thanks, Arliss."

"I'm doing my job. When Narissa or one of the other Eyes asks to see you, you can tell them so."

"Hae," Thainna agreed.

We're all so eager to please the Crest, aren't we?

Arliss gave Thainna some breakfast and then sent her on her way. The cook had plenty of work to do, which now included a journey out into Dormaen. Thainna took her handful of steaming rye cakes back to her room and wolfed them down, but the heavy meal didn't sit easily in her stomach. How long would the Crest wait before he expected progress with Rikard? Days? Weeks?

Thainna still had no idea how to control Captain Mazrem. Bully him with her fear and anger? How long could that last? Rikard was strange and unpredictable. He could see into Thainna's mind, too. It was probably best to keep away from Rikard Mazrem entirely, but Laurael's orders made that impossible. Even if she could, distance would only make following the Crest's orders equally impossible.

I can't do this.

The thought was more than depressing; it was terrifying. There *had* to be a way, or Thain would suffer the consequences of her failure. Thainna pulled out the jars that Narissa had provided and laid out the drams along the edge of her bed. Rikard didn't seem the type to be easily split on any of them. His interactions with Terra were difficult enough without adding ophellion into the mix.

Cardak, maybe? Thainna was pretty sure that cardak was some sort of narcotic, but Rikard wasn't interested in anything like that.

Does Rikard know he's mad?

There were more visitors in the days that followed. On the fifth day, Rikard didn't know two of them: a Nianese man named Liam Io and another historian, Huron DuRainne. Laurael assured him that they were both prominent, important men, but Rikard had no more to say to them than he had to the Moon Court knight, Sir Gallard.

The day's final visitor, though, was the one Rikard was at once anxious and eager to see. As the dinner hour approached, he found himself walking back and forth along a gallery of marble carvings. Laurael was off taking care of final preparations, but both Gaius and Thainna stood to either side of the door, watching Rikard pace. Even though supper was less than an hour off, Gaius snacked on a handful of sugared rose petals. Thainna watched but tried not to look like she was.

They smell like perfume. What do they taste like? Rikard heard her wonder.

"Why so nervous, Father?" Gaius asked. He wiped the white sugar from his lips with the back of his hand.

"I haven't seen Saul in thirty years. I wonder about him. Did he marry?"

"A few years after the war. He has two daughters, as well. I'm engaged to the older one, Sierra," Gaius said.

Laurael had told Rikard of his son's engagement, but not that Gaius was promised to Saul's daughter. Rikard sheared off from his pacing and bounded over to seize Gaius in a hug.

"What? Why have you thought nothing about it?"

"It's not very important," Gaius said, taken aback by Rikard's sudden exuberance.

"Why haven't you married her yet?"

"I've been busy, Father."

Too busy to get married? Laura said the same thing, but it made no more sense now.

"With what?" Rikard asked. "Gaius, family is the most important thing in... in ever! They will love you and you will do anything for them!"

Nearby, the foster nodded to herself and Rikard felt her agree. But she saw him looking at her and quickly turned away. A red, raw blade of frightened distrust drove him out of her thoughts. Rikard touched his fingers to his temple. It stung, but not enough to quell his joy. Gaius was engaged to Saul's daughter!

A servant in a smart black-trimmed tabba appeared at the door. "Lords Mazrem, General Darius has arrived. He's waiting in the triclinium."

Rikard shoved past and ran down the hall to the dining room. His boots clapped on the polished marble and slid as he came to a squeaking halt. Saul stood in the triclinium, handing Laurael a brightly striped amphora. He was older, much older than the young squire that rode beside Rikard into Fiore, but his face was still round and boyish.

"Saul!" Rikard shouted.

At the sound of his name, Saul Darius turned and grinned. The two men embraced tightly, laughing and thumping each other hard on the back until Thainna caught up and made a small, politely disapproving sound.

"Gods, Rik! It really is you," Saul said happily. He gave his one-time master a final squeeze and then led him over to a trio of Carcaen women standing beside Laurael. "This is my wife, Althea, and our daughters, Sierra and Celeste."

Celeste was the very image of her slender, long-boned mother, but Sierra looked much more like her father, rounder of face and wearing a perpetually broad, cheerful smile. All three women curtsied gracefully to Rikard. When Sierra rose, her eyes lingered on Gaius, but he avoided her gaze. Rikard took the girl's hand and kissed it. Sierra blushed prettily and giggled.

"Gaius told me you're going to be my daughter," he told her. "You're very lily-bee."

"Pretty," Thainna whispered from behind him, just loud enough for Rikard to hear.

"Very pretty," he repeated.

Sierra's blush deepened.

"She is, isn't she?" Saul beamed at his daughter and winked at Rikard. "Maybe you can convince Gaius to take some time away from the archouse and actually marry my girl."

"You know how young men can be," interrupted Laurael before Rikard could answer. "So dedicated to their duty. You were just the same! You remember, Althea."

Saul's tall wife laughed and nodded. "Hae, I do. Nothing would keep you from marching into Fiore at Captain Mazrem's side, Saul."

"Ah, hae," agreed her husband. "But I was young. And I came back to marry you, my dear."

"It was difficult to leave," said Rikard, nodding. "Gaius was only six slivers... months old when we received Tychon's orders."

The others must have felt his bitterness or heard it in his voice. No one answered, but the silence didn't last long. Laurael invited everyone to lay themselves on the three long couches. After a moment of indecision, Sierra reclined beside Gaius. She lay further away from his son than Rikard would have liked, but maybe they didn't know each other well yet. He and Laurael certainly had not when they were first married. Rikard looked over at his wife. He caught her eyes and smiled.

Thainna folded her pale legs under her and sat on a cushion on the floor beside Rikard. He touched her shoulder and the girl jumped as though he had burned her, but Thainna was simply surprised, not frightened.

"Thank you for the word. *Pretty.* I'll remember it."

"Hae, my lord," Thainna replied quietly. "I'm happy to help."

"You are?" Rikard asked in surprise.

The red-haired foster blinked up at him.

"What?" she asked.

A dozen men and women served food and drink, talking loudly and announcing what was on each plate, in each decanter. Glass clinked and copper rang. The triclinium was full of noise, so Rikard guessed that Thainna hadn't heard him. Terran ears were so very... limited.

"You said that you're happy to help, but you don't feel happy."

"Get out of my head!" Thainna snapped, then mastered herself and continued in a calmer voice. "I only meant that I'm glad to do my duty, Captain Mazrem."

"Then why aren't you happy?" Rikard asked her. He was even more confused. Despite her protestations of being *happy* and *glad*, Thainna only grew more upset with each word.

"Maybe I don't want to be here... Maybe I want to go back to my own family!" she hissed under her breath. "Or maybe because you tried to strangle me when we met!"

Rikard hadn't thought about their first encounter in days, but Thainna just forced herself to smile tightly as the cook presented a peacock painstakingly redressed in its own colorful plumage and stuffed with truffles.

"I'm sorry, my lord. There's no reason for anger," Thainna said politely. "Please, enjoy your supper."

Her words had the slippery-cracked feel of lies, but the foster girl's mind flitted from one feeling to the next so quickly that Rikard could barely follow.

"Uh... hae," he stammered.

At least the food smelled delicious. Since Rikard's return home, he had eaten better than ever before – even better than his wedding day – but this feast surpassed it all. The peacock was only the first dish in a parade of exotic foods from every corner of the Carcaen Empire. Rikard felt his own not inconsiderable appetite whetted all the more by Thainna's hunger.

"Everyone is talking about you, of course," Saul said. He had to speak up to make himself heard over the clatter. "You're the greatest hero in history, Rik. The Lyceum keeps talking about making you a god!"

"Me...?" Rikard asked. He didn't like the idea. "No, men do not become gods!"

"Most men don't disappear and take an entire army of Fiore barbarians with them!" Saul laughed. He glanced at Thainna and her distinctive fiery hair. "No offense to you, honey."

"Hae, my lord," she said politely.

"Tell me more about afterward, Saul," Rikard said. So much still didn't make sense. "In the vine-fall opens, I spoke to Alexander Ferro, but he asked for more answers than he gave. What happened after Njorn Pass?"

Saul cocked his head at Gaius. "You haven't told your father about it?"

"The basics. Things have been busy. Besides, what could I tell him that anyone else in the world couldn't?"

"We've discussed the political ramifications of his victory," Laurael added. "However, as neither of us were actually present at Njorn Pass, we haven't been able to share those particular details."

"I want to know," said Rikard.

"And you deserve to. Lucky for these gentle ladies, it's a short and simple story." Saul considered for a moment. "You know well how it began, Rik. The Fiori came on us in the night, in the middle of that storm, and one of the scouts came to our tent. You'd taken to sleeping in full armor and so you went straight away to the battle. I was on your heels, but the Fiori were everywhere and I lost you in the snow. I saw Nikas – Captain Hern – and stuck close. By the time I finally found you, Rik, you were up on that snowdrift and drawing a pact circle. No one could hear what you were saying through the storm and the battle."

"Hae, I remember," Rikard said.

He did. So much snow and so much blood... He glanced down at Thainna, the girl who – as she just reminded Rikard – he had tried to kill. After thirty years of constant war, it was a difficult instinct to overcome, and the girl *was* Fiori. Still, that did not mean he was forgiven.

"There was a great, bright red light. I thought you'd called down a great fire or somesuch," Saul went on. "It filled the Njorn Pass. When it was gone, so were you and all of the Fiori. There were just footprints and blood and spears sticking out of the snow. And your sword, of course. Do you know what happened to all of those Fiori, Rik?"

"Stumble tried to explain once, but I couldn't hold it steady," said Rikard. He looked down at Thainna, but her green eyes were turned away. "Flickerdim and the others pulled them toward Alterra, but not *through*. I think the Fiori broke against the veil."

Saul's brows shot up and his wife blanched.

"At any rate, they were gone," he said quickly. "It took us some time to understand what had happened. When we finally did, when the scouts came back and reported that we were alone in the pass, Nikas took command. We still had the blizzard to contend with, so he had us collect those wounded who could still walk and we marched out of the pass."

"How many survived?"

"A little more than five hundred knights and maybe seven thousand soldiers and support made it out of Njorn Pass. Less by the time we returned to Carce."

"So few?" Rikard breathed. "We entered Njorn Pass with seventeen thousand men. Thirty thousand marched from Carce when the campaign began!"

"It was a terrible blow to Carce and to the Verita et Illumina Lansinos," Saul agreed with a nod. "The survivors were divided up among the courts and we started rebuilding our numbers. Emperor Tychon put Nikas in charge of the Moon Court and then Castor inherited the Sun Court a few years after that. I was knighted when we returned, and then the emperor gave me charge of the whole bloody Star Court."

Rikard was happy for his friend's fortune, though he wasn't sure what he thought of the emperor's decision. Saul was a good man, but not a clever or strong-willed one. Not one Rikard would ever have placed in command. Gaius felt much the same, he sensed.

Saul looked between the Mazrem men and gave Rikard a wide, lopsided smile.

"I know what you're thinking, Rik," he said.

"You do?" Rikard asked, surprised. "Can you reach me?"

"Eh? Don't think so, but I'm a career soldier, Rik. I was never on the command road," he said, shaking his head. Althea stroked the back of her husband's hand comfortingly. "It's all fine, my love. I know my own faults. I'm not a quick man."

"But you still took the promotion," Gaius said. His voice had a sharp, bitter edge.

Saul blinked. He laughed again, but now it sounded nervous and uncomfortable. "Why didn't *you* take it, Gaius? You and the emperor are close. I'd be happy enough to give up command. Truth be, it's a good thing we're at peace. I can schedule guard rotations for the emperor, but not much more."

"For the emperor?" Rikard asked curiously.

"The Star Court provides the knights for Emperor Tychon's guard these days. Castor's never been happy about the arrangement, but there's not much he can do about it. It's not my doing." Saul paused to pour thick strawberry sauce over a slice of duck meat and take a few bites. "This is delicious, Lady Mazrem. You always set the most lavish table."

"Thank you, Saul."

"Well at any rate, the decision wasn't mine or even Emperor Tychon's. The Lyceum called a vote early on after they were first convened. Most of the surviving Sun Court was men who had remained behind during the war in Fiore. A consul on the Lyceum, Nieve Centra, argued that the Star Court better knew battle and sacrifice than the Suns. I never agreed with Centra. Neither did Castor – it was just about the only time we've ever sided together – but we were outvoted by the rest of the Lyceum."

Rikard drank from a bowl as he thought. The soup was rich and salty, with chunks of melting cheese floating in it. It was almost too much to take in. When did VEIL get involved in politics?

"Speaking back to promotions, they're saying that Emperor Tychon is going to make you legens," Saul said. "Is it true?"

"Hae, it is," answered Gaius.

"Are you going to accept it, Rik?"

"I don't know," Rikard admitted. "I don't want to accept anything from that man."

"My lord, please," said Laurael. She spoke softly into his ear. "Emperor Tychon has been generous to everyone at this table."

Rikard fell grudgingly silent on the matter. He did not like Castum Tychon, but he liked upsetting Laurael even less. For all of his other faults, Saul was sensitive to the moods of those around him and moved the conversation along to something else.

"Enough about things here, Rik!" he said. "Gaius told the entire Lyceum about some kind of civil war in Alterra. That's why they took you? To win their war? What do Alterrans have to fight about? That entire world of theirs is made out of dreams and thoughts. They should have anything at all that they want. Quite literally, hae?"

"It's not... No, it's not like that. Alterrans don't think the way Terrans do. They can't change their thoughts as easily as we can," Rikard told his guests. They listened attentively – even Thainna. "All new things in Alterra, all new dreams and memories, come first from Terrans."

Saul was still curious. "What about this war? It's about us, I've heard. What does that mean?"

"It's... it's hard to explain. Everything goes two ways. Our worlds are twins. The Alterra are strong in our world. They can do things we can't."

"Hae," Saul said with a nod.

"The same is true in reverse. Terrans can do things there that the Alterrans can't do themselves. Change ideas, have new dreams," Rikard explained with some difficulty. Remembering the details was like trying to catch fireflies with a spoon. "Because of us, Alterra is a changing place. Every song, every day, that whole world changes."

"So you say. I follow, but I still don't understand how that led to a war," Saul said.

"There are Alterrans who don't want their world to be so... influenced. The Shatter. They want things to be... to be..." Rikard tried to find the right words.

It was painstaking work. What seemed so obvious and clear in Alterra was hard to put into speech. He smiled mockingly at himself.

Was this what it was like teaching me in those first days, Stumble?

"The Shatter don't want us to shape Alterra anymore. Long, long ago, when there were few Terrans, Alterra was without form. A starless sky. The Alterra lived without body or... or mind. Just... existed as blank as paper. The Shatter want that back... The still silence. Perfection, as they think of it."

No one ate. Every eye in the triclinium, even those of the stilled servants, was on Rikard. He felt their shock like splashes of cold water. They knew nothing about the war that raged in Alterra. Why? How was that possible? The questions pulled the frayed parts of his memory, tugging on a thread that seemed important, but that might unravel everything if pulled too hard.

"They are fighting over us, what to do with us," Rikard said. "The Shatter want the worlds separated. Without us, all Alterra will return to the primordial emptiness. No pacts, no prayers. They want to sever all bonds."

"You fought for the other side?" Saul asked.

"I do. I fight with the rages and curiosities, singes and dires. I fought for Uprising, the Alterra of the tree-tower. The ones who hear our pacts and honor our sacrifices to them. But there were oceans of bitter tears and we were losing."

Saul sat up, eyes wide, and whistled. "Bloody hell, Rik. Bloody hell. I'm happier than words can ever say that you're back from all that. May the Alterra fight their own damned wars until the stars burn out."

The triclinium was quiet for a moment. The servants resumed their work, removing empty dishes and replacing them with full ones. Slowly, Rikard and his guests continued eating. Another cook came in to show off a huge cake decorated with sugared violets and roses, all glittering as though rimed with frost. Laurael nodded her approval and struck up conversation with Althea and her daughters, suggesting that a more extravagant version of the cake might be suitable for Gaius and Sierra's wedding. Saul sidled down his couch, closer to Rikard.

"Rik?"

"Hae, Saul? Gods, it's good to see you again."

"This war... if these Shatter win – and it certainly sounds like they are winning. Maybe that's for the best, hae? Who wants to make pacts with the Alterra anymore? No one wants to be pulled away for thirty or sixty years to fight in some mad, unending war," Saul said slowly. He gestured to his wife and daughters. "You missed so much. Maybe it's for the best if those Uprising Alterra... lose. Maybe our worlds should just go their separate ways."

Rikard stared. He could not believe what he was hearing. *You want this? The Shattered path...? The broken road?*

"Rik? Hae, Rik? What's wrong?"

Saul shook him and Rikard started, bristling with fury. *Lost, all would be lost...!*

As the molten rage coursed through him, Rikard tried to bridle it like a wild horse. Saul was his oldest friend. But the need to fight the Shatter on all and any field ran deep and hard as bedrock. The rage lanced out, razor-sharp, and arrowed out invisibly at Saul. His friend's body went slack and he grunted in pain. Rikard's stomach turned into a knot of ice and he yanked his anger back, but Saul shook his head, eyes glazed.

"What was that? Sorry, Rik, I lost track of things for a moment there," Saul slurred.

He rubbed his face hard enough to redden the skin. Rikard knew the feeling, the pain – *the attack* – from experience. A sharp, burning needle buried somewhere impossible to reach. It would fade, but not for hours. Rikard dropped his gaze, ashamed of what he had done.

From her seat at the foot of the couch, Thainna looked up at Rikard quizzically. After a moment's confused contemplation, she stood and snapped her fingers to get everyone's attention.

The foster bowed and addressed Lady Mazrem. "I'm sorry, my lady, but I'm afraid I must call an early end to the night. Captain Mazrem needs to rest."

"I think I might have had a little too much wine, myself." Saul chuckled. He stood unsteadily and embraced Rikard, wincing as he did. "Take the legens position, my friend. VEIL needs you."

Rikard made quiet, mumbled farewells to Saul's family. Laurael touched his arm.

"My lord, Gaius and I will see our guests to the gate," she said. "I will find you in our bed soon."

"Hae, Laura."

Rikard kissed Laurael and let her go. Together, his family and friends exited the triclinium. Thainna appeared at Rikard's side.

"Let me check you over and then to bed," she said.

The foster gestured for Rikard to come with her. He wanted to fight, to tell Thainna that he didn't need to be put to bed like an unruly boy, but he just couldn't summon the will to argue.

Rikard followed the slender, pale Fiori girl through the halls of his unfamiliar house. She opened the door to the bedroom and waved Rikard inside. He dropped onto the edge of the monolithic bed. Thainna fumbled an emberbox from the nearby table to light a few lamps, then slipped it into her tabba. She sat on the edge of the dais.

"What happened?" she asked. "I saw that look on your face tonight."

"I don't know." Rikard crossed his arms over his stomach. The sick knot of pain in his gut felt too big, too confusing and complicated. He wished he could just cut it out.

"What's wrong?"

"Too many things. I don't have enough words for all of them," Rikard said. But Thainna was a foster. Maybe she could help with the pain.

"Is it the things I said to you before? About..." Thainna whirled her finger around her ear. Rikard wasn't sure what she meant and reached for the rest, the words that went unsaid. *About you being in my head. I hate it. I can't let you. What if you see?*

Rikard frowned. "You don't like it when I listen to the things you think."

"I like it fine when you listen to me talk, just not in my head," Thainna said, then raised her red eyebrows. "Did you pull that out of my mind again?"

"Hae," he confirmed.

"You don't really understand the irony there."

"No."

Rikard looked down at his hands. The little crescent cuts in his palms – the marks of his furious tantrum against Emperor Tychon out in the jasmine garden – were fading, but he could still see them.

His knuckles were bruised from fighting with Nikas and then again with the Lyncean guard, Karl. Rikard shifted his gaze to Thainna's hands, resting on her knees. They were small and Fiori white, with rough nails and cracked cuticles. But there was no mark of violence on them.

"You have ordinary hands," said Rikard.

"Hae, I guess so."

Thainna put her hands in her lap and examined them. Rikard returned to staring at his own.

"Thainna, why do you make my visits short? I want to see more. More people, more of Carce. I died. I've been gone so long. I fought. Bled. Lost in high winds. There are things I don't... I can't..." Rikard tugged at his hair as though if he could just pull hard enough, he could wrench the thoughts beneath free for Thainna's inspection. "I want to see... more. Why won't you let me?"

But the foster was obviously having trouble following Rikard's conversation. Her face scrunched up like a piece of paper about to be thrown away.

"I don't know if that's a very good idea," she said. "You're not... healthy. I don't think it would be good for you, Captain Mazrem."

Rikard stood up and ripped open the front of his saela with a sharp jerk, snapping free the knotted cord buttons and sending them flying across the room. He tore off the bandages beneath and then pointed angrily to the stitched spear wound in his side.

"It does not bleed anymore, Thainna!" he said. "I will not die that easily. I'm a soldier of Carce, a VEIL knight! I'm not so fragile that I cannot talk."

Thainna leapt back, terror naked on her thin face. When Rikard remained still at the bedside, she calmed – much to his relief. The girl was as prickly as a porcupine.

"Look, it's not my choice to make, Rikard," she told him after a moment.

"But you're my foster!"

"It wasn't my decision to keep you out away from the public. It was your wife, Lady Mazrem. I can't go against her wishes."

"I... what?" Rikard could not believe Thainna. Despite his prior resolve, he reached out, but found honesty in Thainna's thoughts. "Why would she do that?"

"I'm sure she's just being protective."

"Hae..."

They sat there in silence for a moment until Thainna sighed and picked up Rikard's discarded saela and dressings.

"This was really unnecessary," she said with a long sigh, then smiled at him. "You sure like making a point."

Even though he wasn't reaching for her thoughts, Rikard plainly felt the wobbly, shaky nervousness that clung to the foster like a sticky film.

"There's something wrong with me, isn't there?" he asked softly.

Thainna rolled up the torn cloth and wrapped her arms around the bundle. "Hae, there is."

Rikard sat once more and held out his hands. "I don't know how to say things. I don't know how to..."

He curled his fingers into hooked claws and pulled them in close to his chest.

"It's a lot more than that," Thainna said under her breath.

"What?"

Thainna frowned at Rikard. Her words weren't meant for him, he guessed.

"You've been gone from Terra for a long time," she said. "You're completely inhuman."

Rikard narrowed his eyes at her. "I thought you wanted to help, foster."

"I do! Don't rush in!" Thainna snapped. "Believe me, I do want to help. But the problem isn't your physical health. It's probably why Lady Mazrem wants to keep you in, too. There's something wrong in here."

Thainna approached the bed and very gently touched her warm fingertips to his temple. The feel of her made Rikard feel oddly light and feverish.

"It's your mind that needs healing, not your body. I don't think you're really mad, exactly, though I'd bet laurels that I'm one of precious few around here. You answer everything with anger and violence, Rikard. It's scary, even when you *don't* actually hit people."

Rikard slumped. Though he had not struck Saul with his fists – not as he had Karl – Rikard had hurt his friend. It was only a reflex, but a dangerous one. As a younger VEIL knight, how many times had he pitted wills against men just like that, criminals who fought and killed simply because they knew nothing else?

"You're right," Rikard said. His throat was so tight that his voice cracked. "I did... I hurt Saul tonight. It was..."

Rikard made a shoving motion, shook his head and tried again. He pushed all his fingers together into a point. Thainna chewed her lip again.

"I don't understand," she told him. "You never touched General Darius, did you?"

"No, not with my hands. Do you remember when I first saw you, when I grabbed you?"

"Hae, how could I forget?" she asked dryly. "It was one of the more memorable nights of my life."

"I hurt you."

"You were strangling me, Captain Mazrem."

"No, here," he said, touching Thainna between the eyes. She flinched, but she remembered the encounter quite loudly. "I sent my anger on you, honed and sharpened. I did it to Saul and I did it to you. I was surprised and I lashed out. I... I am sorry, Thainna. I'm sorry I hurt you."

"It's alright, Rikard," Thainna answered. "You thought I was your enemy."

"Saul isn't my enemy. Neither is Nikas."

"Neither was Karl, but you still attacked him." Thainna held up her hands when Rikard tried to respond. "No, wait. I think I understand. Really, I do. You spent thirty years in a war, in another world. It's hard to come back to something else. It would be like... like living your whole life in the Rows and then suddenly being asked to work in the imperial palace. Everything is so different."

"I suppose so." Rikard wasn't quite sure, but Thainna's idea had the thick weight of truth.

"You just need to learn to be Terran again," Thainna said with a shrug. She burst into laughter. "Listen to me! I'm advising Rikard Mazrem on how to be human!"

He had no idea why that was funny, but her giggles were contagious. Rikard found himself smiling and then laughing, too. When he finally stopped and wiped the tears from his eyes, Laurael stood in the door with her perfectly plucked eyebrows drawn up into high, surprised bows. With some effort, Thainna stopped laughing and stood.

"Lady Mazrem, your husband is well," she said. "I believe that the wounds should breathe at night, so I'm leaving them uncovered. Please, be gentle with him."

"Hae, foster. I am always very careful," said Laurael.

Thainna bowed and left the bedroom.

24

WHISPER

> "Is war our fate? It seems in our nature ever to reach for more than we have. More than we need, perhaps. Is humanity condemned never to find satisfaction, never to find a lasting peace?"
>
> — OUR RED HISTORY, BY AVILLA SALLUSI

THE SKY over Dormaen was full of stars, twinkling and flickering through the smoke of lamps and candles burning in the city below. Gaius followed his mother out across the grass, listening to her chatter with Saul and Althea. He held Sierra's hand. It felt delicate and tiny in his grasp. Fragile.

Gaius hated it. He had absolutely no desire to marry this wilting little flower of a girl. Sierra Darius was a well-bred woman from a reputable family. A perfect political match, as his mother reminded him, but what did that matter? The Mazrem family rivaled even the Emperor Tychon in power. Gaius Mazrem was already heir apparent to the imperial throne. So what more could marriage to Sierra Darius possibly earn him? Respectability, Gaius supposed, and legitimate heirs.

But heirs mattered only when he died, and the inevitable end to his life wasn't something that Gaius particularly liked to dwell on. Respectability and proper form were his mother's concerns, not his. Besides, none of it mattered at all if Emperor Tychon passed the imperial crown on to Rikard. If Lady Mazrem kept the secret of her husband's madness as well as she hoped to, then it seemed inevitable. If she didn't, then the entire Mazrem family would be disgraced and the emperor would choose some other, more suitable heir than Gaius.

Either way, it was all falling down around Gaius' ears and still he had to smile at Sierra, to pretend he actually cared for her. At the gates, she took his other hand and gazed lovingly into his eyes. Gaius fought down a grimace.

"I'm so pleased for you, my lord," she said in a breathy, wispy voice.

"You are? Why?" Gaius asked. Things didn't seem to be going well for him at all.

Sierra giggled as though he had made some wonderful joke. "Your father's return!"

"Oh, hae. Sure."

"Perhaps with Lord Mazrem taking control of VEIL, he'll free some of your time. We can finally be married. I pray every day that I'll be a good wife to you."

Gaius grunted noncommittally. A dozen pretty maids waited for him at home and none of them expected anything more of Gaius than a show between the sheets. He acquiesced to a short kiss with Sienna as a few of the knights guarding the wall stepped forward to escort General Darius and his family away. When they were all out of sight, swallowed up by the night, Gaius turned to make his way home. His mother fell into step beside him.

"You seem particularly out of sorts tonight, Gaius," she said.

"I'm surprised you even noticed, Mother," he said. "You seemed quite busy pleasing everyone else."

"Saul Darius is a very important man," Laurael reminded him sharply. "We need his friendship and a union with his family."

"What for? They're far less powerful than we are. We don't need Darius!"

"Don't be naïve, Gaius," his mother told him. "Even the emperor needs his generals. Men in power make enemies and no one can watch his own back."

"Maybe," Gaius said sullenly. "But if you'd let me take the promotion, *I* would be general of the Star Court! I wouldn't have to sugar up Darius."

"Did you hear nothing that I said? If you let yourself be promoted over Saul, you'd leave him with nothing. General Darius isn't a wily man. He would not himself be a very dangerous enemy, but he's also a likable man with many of his own allies. Better to have his friendship than enmity, Gaius."

They passed beneath a pair of ivy-covered pillars, silvered in the moonlight and casting a deep violet shadow. The blue-lit shrine loomed just off the path, hunkered down in the night like a hunting cat, back arched and tensed to pounce. Gaius tapped his thumbnail against his bloodcap and scowled.

"Well, I didn't take General Darius' job," he said. "Do I have to marry his girl, too?"

"Hae, you do. I don't know why you object so strenuously, Gaius. Sierra's a pretty girl. She's docile and as easily pleased as her father. She's healthy and young. Though she's growing less so with every day you delay. Some proper sons would make you a better heir to the emperor."

"Always in such a rush, Mother. If you really wanted grandchildren so badly, perhaps you should have given me a few brothers or sisters."

"You're a cruel boy," Laurael said. "I was a young woman when your father left and you were an infant. I didn't have the opportunity to bear you brothers."

"How lucky for us, then, that General Darius whelped a little more successfully. Emperor Tychon never married, as you know perfectly well. I don't particularly see why I should."

"Castum Tychon has far too many exotic tastes," Laurael said primly. She leveled an icy look at her son, all but daring him to remind her that thirty years ago, *she* had been one of those tastes. "He should have found himself a wife long ago and produced himself a true heir."

Gaius laughed. "Not likely. You'd have killed the bitch and any of her pups to be sure of my claim to the throne. Bloody hell, you've probably been keeping yourself pretty just to make sure Tychon pines after you, instead of someone a little more marriageable."

Laurael smiled mysteriously and Gaius belched in answer. The large dinner squeezed his stomach uncomfortably in the confines of his saela. He flicked open the buttons and sighed contently when he could breathe freely.

"It doesn't really matter anymore. So far, you've said and done nothing to ensure that Father isn't going to take everything."

"I can control your father. You are my son, Gaius, born of my own flesh and blood."

"And a little bit of Father's."

"Rikard is just a man. I could have been married to any man. But only you are *my* son. I've not worked so long and so hard to give up your throne to a man I haven't seen in thirty years."

"You've preached this all before, Mother. What are you actually going to *do*?" asked Gaius.

Lady Mazrem stopped at the door of his house and kissed her son's cheeks, a touch of her cool, waxed lips against his sweaty skin. "Sleep well, my son, and have no worries."

Gaius briefly returned his mother's embrace. "Hae, Mother, as soon as I have nothing to worry about."

The sky was full of racing clouds, hurricane and hubris in bright sunset orange. Razor winds cut at them, tearing out streaks of flat, slate gray like colorless wounds. Bright skyfire leaked away through the empty slashes.

Stumble flattened his cheese-shape into an eerie midnight mist and raced through the leaves until he felt Flickerdim nearby. The shadow-serpent coiled through the deep dreams lurking under the broad leaves of the tower. Flickerdim's star-flecked scales took on a distinctly green hue. Stumble curled his tendrils around the older Alterran and clung close.

What's happening? I saw a longing-flower and... and now it's gone! It's gone, Flicker. Why? Stumble panicked. *How did the Shatter get so close?*

Time grows short, Stumble. They have drained the Black Teeth and entered the Skeltersky Morose. The Shatter are closing in, infiltrating the tree-tower.

How long until they take the Uprising?

Flickerdim closed his inky black eyes and wove his head back and forth in a complex knot. His throat flared into feathery gills as he tasted the air for change. The nebulous fronds flickered through a dozen colors and numbers and then were gone. The old Alterran general slithered along the branch and the bark-stone beneath his midnight scales trembled like a plucked harp string.

How long? he asked again.

I don't know. Flickerdim stared out between the branches. His eyes were turning a gray-ground pewter color.

Stumble had never known a wisdom – especially one as old as Flickerdim – not to have an answer. It was against their nature not to know. But if there ever was something that they did not know, Stumble supposed it would be wise to admit it.

High above, the Alterran sky was empty as a drained glass.

Laurael returned to her bedroom to find Rikard and the foster girl laughing at some joke. The joke, she suspected, had been Thainna's. Even before his disappearance, Rikard was a serious man and his years in Alterra only made him more so.

Thainna went immediately quiet, made her report to Laurael and then politely left. As was proper. Rikard, however, continued giggling like a boy half his age. Less than that, she supposed. How could she ever hope to fathom a man who was somehow younger in body than the son he had sired? Laurael found herself annoyed at Rikard, and not for the first time that evening.

"It's improper to be so familiar with a servant," she snapped.

"Thainna isn't a servant," Rikard said. "She's a foster of Surma. She doesn't blind for us... work, I mean."

"That girl *is* a servant, even if not one that we hired. More so, perhaps. Anyone here can leave when they like, but Thainna's a foster. She's sworn her entire life to Surma's service."

"It's not so different than being a knight, then."

Rikard sat back on their bed. Cleaned, shaved and beginning now to fill out his thinned frame, he was quite a handsome man. Another woman – one younger and less ambitious – might have been swayed by his looks.

Laurael sat on a stool and lifted a mirror in front of her face. Young or old, beauty was of much less importance for men. A man could raise himself up by wits, strength of arms or any one of a dozen different qualities. But a woman had fewer paths left to her. Laurael caught her reflection in the pale amber lamplight. Flawless, just as she had to be.

She felt something warm against the side of her neck. Rikard had crept up silently behind her and kissed her throat just below the ear.

"I remember some things that were lost to me," he whispered.

"Take your time, my lord. I would not dream of rushing you."

"Help me remember the rest."

Rikard circled his arms around Laurael, fingers questing for the clasps of her extravagant tabba. She stood and pulled away. In thirty years of chastity, she had only occasionally regretted the loss of such intimate touch.

This wasn't one of those times. Rikard's skin was uncomfortably hot, damp with sweat and somehow clingy against hers. Her young husband watched Laurael reverently, still kneeling down on the rug-strewn floor.

"The day has been long, my lord. Surely you're tired and would like to rest."

"I've rested a lot lately. I'm not tired, Laura."

He stood and hooked his arms around her again. He pulled her close. Laurael kissed him shortly, but nothing more. After a moment of stillness, Rikard released her with a frown.

"Laura, what is this? This... bleak? What's wrong?"

"You've been through so very much, my lord. I wish only to care for you."

"Then care for me," Rikard said. He went to the bed and smiled shyly at her. "Laura, please be with me. Here."

Laurael leaned on the corner post of the bed. She would have to lay with him sooner or later. Rikard noticed her hesitation and hugged his knees to his chest like an upset child. Before his disappearance, Laurael did not recall ever thinking him particularly boyish, but something in the last three decades had stripped away the usual mannerisms of adulthood.

"I took words from Thainna about it," Rikard said. "About how you protect me. She said that you told her to make Saul and Marus and the others leave."

"She told you that?" Laurael's already faltering opinion of the skinny foster dropped another notch. "You've been so wounded, so changed by your time in Alterra, my husband."

"I *chose* to serve VEIL and Carce, Laura. Please, don't keep me from them."

"The foster agreed with my choice. Do you doubt her wisdom?"

"I... don't know."

It wasn't the answer that Laurael had hoped for. She pushed on.

"Be reasonable," she said. "I know you're eager to see more, but you are only newly returned! You have spent more time in Alterra than the world of your birth, my lord."

Rikard's brow creased, but he didn't look entirely convinced. His unbound black hair fluttered in a warm breeze.

"But I want–"

He was going to argue all night. Laurael knew how stubborn her husband could be. She sat beside him on the bed and brushed her fingers through his hair, hooked them around the back of his neck and pulled Rikard into a long kiss. Any thought of argument was forgotten, drowned out in his tide of youthful passion.

"I know what you want," Laurael said. "I can show you all that you've forgotten, my lord, and remind you that it is sweet."

Even in his greatest hunger and weariness, Rikard was never so keenly aware of his own body. His wife's kiss fanned the embers deep inside him into something livid, vital. He was awkward and guilty that he could not remember the details of joining, but the honeyed surge of fire inside him seared away all sense of shame. Laurael's touch drew lines of light along his skin, tracing a fullness that seemed ever on the verge of bursting from his very core.

Laurael guided him with steady confidence, a skilled rider astride a wild and unbroken mount. Rikard fumbled like a youth, but Laurael calmly corrected his every faltering touch. She took him gently and smoothly into her soft, perfect body and his world exploded into velvet sensation.

Rikard searched with trembling hands and uncertain resolve to turn his pleasure back on the woman he loved, but Laurael took his wrists in slender fingers and whispered at him to be still, to let her love him. Care for him, just as he had asked. Rikard's heart seemed at once too small to contain the things he felt and too large to fit in the too-constraining cage of his ribs.

Laura. My lady, my love! The worlds I would give and call and destroy to feel your love, to touch your heart, your body. You saved me a million times. Every memory of you was a spire of diamond rising above the howling storm. Feel me, Laura, feel my need for you, my love! Feel me, reach for me...!

Rikard reached for his wife, pouring such love into Laurael that the echoing surge from his body seemed small – though certainly pleasant – in comparison. But something was wrong. It was like pouring a cup of water down an empty well. His flood of need and feeling were received, but met with nothing in return.

Sweating and exhausted, Rikard collapsed back into the twisted sheets. What was wrong? Though he could remember little about their lovemaking before leaving for war, he was certain he could not forget something like this... this failure. What happened? What had he done wrong? Still holding Laurael in his arms, Rikard felt terribly alone.

"Laura, I love you," he whispered.

"I love you, too, my lord," she responded promptly.

But he felt nothing from her. His wife was cold and barren as stone. Was Thainna right? She said that he was... frightening. Had he hurt Laurael, scared her away with his strangeness? What if he wasn't a man she could love anymore? Rikard kissed Laurael gently and stroked her cheek.

I will be better. Stronger. Good and proper. I will be the husband you loved thirty years ago, he swore silently, knowing his wife could not hear him.

Later, Laurael lay with her head pillowed in the hollow of Rikard's shoulder, panting and trying to catch her breath. Loveplay was a sport for much younger women.

Rikard's ragged breath evened and then fell into a deep, sleepy rhythm. Something behind Laurael's eyes throbbed dully and made her ears ring as though she stood under a vast bell, recently struck. But the pain wasn't quite enough to make it worth calling a servant to bring her willow tea.

Perhaps that meddling foster girl would have a better suggestion, anyway.

Thainna was proving to be a problem. What should have been simple support of Laurael's decisions was becoming something else entirely. Thainna told Rikard things that were not her place to repeat. What did she want? Perhaps only to help a hero. Or perhaps more. Laurael would have preferred to dismiss Thainna, but she could not risk the insult to General Hern and to the priests of the Surmaen temple.

And the foster wasn't the worst of Laurael's problems. Gaius grew more resentful with each passing day, and with good reason. Rikard's return threatened everything she had worked for. Disrespectful and sullen though he had been, Gaius was right to question his mother. How could she correct the disastrous path Rikard had unwittingly set his family upon?

Why did you have to return, Rikard? Why didn't you die as you were supposed to?

The idea stuck. With Rikard dead to all of Carce, everything was perfect. If her husband returned to his grave, all would be as it had been.

If he were dead.

The details could wait. Pleased to finally have a plan, Laurael gently unwound Rikard's arms, turned away and fell asleep.

"Remarkable. And she swears this is true?" asked the Crest. He sat forward on the looming Jade Throne. His eyes gleamed fever-bright with fascination.

"Not as such, but Arliss assures me those are Thainna's exact words. Rikard Mazrem can hear thoughts."

The Crest sat so still on his throne that Narissa wondered if he had fallen asleep. She jumped when he finally stirred. In the dim light of the single lamp, he looked like a statue, some relic of an era long past. Or yet to come... The Crest had been all but unknown before his sudden rise to power and his reign over the House of Five Dragons had been like no other.

"Can Captain Mazrem only hear thoughts formed into words? Or can he see things, imagined or remembered?" he asked.

"I don't know. Arliss didn't say and so I doubt that Thainna told her. She mentioned that the girl's growing rather familiar with Captain Mazrem, as well."

"I'm not surprised. She has a certain base charm. That was why I assigned her, after all."

"I thought it was for her loyalty."

The Crest laughed and nodded.

"That, too," he said. "Tell Thainna that I want more details. And so speaking, how is the great hero? It's been over a week since his return and he's not made a single public appearance."

"Arliss says that Captain Mazrem is quite mad, that his mind's been scrambled."

"I've heard that. What does Thainna think?"

"She believes that Captain Mazrem's been deeply affected by thirty years of war in Alterra, but that he will recover."

"Good. I have limited uses for a madman." The Crest coughed. He touched his fingers to his chest and grimaced. "Has she been able to exert any control over Rikard Mazrem?"

"Not yet, but it's a step forward," Narissa said. The Eye wished she had better news, no matter how many steps removed from the original source. "Arliss reports that Thainna may be able to use Captain Mazrem's abilities against him. She says that he's injured or at least discomfited by fear."

"Interesting. Has she tried the drams you sent her?"

"Not that I'm aware of, no."

The Crest looked annoyed. "Anything else? Sex?"

"I don't know."

"Tell Thainna to report directly to you. I want details and I want results. Now."

"Hae," Narissa said with a deep genuflection. "I'll send for her and have more information within the week."

"Do that."

Narissa hesitated. "She'll want to see her brother."

"I care very little what Thainna wants," the Crest snapped, then suddenly smiled. "No. Let her. Perhaps she needs a reminder of her priorities, lest she grow too fond of Captain Mazrem."

25

BLUE SKY

"We are all honored to welcome Captain Gaius Mazrem into the Lyceum as the youngest consul in the history of the Carcaen Empire. Let him bring us the wisdom carried by his revered name."

— ULLIN CRAESS

ARLISS CAUGHT her at the door of the servant's longhouse. Thainna slowed and shifted her satchel to the other shoulder so that the fat cook could walk comfortably beside her.

"I didn't see you in the kitchen this morning," Thainna said. She smiled at the older Talon. "Were you sleeping late?"

"No," Arliss hissed under her breath. "Wipe that smirk off your face, girl. You're to report to Narissa at once. The Crest isn't pleased with your work."

Thainna jerked to a halt, staring at Arliss.

"What?" she asked. "But I just gave a report. An important one! Shouldn't that be good enough?"

"Hae, so any sane man would think, but the Crest isn't a sane man! You have to go to the temple straight away."

"I can't go now!"

Thainna snapped her mouth shut as a porter brushed past, carrying a basket of flowers perched atop his shaven head. Arliss grabbed Thainna's arm and towed her away, safely behind one of the storehouses.

"You *have* to go," Arliss hissed.

"But I can't. Rikard has more visitors today," Thainna said. "I'm supposed to stay with him. You know that! I can go there tonight, after Rikard's asleep."

"You can't seriously think to ignore the Crest's order!"

"I'm not ignoring it," Thainna said. That was the truth, after all. "I just can't go right now."

"What about between visits?" Arliss suggested desperately.

"Even if Lady Mazrem would lend me a chariot, I couldn't do it. Rikard is supposed to speak to General Castor today and three more Lyceum consuls. There just isn't any time, Arliss. The Crest will have to understand. I'm doing what he told me to. I'll go as soon as I can, I promise. Will you tell Narissa?"

"No," Arliss answered. She shook her head. "Absolutely not. Do I look like a fool? I'm not going to deliver a message like that!"

"I'll take care of it myself," Thainna said. "I'm sorry I asked. This whole thing is my job, not yours. I'll go tonight."

"Hae," Arliss said. The cook looked as though she wanted to say something else, but turned away instead and hurried back into the servant's kitchen.

The day felt strange. Not alien and otherworldly like the ones that came before it, the days since the Crest dropped Thainna into this insane situation.

All through Rikard's meetings with the Lyceum delegates, he seemed distant and distracted. Despite his many protestations the night before, Rikard didn't appear very interested in lingering with his guests. Even his evening visit from General Castor surprised Thainna.

"Castor," Rikard greeted the Sun Court general shortly.

"Lord-Captain Mazrem. You look surprisingly intact, all things considered."

"Hae, considering you and Tychon bought the empire with my blood and that of my men!"

He met General Castor in the atrium, like most of the others. The thick foliage let Rikard and his visitors maintain the illusion of privacy even as a dozen nearby guards and knights ensured their safety. Standing just on the other side of a fan-leaf palm, Thainna cocked her head and frowned. Lady Mazrem was off giving Castor's wife a tour of the estate. Gaius was probably nearby, but Thainna couldn't see him.

General Cadmus Castor was even taller than Rikard, and much older. The body under his rich red saela was leaner, thinner than the younger knight's. Castor's graying hair receded to sharp peaks at his brow and temples, making him look like a hunting bird. The Sun Court general stood well back from Rikard, arms crossed over his chest.

"You're a VEIL knight, Mazrem," he answered coldly. "Blood is our coin. You always knew that."

"A price paid by other men while you waited comfortably back in Carce! You've never known anything of blood, shed or drawn!"

"I came to pay my respects, Mazrem. Why don't we get on with it? You turned a disastrous loss into the most resounding victory in history. You must be proud."

Thainna peeked between the palm leaves. Rikard's temper certainly seemed to be getting the better of him – again – but she didn't hear any screaming yet. Rikard Mazrem stood still, facing General Castor with his hands balled into fists at his side. Castor regarded the young hero with a raised brow.

"Was it worth it, Castor?" Rikard asked. He leaned in close, but kept his hands at his sides. "Were Tychon's orders worth the thousands of good men that died?"

"We all followed our orders, Mazrem. The Sun Court served in Dormaen with honor. We protected Emperor Tychon with our lives every day," Castor said without hesitation. "But you and your boys won the day. I know your opinion of the Sun Court. Well, congratulations. Now it's the opinion shared by all of Carce. Cowards, they said, too afraid to march into Fiore. We only followed imperial orders."

Rikard's jaw worked, but he said nothing. Castor took a step back and looked away, out across the emerald bounty of the atrium.

"Besides, the Star Court's become the imperial guard since you left. How does that taste, Mazrem? Your men took what I deserved, even though they never wanted it."

"Is that still what you want, Castor?" Rikard asked quietly.

"What makes you think I want anything more than to pay my respects, Mazrem?"

"I feel it in you."

General Castor lifted his sharp chin. "Hae, then. The emperor's offering you legens and I doubt you'll decline. When you take the promotion, put the Sun Court back in charge of Emperor Tychon. Let us protect the heart and head of the empire. You don't want the Star Court managing the palace guard and the Suns have proudly served for generations. Put things back to rights, Mazrem."

"Why do you snow... ask this from me, Castor?" asked Rikard in frustration. "Wouldn't it be better put to your emperor?"

"Tychon would never risk insult to your family or your court, Mazrem. That wouldn't be politic. But if the order comes from you, then there's no insult."

"I'm not... I can't make such decisions, Castor. I'm just a soldier."

Castor scowled and raised his hand as though he might actually hit the younger knight, hero or not. Rikard tensed, half-crouching and pressing his thumbnail against the clasp of his cannula. The moment stretched taut before both men thought better of their actions and relaxed fractionally.

"You don't know the difference between pride and honor," said Castor. "You begrudge me what you care so little for yourself."

"I think we're at the end of respects!"

"Hae, then. I'll find our wives and make my farewells."

General Castor stalked away and quickly vanished into the jade shadows. Thainna was still recovering, surprised the argument had somehow managed not to turn into violence, when Gaius stepped out into the garden, drinking from a glass of pale wine.

"You certainly don't pull your punches at all, Father," said Gaius. "And you don't have much love for that bitter old nut, do you?"

"Castor loves his honor like a shiny bauble. A glass star! It sits on a shelf, never touched, never used but so... bright and fragile."

"That sounds a little cynical."

"He is no friend to you, either," said Rikard sadly, shaking his head at his son.

"No, he's not. The whole Sun Court is sore over being deposed and that means trouble for the Moons and Stars, of course."

"I don't understand."

Gaius finished off his drink and left the empty glass perched precariously on the edge of a marble planter. He combed fingers through his long black hair, so much like his father's. Thainna crept closer and pulled down the edge of a palm frond. Was the hair closest to his scalp a different color? Lighter? Did Gaius Mazrem *dye* his hair?

"There's not a lot of cooperation between the courts," Gaius said. "That's all."

"That's all?" Rikard repeated. "What's being done?"

"What can anyone do? Just don't get caught up between Suns and Stars. I overheard Castor's little suggestion, though. The man is obsessed. He's been politicking for decades to reposition the Suns in the imperial court," Gaius said. He patted his stomach. "Well, I'd better find Mother and see if Castor said anything to her about your argument. You're going to get an earful if he did, Father. See you at dinner!"

Gaius left Rikard alone in the atrium, looking lost and angry. Thainna emerged from her hiding place and circled wide to make sure that Rikard saw her before she spoke. She didn't want to startle him.

"Rikard?"

The knight looked down at Thainna.

"You were close by," he said. "But you didn't stop my argument with Castor. I thought you would."

"You didn't lose any time in fighting with him. Was that why?" Thainna asked. "To say your piece before I jumped in and cut you off? Well, you didn't seem about to hit him or spike him with your mind, or... whatever you do. So I kept quiet."

"You're surprised."

"Hae," Thainna admitted.

Rikard sighed and scrubbed at his eyes.

Thainna perched on the edge of a huge pot with a wide brim. "Are you alright, Captain Mazrem? You've been out of sorts all day. You were better off when I left last night."

Rikard leaned beside where Thainna sat. He looked tired. "I am not the man I was when I left Terra."

"I think that's what I said. It's been thirty years in another world. I expect that would change anyone. That's normal, I think. I mean... I guess it would be, except that you're the first it's ever happened to."

"I was with Laura last night," Rikard told her heavily.

"With? You mean... together? Abed?"

Thainna wondered why a married couple doing what they had obviously done before – at least enough to have a son together – merited such unhappiness.

"I... heard only empty echoes," Rikard answered her unvoiced question.

"Echoes? What do you mean?"

"That I am not the man Laurael married, not the one she loved. I need to be different. I want to be who I was."

His every word felt stripped down, as raw as a skinned knee. Or was she just imaging it? Worse, was Rikard putting those thoughts into her head? Thainna shifted a little further away and contemplated more distance, but it wouldn't save her from Rikard's strange abilities.

"Time changes people," Thainna said. She inched closer again. "It's probably changed your wife, too. Look at your son. He's older than you are!"

"It's unnatural."

She laughed aloud. "I suppose so, but so is everything else!"

"I don't understand."

Rikard sounded sulky. Thainna guessed she probably shouldn't have laughed at him.

"You walked through half the city before Sir Gallard found you, hae?" Thainna asked. "Nothing here is natural, not like grass in a field or clouds in the sky. The whole world we build is unnatural, if you want to look at it that way. What about fosters? It's natural to die from diseases and injuries. Stitching them up and treating them with medicines is hardly natural."

Thainna felt like a fraud talking about it. The thought had been Thain's, not her own, discussed at length during one of her many visits to the fostral. It was far from natural for him to still be alive, Thainna's twin decided, but that made him no less grateful for every breath.

"Maybe. But it's not the same. I don't want to be... this," said Rikard.

"Then don't," Thainna replied with a shrug. "Besides, my point is only half about you. It was also about Lady Laurael. She's thirty years older than when you left. Maybe she's changed, too. Bloody hells, who can even say she's been faithful to you?"

Rikard snarled like an animal. "Don't you dare say such things about Laura!"

Thainna jumped, but Rikard didn't grab her.

"Do you know?" she asked, quietly in case anyone was listening. The guards might still be nearby, concealed in the foliage. "Do you really know? Have you looked inside her mind?"

"No! I would never break the silver crown... I would never do that to Laura! She is my wife and I trust her. It would be a violation to reach into her."

"But it's fine to do it to me, hae? To... reach into me?"

"She's my wife!"

Thainna could think of nothing to say to that. It was hardly fair to expect Rikard to treat Thainna with the same deference that he did his own family. She didn't give him the same trust and respect that she gave Thain, after all.

"Fair enough, I suppose," Thainna said. "Reaching? Is that what you call it?"

Blinking, Rikard struggled to catch up with the change in conversation.

"It is... a word," he answered. "Words don't lock, don't fit quite right. But, hae, I suppose."

"Why do you call it that?"

"It's the closest sound I know. I just reach for other things, besides the ones Terrans say. I reach into the bowl that holds the words and find other things, too."

"If you want to be like you used to be, like a normal Terran, then you've got to stop talking about the rest of us as though we're another race." Thainna paused as an idea crept over her. What if, after so long, he *had* become something else...?

"No, I'm not Alterran," Rikard said.

"Well, you've lived longer in Alterra than Terra, hae? I wasn't sure. You got that question from me, didn't you?"

"Hae. You were thinking about something else. A boy who looks like you. Thain. Who is he?"

"My brother," Thainna told him. "My twin."

"He's... sick. You worry about him. Always."

"Our mother was weak after delivering me and died giving birth to Thain. He had no air. He's been ill ever since he was a baby."

"You think of him a lot."

"You think about your wife and son a lot."

Rikard smiled and looked out into the dense, overlapping greenery of the atrium. "I love them. I would do anything for them."

"And I would do anything for Thain."

They sat together in silence until a guard came to fetch Rikard for dinner. Thainna remained alone in the atrium for a while longer, swinging her feet over the edge of the planter. For all of his strangeness, Rikard wasn't a bad man. When he wasn't strangling her or smashing another man's face in, she rather liked him.

"I want to see Emperor Tychon."

Laurael paused with an olive halfway to her mouth. She replaced it delicately on her plate.

"Bastil will make the arrangements, of course," she said. "What's changed your mind, my lord?"

"Maybe he's just tired of your harping," Gaius said. He hadn't stopped eating.

"Be kind to your mother, Gaius," Rikard told his son. He pushed a caper around on his plate with the tip of his bloodcap. The oily brine left a shiny snail-trail across the porcelain.

"No, I just... I want. Young men make mistakes," Rikard said. "The war on Fiore was a costly mistake, but... but for all his acid,

Castor made a good point to me. Every knight knows that he will be asked to spill blood – his own and his enemies. You... we have had thirty years of peace, a strong empire. Emperor Tychon has done that much."

"Of all the men to change your mind, I can't believe it was old Castor," Gaius laughed.

Rikard looked over to his wife. Laurael felt his eyes on her and smiled. She approved of his decision. He had pleased her. Rikard was certain that his happy glow was visible all across Dormaen.

26
NUMBERS

"In the days since the battle of Njorn Pass, Alterran pacts have fallen out of favor. Instead, the knights of VEIL focus on feats of personal strength and valor. The costs of an ill-considered or hasty Alterran pact are too high."

— AFTER NJORN PASS, BY ALEXANDER FERRO

AFTER THE EVENING'S WORK – which was a shorter task now that Rikard's wounds no longer required bandages – Thainna made her way down the hill to the gate. It was not yet full dark. The horizon was still stained the deep violet of a rich woman's tabba. A fat gibbous moon hung low over the city. Karl was on guard duty under the command of a stocky Star Court knight at the wall that closed all of the Mazrem estate.

"Hae, Thainna!" Karl called. He waved to her. "Where are you going tonight?"

"Just down to the temple of Surma."

"Do you need an escort? The crowd's thinned a bit, but there are still a lot of people."

He gestured to the road that ran outside the gates. The throng lingered outside. A middle-aged father carried his daughter on his shoulders and pointed at the tall wall, still too high for the young girl to see over. A group of girls in the plain tabbae of students sang an awkwardly rhyming song in praise of Lord-Captain Mazrem. A hundred other people milled aimlessly, content simply to wait on the fringes of history.

Thainna shook her head. "I think I'll be safe enough."

Though she didn't think anyone in the peaceful crowd posed much of a threat to a girl born and raised in the Rows, the company would have been nice. But Thainna didn't want a Mazrem guard following her into a meeting with an Eye of the House of Five Dragons.

"Will you be out long?" asked Karl.

"Hae. I've got to walk out to the temples and back."

"Why are you going out so late? Is everything alright?" Karl asked, sounding worried. "Is there something wrong with Captain Mazrem?"

"No, nothing like that. I just ran out of medicine and I need to get some more before morning," Thainna lied quickly.

"But walking? Do you want me to call you a horse or a chariot?"

Thainna considered, but shook her head. She didn't want either Bastil or Lady Mazrem to learn of her journey.

"Alright. I'll tell Commander Sirrus to expect you later," Karl told her. "They'll open the gates for you."

"Thanks, Karl."

He held the gate open long enough for Thainna to slip through. The iron clanged shut behind her before anyone else could try to get in.

Summer tottered and tipped on the cusp of autumn, giving the night a crisp edge. More candles and flowers, dried and fresh, portraits and rolled-up paper prayers lined the walls of the Mazrem estate.

Just like the monument to Rikard in Mazrem Square, Thainna realized. They wanted to see him as much as he wanted to see them.

Dormaen was bright and lively, the early evening full of revelers and travelers. Some recognized Thainna's costume and nodded respectfully, but most paid her no mind. For the first time Thainna could remember, she actually enjoyed walking through the city. Her feet felt fine and she wasn't hungry.

Unhindered by her old jealousies, Thainna found herself admiring the expensive tabbae of the other Everstone residents and the delicious smells of cooking food. It was like walking through a play, a vast stage set out just for her. None of it was real, of course – Thainna herself was only acting the part of a foster – but it was still fun.

Beyond the Everstones, Dormaen's citizens dressed less richly, but the sense of summer and celebration was no less. Merchants with carts full of portraits and carved soapstone busts of Rikard Mazrem were closing up shop for the evening, but still managed to call in a few last-moment customers. Flower vendors and chandlers stayed open longer, selling to those bound for the Everstones or Mazrem Square.

The night wore on and the crowds lessened as Thainna made her way out into the temple district. Only a few beggars lingered among the blue columns of the Surmaen temple. Even those were being gathered up and hurried away by a pair of soldiers. The armored men paused to wave at Thainna as she climbed the steps.

Inside, a priest dressed in a dark blue tabba appeared.

"Mana Vahn," he greeted her in clipped tones. "Mana Narissa is waiting for you."

Mana Vahn? He recognized Thainna and must have been aware of her deception. The Crest's deception. She followed the priest into a room much like the one in which she had received Narissa's original instructions.

"Wait here."

Thainna nodded. The priest glowered and slammed the door shut behind him. Thainna wondered what was twisting his tabba. That she was late? That was the House's fault, not hers.

It was just as well that there was no chair in the barren stone room. Thainna didn't feel like sitting. She paced as she silently berated Narissa and the Crest for their ludicrous demands. Without the sun outside and ticking time away only by her angry steps, Thainna had no idea how long Narissa kept her waiting. More than a few minutes.

When the priestess finally burst into the room, her long hair was unbound and damp. Narissa wore her tabba only half closed. The fine cloth whipped and snapped with her quick stride. Narissa closed the door with a surprisingly loud crack and bolted it behind her.

"What in the bloody blazes are you doing here?"

"What? You called me here!" said Thainna.

"This morning! You were supposed to be here this morning, Talon," Narissa said. She swiftly composed herself and finished sashing her tabba closed.

"I was busy."

Thainna put her hands on her hips and stared back defiantly. This was *not* her fault and she would not be so easily cowed.

"Busy doing the job the Crest gave me," she said. "Rikard was in meetings all day and I have to stay with him."

"Your first loyalty is to the House of Five Dragons, child."

"This is stupid! It's just a meeting, an update. I'm only late because I was doing what you told me to in the first place!"

Narissa turned away, wringing her slender hands. She took a deep breath and faced Thainna again. "You don't understand."

"No, I don't!"

"The Crest, in his kindness, had arranged for you to see Thain today. But you failed to arrive when expected."

"What?"

Thainna's self-righteous anger drained away and left her deflated, hollow. Thain? And she missed him to stay with Rikard... Thainna flushed hotly with sudden anger at Rikard for keeping her, talking about Thain when she could have *been* with her brother.

"Arliss told us how familiar you've become with the great Captain Mazrem. The Crest grew concerned that you might have forgotten which man holds your loyalty." Narissa had Thainna on the defense and knew it. The Eye looked down at the girl. "He was very angry."

Thainna's knees turned to cold, prickling water. "Is... is Thain...? Did the Crest hurt him?"

"I don't know."

"Can I still see him? Where is he? Is he here, in... in the fostral? He's sick. He needs care!"

"I have sent notice to the Crest that you finally arrived. If you please him, perhaps he'll let you see your brother. What have you to tell us?"

"I... I don't know. I already told Arliss everything!"

"Tell us more about what Captain Mazrem can do. Can he only hear thoughts or can he see into them, as well? Can he sense those not yet formed into words?"

"Hae. He's answered questions I haven't even figured out how to ask. He picks up on vaguer things, like feelings. And... and he saw Thain's face when I was thinking about him, at least well enough to tell that we look alike."

"Do you believe his abilities have compromised your position?"

"I... I don't think so. Rikard knows there's something strange about me, but I don't think he really cares. He's focused on his own problems."

"What problems are those?"

Thainna hesitated before she answered. She didn't like spilling Rikard's secrets, but were they really secrets? It was only Rikard's inability to communicate that made them so. Thainna's persistence had earned her that information. Why didn't Laurael and Gaius know? But it didn't matter – Thainna had to tell Narissa. The Crest had Thain.

"Rikard has trouble just speaking to people," Thainna reported unhappily. "He gets confused and then violent. He attacked some people. He's hit a few, but Rikard also said that he's hurt them in different ways, like General Darius. The same way he reads others – *reaching*, he calls it – he seems to be able to turn it around somehow and use it offensively. Rikard did that to me when we first met in the Rows."

"What was it like?" asked Narissa.

She doesn't care if I'm alright, just how it felt to have my mind carved open.

"I don't know exactly," Thainna answered. "I don't remember much, really. Rikard only told me about it later. There was some pain and... I don't know the words to describe it. Just wildness in my head. It scattered my thoughts, but he *was* trying to strangle me. When he attacked Darius the same way, the general didn't seem to realize what was going on, either."

"Do you think it's useful?" asked Narissa.

"I... I guess so. As useful as any weapon."

"Do you think these attacks constitute sufficiently embarrassing occurrences to hold over Captain Mazrem?"

"I don't know. One of them was against General Hern and another against General Darius, but no one's done anything about them. I think it's embarrassing, but Lady Mazrem's kept everything under control."

Narissa stood silently at the door, nodding thoughtfully to herself. Thainna waited nervously. Was it enough? She wanted to see Thain. It was just a stupid, silly mistake that had kept her away that morning... Thainna rocked up onto her toes and back. The leather of her sandals squeaked loudly in the small room.

Narissa raised her eyebrows at Thainna and the young Talon stopped moving.

"I will speak to the Crest," said Narissa at last.

"I'm here and I've given my report. Can... may I see Thain now?"

"That decision belongs to the Crest. Wait here."

Narissa left her alone in the cell again. Without her anger to occupy Thainna, the minutes crept by, as slow and cold and vast as glaciers. She looked out the window, but the narrow street outside remained dark and silent.

The night crept onward. A pair of black-robed priests of Saerus marched down the road. They droned a deep prayer to the death-god, but the thick glass of the window muffled their words and turned them into a thin, spiteful buzz like that of a trapped fly. When they were gone, Thainna was almost disappointed. They left her alone again, waiting.

Thainna sat in the corner furthest from the door, pulling her knees up to her chest and hoping the Crest hadn't hurt Thain. No, he would never bloody his own hands. He would have somebody else do it. Some Talon or Flame, and they would follow their orders, even if it meant beating a sick boy. The price of disobedience was too high...

The door abruptly thumped open, startling Thainna. Narissa had returned, followed by a pair of large Lyncean men not wearing priestly blue. They dragged a third, smaller shape between them. Thainna jumped to her feet.

"Thain!"

He raised his thin white face, a pale moon rising amid the midnight of his captor's black clothes. "Thainna?"

Thain could not see well in the darkened room and stumbled. Thainna dashed to her twin and the two men dumped him into her arms. She struggled to remain upright, staggered back a step and then sank to her knees on the hard floor. Thainna cradled Thain against her chest. He looked up at her.

"Thainna!" he said and smiled at her with thin, cracked lips. He brushed his fingers through her hair. Thainna realized that she had forgotten to braid it that morning. "You look pretty."

"I look like a drowned squirrel," she told him, choking through her tight throat. "I always do."

"No, you look really good. Healthy. You've put on some weight." Thain's voice grew softer, more frightened. "Thainna, what's going on? What's wrong?"

Narissa and her two thugs hung back. They barred the door but otherwise let Thainna have a private moment with her brother. She swallowed hard and gently stroked Thain's bony shoulder. He still wore the papery blue-white tabba of the fostral.

He must be so cold.

"I got a... a bloodmark about a week ago. The Crest sent me to go put reins on Rikard Mazrem. I... They took you to hold over me, to keep me on task. I'm so sorry!"

Thain gasped. "A bloodmark? For Rikard Mazrem? Really?"

"Hae."

"You're getting important, aren't you?" Thain said with a coughing, halting laugh. He touched Thainna's cheek. "I'm really proud, but I... I hope it's going well. I don't want to stay there forever. Believe it or not, I actually miss the fostral!"

"*There?* Where did they take you, Thain?"

"Does it matter? I can't leave until you're done."

He twisted to look back at the other House agents and Thainna saw a series of deep scratches on the back of his shoulder. Nail marks? What were they doing to him?

"Do you think you'll be long?" Thain asked in a small voice.

"I... I don't know. I'm trying."

"It's time for you to go home," Narissa announced. She nodded to the two huge men and they stalked forward, reaching for Thain.

Thainna did not let go of her twin. "Wait, not yet. Please!"

"It's time to go," Narissa repeated.

The Lynceans allowed Thainna a moment to release Thain of her own accord, but she had no intention of letting him go. One of the huge, pale-haired men seized Thainna and yanked her back while the other roughly hauled her twin up. Thain didn't pull his feet under him quickly enough and cried out weakly in pain as his arm twisted. He struggled to stand.

"Let go of him!" Thainna cried.

She reached for Thain, but the thug who held Thainna jerked her back. She threw herself toward her brother again and the Lyncean threw her easily to the floor. Thainna banged her knees on the floor as her captor helped to drag Thain to the door. She jumped back to her feet, but Thain shook his head.

"Don't, Thainna! It won't help me. Do the things that *will* help."

Thainna stopped and dropped her outreaching hands. "I'll take care of this. I'll have you back home soon, I promise!"

Her twin smiled bravely as he was led away. The door slammed shut behind him. Thainna pressed her cheek against it, listening, but heard nothing on the other side. She closed her eyes and fought back stinging tears.

"I assume that you'll redouble your efforts to win over Captain Mazrem to the House's cause," said Narissa archly.

"The Crest's cause!" answered Thainna angrily, turning away from the door. "Hae, you've delivered your bloody reminder."

"Good. Do you need anything to further your work?"

"No, you've sent me enough drams to kill a horse," Thainna spat, then considered. "None of the jars were labeled. I recognized the ophellion and cardak, but I have no idea about the rest."

Narissa gave her a look of mild surprise.

"You don't know them?" she asked.

"I said I don't deal in drams."

The Eye made a small, dismissive gesture. "I also sent you substantial quantities of jession, illak and bluoring."

Thainna knew most of those names, but the last was a mystery. "What's bluering?"

"It's an expensive substance. I'm not surprised you haven't heard of it."

"You just acted surprised a minute ago," Thainna pointed out.

Narissa ignored her. "It's a stimulant and a rather potent one."

"Doesn't that seem a little counterproductive? Don't you want Rikard dosed into docility?"

"Be sparing in your use of the bluering. Just a little will make him alert but suggestible. The point is to split him and make him willing to do anything for more. Bluering is good for that. It's the white powder in the green-sealed jar. It will dissolve in almost any drink, but even a little has a strongly sweet flavor. Make sure it will go unnoticed. You know how to use the others?"

"Hae, I think so."

Narissa opened the cell door and led her into the hall outside. "Work swiftly and deftly, Thainna. Your brother's safety depends upon good results," she said, and then vanished down a darkened hallway.

Thainna wasted no time bolting through the temple and out into the sterile silver starlight. She ran down the street until she was out of sight of Surma's temple. Hiding behind a small curved-roof shrine to Suzukarri, Thainna slumped against the wall and hugged her arms around herself, choking on furious tears.

It didn't matter what drams Narissa gave her, how low Thainna wore her tabba, what secret she might be able to uncover about Rikard Mazrem. It would never, ever work. The man was proud and upright, otherworldly and erratic. Rikard needed only reach into her mind to find the truth. Against the man who had single-handedly destroyed an entire nation of her ancestors, Thainna had only her fear for protection.

At least I have plenty of that.

Aelos Vahn stared at the open ledger without seeing it. The light of a single candle made the numbers on the page jump and crawl like fleas. He leafed back to his daughter's column. The work of her young life counted out on a single page – her bid for the Auction, to put her twin on the throne of the House of Five Dragons.

To fix everything.

It was less than a man in the Everstones carried in his wallet. Aelos traced his finger down the line of numbers. So few. What did Thainna think she was going to accomplish? The young always believed that they could change the world, but enough time always turned the young into the old, just like him.

27

AUTUMN DANCE

"The greatest man in history has been returned to Carce and his family keeps him locked away. I call upon Emperor Tychon and the Lyceum to let us see Captain Mazrem. Let him see us. Let us show him our gratitude and remind him what he sacrificed so much for."

— AVILLA SALLUSI

RIKARD WAS STARING into the mirror in consternation when he felt Thainna's familiar presence nearby. She prickled with fear and fury, but that wasn't unusual for the girl. He smiled into the mirror at her and then put the razor to his cheek again.

"What are you doing?" Thainna asked.

She carried a steaming cup of tea in her hands, but didn't seem to be drinking it.

"Shaving," Rikard answered shortly. It was too hard to speak while holding his face tautly rigid as the task demanded.

Thainna put the tea down on the table beside him. She pulled over a chair and sat down gratefully. The foster looked tired. Rikard put down the razor again, too distracted to try again just yet.

"I brought you something to drink," Thainna said. "It… it will help you heal more quickly. I went to your bedroom first, but Lady Mazrem said you had gone. What are you doing here?"

Here was one of Laurael's frilly dressing rooms. Thainna was faintly unsettled at seeing a renowned warrior in such soft floral surroundings. Rikard smirked at the sentiment. Even a soldier could not be in the field every day of his life and he was glad to be home. In fact, he liked being surrounded by reminders of his wife.

"I told the dressers to stop shaving me. I can do this myself," Rikard explained. "But Laura said she couldn't bear to watch me slice up my face, so I came here."

Thainna picked up the razor and raised an eyebrow at Rikard's still-whiskery face. "How long have you been at it?"

"Only about a smaller singing… an hour?"

"An hour?"

Rikard held out his hand for the razor. Thainna handed it back and he turned it over carefully, frowning at the blade. "Hae. I don't remember very well and I don't want to return to Laura with cuts all along my cheeks like a Jumaari gladiator. Can you show me?"

"Show you? I don't shave!" exclaimed Thainna, blushing red as an apple.

"Your father, Aelos. You've seen him shave, hae?" Rikard asked. She nodded. "Can you remember it for me?"

The half-Fiori girl squirmed in her chair, but did as she was asked. Rikard reached and found the memory in the forefront of her mind.

A thin, whiskery Carceman crouched down in front of a filthy shard of mirror propped against the wall of a narrow alleyway. He scraped a crooked knife up his cheek and swore dispiritedly at the poor results. The man was aged well beyond his years. His clothes, his skin, his hair were all filthy. Everything was dirty, broken.

Rikard withdrew and stared at Thainna.

"That… that's your father? That's your home?" he asked, aghast.

Thainna blinked at him and then screwed up her pale face in an expression of sudden shame. "You wanted a memory. Isn't it good enough?"

"Hae, it helps. But–" Rikard said, but stopped when Thainna turned away. "That place, the Rows... That's where you live?"

"What does it matter where I come from?" Thainna asked with sudden and surprising fire. She scowled at Rikard. "I'm here and haven't I helped you? Haven't I been a good foster?"

"Hae," he replied haltingly.

Why was she so upset...? Priests came from all manner of backgrounds, many of them poor. So did soldiers, Rikard thought. The Mazrem name was an old one, but not a wealthy one.

At least, it didn't used to be.

Rikard did not understand and was tempted to reach into her mind again for answers – surely the ones he wanted were in the front of Thainna's mind – but it would only upset the pale-faced girl even more. Rikard found himself reluctant to do so, even to satisfy his own curiosity. Thainna was right. She had been a good foster and a great deal of help. He put a hand on her shoulder.

"I'm sorry," Rikard said.

Thainna looked up at him through her hair. Her green eyes were rimmed in red and looked uncomfortably swollen. He was struck again by how weary Thainna seemed to be.

"It doesn't matter," Rikard said. "I'm glad you're here."

She choked on a sob that turned into a laugh. "And that you didn't kill me?"

"Hae."

Rikard suddenly wondered what Thainna had been doing in the Rows that first night, dressed in dirty rags and sneaking through the darkness. Visiting her father, the despondent loafer in her memories? There certainly seemed to be little love between father and daughter. Perhaps seeing her twin brother? But no, Thainna said that he was sickly and remained in the fostral for care.

Rikard returned to the mirror and lathered his cheeks with a thicker foam of soap than Aelos had been able to achieve. Carefully scraping the edge of the razor along his cheek, Rikard was satisfied with the slightly stripped, raw sensation against his skin. Thainna watched him complete the task and then nodded.

"Well, you didn't slit your throat," she said. "If you'll just open your saela, I can look over your stitches and send you back to your wife. Who are you seeing today?"

"I'm not sure. Last night, I told Laura that I want to see Tychon. Bastil is sending word."

Rikard unbuttoned his saela. The skin over his ribs felt tight, but otherwise fine. Thainna checked the stitches, then rubbed in a new layer of salve. When she was done and resealing the medicine canister, there was a knock at the door. Before either could answer, Gaius came inside and dropped into the chair Thainna had just vacated.

"Morning, Father. Well slept? Bastil's gone up to the palace to ask after some of Castum's time. In the meantime, there's a whole throng of others waiting to see you... What in the name of the gods are you doing? Are you shaving?"

"Hae. I finished," Rikard announced proudly.

It wasn't much of an accomplishment by most Terran standards, he knew. Rikard laughed suddenly at the childishness of it all, startling Gaius.

"Don't you know it's dangerous to shave yourself, Father?" his son asked. "You could slit your throat."

"Your mother said the same thing."

Gaius grunted.

"You can close your saela now, Lord Mazrem," Thainna told him. "Don't forget to drink your tea."

Thainna bowed to the two men and excused herself to get some breakfast. Gaius watched the slender foster leave with a grin on his face that made Rikard uncomfortable. When Thainna was out of sight, Rikard picked up the tea she had brought. It smelled sweet, sugared. He sniffed the dark liquid and wrinkled his nose. He put the tea down. Was that how medicine was supposed to smell?

"That foster's gaining a little meat. It suits her." Gaius sniffed the teacup, too, and his brows shot up. "*This* is what she wants you to drink? She's got better taste than I thought. Do you mind?"

"Not at all," Rikard said. "I don't want it."

In the mornings that they had spent together, Gaius showed absolutely no interest in tea, but Rikard supposed that it was better than beginning the day with wine. His son brandished the cup in a mock salute and drank it down.

It was several more days of gradually lengthening audiences before Bastil's visits to the imperial palace brought back a response. After a boring speech of thanksgiving from another Lyceum consul, Rikard and Laurael took their lunch outside, among white and lavender lilies. A black-armored Star Court imperial guard followed Bastil into the garden where his lord and lady sat, quietly enjoying the amber afternoon sun.

"Emperor Tychon would be pleased if you would join him for a performance in the imperial palace tomorrow evening," Bastil informed them, suitably seriously. His pride was a quiet thing, private and personal. Nothing like General Castor's brittle armor of ego, Rikard thought.

"Please tell the emperor that it would be our honor," Laurael said.

She kept her pretty smile in place long enough to wave Bastil off and send the knight back to the palace. The imperial guard saluted and bowed before departing. When he was gone, Laurael twisted a cream-colored lily off its stem. She turned it over and balanced it on her palm.

"A week before any response! Tychon is stalling," Laurael said. She flicked the lily away into the garden. "But even he couldn't wait forever. He must deal with us. I'll need a new tabba."

Laurael's garden inspiration was difficult to communicate to the tailors, but the next evening, Rikard thought his wife looked lovely. A little overwrought, but lovely. The new tabba was layered in sheer white, gold and cream, sparkling with tiny crystal beads and sashed in an elaborately cross-tied length of gossamer in verdant green. The dressers straightened Laurael's hair with a pair of hot, flat iron plates and oiled it until it gleamed.

As beautiful as she looked, Rikard was privately glad that his VEIL saela was appropriate dress. It wasn't very comfortable, but it looked more so than Laurael's tight-cinched tabba and certainly took less time to prepare.

That wasn't to say that the dressers failed to fuss over Rikard as well. They inspected and brushed clean every inch of his new saela, combed his hair and even buffed his nails with a piece of wool. Thainna checked his healing injuries and assured Laurael that her husband would not bleed through his nice clothes. The foster bowed and reminded Rikard that she would look in on him when he returned later that night.

The early autumn twilight was a rich violet color, speckled with shining stars like the beads on Laurael's dress. Gaius met them outside the main house, already pulling himself into one of a pair of waiting chariots. A hostler tightened the kajja's bridle and then handed the reins to Rikard. Quilted red padding lined the chariot, like a jewelry case, to protect the expensive, valuable things inside. Rikard helped Laurael up into the chariot beside him and held the reins uncertainly.

"Do you remember how to drive?" Gaius asked. He flicked his reins expertly and the kajja trilled, scraping its claws impatiently on the paving stones.

"Hae... I think so," Rikard replied reluctantly.

Not that he had much occasion to drive, even before the war in distant Fiore. Like all knights, he learned the basics, but little more. The rocky, icy mountains were difficult to ride across, much less traverse by chariot. Rikard gave the reins a small, experimental tug. Even when his driving lessons were fresh and new, they had been with horses, not these huge, sunset-hued birds.

"What say you to a little race then?" suggested Gaius. "A little friendly competition?"

"A race...?"

Rikard had no chance to ask for details. His son snapped his reins once and whistled. His kajja lunged and leapt into a low, smooth run. Gaius raced down the drive, hurtling toward the front gates. The guards shouted, clambering and barely managed to yank them open in time. Gaius called back to his parents, but the distance between them swallowed his words.

Rikard tried mimicking Gaius' commands as best he could, but the kajja only looked over its copper-colored shoulder at Rikard and clacked a long, hooked beak at him. Quickly bored, the bird began preening its bright feathers. Beside Rikard, Laurael sighed. He shook the reins again and clicked his tongue, but still the kajja would not move.

Gaius was already out of sight down the road. Since the usual Terran methods were as useless as ashes in his hands, Rikard reached into the kajja's simple mind, playing his own desire over the bird's, like plucking the strings of a harp.

Go, run there... Fly? he added as a questioning afterthought.

Rikard wasn't sure if the tall, lanky bird could take to the air, even when not tethered to a heavy chariot. He didn't know the route to the imperial palace, not through the unfamiliar streets of the new Dormaen, but he felt along the kajja's nerves and found a sharp sense of smell. Smoky-bright and sharp-sour city smells, but the brother-scent was still young and thick. The kajja smelled her sibling, the one that pulled Gaius' chariot.

Follow him, Rikard instructed.

The kajja sniffed the air, hissing softly. She caught a scent strong enough to track, trilled triumphantly and leapt into motion, jerking the chariot behind so abruptly that Laurael cried out in surprise and grabbed onto Rikard's arm. Even through the sleeve of his saela, her nails bit into his skin.

They raced out through the open gate. Gawkers outside cheered as they thundered past. The smell of the other kajja drifted this way and that on the restless air. Following it, the chariot wove an erratic path through Dormaen, bumping down into the gutters and then jumping out again. Every pop and shudder made Laurael shriek and cling tightly to her husband.

The road was full of people, many with thoughts of Gaius' recent passage still resentful in their minds. Some of them filtered cautiously back into the road, numerous enough that Rikard had to yank back on the reins several times and think jerky *stop* commands to his kajja. He swerved around another chariot, close enough that he could have reached out and touched the driver's tabba. The other man swore until he recognized Rikard and his grumble rose to a cry.

"It's Captain Mazrem! Rikard Mazrem!"

The crowd took up the chant all along the street, shouting his name and raising their fists into the air. Just as at the Moon Court archouse, their jubilation made Rikard feel light-headed, as though he floated through whipping clouds. Hot and heady, not unlike the rush of battle. Spurred by her driver's burst of borrowed enthusiasm, the kajja sprinted through the close crowd.

Rikard rounded a corner so fast that the chariot tipped up onto one wheel and Gaius came into view just ahead, but so did the great white domes and spires of the imperial palace. The gates – taller and broader than those of the Mazrem estate and gilded even more brightly than the kajja's plumage – stood open and flanked by rows of VEIL knights in armor of black leather and shining steel.

Rikard urged his kajja onward and raced through the gates just seconds behind his son. Gaius grinned broadly when Rikard pulled to a stop beside him.

"You won a war but you can't win a simple chariot race? I think the empire's in trouble!" Gaius said with a wink.

Rikard had no answer to that and covered his embarrassment by helping Laurael down from the chariot. She avoided his gaze and went to Gaius. She patted her son's shoulder and congratulated him on his victory.

Rikard used the moment alone to inspect the palace, the first place other than his own home he had seen in weeks. When last he had seen it thirty years ago, the royal palace of Carce was a lovely, sprawling house of red and blue, surrounded by well-trimmed box-wood hedges. But like the rocky Everstones, the palace had grown like a single flower left to seed for three decades until it filled the entire garden. This citadel was not just the center of a single small kingdom, but the axis of a vast empire that spanned all of Terra.

Delicately tapered towers lined a long courtyard ten times the width of the street outside. The air was full of the gentle sound of fountains carved in the graceful shapes of leaping carp and crouching lions with crystal claws. In the midst of it all rose the tallest building Rikard had ever seen in the Terran world. He thought at once of the Uprising, of the great white tree that dominated the eastern sky of Alterra. Tychon's imperial seat was almost a city unto itself, a mountain of marble and quartz and alabaster touched here and there with brighter green and gold. A vast dome capped the palace, gilded and shining like the rising sun. Depictions of men and animals fought and frolicked in carved friezes, all far larger and lovelier than their real-world counterparts.

Rikard would have liked to inspect those carvings more closely, but a steward – probably one of many in a place so immense – cleared his throat. He waited a polite distance away, wrapped in a long formal tabba pinned at one shoulder with the imperial lion and laurel crest. He wore the same expression of gravity that Rikard had grown used to seeing on Bastil. The royal steward bowed deeply to Rikard.

"Lords and Lady Mazrem, his Imperial Majesty bids you a warm welcome. If you'll follow me, I'll escort you to the stage."

"Stage?" Rikard asked curiously.

A drama? He had never seen one before. Rikard offered Laurael his arm and she took it, still pointedly not looking at her husband. Her smoothly oiled hair was disheveled.

"Hae, Lord Mazrem," said the steward. "Emperor Tychon has arranged a performance of dancers for your entertainment."

Rikard had never seen one of those, either. He had danced with Laurael at their wedding, of course, but professionals were something else entirely. Or so Rikard assumed. He pulled Laurael along excitedly as the steward escorted them across the courtyard and into the palace.

The halls were paneled in exotic hardwoods and wide enough that Rikard could have driven his chariot inside while still leaving enough room for the steward to walk beside him. Great polished columns lined the distant walls like the trees of some impossible forest. Jasper capitals beautifully carved in the likeness of laurel leaves only heightened the illusion. Rikard stared.

"You were not half so impressed at home," Laurael reprimanded him under her breath.

"It's not half so impressive!"

Laurael scowled at Rikard.

They arrived at a wide, semi-circular room with a floor angled down like the slope of a hill and set with rows of white-cushioned seats. Most of these were already filled by people in long formal tabbae. Another man in imperial dress whispered with their guide for a moment and then raised his voice.

"Lord-Captain Rikard Mazrem, his lady wife and his son," he announced.

The attendant nobility stood together, all applauding. A few of the younger Carcaens cheered and whistled, but were shushed by their older and more gracious companions. The steward caught Rikard's attention.

"His Imperial Majesty has arranged seating for you and your family up front."

"Where is Tychon?" Rikard asked him.

"There is the emperor's seat." The other man pointed to a small balcony on the far wall of the theater, hung with velvet bunting in red and gold. A gilded throne sat empty on the balcony.

After all of the fighting to get Rikard into the imperial palace, Tychon wasn't even there. Rikard looked up into the royal box seats. Perhaps not so much had changed since he left Carce thirty years ago. Emperor Tychon still lived apart from his people. Above them, like a god.

Rikard allowed himself to be guided down the stairs to a trio of empty seats. Aside from Tychon's throne, they were the only ones in the entire theater. Laurael seated herself gracefully between her son and husband. On Rikard's right, a Carcaen woman in a filmy tabba of sunset-orange smiled at him.

"Welcome home, Captain Mazrem. I'm so glad you could join us," she said. The woman extended her hand, an awkward gesture when she was seated next to him. "I'm Cerris Ael. My brother was one of the knights who made it home because of you. Harlaen. Do you remember him?"

Rikard didn't, but Cerris did. She wore the memory as boldly as her revealing tabba and he almost had no other choice but to look. Her brother was gone, but she remembered him so clearly. Sir Harlaen Ael, a round-faced man with an infectious smile.

"Hae, I remember him now," Rikard said.

Cerris' red-lipped smile widened.

"He spoke of you every day for the rest of his life. Even when he died, he thanked the gods for you, Captain Mazrem, for returning him home to Dormaen instead of dying up there in the Fiore snow. Ah, speaking of Fiore!"

Unseen servants had shortened the lantern wicks, sinking the theater into deep shadows. Rikard followed Cerris' gaze to the stage. A pair of young women stepped from the curtained recesses that flanked the stage, one from each side. They were Fiori, with the same slender build and flaming red hair as Thainna. Rikard stared and felt a hot flush creep into his cheeks. The two women wore only their own luminously pale skin.

The dancers came together in a pair of svelte, graceful strides. Despite their nudity and beauty, there was nothing sexual about their performance. One woman darted her hands at the other, with fingers oddly curled, as though she should have held something. Her partner flipped away acrobatically and then circled back in a series of leaping twists that flared her fiery hair like the petals of an exotic flower. The first dancer kicked high, stepped to the side and snaked behind her partner.

Their dance was all too familiar. Though they were smoothed and rehearsed, Rikard recognized those movements – the sinuously graceful leaps and twirls. Small steps, high up on the toes like a prowling cat, made for moving across the icy, craggy ground of the snow-bound Fiore mountains. Thousands of soldiers and knights had died locked in that beautiful, terrible dance.

It was lovely to watch, but eerie, like finding Thainna that first night in the Rows. Wrong somehow. Martial skill that should have been deadly dangerous reduced to a mere show, performing like chained bears. Rikard shifted in discomfort that had nothing to do with the soft seat beneath him or even the proximity of the sensual Cerris Ael. The Fiori were his enemies, so why should it bother him? He had no answer, but couldn't shake the feeling.

All around him, the other nobles shared none of Rikard's unease. They watched the Fiori women's fighting dance with the fascinated disdain of an owner observing a pet.

By the time they completed their dance, the Fiori shone under the dimmed light with sweat and were panting hard. Their audience applauded appreciatively. The two women bowed and then retreated from the stage. Rikard sat quietly, thinking, until Laurael repeated his name a third time and finally roused his attention.

"Hae?" he asked.

"Emperor Tychon's sent for us."

Laurael gestured to a woman who waited beside the stage, a few feet away. She wore the imperial crest, just like the steward and herald. Rikard nodded and stood. Overhead, the balcony remained empty.

"I so very much hope to see you here again, Captain Mazrem," Cerris said. She offered her hand again. Rikard took it briefly and then turned back to his family.

"Harlot," Laurael grumbled under her breath.

Gaius chuckled and winked. "Never fear, Mother. Cerris can't afford the care you have. She'll be a baggy old crone in a few years."

"Why don't you like her?" Rikard asked, surprised. Cerris had seemed kind and sincerely grateful.

Laurael declined to answer that, which only made Gaius laugh again. He put his mother's hand on his arm.

"Come along, Mother," he said. "Tychon wants to see us."

Gaius sobered at the icy look Laurael shot him. She gave the lingering servant a brittle smile.

"Thank you for waiting," she told him. "Please take us to the emperor."

Other guests tried to stop Rikard as they left the theater. Even as Laurael greeted each by name, their escort gently but firmly informed them that Emperor Tychon was waiting. Outside, she led Rikard and his family through a manicured miniature orchard and then into a labyrinth of more gigantean halls. After what seemed a full day's march, they finally arrived at a library. Warm firelight flickered through open doors.

"His Imperial Majesty is inside. I will be waiting here when he's done with you."

The guide's words sounded slightly ominous to Rikard, but he felt no fear or malice from her. Laurael and Gaius certainly didn't seem to think anything of it, so he followed them inside.

The library was vast, every wall lined with shelves that rose so high that the upper reaches were lost in shadows. Rikard had never seen so many books. Titles glittered in gold leaf on the leather-bound spines, dancing in the firelight like the Fiori girls in the theater. *Accounts of Njorn Pass, The Still Wind, Maiden's Song, Our Red History, Poetry of the Po'Mar Lowlands, Beyond the Veil*, Rikard read. There were thousands of others – perhaps tens of thousands – many marked in languages he could not read.

In the library's center sat Emperor Castum Tychon. He looked... old. Tychon's once-black hair lay now like white mist settled against his brow. Fifty-nine years of life had carved deep lines into his face.

Almost sixty. A lifetime. Sixty years. Anything more is just greedy. The thought echoed as though across a great distance.

Tychon's taste hadn't changed much, however. The emperor's evening tabba was of a loose, comfortable cut that nevertheless glittered with threads of woven gold. Rings adorned his fingers and his wrists were hung with a dozen thin silver bangles. Even his ears were pierced and studded with gems.

Tychon closed the book he had been reading and laid it aside, stood and embraced Gaius. He kissed Laurael's cheek and nodded gravely to Rikard.

"Captain Mazrem, Carce's greatest son," said the emperor. "We are so pleased to have you home once more."

"Thank you. It's good to be home, though it has changed a great deal since I left," Rikard answered carefully. He was pleased when the correct words came to him.

Tychon smiled and invited them to sit. "What did you think of the dancers? I thought you might particularly appreciate them."

"I have never seen anything like it," answered Rikard. "They've turned battle into dance. It is... very strange. Why didn't you come to watch?"

"I've seen enough Fiori war-dances to last a very long lifetime," Tychon told him with a dismissive wave of his bejeweled hand. "I outlawed the Fiori battle arts. They taught their women to fight, you know. Barbaric!"

Rikard touched Laurael's powdered cheek. He couldn't imagine sending his wife into war.

"But you let them... dance?" he asked.

"They think they're quite clever, turning their martial art into dance," Tychon said. "I permit the Fiori their little deception. Such small rebellions keep them from a greater one. And their girls are quite lovely, it must be said. How are you, Rikard?"

The emperor's casual familiarity seemed terribly out of place, so different from Rikard's dim memories of the fervent young king who sent thousands of VEIL knights and soldiers to die in Fiore. Had time changed him so much?

"It's good to be home, as I said," Rikard replied. "Terra has become very different in thirty years."

"Years spent fighting in an Alterran civil war, I've been told. How terrible. And over us? Tell me, Rikard, what's that all about?"

More smoothly than he had with Saul, Rikard explained the Alterran war to his emperor: the battles waged over the fate of worlds, the Shatter's desire to turn away from Terra, to sever all ties between the worlds and their people... those few fragile bonds which still remained. A world torn between stability and tumultuous change in which Rikard had served as a warrior of chaos. Much like Alexander Ferro, Emperor Tychon seemed interested in only one particular point.

"After the great expenditure of power to bring you through to Alterra, they sent you back early, with their war not yet won?" he asked. "That seems odd."

"Hae, Majesty. I don't know why. I... I think I was told. It might even have been my idea. But passage through the veil is difficult and there are things I still don't remember."

"Have you asked?"

Rikard shook his head. "I have as... as best I can, but found only silence. If Flickerdim hears me, then he is not answering."

"An Alterran ignoring you in a time of need? I'm not surprised. They will come to you when *they* wish."

"If Flickerdim is still alive but silent, then I believe it is for a reason. He is an old and great wisdom."

"Your faith is commendable, I suppose. Do you think that you'll remember what they wanted?" Emperor Tychon sounded curious, but not terribly concerned. "Well, little good ever came from discussion with the dream-eaters. Perhaps it's for the best."

Rikard leaned forward and rubbed at his eyes until his vision swam with spots of exploding color. He wanted to remember. He *needed* to. It was important, vitally important...! But no one else seemed to think so. Why couldn't he remember? Why didn't Flickerdim tell him?

"There's a foster working with my father. I'm sure she'll help, if she can," Gaius supplied when it became obvious that Rikard had no answer to give the emperor. "A Fiori girl, of all things."

"Half-Fiori," Rikard corrected automatically. He opened his eyes and looked at Tychon. The spots had not faded and the emperor floated in a haze of red and green. "Don't you worry, Majesty? All of Alterra is at war!"

"I am emperor of Terra, Captain Mazrem. *This* is my world," Tychon said. He lounged back in his chair and waved his hands, taking in the library, the palace and the entire world beyond. "Let the Alterra make whatever war they like. I will shed no tears."

"But they're our allies!"

Rikard's voice was rising and Laurael placed her hand against his arm.

"Please, my lord," she said gently. "We are guests of the emperor and his loyal subjects."

Rikard jerked away. "Laura, no! Why isn't anyone else concerned? You're all so busy celebrating me that you don't even see the war burning just beyond the veil! It's been waged for thirty years. Why does no one know about it? They fight at the Uprising over us, *for* us. Surely even that tears sky for you, Tychon! If the flatlands bloom and sunder the spire, the walls break..."

Rikard trailed off. The other three stared at him and shook their heads as though at the inevitable stumbling of a clumsy child. He wasn't making sense anymore and even if he did, they weren't listening. The Alterran war was unimportant, far away.

"You barely cared about a war in your own world!" he snarled at Emperor Tychon. "It was naïve to think you might give a single drop of blood about theirs!"

Rikard started to rise, to storm out of the library, but Laurael's fingers wound around his wrist like tree roots through stone. He had embarrassed her, Rikard realized, and felt a sharp, heartsick stab of shame. Gaius watched the whole thing with a slightly surprised smile, as though it were all some amusing play. Like he was watching the Fiori dancers.

Tychon didn't look at Rikard for a long moment. He twisted a ring adorned with a huge ruby around his middle finger. The air hung heavy with anticipation. Tychon looked... tired. Not angry or hurt by Rikard's words, simply wearied by them.

He just wants us to leave so he can go to bed, go to sleep.

Rikard looked down at the book on the table beside Emperor Tychon. The cover was emblazoned with a nude woman kneeling in the petals of a lotus.

Well, perhaps not to sleep yet, but certainly to bed.

"We are promoting you to legens." Tychon still didn't look at Rikard. "We could do no less for the hero of Carce, but we remind you that the war is over, Legens Mazrem. Terra is at peace and we intend to keep it that way. We have spent enough of our lifetime fighting, legens, and so have you. It's time to enjoy the fruits of our youthful labors, hae?"

"Hae," Rikard agreed through gritted teeth.

"We understand that you're still suffering Fiori injuries, Legens Mazrem. VEIL has survived thirty years without you and a century without any legens. Take your time in recovery. Your men will be there when you're ready."

Fatter and lazier with each passing day, the emperor thought, as thick and sour with contempt as curdled milk. *Do with them what you will. Carce has no more need for knights or Alterra. Just leave us alone. Leave us in peace, hero.*

"We fought for you," Rikard said. "We died for you, for Carce! We bled and sacrificed for the empire that you built!"

Rikard wanted to scream and cry, like the child they thought him. It wasn't fair! Laurael told him to forgive Emperor Tychon, to be thankful for the good done and forget the rest. How could he? Tychon cared nothing for the men who had given so much for the empire or for the Alterra who shared their twin existence, who died alone and forgotten beyond the veil. All the old man wanted was peace and quiet to enjoy his rich, lavish life.

Rikard rose and bowed. "I... Thank you, Majesty."

Every word burned. When they were done, Rikard turned on his heels and stalked out of the library. He could hear Laurael behind him, speaking softly to the emperor.

"He's still a little fragile, but he's recovering."

"*That's* the man you left to hold in memory?" hissed Tychon, also quietly.

"Enough, Castum," Laurael said. "Rikard is as important to you as he is to me. Give him peace and he'll give you the same. He's a simple man."

"A simple man that you've just made legens," interjected Gaius, speaking up for the first time.

"Go find your father, Gaius. Castum and I can handle this. I'll see you in the orchard."

"Mother–"

"Go make sure the new legens doesn't lock himself in a closet or something," said Tychon.

Rikard hadn't meant to eavesdrop and vaguely remembered that he should feel guilty for it, but they were talking about *him*. He was too angry to make himself care much about social niceties. He retreated down the nearest hallway and found the woman who had escorted him to the library. She bowed and greeted him, cool and professional. Rikard said nothing in reply. He leaned against one of the tree-trunk columns and waited.

Gaius found him only moments later. Rikard did not look up at his son's approach. He didn't need to see his son's face to sense the anger and displeasure that mirrored his own.

"There you are, Father. Mother will be along in a little while to collect us like so many parcels. We're to wait for her in the orchard."

"Hae, I know," Rikard grumbled.

Gaius was quiet for a moment. "You heard, then?"

Rikard pushed himself upright.

"Which way is the orchard?" he asked the waiting servant.

"I know the way," Gaius said and flicked a finger at the woman. "Go find us something to drink, sweetheart."

Gaius and Rikard walked together in sullen silence out to the small orchard. It was getting late and the starlight transformed the first autumn apples into great silver-black pearls. Gaius plucked one down from a sculpted branch and took a crunching bite.

"You're not pleased," he said. "Don't you like your promotion, Father?"

"You don't like it."

Gaius bit into the apple again and then he dropped it to the ground, only half eaten. It thumped into the neatly cropped grass at their feet.

"Ever since I made captain, Mother's had me turn down every single promotion," said Gaius. "You've been back a couple weeks and she's happy enough to let you jump right up to legens."

"I don't want to be legens," Rikard argued.

"You didn't protest."

"I didn't want to embarrass Laura any more than... than I already did."

Gaius quirked a smile. He didn't really believe Rikard, but he shrugged. "You still don't care much for Tychon, do you? I'd not say it here, though. We're up to our asses in political muck."

"I don't understand. I never understood politics." Rikard hated the petulant tone of his own voice.

"Tychon waited a week before inviting us here, to a theater full of Dormaen's aristocracy," Gaius explained. *He* understood. "The emperor never came himself. He's showing you – and everyone else – who still calls the plays."

"But he made me legens."

"Tychon isn't stupid, Father. He wants to put you in your place – which *is* below him – but he doesn't want to make an enemy of you, either. If he takes something away with one hand, he has to give something else with the other."

The imperial servant returned then, bearing cups of cold wine. She offered them to the two VEIL knights and then retreated to wait for other orders. Or to listen to them, perhaps. Gaius worked on another apple and guzzled his wine in a few long gulps. He and Rikard waited together in silence for the better part of an hour before Laurael came to collect them.

After a much slower and quieter ride home, Gaius made curt goodnights to his parents, then left to find his own bed. As they wound slowly up the graveled path, Rikard put his arm around Laurael. She was cool and stiff at his touch, like a statue only grudgingly given life.

"What did you talk to Castum about?" Rikard asked.

"Only you, my lord. Details concerning your return to VEIL," Laurael replied. "After your outburst tonight, Emperor Tychon worries for your health. He hopes you're well enough to rejoin your knights soon."

"But he doesn't question my ability?"

"No. Of course not, my lord. You're the greatest hero ever born to Carce. Who better to lead VEIL?"

"If Tychon doesn't like the things I say, thinks that I'm unfit or unwell, he should keep me away from VEIL," Rikard said. "I could be dangerous to him and to the empire. Unless he thinks I can't do any harm there."

Laurael pulled him to a stop and turned to face Rikard. "Even if Castum Tychon is foolish enough to think that, he's wrong. You are an important man. You can still do a great deal of damage."

Rikard kissed her hands and then her lips. "Thank you, Laura."

28

REACH

"Not all beginnings are written on the first page."

—OUR RED HISTORY, BY AVILLA SALLUSI

RIKARD'S late return meant that Thainna didn't find her own bed until even later. When she finally fell down into the increasingly familiar softness of her bed and pulled the blankets tightly around her, Thainna didn't sleep well. Her dreams were full of unsettling images of Thain, crying and rattling in jade chains.

Thainna woke abruptly, but the clattering noise didn't stop. She sat up, rubbing her eyes. The light coming in through the window was still dim and the pink color of the shiny interior of a seashell. It was far too early. What had woken her?

There was someone else in Thainna's room. Sleep blurred her vision and it was little more than a thin shadow, but it held something cradled to its chest and was dashing away toward the door.

Was she being robbed? Here, in the Mazrem house? It seemed impossible, but Thainna recognized the furtive escape as one she had made too many times.

She kicked her blankets off hard enough to fling them across the tiny room and onto the thief. The flimsy barrier didn't stop the man – Thainna could see now that it *was* a man – but it slowed him just enough. Thainna leapt from her bed and tackled him to the floor, smashing her temple against the doorframe in the process. Thainna saw stars but felt skin under her fingers. When she tightened her grip, hard enough to turn her knuckles white, she heard a low moan of pain. The intruder stilled.

"Stop, please! Please," he croaked.

"Give it back!" Thainna cried. She shook the blanket-covered man.

A knob-knuckled hand emerged from under the cloth, holding the jar of expensive bluering. Thainna snatched it back and replaced the jar beside her bed. One of the others, the cardak, lay broken and its dark contents scattered across the floor. That must have been the noise that woke her up.

Thainna had not released the thief. She shook him again.

"How did you get in here?" she asked. "What the bloody hell do you want that for?"

The man wriggled free of the blanket, though not her grip. He was a middle-aged Carcaen with a narrow, drawn face and thinning brown hair.

"Caelin?" Thainna gasped, startled. "What–?"

There was a loud banging at the door. She released the other Talon.

"Thainna?"

She recognized Bastil's voice outside.

"Thainna?" the steward called through the door. "Is everything alright? I heard something breaking!"

"Fine! All fine," Thainna shouted back.

Caelin probably left the door open, giving himself an easy route of escape, but it had been kicked or shoved shut at some point during their struggles. There was a pause outside.

"If all is well, tell me what I called you when you first arrived here," Bastil said.

What *had* he called her? Thainna thought, grasping at the memory that felt like a lifetime ago. The last thing she needed was the house steward bursting in and demanding explanations...

"Thinny!" she cried. "You called me *Thinny*. I'm alright, Bastil. Everything is fine."

Both Talons held their breath and listened until Bastil's footsteps faded into the distance. When they were alone again, Thainna swatted Caelin's bony shoulder.

"What are you doing here, you bloody old badger? You're supposed to be working Gaius, aren't you?"

Caelin squeezed his eyes closed and Thainna worried for a moment that he might cry. His face was red, but it seemed he had wept his last tears. His eyes remained dry.

"Hae, I'm supposed to be, but that man's appetites are bottomless," said Caelin. "Lord Gaius told me to get him some more bluering."

"More? I heard you were supposed to get him split on ophellion. When did he have bluering?"

"Lord Gaius said you gave it to him. Didn't you?"

"Me? No, of course not! I'm on Rikard, not Gaius. Bloody hell, I did give Rikard some tea spiked with bluering about a week ago. He never seemed affected, so I didn't bother giving him more... Did Gaius drink it?"

"Hae, must have done. Please, I need more."

Thainna scowled.

"Why do you need it from me?" she asked. "Why don't you get it from the House? Why are you stealing from me instead of talking to the Eyes?"

"I've tried," Caelin said, shaking his head. "I've gone asking, but they won't give me anything. They say the bluering's too expensive.

Your work is more important, hae? I didn't think you'd give up the drams willing, not with such an important job, but I had to... Milla's waiting for me to be done here."

He said it with such despair that Thainna felt ashamed, though the whole thing certainly had not been her idea. The Crest had taken Caelin's wife, just like he had taken Thain. She pulled the jar of bluering down again and handed it to Caelin. He reached out for it hesitantly.

"But what about your job, Thainna?" Caelin asked. "The Crest took someone from you, too."

Thainna pulled the other jars out from under her bed. Even with the loss of both the spilled cardak and bluering, it was an impressive collection of drams. Caelin seemed to agree. He picked up one and, after a permissive nod from Thainna, worked the stopper free. After a sniff of the contents, he whistled softly.

"Jession?" Caelin closed the jar and handed it back to Thainna. "Good stuff, I hear."

"I gave Rikard the bluering, but he didn't seem to give two beans about it. It was the best I have. If you need it for Gaius, take it. Maybe the Crest will call that good enough and let you go home with your wife, hae?"

It seemed that Caelin still had a few tears. He hugged Thainna gratefully and a few dropped onto the shoulder of her tabba, warm and not altogether uncomfortable. The older Talon babbled his thanks and then hurried out the door, eager to continue – and to finish – his work. A moment later, his gaunt face appeared in the door again.

"Good luck in getting your father back home," said Caelin.

"It's my brother, actually," she told him. "But thanks."

Caelin nodded and then vanished once more. Thainna considered trying to get back to sleep, but dreams of being locked away from Thain were no better than the waking reality.

She closed the door behind Caelin and swept away the spilled cardak as best she could with a dirty tabba. Thainna wrapped up the broken pieces of the jar in the cloth and shoved them under her bed, along with everything else she didn't want the other Mazrem servants to find, including the satchel full of small but expensive trinkets she had stolen. Whatever else might happen, she still had the Auction to think about.

Satisfied with the results of her cleaning, Thainna collected a freshly laundered blue tabba from a basket beside the door and headed for the bathhouse. She wanted to stop to get some breakfast from Arliss, but decided grudgingly against it. She wasn't hungry. It still amazed her.

When she arrived at the bathhouse, Thainna was surprised to find she had it to herself. The cooking and grounds staff were already hard at work, but it was still early and the rest of the servants were probably just beginning to stir. Lord and Lady Mazrem would not be awake for hours yet.

Thainna stripped out of her clothes and slid down into the huge tub. The water was warm, but not hot and the languid heat tugged Thainna back toward sleep. She waded over to one of the wide, shallow steps that lined all four sides of the bath and sat. If she fell asleep, she probably wouldn't drown there. Thainna combed soap through her hair and laid back on the step to let the steaming water rinse it away.

It was not completely without fear that she had let Caelin take her bluering. The loss meant one less tool left to somehow get Rikard under her control. But Thainna didn't think the bluering would have worked, anyway, and doubted any of the other drams Narissa had given her would be any better.

Floating in the warm water and her blissful lack of hunger, Thainna despaired. She would never get Rikard addicted to anything. He had weaknesses – plenty of them but drams were not one of them.

Narissa seemed certain that Thainna could seduce Rikard away from his wife. The priestess didn't know Laurael very well, Thainna decided. Despite being more than twice Thainna's age, Lady Mazrem held herself with the graceful air of a natural seductress. Every single thing she did was lovely, beautifully practiced. Besides, it was obvious in Rikard's every look and word that he hopelessly adored his wife.

That left blackmailing Rikard. The very idea made Thainna's heart speed in her breast. She liked Rikard, Thainna supposed, though it was difficult to say. The man was as strange and distant as a mountaintop. Thainna combed through her memories of the past days. Was there *anything* she could give the House of Five Dragons? Only Rikard's confusion, which faded by the day.

Nothing useful. Thainna pressed the heels of her hands against her eyes. She would not cry. There *had* to be something she could do. Something...

When she finally opened her eyes, Bastil stood at the edge of the bathing pool. The stern-faced old Carcaen gestured impatiently as Thainna started, spluttering and splashing. She struggled upright and tapped the water from her ears.

"Get dressed," Bastil said. "Legens Mazrem wants to see you."

"Legens?"

Thainna only vaguely recalled Rikard mentioning his new rank the night before. It had been very late. Was he finally accepting the title? It would make the knight even more powerful – if only in name – and that much more valuable to the Crest.

"What does he want?" Thainna asked.

"My lord didn't say," answered Bastil.

Thainna climbed up out of the bath and squeezed the water from her hair. She wound it into a coil at the nape of her neck and belted on her tabba.

Bastil remained a little longer than was strictly necessary, but Thainna doubted that he was trying to leer at her. He looked as though he wanted to ask about the morning's disturbance, but his good manners – or some other pressing business – won out over his curiosity. The steward left without asking Thainna any questions.

She laced up her sandals and hurried out of the bathhouse. Thainna assumed that the new legens wanted to meet her in the triclinium or maybe his bed chambers, but a maid shushed her at the bedroom door and waved her off. Lady Mazrem was still sleeping, she said, and sent Thainna outside to the east veranda.

Rikard stood on the veranda with his back to the door. He hadn't been awake for long, Thainna guessed. He wore his pants laced around his hips, but the knight's saela lay over the arm of a nearby couch. His long black hair was mussed, not yet combed or tied. He stared out across Dormaen.

The Mazren River was just visible in the distance, blurred by smoke and the general haze of the city into a pewter ribbon across the horizon. The sun was little more than a golden-pink arc of light above the hills to the east of the Kaelos Valley. Most of the city had extinguished the streetlamps, but thousands of shops, streets and homes still glittered with bouncing points of light like dancing stars. A cacophony of voices, squeaking doors, creaking wheels, cracking whips, hooves on the stone roads and roof tiles expanding in the warming morning all blended together into a lively thrum, audible even up on the slopes of the Everstones. Like the humming of a beehive, Thainna thought, so vitally alive. She had been born in Dormaen and suspected that she would die never seeing another city. It was her whole world, but Thainna suddenly realized she had never really considered it beautiful. Under the blushing early autumn sunrise, she had to admit that it was.

"Thainna, come here. Please."

Rikard said it so softly that Thainna wasn't sure that she had heard him correctly at first. She went to Rikard's side and looked up at the tall, hawk-faced knight. His cheeks were shadowed by a day's stubble and his dark eyes looked haunted.

"Do you see the river there?" he asked.

"Hae. That's the Mazren River," Thainna answered.

"My grandfather's grandfather took his name from that river. It used to run through the center of Dormaen, like a vein of quicksilver."

"Pata said that they had to reroute it to the east side of the valley to make room in the city. That's where the Rows are now. The ground there is bad. Half of what anyone's managed to build just falls over inside five years."

Rikard nodded once and continued his contemplation of the city. Thainna tried to think of something to say, something helpful. Something Thain might say. Rikard must have heard her thought. He looked down at the small half-Fiori girl.

"Thainna, you have been the best candle... the best friend I've known since my return."

"You only came back on the calends, Rikard," she reminded him. "You've been here in this house most of that time."

Rikard turned to face her and knelt. Thainna very nearly ran away, half afraid that this was some strange new alien, Alterran response, but managed to hold her ground. Rikard wound his arms around her waist and buried his face against Thainna's stomach, clinging to her like a child. She was sure her eyes went wide enough that they could have dropped right out of her head.

"Something's gone wrong," Rikard said into her stomach.

"What? Rikard, I... I don't read minds like you do," Thainna stammered. "What are you talking about?"

"Tychon's made me legens of VEIL," Rikard told her. "He called it a reward, one befitting my deeds. But he lied."

Rikard clutched at Thainna's tabba so hard that she worried he might rip it. His voice was hoarse with despair.

"He thinks nothing of them, the knights who fought and died in ice for his empire! Not those who fell or those who live. Fat and lazy, those are his thoughts. Bullies and brutes."

Thainna wavered. What should she tell him? Comfort or truth? She remembered Ortho, the knight who had hit her in Mazrem Square. Rikard was on his feet in a heartbeat, still clutching her close, but now face to face.

"Truth, Thainna," he begged in a thick voice. "Please! I choke on the lies."

She bit her lip before answering. For all that he had done to shape the world, for all that he *was*, Rikard knew less about it than those who lived in it now.

"The emperor is right," Thainna told him. "You've been gone for thirty years, Rikard. You don't know what VEIL's become. I don't even know for sure what it used to be. Your war was years before I was even born. All I have are stories and Pata was never very good at telling them. Whatever VEIL was, I don't think it's like that anymore."

"We fought for peace, Thainna," Rikard said. "At first to defend Carce's borders, then for the other nations! We were a state of scholars! How many Carcaens died on Lyncean swords?"

Rikard's fists tightened in her tabba. A week ago, she might have read violence in the gesture, but Thainna surprised herself... She wasn't afraid. Rikard was angry, but not with her.

"And then for unity, hae? Just like Emperor Tychon told you to. Well, it worked. There hasn't been so much as a Nianese squabble since Njorn Pass," she said. "But what do you think VEIL's done in the last thirty years? They're bored. They're both feared and afraid. They're powerful."

"There are still enemies to fight, aren't there?"

"Like who?" Thainna asked. "The House of Five Dragons? Why bother? VEIL is just as dirty."

She snapped her mouth shut, but Rikard furrowed his dark brows deeply.

"The House of Five Dragons?" he asked. "What's that? I... don't know the name."

"It's a syndicate of criminals," Thainna explained quickly, not lingering on the details even in her own thoughts. "The largest in Carce, made up of hundreds of thieves and money-shavers and blackmailers and murderers. Maybe thousands. They have... they have great power in Dormaen, Rikard. The House has people everywhere. The Rows, the temples, the markets and the colleges and laweries, here in the Everstones. Probably in the Lyceum and imperial palace, too. And surely in VEIL."

"And VEIL allows them to remain?" asked Rikard.

"VEIL doesn't care," Thainna answered. "Why should they? The House of Five Dragons is rich and controls so much. Better to be their allies than enemies. Any House spy in VEIL is just bringing in two paydays! It's to their profit."

Rikard shook his head. "Someone *must* protest. What could a knight of VEIL have to fear from this... this House of Five Dragons? Even the roughest iron... street tough can raise nothing against a VEIL knight with the Alterra by his side!"

Before she could stop herself, Thainna laughed. It was a hard, bitter sound.

"I'm sure there are some knights not taking House money, or buying House women, or split on House drams," she said. "But even if they wanted to fight the House of Five Dragons, no knight would bleed for it. Maybe back in your day, Rikard, but not anymore. No one calls on Alterra anymore. I told you, they're afraid. No one wants to end up like you."

Rikard stared at Thainna as though she had grown a second head.

"I don't understand," he said. "What is a VEIL knight without the Alterra? Show me!"

Thainna was forming the words to do just that when she felt Rikard's presence in her mind. He was a heavy, insistent pressure right behind her eyes, pushing somehow deeper than her skull could possibly contain. It wasn't painful, but it was deeply intrusive.

Thainna felt vulnerable, peeled open like a piece of fruit as Rikard peered into her memories. She cried out sharply.

And then he was gone. Thainna felt suddenly as limp as a sack of wet sand and fell against Rikard. He caught her easily in his arms and carried her to a couch. Carefully, he laid her down, pillowing her head on his folded saela. Rikard remained crouched beside Thainna.

"I'm sorry," he said in a low voice. "I needed... but I'm sorry. I shouldn't have, not without permission."

Thainna felt strangely boneless and yet like she was floating on something soft and... stringy? It was impossible to put the sensation into words. Thainna was half tethered to her body, half soaring free like a flown standard. She was high above the world even as she sank deep into it. Beside it, within it... She couldn't speak for a long moment. When Thainna finally found her words again, her tongue was heavy and unresponsive in her mouth.

Is this what it's like to be Rikard? she wondered.

Hae.

Thainna clearly heard his answer in her mind, as easily as she knew her own thoughts but just as clearly those of another. Rikard's short, simple word was more... brown than her own, she supposed, like turned soil. His mind was thinner, too, stretched and layered. Tempered, perhaps, like the folded steel blades that the Nianese favored.

Are you listening... feeling me, Rikard?

Hae, he thought.

...Please stop.

Sharing her mind with Rikard was not altogether unpleasant, but there were too many things he could not know about her. Unwelcome panic prickled through her like rippling black thorns and Thainna cracked her eyes open just in time to see Rikard recoil. Fear had not lost its sharp edge against him, it seemed. Thainna sat up and smiled sheepishly at him.

"Now I'm sorry. I didn't mean to hurt you."

Rikard touched his forefinger to his lips. It seemed like a strange gesture, but when he dropped his hand again, he was smiling back at Thainna. "Now we're even."

"Did you see what you needed to?"

"Hae," answered Rikard. His smile fell away and Thainna almost regretted asking. "The bond with Alterra is all but broken. Even when Mask fell, I never... I didn't realize it was so bad. No one in Terra knows about the war. Stumble and Flickerdim fight in defense of a brotherhood that's been forgotten. How did we drift so far away? They... you all keep talking about how I built the empire. But without the Alterra, I could have done nothing. VEIL is so afraid of blood now, of what they may have to give up."

"We thought you were dead and no one else wanted that to happen to them," said Thainna. "You lived, as it turned out, but we're not so sure that death wouldn't have been better."

"How can you say that?" Rikard asked.

He peered at her curiously. In his dark eyes, Thainna could clearly see the temptation to simply reach into her thoughts for the answer. She couldn't lie to herself – it *was* tempting. That mental bond was a much more effective, intimate sort of communication than any words.

Intimate? Don't even think that, stupid girl, Thainna told herself firmly.

"Thirty years fighting in Alterra, in an alien world," she said instead. "Twice that or more if they hadn't sent you back. Bleeding gods, you didn't age at all while you were gone. Your own son is older than you are. Nothing can be worth that!"

"That's why Nikas was so upset when I saluted the Alterra," Rikard said in wonderment. He sat down next to Thainna. "They're afraid of Alterrans. Because of me? Because of what happened to me?"

Thainna nodded.

Rikard drew a deep breath. "I think that I understand. Thank you, Thainna."

A maid emerged from a nearby door bearing Rikard's breakfast. He accepted the tray from her and set it down on the cushion next to Thainna. She moved to stand, but Rikard laid a restraining hand on her shoulder.

"Is there something else you need?" she asked.

"Hae, there is. Are you hungry?"

Thainna was about to tell him no when her stomach grumbled loudly. "Well, I wasn't, but I guess my guts have their own opinion."

Rikard offered Thainna a plate of sliced green melon and she accepted. The servants in the Mazrem house ate well, but not half so lavishly as their masters. The melon was as crisp and sweet as honey. Thainna had never tasted anything so delicious.

"Did you just want to share some breakfast, Rikard?" she asked when she had finished off the melon and concluded that licking the plate clean might be a little too rude. "Do you want me to go now?"

"No. I want to fix this, Thainna. All of this. I'm going to report to the Star Court archouse today to take my new position in VEIL. I want you to come with me."

"I'm flattered, of course, but why? I'm just a–" *Thief*, Thainna almost said, but corrected herself. "–a foster. What could you need me for?"

"I begin to understand that I have broken... that I have enemies, Thainna. I believe that my health will make an easy target."

"You want me to tell them where to stick it if they claim that you're in no condition to do... whatever you want to do?"

Rikard laughed. "Hae. But that isn't all. I feel something inside you, Thainna, something harder than I knew. Your concern for your brother makes you twice as watchful, as careful. I don't understand the shape of it, but Thain is your twin, like Saerus to Surma. It must be good fortune. You remind me of Stumble."

"Stumble? Who is that?"

"A young Alterran, a curiosity. He's a good... man, I suppose. Stumble and I were friends. He taught me the ways of Alterra when I first arrived. We fought together for many years. I want you near me, as Stumble always was. You will see things that I will not. And you tell me what no one else will."

Thainna blushed and nodded. "Hae, then. When do we leave?"

"I need to talk to Laura first." Rikard stood and pulled on his saela. He fastened the knotted buttons and straightened his sleeves. Did he look nervous? "Get anything you might need and meet me at the front gate."

"I'll be there soon," Thainna promised.

At first, Laurael was relieved to find herself alone in bed. Rikard had kept them both awake late into the night and she had no particular desire to begin the new day in such a sweaty fashion.

A cold wave of doubt doused her pleasure. Where *was* her husband? Their visit with Emperor Tychon had not gone well. Rikard's childish departure had only strengthened Tychon's conviction that the young knight would turn on him. She argued with the emperor for almost an hour, trying to convince him that Rikard had no design on the throne, but was not at all certain of her success.

Blood of the gods, Tychon is like a jealous child brooding over his favorite toy. He reads envy in every glance and thinks everyone is out to steal what is his.

Still, she couldn't be too angry. Tychon's paranoia played quite well into Laurael's hands. The emperor was worried about entirely the wrong Mazrem. Rikard had no ambition, but Laurael thanked the gods every day that their son more than made up for that particular failing.

Gaius could be a difficult boy, but what young man was not? He would be a fine emperor, if Rikard didn't steal VEIL and the Lyceum out from under him.

Laurael sat up in her bed and called for a dresser. A moment later, the door opened, but instead of one of her girls, Rikard strode into the room. His long hair was still sleep-tousled, but he was already dressed. Laurael's young husband sat on the edge of the bed and kissed her. Especially when compared to his desperate, needy lovemaking of the night before, Rikard seemed to be in high spirits.

"I'm going to the Star Court today," he announced.

Laurael kept her expression carefully neutral. "Are you certain, my lord? You're not to strain yourself, you know. The foster girl has said it herself."

"Thainna's coming with me."

"Is she? Well, then I'm sure you're in good hands. Will you be gone long?"

"Most of the day, I think."

"After thirty years alone, I suppose I shall survive a little longer," Laurael said with a sigh. "Return as soon as you may, my lord."

"I thought that I would bring Gaius along, too. He's a VEIL captain, after all."

"Let our son sleep. Making his own time is one of the privileges he's earned. When he wakes, I'll send him to join you."

Rikard cocked his head and looked as though he might protest, but only nodded. He gave Laurael a lingering kiss and turned away to leave.

"Comb your hair," she snapped. "You can't appear at the archouse looking like a Rows vagabond."

When Rikard had pulled his black hair into some semblance of order, he bade her a final farewell and left. Laurael lingered in bed until the dressers arrived to arrange her hair and makeup. When the oldest girl finished lacing her corset, Laurael sent her to fetch Gaius.

"Breakfast?"

Arliss offered Thainna a heel of dark bread smeared in cheese curds, but she waved it off.

"No, I've already eaten. Are you expecting anyone soon?"

"You're pretty early. Breakfast for most is in about half an hour. Bastil hasn't come through yet, but he's a late eater. Foolish man, he's all skin and bones! I notice you've put on a little fat," Arliss said. "Not that you couldn't use a little more..."

"I had breakfast with Rikard," Thainna told her. The cook's eyebrow shot up. "He's taking me with him to the Star Court today. Can you take a report to the House for me?"

"Is it important?"

"Hae," said Thainna. "You were right before, when you said... Anyway, I have to send news as often as I can. I need to tell Narissa that I'm finally getting somewhere."

"I can't get away until after midday. What do you want me to tell her?"

"Rikard said that I remind him of an Alterran friend of his and he wants to keep me nearby. He seems to trust me."

Arliss blinked and shook her head, disbelieving.

"I think that's the angle I can work on him. Tell Narissa that I tried the bluering, but it only hooked Gaius, not Rikard." Thainna thought for a moment and then corrected herself. "No, don't tell her that. Tell her I need some more of the ophellion and bluering instead."

"You just said you weren't using them," Arliss said, suddenly suspicious. "You're not split yourself, are you?"

"No! It's for Caelin, but please don't tell Narissa that. Caelin said the House has been turning down his requests because they're low priority or something like that. But Narissa said the Crest will give me anything I ask for."

"Hae, then."

"If she sends you back with anything, just give it right to Caelin. I don't know how long I'll be gone today."

The older woman nodded. "I'll do that. Take care of yourself, Thainna."

Thainna was waiting for Rikard at the front gates, chatting with one of the household guards. Another guardsman held the reins of a kajja hitched to a chariot, though not the one Rikard used the night before. When he neared, Thainna broke off her conversation and approached.

"I had one of your men bring this around," she said, pointing to the chariot. "They want to know if you'd like an escort."

"No. I just want to get underway."

Rikard found himself unexpectedly impatient. He climbed into the chariot. Thainna gestured to the guard she had been speaking to.

"No escort today," she said. "Can you get the gates?"

"Hae, Mana Vahn."

He jogged down to the bottom of the hill and waved to the other men. Thainna stepped up into the chariot with Rikard. She felt very small and very warm next to him. The guards below heaved the gates open and saluted Rikard as he drove past.

The outer wall of his home was a jumble of flowers, candles and more. Curious, Rikard slowed the kajja to a walk. What was all of this? Offerings…?

"All of this is… for me?" he asked.

"Hae. I'm a little surprised Lady Mazrem hasn't had it all removed yet," said Thainna. "I don't know, maybe she has and they've put down more. They keep trying to make you a god, you know."

Rikard scowled. "Laura told me."

"Of course, most of the people in Dormaen don't need a Lyceum dictum to worship you."

Rikard darted a shocked look down at the flame-haired girl.

"Do you...?" he asked.

Thainna blushed. "Me? No, I've never worshiped you. I don't visit the temples much, except the fostral."

"But you're a spring-thrice... a priestess!"

"Hae, right. A priestess." Thainna looked away, at the offerings. "You're not offended, are you?"

"That you don't pray to me?" Rikard laughed and shook his head. He silently urged the kajja on, out into the street. "No. I don't want to be a god. I just want to be a man. A husband and a father and a knight. That's hard enough."

Laurael's face paint was dry and her dressers had long since retreated by the time Gaius staggered into her dressing room. His eyes were red-rimmed and slitted against the pale sunlight as though it might blind him. Gaius' cheeks were ruddy and rough with dark whiskers.

"What is it now, Mother? Are you out of other men to annoy?" he said sourly. He swept a faltering bow. "I'm at your disposal, great lady."

"You're drunk," Laurael snapped.

Gaius raised a finger and waggled it at her. "No, Mother, I *was* drunk. Now I'm hung over. But I had a nice tall cup of bluering. Maybe you'd like some, Mother? It might sharpen your mind. I'm certain you need it as much as I do. After all, we're about to lose everything."

"You're babbling, Gaius."

"Hae? Are you quite sure you're awake, Mother? You seem to be dreaming," her son said. His breath stank like burnt sugar. "Despite Father's blatant disrespects to Tychon, the old scab *still* made him legens! Why? Because the worlds might collapse if some poor, deluded soul didn't worship the great Rikard Mazrem!"

"Gaius–" Laurael began, but he cut her off with a petulant cry.

"I wanted to be emperor, Mother! But Father might as well have robbed me of the throne!"

Gaius fell to his knees on the rug-strewn floor and hammered his fists against his thighs. Laurael knelt and put her arms around her son. She kissed his fever-flushed cheek.

"Your father will take nothing from you, Gaius," she whispered in his ear. "Nothing! I swear it on my blood. I've spent my life ensuring that you will succeed Tychon. Rikard will not interfere."

"If it was up to him, I'm sure he'd agree. The man is too humble by half. He'd not take an offered acorn! But it's not going to be his choice, is it? It's up to Tychon and the Lyceum!"

"They will choose you, my son. There will be no other choice."

She stroked Gaius' dark hair. It needed to be dyed again. She would tend to it herself. No one else ever got it right. Gaius pulled away and turned to face Laurael, his expression puzzled.

"Why?" he asked. "What are you going to do?"

"I'm going to kill your father," she said. "Tychon will appear responsible for it. The emperor is already consumed by fear for his throne. It will not be a stretch of reason that he might eliminate such a rival. His paranoia of usurpation will brook no other conclusion. Castum Tychon is the only man in Carce who doesn't love your father."

"Except us."

Laurael shrugged. "The Lyceum will remove Tychon from the throne. When that's done, who better to take control of the empire than the son of the martyred Rikard Mazrem?"

Gaius pressed his lips together into a flat, thoughtful line. "Can you do it, Mother?"

"Hae, of course. Haven't I always taken care of you, Gaius?"

It was a mother's right and responsibility to comfort and provide for her child. Laurael would gladly burn the worlds to ash to make sure they were safe for Gaius.

29

VERITA ET ILLUMINA LANSINOS

"Our strength holds worlds together."

— A VEIL AXIOM

THE NEW BOY hit the ground with a thump and groan. He clutched his hands to his stomach and curled into a ball on the trampled grass like a newborn kitten. The tiny mewling noises he made did nothing to dispel the illusion. Ortho kicked the young squire one last time. The boy wailed.

"Stop your bawling and get up," Jaesun barked.

Other knights laughed as the new squire tried to regain his feet. He was an Ocrissian, slender and long-limbed like a dancer. Ortho shoved him back to the ground with one boot and Jaesun nodded.

Ortho grinned down at the Ocrissian squire. Ever since the incident with the fake medal, the entire Star Court had been laughing at Ortho and it was good to finally have someone smaller, younger and less experienced to beat on.

"Get on your feet," Ortho told the boy, then kicked him again. "Do you think a Fiori barbarian is going to back off?"

The squire's legs lashed out again, but not trying to stand. He missed Ortho and kicked one of the other knights, a brawny Lyncean named Walthere. With a startled grunt, Walthere tumbled to the ground. A dozen other knights laughed uproariously and a few called out bets.

Walthere was furious. He twisted his body in the grass and grabbed, but the boy wriggled like a wet fish and squirmed out of his grasp. The others had backed away, including Ortho and Jaesun, unwilling to get in Walthere's way. The squire was slimmer and faster than the huge Lyncean, and was back on his feet in an instant. But he had only a moment to savor his small victory before Walthere jumped up, too. The Lyncean's usually pale cheeks were flushed red with rage. Ortho smirked. The boy had just made a bad enemy.

Realizing that his gamble hadn't paid off, the squire spun on his heels to bolt for safety, but Jaesun shoved him back into the middle of the encircled knights.

"Fight, you coward!"

The Ocrissian stumbled back, almost falling again. He regained his balance just in time to see Walthere's punch, but not in time to avoid it. The Lyncean's blow connected solidly and the squire staggered and fell, bleeding freely from his split lip. The other knights took a quick step back.

"Walthere, get back. Gaeren, get a templar out here to clean this up at once!" Jaesun shouted.

Gaeren, a Carcaen knight about Ortho's age, hurried into the archouse. Ortho polished his cannula on the breast of his saela and cursed Walthere's short-sighted anger. Instead of an entertaining fight with a few good bruises and maybe some broken bones, they were waiting tensely for some old woman to clean away the blood. Ortho scowled at Walthere's back. The hulking Lyncean seemed to feel eyes on him and turned.

"Nice work on that boy," Ortho told him.

Walthere grunted and turned away, hastily scrubbing the blood from his knuckles with a handful of grass.

Gaeren bounded down the stairs of the archouse, taking them two at a time, and sprinted across the training yard to Jaesun. When he saw that Gaeren was alone, the squadron commander scowled.

"I told you to bring a templar. Where's Tes Ren?"

Gaeren skidded to a stop, panting and red-faced.

"I went and... I saw... and he asked..." the knight panted, trying to breathe and speak at the same time and doing neither very well.

"Hae? Saw what?"

"It's Captain Mazrem! He's here!" Gaeren finally choked out.

"Gaius Mazrem?"

"Rikard Mazrem, sir! He's just arrived and he was speaking with Tes Ren. He's on his way out here!"

No sooner had Gaeren finished than a trio of figures appeared on the landing at the top of the stairs. One was the familiar white-robed bulge of Ren, a senior templar of the Star Court. The other two were less familiar, but not strangers. Ortho recognized Captain Rikard Mazrem, tall and strikingly handsome, just like his statues. He knew the Fiori girl in the fostral tabba at his side, too, but couldn't immediately place her.

"Fall in!" Jaesun ordered.

The nearby knights scrambled into a crooked line. Ortho couldn't tear his eyes off Captain Mazrem and was the last to take up a position at the end. Well, almost last... The Ocrissian squire limped into place beside Ortho. The boy's eyes were glazed and his face swollen. Blood from his lip dripped down his chin.

Rikard Mazrem strode down the stairs, followed closely by the two women. He stopped in front of Jaesun, who saluted smartly. Captain Mazrem returned the gesture and peered down the line of knights.

Their famous visitor had not gone unnoticed. The archouse windows were full of faces. More knights and templars gathered on the stairs, watching and whispering to one another. Ortho shifted his weight uncomfortably and straightened his saela. Was Captain Mazrem looking at him? No, he realized, but the Fiori girl was. She stared, a frown tugging at her lips. Why did she look so familiar?

"Captain Mazrem, it's an honor," Jaesun said.

Rikard Mazrem looked right past him and fixed his eyes on the squire at the end of the line, then tracked beads of red dotting the grass. He knelt and touched his fingers to a tall blade of grass. They came away red with smears of the boy's blood. Ortho gasped and heard the other knights doing the same. He was actually *touching* the blood...?

Captain Mazrem strode to the end of the line and reached for the squire, tilting his chin up.

"Gently, Rikard," the girl told him quietly.

Ortho doubted anyone else could hear her warning. Captain Mazrem nodded and touched his thumb – gently – to the squire's split lip. More blood. Fear rose sourly in Ortho's throat. Captain Mazrem shot him an unreadable look, and then returned his attention to the squire.

"What's your name?"

"Tyne, sir. Tyne Inos."

"You know this man. He is your brother. Who will stand forth and heal his wounds?" Captain Mazrem called to the crowd. An unhappy murmur ripped through the courtyard. "No one? You will shed this man's blood, but you won't bleed for him?"

Captain Mazrem flicked open the cannula on his forefinger. Ortho took a step back from the line. Most of the other knights had done the same, or seemed on the verge of bolting.

Jaesun slapped his fist into his open palm.

"Hold your line! This is Rikard bloody Mazrem before you. Hold, damn it!"

Reluctantly, Ortho and the rest reformed the line. He smelled the salty copper tang of Tyne's blood.

Captain Mazrem lightly touched his thumb to the bead of blood welling up at the gold-capped tip of his forefinger, mixing his blood with the squire's and then drew a small red circle on the boy's forehead. Tyne froze, terrified.

The Fiori girl touched his arm and Captain Mazrem looked down at her. She raised her eyebrows quizzically, but said nothing. The captain seemed to take some meaning from her look, however, and nodded. Captain Mazrem sighed heavily and then turned to address the entire courtyard.

"General Hern told me that you no longer make this gesture, this sign," he said, pointing to the circle over Tyne's eyes. "Thainna says that you're afraid, that the men of VEIL no longer make pacts with the Alterra!"

"With respects, Captain Mazrem," Jaesun responded, bristling visibly. "We fear nothing!"

"Legens. Emperor Tychon has named me legens over all of the courts of VEIL, Commander Jaesun. You all fear blood and the Alterra. You will not even heal one of your own! Why? Without Alterran aid, thousands of knights and soldiers would be nothing more than bones in the snow of Njorn Pass. There would be no Carcaen Empire!"

"That was your sacrifice, Legens Mazrem, not the Alterrans'," Jaesun said stiffly. "For which we have–"

"Without the Alterra to hear my plea, I would have been a madman weeping and bleeding in the snow. We are knights of Carce! We do not fear blood and we do not fear sacrifice. We give of ourselves willingly for the empire and for our allies, for Terra and Alterra alike!"

Beside Ortho, Tyne cheered. Perhaps half of those watching the proceedings echoed him or applauded. Hundreds more shifted uncomfortably and gave one another significant glances. Jaesun was one of the latter. His nostrils flared and a red flush crept up like a rash along his thick neck.

"Thank you for the inspiring words, legens," he said in a grating voice. "As you say, we're giving of ourselves and should return to training."

"Training?"

Now Legens Mazrem's voice dropped dangerously low. Ortho strained to hear. Mazrem's face darkened with sudden fury, as ominous as storm clouds. His Fiori companion's eyes widened and she tensed visibly.

"Sir Gaeren told me very little about what happened out here," said Legens Mazrem. "What he did *not* say was much more informative. I know what happens here. Men who thrash each other and anyone else they please!"

"Legens!" Jaesun protested.

"VEIL wasn't always like this. It won't always be like this. You watched while your own men beat a young squire, commander. You encouraged their brutality. Leave this court at once!"

"What? You can't do this!"

"Go from VEIL, Commander Jaesun. Go with my best wishes, but go."

Jaesun's eyes bulged and he spun away, spluttering in fury. The training yard erupted into a riot of cheers, dismayed cries, loud hissing and applause. Ortho closed his mouth with an effort. By now, most of the knights and templars had poured out into the courtyard to watch. Legens Mazrem made a sweeping gesture that took in the courtyard and archouse.

"Brothers of the Star Court!" he called.

"Hae, legens!" came the loud, scattered replies.

There were other voices, but Ortho could not make out the words. He couldn't find breath enough to speak a word of his own.

"We have lost our way. We've forgotten who we are. Men of steel, men of blood, men of two worlds!" Legens Mazrem raised his right hand, still stained red. "We have made our pacts with the Alterra and we must honor them."

Rikard swung his hand in a broad, flat arc, flinging drops of his blood and Tyne's. The moment hung, as grave and still as a stone frieze, and then the air filled with fire. A sheet of flame rippled out from Legens Mazrem's fingertips, following the sweep of his hand baking the yard in hot red radiance. Even twenty paces away, the rush of blazing wind ruffled Ortho's hair. As quickly as it appeared, the wave of fire was gone. The air smelled acridly of smoke. General Darius stood on a high balcony, his expression unreadable at this distance.

"The life of a VEIL knight is not an easy one," Legens Mazrem told the assembled Star Court. "Take the day to yourself, brothers. Consider your choices here. Many of you joined our ranks after my time. Perhaps you don't truly understand what I will ask of you. This is not a life meant for every man. If this court is not the place for you, then go in peace from our gates."

The crowd murmured and stirred. Legens Mazrem held up his hands and they quieted once more.

"Any man who elects to leave VEIL will go with the love and prayers of his brothers, and a year's pay to begin his new life. I would not send any of you into the Rows to scratch a living from the mud! If you wish to go, notify General Darius. For all those who remain, return to this yard tomorrow morning to begin again!"

Legens Mazrem leaned down and said something to the Fiori girl. She listened and then nodded. Rikard Mazrem strode across the yard and into the archouse, glorious as a god. A rolling thunder of applause and boot-stamping, cheering and shouting followed him, shaking the tall stone wall of the Star Court.

When he was gone, the rumble took on a new, curious note as knights and templars turned to one another, already deep in discussion of what had just happened, wondering who would go and who would stay. The legens' Fiori companion pushed her way through the crowd to Tyne. Ortho lingered, wondering at her business. The dazed Tyne bowed deeply.

"Hae, mana," he greeted her.

"Rikard sent me to take a look at you. Tyne, right? I'm Thainna Vahn," she introduced herself.

The name meant nothing to Ortho, but he still couldn't shake the feeling that he knew the girl. Thainna gently inspected Tyne's face. She didn't seem to be doing anything, as far as Ortho could tell, just looking.

"Does it hurt?"

"No, mana," Tyne answered.

Thainna raised her red eyebrows at him and the young squire flushed.

"A little, hae," Tyne admitted.

"Where?"

"Just my jaw."

Thainna smiled at Tyne and lightly probed the side of his face, up to his temples.

"Nothing seems broken," she said, then touched her finger to the bloody mark the legens had left. Ortho couldn't believe it. "Can you feel this at all?"

"Hae, I can. It's sort of... warm."

"Well, it *is* blood." She rubbed the sticky redness between her fingers. "No, this has gone cold. Are you going to stay with Rikard?"

"Hae!" Tyne nodded enthusiastically, then winced and put his hand to his bruised jaw. "If he'll have me, I mean."

The foster laughed. "I don't think you have anything to worry about. But Rikard's not talking light when he says he's going to ask a lot of you. Why don't you go get some rest? Tomorrow's going to be a long day, I'm sure. If the pain gets any worse, tell a templar."

"Hae, mana."

With one last bow, the squire departed and Thainna whirled to face Ortho. He offered her a deep bow. One much better practiced than Tyne's, he thought. A foster did not demand such respect from a VEIL knight, but she was obviously someone of importance to

Legens Mazrem, and so to the rest of Carce. When he straightened, Ortho found Thainna's eyes narrowed to glowering green slits.

"Have I–?"

"Don't you remember me, Sir Ortho?" she interrupted.

"No, mana," Ortho stammered. It was mostly the truth. "I'm certain I would remember meeting such a beauty."

Thainna laughed, but the sound was nothing like the sweet laughter she had given Tyne. This was bitter and twisted by anger.

"You called me Senna then. I sold you something, a medal you thought belonged to Captain Mazrem. And you gave me this in return."

She turned her face to show him a faint yellow bruise. It was barely visible against her milk-white skin, a pale twin to the dark welt on Tyne's jaw. Ortho started. Senna? The dirty girl from Mazrem Square? It didn't seem possible.

Thainna stepped in close, standing up on her toes to hiss into his ear. "I know what kind of knight you are," she said. "If you stay, then Rikard will know, too. Take your pay and go. VEIL doesn't need men like you."

Ortho could only stare in stunned silence as Thainna stalked away.

Flickerdim's dimming crescent moon eyes widened and Stumble tightened his wispy tendrils into stone, taking his favorite malachite nightingale shape once more. The curiosity hopped excitedly from one half-coalesced talon to the other, chirruping in exultation.

He did it! He's going to bring them back to us, rekindle the flame! But he never remembered the plan, Flickerdim. You never told him, even when he asked. How did he know what to do?

He had to come to it on his own. He must have passion in the days to come, more than any simple order. He always knew that, Flickerdim thought, as though he had known all along. Perhaps he had. *And he knows that we need the Terrans. Without them, we are naught but formless dreams. Without them, our world breaks. He had to feel it, not simply remember it. Nothing lesser will do.*

Flickerdim's darkness-scaled head detached and floated free for a moment as he craned it up to look into the Shattered gray sky. The old wisdom carefully worked free a strand of night-shade from his body and twined it around their branch of the Uprising. The midnight black coiled down the tower and puddled heavily as guilt on the blade-fire ground of the Uprising. It boiled like tar for a moment, then suddenly stilled and went as smooth as ice.

Why isn't anything better yet? Stumble whimpered.

It's too soon... and perhaps too late to save us. He has told VEIL to strike a new bargain with us, but how many will leave? Some are taken by the beauty of it all now, but many will cool in time. A short time. They are frightened of us, of what we take, what we need from them. The Terrans can't see us, the world they've created here. They don't know its worth. They must believe, and these men lack faith.

Stumble's beak sagged down onto his chest. He nudged it back onto his face with the crest of one wing. He cocked his head this way and that, looking.

The girl does. She knows. She believes, doesn't she? She has seen into his heart!

Flickerdim flicked his tongue and didn't answer.

"You just about stopped my heart, Rik," Saul said.

"Sorry, Saul."

The general sat behind his desk and gestured for Rikard to take a chair.

"Tes Ren," Saul said, "can you please go get the legens something to drink? Starting riots is thirsty work, I'm sure."

The templar bowed and left the study. Saul rested his elbows on the desk and steepled his fingers under his chin. Rikard felt his friend's conflicted, tangled thoughts like a snarl of brambles.

"A year's pay, Rik? You're kidding, hae? Do you have any idea what that is going to cost? You're going to make the same offer to the Sun and Moon Courts, aren't you?"

"Hae," Rikard answered. "Saul, it must be done. Your men were beating one of their own and called it training."

"It's not completely without merit, Rik! It's a rough lesson, I'll admit, and not exactly how it was done in our day... but you can't argue with the results. VEIL knights are still the toughest fighters in Carce," Saul protested.

"It's not just about results. A war fought by monsters has no victor!"

"Bloody hell, Rik, is that what this is all about? The Fiori war?"

"Of course not. It's just as I rang... as I said, Saul. This is about VEIL, about the empire! I saw Emperor Tychon last night. Do you know what he called us? Lazy bullies! Based on what I've seen since my return, I can't say he's wrong."

Saul recoiled as though struck and Rikard almost regretted his words. But they were true, no matter how they stung. Did Saul think it hurt any less to say than to hear?

"We have a chance to fix all of that," Rikard said. "But I need your help, Saul. I need you to back me on this. If things are as bad as Thainna tells me they are, there's going to be opposition."

"Is Thainna that foster girl who came with you today? What did she say?"

"She's the one who told me about things in VEIL, about the House of Five Dragons. Thainna says they're everywhere, even inside your archouses."

Saul paled a shade and stared intently at Rikard.

"Can't say I've heard anything about that," he said quietly. "It's dangerous to go around telling people that you have."

Ren returned, carrying cups of water that smelled of lemons and sugar. Rikard pondered the strangely circular statement from his one-time squire. Sensing the tension in the room, the templar served them and quietly retreated, closing the door behind her. General Darius rested his chin in his right hand and drummed his bloodcap against his cheek.

"You really want to do this, don't you?" he sighed. "You're right, Rik. You usually are. You're going to set the world on fire, old friend. Backing you might not be the brightest move I've ever made, but the other generals certainly never accused me of an overabundance of thought. Hae, I'm with you, Rik. With the Alterra, against even the House. To the end, I'm with you."

Marus' toe caught on a stone in the road and he stumbled, swearing. He clutched the packages to his chest, but the top one slid and smashed to the ground with a muted tinkle of broken glass. The little glass rose for his mother, dashed to a hundred pieces inside its insufficiently protective velvet wrapping. Marus swore again. Why didn't he think to buy her something a little hardier?

It wasn't much further to the archouse, but the roads were busier than usual. Another mounted knight very nearly trampled Marus as he crouched to retrieve the broken rose. It was useless now, but no point in leaving it for some inattentive passer-by to cut himself on. A shadow fell across him and Marus heard a panicked whinny just in time to pitch himself to one side, scattering the rest of his shopping in the process.

He rolled to his feet with a grunt. The man atop a chestnut mare was a little older than Marus and wore the crimson of a Sun Court knight. He reined his jittery mount to a stop a few paces away and pulled her around, back toward Marus.

"Sorry there, brother!" the mounted knight called down.

There was a circle of blood on his brow that looked like it had been drawn there. Marus stepped closer and shaded his eyes to better investigate, but there seemed to be no wound beneath it.

"I'm alright," Marus called. "Are you?"

"Well indeed!" laughed the other knight. "I've never seen a day like this one!"

"Why? What's going on?"

Marus looked past the other knight, straining onto tiptoes to see over the other people filling the crowded street. He could just make out a knot of young men in Moon Court blue armor and saelae shoving their way out of the archouse gates. One of them streamed blood from his off-kilter nose and screamed obscenities at someone still inside the fenced yard. His friends tugged him away, out into the street. A wagoneer yanked on the traces in his hands, pulling his hump-shouldered ox aside too late. The knight with the bloody face bounced off the beast's long, muscular flank and fell to his knees in the dirty street.

"Those who swore themselves to VEIL just for glory and greed are no longer welcome within VEIL," said the Sun knight. "Legens Mazrem has decreed that they are free to go, of course, but those who pass out of those gates today are knights no longer."

"Legens Mazrem? You mean Rikard Mazrem?"

The other knight spurred his horse a step closer. "Hae, Legens Rikard Mazrem. The emperor named him so last night. He says that it's time to change the Verita et Illumina Lansinos, to remember the honor that was once ours."

Marus blinked. "He... did? Are you sure? How does he plan on doing that?"

"He hasn't yet said, but we know that it's our choice whether or not to be a part of it. The legens has given any unwilling knight the chance to leave, without dishonor and with a year's pay. That lot–" The knight in red nodded to the growing group of bloody-nosed knights outside the Moon Court gates. "–have decided that the life of a VEIL knight is not the one for them. What about you? Will you stay, brother?"

Marus gathered up his fallen packages. Most of them were dirty, many crushed, but that suddenly didn't seem to matter. Rikard Mazrem was going to fix VEIL? Could he? Marus thought back to his last meeting with the great hero. He was so unhinged, so sick. But he remembered Rikard's simple, sincere joy at finding Ephria alive, too. Rikard Mazrem might condemn all of VEIL to a bloody hell – the road to hell was paved in gold, it was said – but Marus decided that he would rather die under a good man than prosper under bad ones any longer.

He straightened and grinned at the Sun Court knight.

"Hae, I'm staying."

Emperor Tychon considered having the pretty young messenger stay, but he dismissed her with a flick of his fingers. The girl bowed and retreated through the gauzy emerald curtains. He beckoned to the other two women, this pair draped across his bed and wearing nothing but the silver collars that he liked so much.

The emperor of Carce fell back into the soft silk covers and contemplatively stroked one of the girls' soft ivory skin. A year's pay? How many VEIL knights would Rikard scare off with his talk of sacrifice and blood, entice with easy money? If the number was too many, VEIL would be hard pressed to come up with the necessary laurels.

The concubine whimpered under his flagging touch and Emperor Tychon was momentarily distracted by her loveliness. She was younger than Laurael and thinner in the lips, but otherwise looked a great deal like the Mazrem widow. Tychon pulled her close and nuzzled her hair, inhaling the lavender scent he ordered her to wear. Just like the oil Laurael used.

Carce was Tychon's empire and he knew how deeply the poison ran. He had poured more than his share. Every decree Tychon made earned him enemies. When he wearied of his enemies, he created the Lyceum to make the laws and take the blame when the provinces didn't like them.

Tychon pulled a girl into each arm. He kissed them both, then sat back and told them to turn their affections on one another. Bringing about this new vision of VEIL would be more difficult than Rikard thought, but still...

The emperor couldn't focus on the women in his bed. Gaius said that his father had no designs on the throne, but if that was true, then what in the worlds was he doing? A fat, lazy army did no harm in peacetime. A fit army was meant for war. What was Rikard Mazrem up to?

"There's news from our VEIL sources," announced one of the Eyes, a fat banker from the central district. He genuflected deeply before the Jade Throne.

The Crest shifted in his seat. His tabba rustled in the darkness like the restless tail of a true dragon. His fingers gripped possessively at the golden-green stone of his throne.

"What is it?" he asked in a brittle voice.

"With permission, one of your Flames waits just outside to deliver the news himself."

"Hae, show him in."

A moment later, a pair of Talons escorted a third man into the room and the Flame prostrated himself before the Jade Throne. His dark hair was in wild disarray. The Crest snapped slender fingers at him.

"Give me your report, Commander Jaesun."

"It's Legens Mazrem!" the knight exclaimed.

Nervously stumbling over his tongue and recoiling fearfully at every question from his master, Jaesun recounted the day's events, Rikard Mazrem's shocking announcement and mysterious plans.

"Changing VEIL?" mused the Crest. "How many of our knights have left?"

"I... I don't know," Jaesun confessed. He thought for a moment, jaw clenched angrily. "Rikard Mazrem is a powerful man and he calls on Alterra with impunity! He can uncover all of your agents, I'm sure. If he finds out that I serve the House..."

The Crest gave him a sharp, dangerous look and Jaesun seemed to think better of whatever he had been about to say. He fell to his knees on the slanted stone floor. His master drummed his fingers on the cold jade.

"It will not stop here. Rikard Mazrem will not be content until he has purified his beloved VEIL. We've just lost every agent inside the courts." The drumming stopped and the Crest pounded his fist on the arm of his throne. "Curse his blood!"

"I can... should I pull our men out? Warn them?" Jaesun asked.

"No, they are lost. You will remain here until I have another use for you."

The Crest dismissed his bought knight with a wave of his hand. Escorted by the Talons who had brought him, Jaesun hurried away. The Crest tilted his head to regard the row of silent Eyes that observed from the deep shadows.

"And what does Thainna have to say about her progress with Legens Mazrem?" he asked in a soft, deadly voice.

30

RED BLOOD

"To all things, there are two faces. Terra and Alterra, day and night, light and dark. Even the gods were born in twins. To all things, there must be two sides. This is the truth of our worlds."

— THE BOOKS OF SURMA AND SAERUS

WHEN HE RETURNED to the Star Court that evening, Rikard found Thainna in one of the empty bunk rooms. In his hurry to address the Sun and Moon Courts, Rikard had forgotten all about her.

The Fiori girl sat under the small window and had a waxed board in her lap, scratching at it with a sharpened length of bamboo set into a bone handle. She hummed tunelessly to herself and didn't seem to notice him at the door.

Rikard realized that he was staring at her. Thainna had lost much of her skeletal, unhealthy thinness, but maintained the whipcord build of her Fiori heritage. The combination of her angular Carcaen features with her strange, snow-white skin and fire-red hair that had so repulsed him upon their first meeting now seemed so familiar, even striking.

A few strands of long, wavy hair had come loose from their coil and spilled down the back of Thainna's pale neck.

Beautiful.

But it was improper to even think such things about another woman. Laurael waited for him at home. Rikard cleared his throat and Thainna turned around. She put the board down on a desk. What Rikard had first taken for sketches were columns of numbers. Sums?

Thainna stood. "So much for protecting you from the villains of VEIL."

A delicate brush against her thoughts reassured Rikard that she harbored no resentment. She was teasing him. Thainna was used to being used and overlooked, he realized sadly. He would not do it again.

"I'm sorry, Thainna," Rikard said aloud. "I was just so tidal... excited, I mean. I didn't mean to leave you here."

"It's alright. Can I ask you about something?"

"Anything. What is it?"

"This morning, you asked the other knights to come heal Tyne's injuries. Not that I don't see the point you were making, but why didn't *you* do it? It seems like it would have been a better demonstration than the fire."

Her curiosity felt so much like Stumble that Rikard didn't answer for a moment. He simply basked in the eager warmth.

"I wanted to, but I couldn't," he said at last.

"Why not?"

"The other knights could have because they knew what he was like before, uninjured. They could have remembered him as he was to the Alterra. A sort of young tree... a sort of guide, I mean, to tell them what to fix."

"But you could see his injuries," Thainna said. "Isn't that good enough? You know what lips are supposed to look like when they're not split open."

Rikard didn't want to think about Thainna's lips.

"Healing is a delicate thing," he said. "If I didn't remember him just right, Flickerdim might have rebuilt him wrong. Human bodies are far more mutable than our thoughts to them."

"I guess I understand..." Thainna shrugged. Her comprehension was inexact, but close enough. "Did the other generals give you any trouble? Since you just got back now, I assume you didn't really need me for anything."

"Castor argued with me, of course," Rikard said. "He thinks that I'm slandering VEIL. And him. The man hates every breath of me, but I hold rank over him now."

That was still a strange thought.

"What about General Hern?" Thainna asked.

"Nikas is too polite to argue with anyone. He won't oppose me, but he's not supporting us, either. I tried to convince him, but it was like... like trying to bend water. The words didn't come easily and I don't think I argued very well."

"No, you didn't," a new voice said from behind them.

Gaius stood in the doorway, holding a cup of sharp-smelling liquor. Rikard had been so focused on Thainna that he failed to sense his son's approach, not even with his ears. Gaius laughed and swayed on his feet. Rikard held out a hand to steady him, but his son ignored him and stumbled over to plop down into the chair next to the desk.

"Have you spoken to General Hern then?" Thainna's tone was steady enough, but Rikard felt her flicker-prick of apprehension.

"Laura said that she would send you to join me this morning. Where have you been?" Rikard asked.

"Mother and I had some things to talk about," Gaius answered vaguely. "By the time I drove out here, you were already gone to tear down the Sun Court. When I heard what happened, I went to go see Nikas Hern. That was after you left his archouse, Father."

"And he wasn't convinced," said Rikard.

It wasn't a surprise. Nikas had been polite but clear in his unwillingness to take sides. Still, Rikard had hoped somehow that Gaius would bring better news.

"Not even one bit. He doesn't want you cutting new sails, not when he's done so well in recent days. You're preaching philosophy to men who want prosperity."

Rikard frowned. His son was so bitter.

"The knights of VEIL are better men than you credit them to be," Rikard said. "Fewer than two hundred have left."

Thainna listened silently. She wanted to say something, Rikard sensed, but would not. Could not, perhaps. Thainna thought of her brother again, the sickly boy with her face. She was afraid for him. That fear was somehow tied to Gaius, but even more to Rikard himself. It wound around her like silk around a spider's prey.

Gaius snorted. "Count your knights again tomorrow morning. Those who already left are only the first wave, Father. There will be more. Many more. The ones who were too frightened or ashamed today will leave tonight. Tonight, your speeches will fade and more will go. Tomorrow, you'll start your work. It'll be too much or too little and more will leave."

"They are good men. Strong men," Rikard repeated stubbornly. "Gaius, you're a knight of VEIL, too. You should have more faith in your brothers."

"I know them better than you do, Father. By morning, you'll know I'm right," Gaius said. He gave his father a suddenly intense, curious look. "I heard something else, too. I spoke with General Darius before I left and he had a very interesting story to tell. I saw something like it at home, in the garden. You summoned that fire without writing a single instruction."

"Is that strange?" Thainna asked.

"More than a bit. Where did you school, girl? If all fosters have your education, they probably kill more patients than a Rows cutthroat. Father, are you sure you don't want a new one?"

"No!" Rikard snapped.

Gaius shrugged and returned his attention to Thainna. "It *is* strange. Blood's the only thing that shows through the veil, that Alterra can see. If we want something from them, we have to write out instructions. Detailed ones, so there are no... misunderstandings. Whatever the common folk may think, VEIL knights don't just squirt our blood indiscriminately."

"We *common folk* don't think you bleed at all," Thainna said.

Gaius gave a short, barking laugh. "Perhaps, but our new legens is here to change all that. Hae, Father? So, how did you summon up Alterran power without writing a full pact? How did the Alterra know what you wanted them to do?"

"They know me. They can feel me, my blood," Rikard explained. "They know what I need. I don't have to write instructions anymore."

"Lucky you," Gaius said. His voice slurred slightly. "What a great gift for a great man."

Thainna gave Rikard a sidelong glance. She started to say something, and then closed her mouth again. Rikard touched her mind as lightly as possible, asking permission, and felt Thainna's hesitant assent.

What? What is it that you want to say but are afraid to?

I'll never get used to this. Is Thain well? If they hurt him, I'll... I don't know. This feels so strange. I feel him inside me. I don't like it. I like it. Don't think that, stupid girl! He can hear. Bloody hell, he probably heard that. And that.

Thainna had no practice in sorting her thoughts for another to reach. They were tangled and jumbled like necklaces in an old jewelry box.

You can hear anyone you want to, hae? she thought. *You only sometimes stay out of my head because you're being kind. Why can't Alterrans do it, just listen in on anyone's mind they like? Why do knights have to write anything at all?*

The knights of VEIL and the Alterra are brothers, but we're still... very different, Rikard replied as simply as he could, but sensed that the answer didn't satisfy Thainna. *I'm different. I was in their world so long that... that sometimes I'm more Alterran than Terran. You have thought so yourself.*

You had a bloody hard time understanding your own kind when you first came home, Thainna pointed out.

I have lived in both worlds and thought both thoughts. The Alterra understand me and... and I hope that the Terrans will, too. But the Alterra can't do what I do. They can't hear the things that I do. They need to read the blood pacts to do as a knight asks.

Thainna seemed to understand, so Rikard withdrew from her mind. Unburdened by Terran speech, their conversation had taken only seconds. Gaius didn't seem to have noticed at all. He yawned and loudly cracked his knuckles.

"Well, that's enough excitement for one day. I'm going home for some dinner. Are you coming?" Gaius asked Rikard.

"Hae. Thainna?"

The foster nodded and followed him through the archouse to the stables outside. When one of the hostlers had helped Rikard to bridle the kajja, Thainna climbed up into the chariot beside him. He whistled softly at the huge bird and they drove out across the archouse yard. There were still knights at the gate as Rikard passed out into Dormaen.

He let the kajja set her own leisurely pace. The early evening traffic was slow and heavy. There was no point in hurrying, even if he could.

"Why didn't you want to ask your question with your mouth?" Rikard asked.

Thainna looked up at him suddenly, as though startled. Her mind had obviously been elsewhere. She thought for a moment before answering.

"I don't trust him. Gaius. Look, Rikard, you can tell me to track ice, but I don't know about that man."

"What?" asked Rikard in shock. "Gaius? He's my son!"

"He was drunk and probably worse. Gaius is jealous and out of control."

"Thainna!"

The Fiori foster gave Rikard a hard look. "Be angry with me if you want, but you said that you wanted me to tell you the truth."

Rikard felt a heavy weight of guilt from Thainna with this statement, but it made her no less correct. Rikard tightened his fist on the kajja's traces, making the leather creak.

"...Hae," he admitted.

"You heard him in there, Rikard. Gaius isn't happy for his father or even that curious about how your pacts work... or don't work. He just wants it for himself."

"He's my son," said Rikard again, but sadly this time.

"How can you avoid knowing these things about him? You can pluck a single thought or feeling from one man in a crowd, but you don't even seem to know what your own family is thinking!"

"I don't have to reach for their thoughts! They give to me... I trust Laurael and Gaius."

"Trust them so much that you haven't told them that you can do any of this?"

"I never tried to keep it a secret!" Rikard protested.

"Are you going to tell them?" Thainna asked, green eyes wide.

"Soon, I'm going to tell all Carce."

"Are you sure that's a good idea?"

"I hope so," Rikard said.

Thainna didn't know VEIL or his family like he did, but still... Rikard couldn't deny that Gaius had some kind of... problem. He was certain that his son understood the depths to which VEIL had fallen. He was always so deprecating, so condescending toward his brother knights.

Is that what's wrong, why he seeks solace at the bottom of a cup? Is he ashamed? Of them? Of himself?

Perhaps the changes to VEIL would change Gaius, too. Rikard and Thainna rode back to the Everstones in silence, each leaving the other alone with their own thoughts.

The next morning proved Gaius right. He tossed a waxboard to Rikard with a shake of his head.

"The court captains have reported more losses. Another hundred left last night."

Rikard caught the waxboard, clacking his bloodcap against the wood as he scanned the tallies. Ninety-eight. Not quite a full hundred and not so many in the grander scheme, but it was still a painful blow.

He ran his fingers over the etched wax. It was rough and flexible under his fingers. Every day, it still amazed him to feel such things. This board would remain even after he left the room. The words, the names and numbers would all stay the same until someone heated and smoothed the wax again. So stable, as unchanging as the road he had followed into Dormaen. Yet so changeable... Rikard underscored one of the names with his thumbnail. But it was easier to change a wax board than change a man's heart.

"A hundred? That's not so bad," said Saul. "That's less than ten percent loss. It's costing us a few laurels now – I'm not sure how many – but we only have to pay them the once. The Lyceum can't object too strongly, can they?"

He sat at his desk, looking out from behind leaning towers of other boards and papers, folded or rolled and sealed in wax of all colors. Most of these lay wherever originally set, unopened and unread. As he had himself confessed, Saul Darius was not a natural leader.

"It's not about money," Rikard said. He looked over the numbers again. "Most of these are from Sun Court."

Saul waved one hand dismissively. "Hae, but forget them. You know, pretty much everyone in Carce thinks you're a hero, Rik. Now more than ever. More than a few civilians have suffered at VEIL hands and they're praising you for cleaning that lot out…"

Rikard shook his head, unsure what to say to that.

"What have you got planned?" Gaius asked, heaving a great a sigh. "What's next, great legens?"

Rikard looked up at Thainna. The foster stood at the balcony door, gazing out over the busy Star courtyard and the city beyond the gates. Sensing Rikard's eyes on her, Thainna turned to face the two VEIL knights.

"Hae?"

"It's not enough, not yet," Rikard said. "We still have more work to do."

Thainna's pale brow furrowed.

"More? I'm getting tired just listening to you," said Saul. "What more is there?"

"The House of Five Dragons… Thainna says they had spies in our ranks," Rikard said. "We must find them, or else they will continue to corrupt VEIL from within."

Gaius scowled. "The House of Five Dragons? These are not people you want to tangle yourself with. You know what they say: *Reach into the dark and you'll get bitten by the shadows.* Or something like that."

"We can't let men like that remain a part of VEIL!"

"They're criminals, Rikard," Thainna reminded him quietly. "They'll lie to you. And they're good at it."

"They can't lie to themselves. I will find them."

31

TRUCE AND TRANCE

"In the early days of VEIL, Alterran understanding of the Carcaen language was a mystery. How was it that we could communicate with the spirits of another world? It was only later scholars came to understand the bond of dreams and desires between Terra and Alterra. They knew our language because they were born out of it."

— OUR RED HISTORY, BY AVILLA SALLUSI

THAINNA WASN'T REALLY sure what she was looking for. Even a real foster had no experience with this sort of exhaustion. Rikard leaned against the wall of General Castor's office, sweating. She touched the back of her hand to his brow and looked at his dark eyes. The pupils were constricted to black points like dots of ink and his skin was warm, but they *had* been out in the sun all day. Did that mean anything? Rikard took her wrist and pulled her hand away.

"Is he well, mana?" Castor asked.

He almost *sounds like he cares,* Thainna thought.

"I'm fine," Rikard assured her.

He stood, wobbled and then steadied himself again.

"What's wrong with you?" Castor asked.

Rikard scowled up at the Sun Court general. "As far as you're concerned? Everything. But I'm not ill, Castor, and I'm not done for the day."

"I'll call the next company into the yard. Is this strictly necessary, Legens Mazrem?" General Castor stressed the title like a curse.

"Hae, it is. Please, summon the knights and warn them of what's to come. Give them their chance to go, if they decide to."

Castor saluted and strode out of the office. Rikard sat on the corner of the general's desk, rubbing his temples. He looked so tired, but otherwise quite pleased with himself. He lifted his head and smiled at Thainna. She couldn't help smiling back. No longer consumed by the disoriented madness that had tormented him weeks before, Rikard's smirk was distinctively boyish.

Like a boy who has found his father's sword and can't wait until he's old enough to swing it.

"We should finish with this soon," he said. "Then the real work can begin."

"You have something even harder in mind? Rikard, I'm supposed to be taking care of you. I know that I'm mostly here to tell off people like Castor, but I actually want to help, if I can. You're already tired."

"I'm not used to reaching so far or so deep," Rikard admitted.

"Not to sound callous, but why not? After thirty years, I thought you'd be used to this sort of work."

"No. War in Alterra is nothing like this," Rikard said and made a strange snaking, looping gesture with his bloodcapped forefinger. "Or at least, only a little. When the Alterra of the Uprising pulled me through the veil, everything I was became something else. Every passion, every dream and desire and fear and memory became my body, like any other Alterran. My allies and enemies were all... what they were. There was no deception. Except the deceptions, but even they were obvious ones. What I reach for now is deeper, harder to find. Terrans are so... complex. We've been at it for days and I feel the strain against my own skin... against my memories."

You don't seem to find it difficult with me, Thainna thought.

You're different, little Fiori, he returned. *Fiori* was no longer tinged with anger or bitterness, but with affection and even a delicate sort of respect. *You invite me into your thoughts, Thainna. You want me here. Sometimes. It's easier to step through an open door than to kick one in.*

"But the knights know what they're getting into, Rikard," she argued out loud. "You gave them a chance to leave. You've instructed the generals to warn them and then you give them another chance to go, pay and all. No questions asked. And their minds are *still* closed to you?"

"Not objecting to something isn't the same thing as wanting it."

Thainna blushed. "Hae, I guess. There are still about three hundred knights left in the Sun Court to go. Are you well enough to do it?"

Hae, I can do it. I want to, Rikard thought. "Let's go."

"Don't push too hard. If you faint, I don't know that I can drag you all the way back to the Everstones. You're very heavy."

Rikard laughed and let Thainna pull him forward a few steps.

"In the old days, I couldn't have done this at all. There were more than twenty thousand VEIL knights then," he said, suddenly sobering. "There are fewer now. And those that remain are... afraid, as you said."

"Like Karl. He wanted to join VEIL, but he was terrified of the Alterra," Thainna sighed. "Still, there are a lot of knights. Your head must be splitting."

"Hae, but it's well worth a little pain. I can't ask sacrifice of my men that I'm not willing to make, too."

I can't imagine any of the generals saying that.

Thainna's thoughts were cool and soothing as water running over hot stones, over Rikard's raw and reddened mind.

Agreeing with her would have been the worst sort of boasting. Rikard looked down at the floor, flattered and unsure what to say or think.

Come now. Time to get back to work, he decided.

They made their way through the red- and gold-tiled halls of the Sun Court archouse once more, back outside. The yard was full of knights in armor and saelae, all talking and pacing nervously. A stout commander saw Rikard and Thainna descending the stairs again. He stood on a painted podium and whistled sharply.

"Company five, form up!" he called.

One hundred crimson-armored knights ordered themselves into ranks. Not very straight ranks, Rikard noticed. In many cases, Emperor Tychon was right... Too many of these men were lazy, self-centered and lacked anything like discipline. But maybe that was only because they had never known anything else. Rikard hoped to give them something more.

The Sun Court knights fidgeted in meandering ranks. Their namesake burned clear and white-hot high in the cloudless blue sky. Though the air was starting to cool with the onset of autumn, the sun beat down on the sweating armored men like great golden blades. To one side, General Castor stood in a ring of his aides, reading over boards and papers.

"How many left?"

Castor looked up at Rikard's approach.

"Five," he answered. "That makes thirty-seven today alone. How many more of my men do you intend to poach?"

"I don't want anyone to leave, general. I want them to stay, just as you do."

"Then stop this insanity, Mazrem."

"Insanity is letting corruption rot the heart of the strongest fighting force in the two worlds, Castor. Terra needs us, and so does Alterra. You have no idea the kinds of things we can do together, but we must give of ourselves to do it. Not take."

"Hae? What are *you* giving, Mazrem?" Castor asked under his breath.

Rikard gave Castor a long, weary look and then paced back across the field to the Sun Court fifth company. He opened his cannula and traced a circle on his brow. Some of the knights had cheered, some very few had returned the salute. Most murmured uncomfortably, just like that first day in the Moon Court yard. Rikard raised his hand.

"Does this bother you, brothers? You know why I'm here, what I want, what I'm looking for. Corruption, cowardice, brutality. Most of you have nothing to fear and fear nothing. I offered you the chance to walk away, to choose a less demanding path than that of a knight, yet you remained! But there is word of spies from the shadows of Dormaen, dragons from the darkness. You know what is being asked of you, hae?"

A general murmur of assent and a slow wave of uncertain nods rippled through the company. They understood. Most of them disliked the idea, but were willing to let Rikard search their minds for anything dangerous. Blood and sacrifice, they remembered. These men were knights, willing to give for their people. Rikard smiled at them and closed his raised hand into a fist.

"What I ask of you, no man should have to give," he said. "What I ask is unfair to ask of anyone. But we are more than men! We are Verita et Illumina Lansinos! Thank you, brothers, for all you sacrifice. Are you ready?"

"Hae, legens!" shouted most of the Sun Court knights. "Hae!"

"You will feel me among you. Be brave. Stand fast and strong."

Feeling the world with his Terran senses was distracting: the sun's amber light, Thainna's stony-sweet scent, the clatter of sword and armor. Rikard closed his eyes.

The courtyard was gone. He cast about in a field of words and winter, worries and wonders. The knights' thoughts were a storm. A hundred uneasy storms over a hundred peaks and valleys of life's highs and lows.

Rikard spread himself flat and thin, a brindle cloud floating on the currents of curiosity and questions. Just like Stumble taught him.

They felt him, as he had warned, ruffling their storms as he passed. Rikard touched the knights' minds as lightly as he could manage. Most of these were good men, or at least not bad ones. They startled at first, rippling like disturbed water. When Rikard did nothing more intrusive than brush his mind against theirs, they gentled. Calmed, the roiling knight-storms coalesced, drawing together and settling down into laurels and willows and oaks, the trees that meant home and life.

Roots wormed down into stone, stable old memories and loves. Family and friends. Some of the trees were twisted or stunted where they grew from misplaced ambitions and scarred losses. Rikard reached among them like a farmer wandering through an overgrown orchard. Leaves flickered as he passed, full of faces and songs and late, drunken nights. Brawls in taprooms and courtyards, clinging fingers of boys and girls eager to give and to take. Springs and summers and autumns and winters. Whispered secrets behind doors – some closed, some wide open. Youthful dreams and cold adult realization that were rimes of thorns, frosty realities that stung Rikard as he blew past.

Flame.

Rikard stopped in a crevice of deep midnight. Two trees twisted in the cold, heaving like weeds at the bottom of the sea, but their bark was cracked like something burned. Embers seethed beneath the charred skin of the first tree and tongues of flame licked out at Rikard, forcing him back with sharp blades of suspicion. Fear.

Rikard brought himself together to build himself better, more precise senses. Mind's eyes. He reached sideways, drawing on Thainna's faith and determination to protect himself against the fear to craft a shimmering, sheltering caul like a Caspian veil. Rikard drifted closer, until the trees were not trees, but twisted, branching serpent-shapes with snatching claws and fierce, hard eyes.

Dragons, in the House of the Five.

Flame.

Rikard turned to the second serpent-tree. And what of you?

It replied only in a sandy, opalescent rustle. This one was more subtle than the first. The second knight's mind was smaller — no, only more closed — with leaves of molten bronze on long, drooping branches. Rikard ignored them aside, revealing the body beneath. Twining serpents, much like the first, but these had huge, empty black eyes like a starless night. Even old Flickerdim would have envied the secrets of such eyes.

One of the sinewy dragons lifted its long, thin neck away from the others. It chuffed gouts of greasy green flame at Rikard.

Get out, *it hissed.* Go away. I am not here.

What are you? *Rikard wondered.*

The dragon-thing turned away, slithering into the formless shadows of its fellows. Before it could vanish, Rikard grabbed for the serpent. The other knight's mind shuddered and the scale-bark slithered, as slippery as oil. Flaming oil. It burned, but Rikard held fast. The serpent hissed and snapped at him with long white-wink fangs of hatred.

What are you? *Rikard asked again. He squeezed. Not hard enough to damage the knight, just enough to hold him still.* I fear, too. I fear for the future of Carce if left in hands like yours. The House of Five Drag-ons. Thainna told me about you.

Recognition. The leaves shivered and several of them blackened as though burned.

Traitor. She said, she spoke. Traitor.

Traitor? *Rikard didn't understand.*

Little traitor!

The knight would reveal no more without reaching much deeper, cutting away into the vital places that were too delicate to withstand such abuse. Rikard knew enough.

But Thainna shuddered once in unease, then more violently in fear. Something was wrong.

Rikard tore his Terran senses open once more. A tall Jumaari knight with scarred cheeks was pushing his way through the crowd toward Thainna.

Rikard shouted and the Star Court knights who had accompanied him converged on the Jumaari, but the man was quick and strong. He shoved and ducked past, charging forward again with his gladius in hand. The other Sun knights fell back with dismayed cries.

"Hold your lines, damn it!" bellowed the company commander, waving his hand over his head. "Munos, Lancer! Get that bloody blade away from him!"

Finally spurred into action, a pair of Sun Court men leapt on their brother, finally dragging him down to his knees. One of them twisted the sword free and it thumped uselessly into the grass. The House spy spat a curse and dug his fingers under the shoulder of his armor, emerging with a short, sharp throwing knife. With a snap of his wrist, he flung it at Thainna's throat.

No!

Rikard snatched at the sharp, shining shard of steel. It was flying far too fast to catch, but the blade was too small, too light to cut through much. It sank into the meat of his hand and sliced free a red ribbon of blood. Rikard flung the short knife to the ground and closed the short distance to the Jumaari spy. The other knights scrambled back, staring at their legens. Rikard flicked blood onto each of the spy's wrists.

Bind him like vows. In trade, I give you the names of the philosophers' dragons, the damned enemies on this very field: Lust and his sister, Greed! Rage hand in shaking hand with Fear! And Pride. Such pride in Castor, even in this low moment...

The man arched his back and grunted as an invisible force – an Alterran force – seized his bloody wrists and yanked them behind his back. Fine silvery-black chains flashed into being around his gauntlets, slender but unbreakable as faith. Rikard snarled and grabbed him by the front of the armor.

You spied on us, corrupted us from within. You tried to kill Thainna! You are the traitor!

Rikard's fury built to a razor edge, sharper and deadlier than the spy's holdout knife. The bound knight screamed and writhed in his grasp.

There was a light touch at Rikard's shoulder, and then another against his seething mind. He looked down to see Thainna – even paler than usual – standing beside him.

Don't, Rikard. Please, don't hurt him.

He tried to kill you. He called you a traitor!

I'm fine... Please, let your men throw him out and I'll take a look at that hand.

Thainna was more upset than she wanted him to know. Somehow, despite the attempt on her life, Rikard sensed a deep, simmer-soft sympathy for the spy. Why?

Rikard gestured to the other one that he had discovered, a Carcaen who stood in silence, perhaps hoping that he would be forgotten. Rikard had not.

"Send him away. Let him find his own way, his own life." Rikard dropped the Jumaari man into the grass. "But this one tried to kill Thainna. Take him to a lawery. He will be tried in court for his crimes."

Black-armored knights led the two House spies away. The Sun company commander ordered the remaining men back into line. Rikard thanked and then released them for the day. As the fifth company filtered out of the yard, General Castor motioned stiffly to one of his adjutants to summon the sixth. He wasn't pleased and refused to meet the legens' eye.

Thainna pulled Rikard over to one of the archouse steps and told him to sit. She inspected his gashed palm in sullen silence. She was angry with Rikard and it hurt. Not as her fear had cut into his mind, or even as the knife had cut his flesh. *This* pain made his heart and gut twist as though ripped by a Fiori spear.

"Thainna, I'm sorry," said Rikard.

"Why didn't you let that man just leave? You've let everyone else go, even the ones who tried to lie to you!"

"He tried to kill you!" Rikard cried. He couldn't help matching her anger. He yanked his hand away from Thainna and shook it at her. "This could have been your throat! He wanted you dead! Why do you defend him?"

A hot blade-edge of pain flared behind Rikard's eyes as Thainna fought down a surge of fear. She bit her lip and took his hand again.

"I think it's fine," she said. "The cut's not deep. I'll get something to cover it. You've been bleeding enough from that."

Thainna tapped one fingertip on the cap of his cannula. As she stood to find some bandages, Rikard caught her wrist in his uninjured hand and tugged her back to the stairs.

"Thainna, I'm sorry," he said again.

"Then tell your knights to let him go."

"I can't. I didn't want him to hurt you, but even if you hadn't been his target, I couldn't just release him. He had no intention of leaving peacefully, Thainna. He'll have a fair trial. VEIL will pay for his defense."

"Fair trial?" Thainna scoffed. "No one gets a fair trial."

"He will, I promise," Rikard vowed impulsively. "I'm legens of VEIL. That must be worth something."

Thainna paused. "Really? You'll do that?"

"I will."

Rikard wasn't sure about the details, but he would find a way. Thainna squeezed his hand gently, gratefully, and then sprinted up the stairs in search of a templar. Rikard watched her go. The pain in his chest had become something much lighter and brighter, but which squirmed no less.

The sixth company marched into the yard, flowing through the archouse doors like blood from a wound. There was more work to do.

Gaius burst through the curtains that covered the reading room door, very nearly tearing one of the blue velvet drapes free of its bronze hooks. Laurael looked up from a scroll draped across her lap. She gave her son a cold look, but laid the paper aside.

"Dust of Saerus, what is it now? I was reading."

"Bleed on that, Mother!" Gaius hissed. "Have you heard what he's doing? What he can do?"

"Your father? Hae, of course. The man tells me more about his days than I ever care to know. He's putting a comb to VEIL and picking out the louses. What do I care? He is busy and leaves me alone to my days. I've business enough to fill them without his boyish lust and babbling."

"And do you know *how* he's doing it?" Gaius almost screamed.

Laurael put her finger to her lips. "Softly now, unless this conversation is meant for the entire house."

"He can read thoughts, Mother, like you read your letters and ledgers!" Gaius' voice was softer now but burned with no less rage. "Father's been pouring through the minds of every single VEIL knight, easy as walking through this library!"

"So?"

"So? *So?* Mother, do you know what this means for us? For me?"

"Hae, I've heard the stories. If your father could pull my designs from my thoughts or yours, he would have done so already. With you and I, he thinks only with his heart or even lower organs. He knows nothing."

"Even if you're right... what then? While he's out of your way, he's in mine! Three hundred knights left on their own and Father's removed another forty-eight. But those who remain love him for it, or think him an even greater hero. His popularity grows every day! All Dormaen knows of what he's done. But no, that's not enough for Rikard bloody Mazrem!"

"Gaius…"

"Father protects even those unfit for VEIL. One of them tried to kill Thainna today! He's arranged a trial for the man, hired one of the best lawyers in the city to defend him. Does anyone admonish Father for it? No! They only love him more. Tychon will never let it stand. You have to stop this!"

"Patience, Gaius." Laurael took her son's flushed cheeks in her hands and kissed his brow. "Have you forgotten what work it is that I do now?"

"Have you found a way, then, to… to kill him? A man to do it?"

"Not yet," Laurael said.

"What? Why not? Don't tell me you can't find anyone! Even Rikard Mazrem must have enemies."

"I can find a man to do anything I wish, though it has been… difficult," Laurael said primly. "The usual House assassins have refused to take the job. Still, it is a matter of timing, not resources."

"Timing? What in Terra are you waiting for? Every day is one more that Father might find out what you're doing, another day that he's out there sowing chaos!"

Lady Mazrem pursed her lips. "It's a delicate matter, my son. Not yet. Not now."

"How can you just–?"

"Return to your father, Gaius. As you say, he can see into our minds if he so desires. Give him no reason to question you," Laurael said firmly. She waved Gaius toward the door. "In thirty years, I have never missed an opportunity to better your lot, Gaius. I will not miss this one. Let me worry about it. You have much more important concerns."

He stiffened. "Like what?"

"How you'll celebrate your martyred father when he's gone. Now go."

"You're a cold woman, Mother," Gaius said. He smoothed his hair and then left Laurael alone in the library once more.

"How many has he found?"

"All of them. Everyone on the books. Six left during the first two days. He found the other twenty-eight, as well as nine knights we had targeted for assorted uses," the Eye reported in her high, delicate voice.

The Crest traced his fingers in circles on the wide arms of his throne. "That's every last man we had inside VEIL. What about the templars?"

"The legens found all thirteen and removed them."

"Where are they?"

The Eye looked over her list. "Twenty-seven of the knights and twelve templars reported back to us. Six knights and one templar tried to run. I set Talons on each of them. None of them made it out of the city."

The Crest's fingers went still on the green stone.

"That leaves one more. What happened to him?" he asked.

"Horrus. He's awaiting trial in a lawery. Legens Mazrem seems to have taken a particular interest in him. Eulian said that he tried to kill the foster."

"Thainna? He better have failed!"

"Hae, my Crest."

"Good, I need that girl alive. Make sure no one else gets that same idea. Have Horrus' family drowned and make sure everyone knows why."

"It will be done."

"And summon Thainna! I need to regain control of this."

32

OF BLOOD AND SACRIFICE

"Alterra is literally a world of Terran dreams, and we fear that world. What does that say about our dreams?"

— AVILLA SALLUSI

RIKARD COULDN'T KEEP himself from prodding the gash across his palm. It itched like madness. He rubbed at the bandage until Saul made a disgusted noise.

"Rik, if you don't stop poking that thing, you're going to get an infection. And then that little Fiori foster is going to take off *my* head for not stopping you. Now, what did you want to talk about?"

"I need to know what's going on in the city," Rikard said. "In the empire. I already know the history, what happened while I was gone. Tell me what's happening now."

Saul rubbed his eyes. "You're relentless, Rik. Hae, then. What do you want to know? Why?"

"We need to do something, Saul. Remember what you told me about Dormaen? The people of Carce are afraid of VEIL, and VEIL is afraid of the Alterra. We must fix that. We have to repair these fraying bonds between us and the people, between us and the Alterra."

"Look, you've already convinced me, Rik. What do you plan to do about it?" asked Saul.

"Make a... gesture. No, that's the wrong word. It rings hollow. We need to do something for the people of Carce and for the Alterra. We must remind them – and ourselves – that VEIL exists to serve the worlds."

"A demonstration, you mean. Like what?"

"VEIL was born of the scholars who first found a way to speak to the Alterra, Saul. We can't forget where we came from. We can do more than fight! We can hold back floods, bring rain to a desert or build a house in a day."

"Don't you think we might want to wait on anything like that? You've already thrown everything into chaos. Nikas Hern is starting to chew on his own feet. You're going to burst the man's heart, you know."

"We can't wait," Rikard said. "We must fix this!"

"Hae, Rik. If you say so, then it is," Saul answered. He drummed his fingers on his desk and gave a small, self-mocking laugh. "I can't keep track of the whole world. Most of the time, running the Star Court is more than I can really manage, especially these days! I can send for some of the templars who know some more. I think most of them are out taking stock in the storehouses, but I'm sure they can spare one."

"The storehouses?"

"Hae. They're checking the new headcount against the supplies. Since that blight out in Erastrasus, everyone is watching their numbers pretty close."

Saul called for his adjutant and relayed the request. When he was done, he smirked at Rikard.

"So where's that Fiori foster today?" he asked. "She's a pretty little thing. I was looking forward to seeing her again."

"You have a wife, Saul!" Rikard admonished his friend.

"And I love her, Rik. But a man never stops admiring beauty."

"Thainna will be back this evening. She said she had some business in the city today."

"You let her go off on her own? After that attack...?"

Rikard picked up a quill from Saul's desk and spun it against the slick metal of his bloodcap. "I didn't want to, but she felt it was important."

Karl offered once again to accompany Thainna into Dormaen, but she turned him down. Not that the Lyncean guard wasn't pleasant company. Karl seemed inspired by Rikard's heroics and redoubled his efforts to become a proper gentleman soldier. He flushed when Thainna suggested that with his employer now in control of VEIL, this might be the time to reconsider knighthood. She took advantage of Karl's flustered stammering to slip out of the gate and into the city.

Her satchel was heavy and Thainna's tabba was stained with sweat by the time she left the Everstones, heading into the closest district of shops. She almost regretted not asking Bastil for use of one of the Mazrem's horses. Surely evading a few questions was less work than her burdened hike.

It took most of the morning to sell the trinkets she had stolen from Rikard's house: the pretty glass lamp, the filigreed emberbox, a small opal-eyed statue of Merra, a pair of delicate finger-cymbals, a set of combs set with rubies and a dozen long-tined silver forks. Thainna was a practiced thief – she took nothing that bore any recognizable marks that might make selling them more difficult. Her second task would be trouble enough.

When she was finished with the shops, Thainna made the long journey into the Rows, the old shores of the Mazren River, the one

Rikard's family took their name from. Rikard was an old name, too, from the ancient Carcaen tongue. It was as if no part of him really belonged in the modern age, Thainna thought. But it was the age he had created.

None of this is fair to Rikard. He gave his life in Njorn Pass, then got hooked into an Alterran civil war. Then they turn him out into Terra and now he has to fix VEIL. Rikard doesn't get much rest, does he?

Neither did Thainna. It certainly was not good to be home... The streets of the Rows were no less broken, smelly or crowded than she remembered. Every building was falling down and the people looked little better. The streets ran dark and fetid with muck – sick blood carrying poison through a dying body.

And I'm here to peddle more poison.

If she couldn't use the drams Narissa had given her, she certainly would not let them go to waste. Not with the Auction approaching. Rikard wanted to fix VEIL... Maybe he would have approved of Thainna's plan to promote Thain and mend the House of Five Dragons. The attack yesterday had shaken her, but served even more as a stern reminder of the importance of taking control of the House of Five Dragons, of winning the Auction and delivering the House into Thain's capable hands.

It wasn't hard to find people who wanted to buy the contents of Narissa's jars, but it took most of the afternoon to find those with the money to do so. After Thainna traded away the last of the jession for a handful of shaved willows, she found herself at the stained, splintered shop door and could put off her final task no longer. She pushed it open.

"Time to wake up and work, Pata," she announced.

Aelos Vahn sat inside the House front-shop, but he wasn't asleep or even lounging under the murky window. He hunched over the splintering table, staring at the open ledger. When Aelos saw Thainna, he jumped to his feet with a look of horror on his lined, dirty face.

"Thainna! What are you doing here?"

"Hae, Pata," Thainna said sourly. "I missed you, too."

Her father scowled. "Of course I missed you, but what are you doing here? You're supposed to be with Rikard Mazrem!"

"You heard about my job, then. You weren't worried when I vanished?"

"You've always been hard to keep track of, Thainna. I figured you were off working," Aelos said. He would not meet her eye. "Eventually, I heard about your bloodmark. And your job."

Was he proud of her? The job should have gone to someone with far more rank or experience. Surely even Pata was impressed... Thainna searched her father's face, but found only surprise and displeasure there. She sighed and tossed a wallet onto the table. It clanked heavily.

"I need to make a deposit."

Slowly, Aelos sat again and reached for the wallet. He untied the cord and gasped at the coins inside. "Where did you get all of this?"

"I stole a few things from the Mazrem house. I sold off the supplies I didn't use on Rikard and–"

"Thainna! You sold them? You can't do that!"

"Why not? I don't have the time to work for myself while I'm on this job, Pata. The House gave me those drams to use. Narissa isn't expecting them back."

"That's House property!"

"And I'm stealing it? The House probably stole it before I did. If it bothers you that much, I'll just ask Thain for a pardon or something when he's Crest."

Now Thainna's father did catch her eye, but dropped his gaze a moment later. "You don't have to do this."

"Don't start."

"Thain's sick! You don't even know if he'll be well enough to run the House. It's cruel, really. He's a sick boy, Thainna."

"Don't be bitter." The desire to fight her father was suddenly gone. "Please, Pata. Just count the money and then I'll go, hae?"

Aelos poured Thainna's money onto the tabletop and separated it into piles. Nervous and excited, she watched the stacks grow, coin by coin, like crooked little towers being built. Still, Thainna felt more than a little guilty stealing from Rikard.

It's not really stealing from him, Thainna told herself. *Laurael probably bought all of this. If he weren't married, Rikard would probably still live in an archouse bunk.*

The idea made her feel only a bit better. Aelos finished counting and swept the money into a covered bowl. He set it on a nearby shelf and then wrote the new total down in the open ledger.

"How much have I got?" Thainna asked breathlessly.

"Almost two hundred laurels today. That brings you up to about nine hundred."

"Nine hundred! I'll have more than a thousand by winter, Pata. That's got to be enough!"

"That's not much money, really."

"It's more than you've ever earned! You keep telling me to run off with it and live better."

"Thainna, it took fifty thousand to win the last Auction."

She felt like her father had just punched her in the stomach. Fifty *thousand* laurels? Thainna couldn't imagine having that much, much less spending it on the Auction. Surely anyone that rich could simply leave the House of Five Dragons.

"How much money is in the House vault?" Thainna asked.

"You know I couldn't tell you, even if I knew. The Crest would have me thrown in the river!"

Thainna grabbed for the ledger, but Aelos snatched it back out of her grasp. She curled her lip at the useless old man. "It doesn't matter, anyway! I just need more than the other bidders. How much have they got?"

"You're contending with Eyes and Flames," Aelos reminded her.

"You're a thief, Thainna. That's all. Unless you plan to steal Rikard Mazrem's entire house and holdings, you can't compete with them. Even if you could, it wouldn't matter."

"Because of the Crest we've got now? Because he won't give up the Jade Throne? I'm so tired of hearing everyone say that! Things *will* change!"

"Everything is changing," Aelos said. He looked at Thainna with drooping eyes and managed an awkward smile. "Even you. Look at you! Dressed up fancy, like a proper lady."

"Like a priestess, you mean."

"You look beautiful. Probably got that Mazrem fellow wrapped around your finger by now," Aelos suggested hopefully. "You said you didn't need the drams."

"Rikard's not like that. I tried to give him bluering once and he didn't even notice."

"What about the jession?"

"I didn't try–" Thainna began, but then frowned as a thought occurred to her. "How did you know what Narissa gave me?"

"I said I asked around after you."

"Hae," said Thainna suspiciously.

Her father's information seemed a little too detailed. Suddenly, Thainna wished for Rikard's strange Alterran ability to reach into his mind. What sort of secrets might she find in the dusty, unused corners of her father's mind? Thainna scowled at Aelos. After so long apart, she was already sick of the old man.

"I have to meet Rikard at the archouse," Thainna said. Without further farewell, she stomped angrily out of the store.

On his mother's advice, Gaius drove back to the Star Court, but the sun was soon sinking into the hills surrounding the Kaelos Valley. Ranks of knights worked in the courtyard, practicing some of the older sword techniques – the left-handed pact forms. At Gaius' approach, the oldest called a stop and saluted.

"Good evening, Captain Mazrem," he panted.

"Where's my father?" asked Gaius shortly.

"The legens rode out an hour or so ago, sir. He's ordered the three courts to convene here tomorrow, though."

Gaius grunted wordlessly and climbed back into his chariot. Rikard could never stay where he was supposed to, could he? Gaius shook his reins and guided the kajja back out onto the road. He bridled at the pointlessness of it all.

Evening traffic ran as slow and thick as chilled honey, leaving Gaius time enough to brood. *I'm Rikard Mazrem's son! I was supposed to inherit this whole world,* he thought angrily. The world may not have been the one Rikard thought that it should be, but it would have belonged to Gaius.

He looked up from the bouncing jewel-hued back of the kajja running before his chariot. The market and central districts that lay between the Star archouse and the Everstones were some of the most affluent of Dormaen. Over the angular city skyline, the pristine dome of the Lyceum was clearly visible, as smoothly white as the egg of a celestial bird-god. Smooth glass shined in every shop and house window, some even in ruby red and deep emerald greens. The people who lined the walkways that ran beside the road wore expensively patterned tabbae and beaded sandals. Many recognized Gaius and waved as he drove past.

Even here, though, money couldn't cover all signs of the deep rot that ran through every inch of Dormaen. Gaius caught sight of a few girls for rent, all garishly dressed and marked by the red bracelets around their wrists. A fat man stood in the door of his bakery, boasting his low prices – still five times what they should have been. Around the next corner, a pair of men in dark clothes waited with daggers hidden poorly under short capes.

What does Father think he can do against all this? He really is mad.

Another thought followed on the heels of the first. *And this is the world that Alterrans — the ones of the Uprising, at least — want to keep close? They're as mad as my father.*

When Gaius reached the broad, gentle rise of the Everstones, he wound the reins around one hand and took the wallet from his belt. From a fold of thick paper inside, he tapped a bit of fine brown powder into his mouth. The ophellion bit acidly on his tongue, but dissolved quickly. Gaius shuddered with pleasure as the dram ran through his body, as smooth and cold and deep as icy waters. It was a bad idea to show up to dinner bristling with anger at Rikard, to give him any excuse to go searching through his son's thoughts.

Back at the house, Gaius found Rikard was already in the triclinium, lying across one of the couches. Thainna lay beside him — not sitting apart or at his feet, as was proper for a servant — listening to him with a furrowed brow. On Rikard's other flank, Laurael fought to keep her smile steady.

"Do you think it's a good idea?" Rikard asked both women.

"Why are you asking me about it? I'm not a knight or a templar," Thainna said.

Before Rikard could respond, Gaius stepped through the door. The foster dropped her gaze, her lips twitching. Was that a smile or a scowl? Either way, she hid it even as Rikard's face lit up. Gaius had no doubt that his pleasure was sincere.

There's nothing subtle about my father, Gaius thought with a mix of irritation and reluctant admiration. Rikard Mazrem was a simple man. He never lied. Gaius wasn't even sure if he knew how.

"Come and eat," Rikard said brightly, gesturing to his son. "I missed you at the archouse today."

Gaius draped himself over the opposite couch and plucked a handful of fat purple plums from a nearby bowl. They were cold and sweet, bursting with flavor. An unfamiliar serving girl — one of those that Bastil had brought in to deal with the rise in visitors — darted a furtive, mousy look at Gaius. He winked and she blushed.

When she had delivered her tureen of steaming soup, the girl fled the room, her cheeks still bright red. Gaius promised himself that he would find her later.

"So what do you want, Father?" he asked.

The pleasantly cool weight of the ophellion blunted the worst accusation from the question. It would get him through dinner, and then he would go home for a dose of sweet-hot bluering...

"I need you to do something," Rikard told him.

So simple and straightforward. Had the man always been like that? When Gaius was a boy, Laurael had rarely spoken about his father except to remind him to conduct himself appropriately. Was it something Rikard had picked up in Alterra? Did Alterrans lie? *Could* they?

"The great hero needs *me* to do something? What's that, hae? Sweep up the rose petals they shower wherever you go?"

Rikard flinched and Gaius almost regretted his words.

"Would... will you come with me to the Star Court tomorrow?" Rikard asked.

"Well, the hours you keep are a little early for me. What time?"

"Noon."

"I guess so," Gaius said. "What do you need me for, Father? Are you lonely?"

Laurael frowned at him, but Gaius ignored her.

"No, I..." Rikard started. He made a strange little gesture with his right hand and tried again. "I want you to join in an Alterran pact with me."

Gaius had just raised a cup of wine to his lips. Even ophellion couldn't blunt *that* blow. Gaius choked, spluttering and pounded his fist against his chest until he stopped coughing.

"A pact? Me?" he asked. "For what? What have you been drinking? Gods only know what those dream-eater monsters will take in return!"

"Please consider it, Gaius?"

Thainna watched the exchange with an absurdly disapproving little frown on her pretty lips. Gaius scowled at her. He didn't see the foster spilling *her* blood to the Alterra.

Gaius took another handful of round plums and set them spinning on the tabletop, wobbling like drunkards. A blood pact...? It was too dangerous to even think about... wasn't it?

Thainna had departed after dinner to visit the baths and wash away the sweat and dirt of the day. But Rikard found her later in the wavering azure light of the shrine. Thainna wore a white sleeping wrap knotted under her arms and knelt before the smooth alabaster altar of Surma. She stood up when Rikard entered, a little surprised but not startled. Had Thainna heard him, or felt him coming?

"Do you need me to leave?" she asked. "Bastil said no one comes here much and I was free to make my prayers."

"No. Please stay."

Rikard nodded at Thainna and she sank back to the floor. He sat back on his heels beside her. The foster touched her fingers to the altar, leaving bright smears of blood on the white stone. A small kitchen knife lay on the fitted stone floor beside the shrine.

"You're bleeding," Rikard said. "What are you doing?"

Thainna held up her hand. There was a small, bloody cut on her third finger.

"Just a little nick. I thought about the things you've been saying. About blood, about fear. No one bleeds for the gods or the Alterra anymore."

"But you understand sacrifice. Are you praying for him? For your brother?"

"Are you in my thoughts again?" Thainna asked with a small smile. She waved off the question before Rikard could answer. "No,

I don't feel you there. Hae, for Thain. He's... Things are worse now. It's complicated. I miss him so much."

"Why don't you bring him here?" Rikard suggested, surprised he hadn't thought of it before. Thainna's separation from her twin wounded the foster deeply. "There's plenty of room and food. You could take care of him more easily if he was nearby."

Thainna's eyes widened. "You would let me bring him here?"

"He could live here, if he wanted," said Rikard. He felt as though he had eaten butterflies for dinner, flittering things that only now realized their new home and had gone exploring. "You can, too. I'd like you to stay here with us. If the temple would allow it, I mean. Laura's done very well for herself, for my family. Two more mouths to feed wouldn't be a burden."

"You would let us both stay?"

Thainna stared up at Rikard with such impossible hope that it made his heart clench. The alleyway that she called home, the one he had seen in her memories, was... horrible.

No one should live like that. Especially you.

It's all I've ever known, Rikard. I'm used to it.

Are you saying no?

Thainna laughed. She wiped her eyes and grinned at Rikard.

"No! I mean, hae. I'm not saying *no*. I want to. I would like to bring Thain here," Thainna said. She gestured around her, then at the wide door that led out into the rest of the rolling estate. "He's never even visited a place so lovely."

"Would it be allowed?" asked Rikard hopefully. "Would Narissa object?"

Thainna bit her lower lip. After a moment, she shook her head.

"Not exactly. But Thain..." The heat of her tears was back, this time in sadness, and Thainna turned her face away.

What's wrong? Rikard wondered.

It's complicated. Dangerous.

...You can't do it.

If Thainna couldn't bring her beloved twin, she would never stay here. Thainna would run home to him, even if it meant going back to her filthy alley. The idea was a horrid one. It hurt like a kick to the stomach. Thainna deserved better than that, but she sacrificed out of love. She would give up anything and everything for her brother.

Rikard brushed his fingers over Thainna's pale cheek and took her blood-streaked hand in his. This girl from the mud and trash of the Rows understood devotion and sacrifice better than any VEIL knight. Rikard was so proud of Thainna that he wondered if his heart could actually burst.

Tears shone in Thainna's coppery lashes. *Maybe in time, after...*

The thought that followed was close and private, tangled in sticky worries like one of Rikard's butterflies caught and coiled in a spider's web. She didn't take her hand from Rikard's and a hot tear fell from her chin onto the cuff of his saela. It sparkled star-bright against the black for a moment before vanishing, absorbed into the cloth.

Rikard stroked his thumb across the back of Thainna's hand. It felt so delicate, but strong. Something of steel and stone carved skillfully into a small, fine shape. Rikard wondered what she was thinking and was tempted to reach for an answer, but the wingy fluttering in his stomach was more fun than knowing. He liked the mystery, Rikard decided.

Thainna had asked him something. She looked at him with a quizzical arc to her red eyebrows. Rikard shook himself from his reverie.

"I'm sorry. I didn't hear. What?"

"What did you come to pray for?"

"Gaius." Rikard reluctantly took his hands back and thumbed open his cannula. He daubed a line of blood onto the snowy white Surmaen altar, beside Thainna's mark. The butterflies turned to lead in his gut.

"I don't know if he will help us," Rikard said. "He hates me. Gods' blood, Thainna. My own son hates me."

"I'm sorry," said Thainna gently. "But I told you there's something sour in him. I wish I were surprised. And with his mother–"

Rikard's head came up. "No. Thainna, please don't. I love her."

"Hae, then."

Thainna turned away with a frown that made Rikard regret his sharpness. He dropped his gaze to the smears of Thainna's blood on Surma's altar.

"It's not going to... do anything, is it?" she asked after a moment. "Those marks don't mean anything to the Alterra, right?"

Thainna didn't sound afraid, Rikard thought, but disappointed. Did she *want* the Alterra to hear her?

"No, not like this." Rikard trailed his finger through her blood, drawing a curving line on the stone. "But if you draw it here. And like this, here... Cross it here."

Thainna tilted her head. "It looks like shortscribe."

"Can you read it?"

"I think so. *Good morning, burning* and *scales*, all piled on top of each other."

Rikard grinned. "Well read. The third one says *dragon*, not *scales*. It's the sign meant to get the Alterran's attention. A greeting, of sorts, more formal than the circle. The scholars worked it out in the old days."

Thainna looked at her blood. "Why *dragon*?"

"I don't know, precisely. Dragons are just a legend. Their name became one for anything powerful and majestic... but now it just seems to mean something dangerous or evil."

"That certainly sums up your relationship with the Alterra. The powerful and the dangerous. Maybe you too, hero of Carce."

"Hero." Rikard sighed. "Saul called me that."

"It couldn't have been the first time. You're the greatest legend in all Carce."

Rikard was not so easily deterred. "I don't feel heroic, Thainna."

"You saved most of VEIL and won a war. You wiped out the entire Fiori army."

"Do you ever hate me for that? I hated you. I hurt you," Rikard said. "In the pass, I would have given everything – and did – just to end it. I destroyed thousands of Fiori."

"I've never even seen Fiore. Pata always said that Therra – that's my mother – didn't miss the mountains. Rikard... it was a war."

"Emperor Tychon began that war."

"And you ended it. It's over and none of that is a reason to doubt your heroism. I don't hate you and I doubt any of the other Fiori do, either. Hae, I know you don't care much for the emperor, but that doesn't mean he's completely worthless. There are forty-nine other nations besides Carce that warred with each other. Now they fight it all out in the Lyceum. It's bloodless and it's boring. Sometimes I think that Emperor Tychon only created the Lyceum to give the provinces a civil battlefield."

Rikard found himself smiling a little. "That's not a bad idea. But you only made my point for me, Thainna. They are doings of the emperor, good or ill, not me. I'm only a soldier."

"That sounds like the defense of a man who doesn't have any better argument."

"Maybe not, but that doesn't change anything. It doesn't feel right. I did only what any other commander would have done."

"But they *didn't*," Thainna said. "There was a lecturn once who said something about Njorn Pass. He wasn't very popular for it, but I think you might like it better than most."

"What did he say?"

"He said that circumstances make heroes, not deeds. I guess he meant that you were in the right place at the right time to do the right thing."

"It was in the hands of the gods, then?" Rikard asked. It made him feel better. Less aggrandized, a little less a fraud.

"Maybe. But I don't agree. Any other VEIL commander could have made the same choice that you did, hae? At any time during the campaign? But they didn't – you did. You were the only one willing to make the trade."

Rikard could think of no argument. Thainna had a point, but one that was hard for him to dwell on. Rikard stood and crossed the shrine to the Alterran door. Opening his cannula, he drew the same mark he had just shown Thainna. It shone black like ink in the blue light of the shrine.

When they had each finished their solitary prayers, they made their way from the shrine. Outside, Rikard caught Thainna's eye.

"You'll come tomorrow, hae?"

"I won't be much help, I think, but I'll be there if you want."

"I do."

Thainna smiled shyly and struck out across the hilly estate. Rikard watched her go and wondered. A hero... Surely a hero could make a small request of the temple, Rikard reasoned. A hero could ask that Thainna be allowed to stay. When she freed Thain from whatever it was that frightened her, he would give Thainna and her twin the life they deserved. Together.

33

CALLING

"History happens in a moment. Years, decades can pass unnoticed between. And then, in an instant, the whole world changes."

— AFTER NJORN PASS, BY ALEXANDER FERRO

"Do you have any idea what we're all doing here?" asked another Moon Court knight.

Marus shrugged and grinned at him. "Not a bit of one. Bloody hell, when was the last time all three courts gathered?"

It was the other knight's turn to shrug. He had no answer. That was fine with Marus. He didn't need an answer yet. The wonder of seeing all VEIL in one place was enough to permanently pin the grin to his face.

The Star Court yard was full of men, crowded with thousands of knights in a mix of black, red and blue armor. The courtyard was never meant to hold so many, but most of the knights didn't seem to mind the close pack of their brothers. Hundreds of them had left when Rikard offered them the chance, but more stayed, curious about what was to come.

The crowd would not be still. Every breath was tense with anticipation. No one knew what their strange, famous legens planned. A restless murmur rose and fell by the moment, speculating and then remarking on the pointlessness of doing so. Rikard Mazrem was nothing if not unpredictable.

Just before noon, General Hern appeared on one of the high half-moon balconies, accompanied by a pair of templars scribbling on boards. A shout rose from the assembled knights. Hern raised one of his hands and bellowed something in reply, but Marus could not hear him.

"What did he say?"

"I have no idea," Marus answered.

The man who had asked was a few years younger than Marus and wore Sun Court red. Struck by a sudden impulse, Marus extended his hand.

"Marus Gallard. Did General Castor tell you what all of this is about?"

The other knight took Marus' hand and introduced himself as Ashus Vorrenum, but then shook his head. "No, he didn't say."

"Nothing at all?" Marus had to lean close and shout to make himself heard over the throng of other knights, all probably asking much the same.

"General Castor spoke to us briefly before we left the Sun Court this morning," Ashus said loudly. His volume could not mask a hitching note of hesitation.

"What did he say?"

"He warned us that the legens would ask something dangerous of us."

"Shut up, Ashus," said another Sun knight.

He thumped his brother knight on the shoulder, making Ashus stumble heavily against Marus. Ashus scowled at the other Sun knight and pushed away a few yards through the crowd. Marus kept pace. Ashus muttered something under his breath.

"What was that?" Marus asked.

"Nothing, sir."

Marus considered pressing the younger knight, but decided against it. The crowd of knights suddenly went still and rigid around them. Marus looked at the balcony General Hern had occupied a few minutes before. One by one, then hundreds and then thousands, the knights took up the chant.

"Mazrem! Mazrem! Mazrem!"

Marus and Ashus joined in, raising their right hands to join thousands of others. Golden bloodcaps shone across the courtyard like a field of tiny suns. High on the balcony, Rikard Mazrem held up his own hand and then swept it down, signaling for silence.

For only the second time that Marus had ever seen – not that he had met the great man many times, he admitted to himself – Rikard wore full armor to match that of the sea of knights below. It looked to be a modern suit, jet black and marked by the shiny silver insignia of the Star Court. The Fiori foster fidgeted beside him in her sky-colored tabba, uncomfortable in front of the vast crowd. The generals of the three courts stood behind Legens Mazrem. From his vantage point, Marus could read very little in their expressions, but he thought that Castor and Hern looked unhappy. The knowledge gave him a secret, guilty little thrill.

You got pretty comfortable in the easy old ways, didn't you? Let's see what you think of a proper leader.

A sixth figure stepped out onto the balcony, a man who looked so much like Rikard that Marus had to squint at him for a long moment before he recognized the legens' son, Gaius Mazrem. Some time passed before the knights managed to quiet themselves.

"Brothers!" the legens called out.

Another roaring cheer and Rikard had to wait before continuing.

"Brothers, you bring pride and grace to Carcel You have endured what no men have before. You have let me into your very hearts and thoughts and do you know what I found there? Corrupt men, hae, that have been sent on to new lives outside VEIL. But I found honor, too. Strong men with pure spirits!"

Another rumbling thunderclap of applause and shouts greeted the new legens' pronouncement and thousands of knights basked in his pride. Marus tried but couldn't manage to school his own grin into something more sober and professional.

"This is the face we must show to Dormaen, to all the empire." Rikard's voice echoed across the courtyard. "We remember our honor and we must be certain that they do! We must write this moment into the book of history in the only ink befitting VEIL knights. In blood!"

"What do you want of us, Mazrem?" cried a man at the front. A hundred other knights echoed the question. "Tell us our orders!"

"I call upon you to remember your origins, my brothers," Rikard said. "Before we of the Verita et Illumina Lansinos were warriors, we were scholars. Men of fine Carcaen tradition in service to both worlds. We served our nation and we will serve her again!"

"We will serve!" shouted the knights.

"The grain harvest from Erastrasus is blighted. It molders even now in the Lyceum vaults, waiting to be burned. Five hundred tons of wheat and millet. Dormaen has grown large and without that harvest, tens of thousands of her citizens will starve!"

Marus nodded. Next to him, Ashus did the same. Everyone had heard the rumors, though few knights had concerned themselves much over it. VEIL was powerful and hungry soldiers were even more dangerous than bored ones. They would be among the last to go without. It was terrible news, but what could anyone do?

"With your help and that of the Alterra, I will cleanse the Erastrasus grain," Rikard announced.

Marus, Ashus and a dozen other nearby knights gasped. Whispers rippled through the crowd of knights. Rikard Mazrem raised his hand again for quiet.

"The cost will be high, brothers," he said. "But it will be well paid to keep Carcaen citizens from going hungry. I call for knights to draw their blood beside me, to make your sacrifice before the gods and Alterra for Carce! We can recover what has been lost. None but VEIL can do this, brothers. It falls to us! Our duty, our privilege. With this act, we give to Terra and Alterra, the worlds that are mother and father to us all! Who stands with me?"

Marus was the first to raise his fist. "Hae, legens!"

"Hae, legens!" cried Ashus.

"Hae!" bellowed the knights. "Hae! Hae!"

But not all of them, Marus noted. Beneath their crested helms, hundreds of faces had gone as white as milk. Many of these wore red armor. The Sun knight who had chastised Ashus kept his hands firmly at his side. Did Rikard know their fear? Did he feel it? The extent of the legens' strange powers were still a mystery to those under his command.

Marus couldn't waste worry on the frightened knights. The loss was theirs. The chance to be a part of something great, finally! After twenty years of wondering why he bothered getting out of bed in the morning, why he had ever joined VEIL... Now thousands of men held fists in the air, pledging blood, memory and their very spirits to Rikard Mazrem. To Dormaen, to Carce and to the Alterra.

"Hae!" Marus shouted again.

I see, I see! The tower leaves shone silvery clarion with elation. All of them rang and shivered in the brazen typhoon. Stumble ducked his stone-feathered head and danced a ridiculous little jig on his short, stripy legs. *I hear them. I feel their thoughts like moonlight. Can you clasp it? He's bringing them back to us!*

Stumble hopped underways along the great white branch and then nipped excitedly at Flickerdim's stormy tailtip. Something far below them rippled softly, like a parent's affection. Stumble fluttered down through the branches to see.

A doorway? The shape was glassy and indistinct, but it arched at the foot of the Uprising, drawn and bowed like a wilting tree but growing stronger with each breath. The emptiness inside the door swam with wispy colors, scents and sounds that bled out, running over the threadbare swell of the fading Uprising like an upended bucket of paint.

A Terran door! Just like in Mask, back when I was only a childish question! Stumble thought.

Flickerdim blinked opaque eyes and tasted the air with his smoky tongue. The door – once so familiar, now as rare as truths – seemed to strengthen everything around it. The Uprising sang with verdant tones and the tree-tower danced, swaying in the unknown wind. Even the storm overhead was darker, burning staccato with flashes of rowan. The blank rents of the Shatter across the sky swirled suddenly, snaking over the Uprising and stabbed down toward the tree-tower like the shadows of swords.

The Shatter see it, too, Flickerdim said. *They are attacking.*

"The emperor isn't going to like this," Gaius said when they had gone inside.

The room pounded with the chanting cheers of the knights outside, even with the doors closed and heavy drapes pulled shut. It was like being inside a drum, Gaius thought. Rikard lingered just inside, eyes half shut and basking in the praise of his men.

No, that's not fair, Gaius thought reluctantly. *He doesn't care about the praise. He's glad to see them happy and inspired.*

Not everyone was so pleased. Muscles rippled in Castor's jaw and the Sun Court general clenched his teeth so hard that Gaius was sure they would crack. He looked like he was trying to eat his own tongue. Nikas Hern detached himself from the other court generals and cleared his throat a couple of times until Rikard's eyes fluttered open and focused.

Thainna smirked and General Castor shot her a withering look. The red-haired foster stopped laughing and looked up at Rikard. The pair held each other's gaze for a silent moment, and then Rikard turned to Hern.

"Hae?" he asked.

"Gaius is right," Hern said without missing a beat. "Emperor Tychon isn't likely to receive news of your decision very well."

"Why not? We only want to help his people. Even if that's not enough for him, cleansing that grain shipment will probably keep them from rioting when winter comes."

"Both true," Gaius said. "But Tychon doesn't care what happens beyond the gates of his palace, Father. Whether Carce flourishes or fails, Tychon doesn't mind so long as the wine and women flow."

A long table of polished hywood ran the length of the room, lined on either side with high-backed chairs. General Hern sat on one and crossed his arms. Unlike the other knights, Hern still wore his standard blue saela rather than his full armor.

"I would not have put it that way," he said.

"I know," retorted Gaius. "You bend like a reed, general."

"And float like one when the drink's running high," Saul Darius added with a chuckle. He nodded to the other generals. "Hae, you worry too much, ladies. The emperor will see reason. Rik assured Tychon that he has no designs on the throne."

"Words are cheap," Hern said.

"Then why are you so rich, old friend, since they seem to be your trade?" Darius countered.

The Moon Court general scowled at him. "An invested salary and the emperor's generosity, Saul. Same as you. Same as all of us."

Gaius looked at his father. Rikard was distracted again. He and Thainna looked at each other as though engaged in some silent, private conversation. Perhaps they were. Did the endless bickering bore Rikard? If so, Gaius could hardly blame him.

"Rik?" Saul snapped his fingers for his friend's attention. When the young legens tore his eyes away from Thainna's, Saul laughed. "Your wife is going to whip you if you stare at that Fiori girl much harder, Rik."

"Enough," Rikard said, but Gaius thought he looked flushed. "I heard you, Nikas, but my words still linger... they are true. I meant them. I don't want the empire, only for its people to prosper and its knights to remember their duties."

Hern tapped his capped forefinger on the bright-polished table. "Mark me, Emperor Tychon will fight you. He will find some guise for his complaint. Are you certain you want to do this?"

"I am," said Rikard evenly. "We must prove our worth to Dormaen and ourselves."

Hern sighed. "Hae, legens."

"Will you join me in this pact, brothers?"

The generals looked at each other, eyes wide with surprise. Saul shook himself all over like a wet dog and nodded to Rikard.

"Hae. I'm with you, of course," he said. "Can't think what your Alterran friends might want with anything between my ears, but they're welcome to it. Cleansing the grain is a good idea, as you say, and I'm too fat and too lazy to weather a winter riot. I'll bleed with you, Rik."

Hern and Castor were pale and silent. Rikard waited a moment, and then nodded to the two generals. "It's a hard thing that I ask. Take your time in considering."

"Thank you, legens," Hern said with a bow.

The clamor outside had finally begun to die down and Castor cocked his head toward the balcony door. "It's time to return our men to their own courts, Legens Mazrem. They'll have preparations to make, I'm certain. If you'll excuse us..."

"Hae, go. They will have questions," Rikard said.

The generals saluted and departed, leaving Gaius alone with his father and the foster. Rikard watched the door swing shut behind the other men and sighed heavily. A moment later, he smiled and took up Hern's seat at the table. He brought his eyes up to Gaius, apparently cheered. The man changed moods like clothes.

"It went well, don't you think? I had hoped for a few hundred volunteers, but there must have been thousands today!" Pleased, Rikard slapped his palm against the tabletop. "Our brothers are not as faint-hearted as you thought, Thainna. They're good men. They need only the chance to be so."

Gaius expected the Fiori girl to bristle, but she smiled back at Rikard.

"You were right," Thainna told him. "I hope they're so eager when the time comes to actually scribe their blood."

"Have faith. They will."

Thainna laughed. "They would follow you right into Alterra if you ordered it."

"What about my son?" Rikard asked. The question was hesitant, almost shy, as though he were not the most powerful, privileged man in the entire world. "Gaius, you haven't said very much. What do you think?"

Gaius sat down opposite his father and didn't offer up an immediate reply. Rikard had shared his plan the night before and wanted his son to approve, to help. It made Gaius feel strangely powerful, a sensation largely lost to him since Rikard's return. But he couldn't enjoy it long.

I don't want power over him, not like this. It's not right. Whatever else is wrong with him, my father is unfailingly noble. Perhaps that is one of his failings. It's not right that he should need approval of this stupid, selfless decision from... from someone like me.

Gaius rested his chin in his hands and regarded Rikard across the table. It was like looking into some kind of magical mirror. Gaius saw all of his own familiar features, even the raven-black hair that his mother dyed. But Rikard wore it all so differently. His face was handsome and chiseled, the face of a man other men admired and followed to their benefit. A nobleman in the truest sense. He was respected not by virtue of birth, but by spirit and sword.

His sword is still in my house. He's never asked for it. He's never needed it.

Gaius' eyes wandered to the door. Only Saul had promised his blood to Rikard's pact. The Star Court general was a good man, but with all the wit of a stone. Hern would not decide until he knew where Emperor Tychon stood. Coward. And Castor... Could his ridiculously stiff-necked sense of honor win out over his hatred for Rikard?

What good was it to disdain such men when Gaius himself was no better? He looked at his father again. Rikard met his gaze with an open eagerness, a raw need that jarringly reminded Gaius that the great hero was still such a young man.

Sometimes. At others, he seems as old as the sky.

"I think Emperor Tychon will fight you every step of the way," said Gaius slowly. "But I think it's a good idea."

"Will you stand with me?"

Gaius took a deep, steadying breath. "Hae... hae, I'm with you, Father."

Rikard jumped to his feet and vaulted over the table. It couldn't have been easy in his armor, but the legens hardly seemed hindered at all, or else too elated to notice. He seized Gaius' hand and pulled his son up into an embrace that clattered like a sack of nails as their armor came together. Rikard kissed his cheek.

Gaius saw tears in his father's eyes. He coughed uncomfortably and thumped Rikard's back a couple of times.

"Hae, enough," Gaius said. "I don't even know if your grand pact will ever happen. There's still Tychon to deal with."

Emperor Tychon waited. His toes curled in their soft doeskin slippers, itching to pace nervously. Stirred by her emperor's agitation, the girl kneeling beside his throne fidgeted uncomfortably. Or perhaps it was the cool marble floor against her bare backside. Tychon ran his fingers through her golden hair, down the side of her neck and over her delicate collarbone. Was there time...?

A sudden breeze made the gauzy curtains billow like smoke. Tychon looked up at the open door.

"General Cadmus Castor of the Sun Court of VEIL," the herald announced.

A pair of knights in steel-studded black armor stood at the tall doors, gilded and emblazoned with the lion and laurel. They saluted as the tall, thin Sun Court general strode into the room. He had changed his blood-red armor for a fine silk saela of the same color. Castor bowed deeply and waited until the emperor gestured him forward.

"We are pleased that you came to us so promptly, general," said Tychon. He gestured to a doe-eyed girl, who came forward and filled the emperor's glass from a crystal decanter.

"Imperial Majesty, I am–" Castor began, but Tychon interrupted him.

"What is Rikard doing? Calling VEIL together, casting out the rot? He's securing and strengthening VEIL. Now he's asking for the entire Erastrasus grain shipment. What does he want with it?"

"The legens has a plan to purify it, Majesty," said Castor. His chin was raised and his back as straight as a column. "He's called for volunteers to join him in an Alterran pact to do so."

"How many have come forward?"

"The commanders are still taking proper numbers, but about six thousand, Imperial Majesty. Perhaps seven. More than half of VEIL."

Tychon closed his eyes and touched his fingertip to the sapphire crown on his brow.

"Seven thousand men?" he asked. "Seven thousand of Carce's knights to bleed together to the Alterra. Why is that, Castor? No one in VEIL makes pacts with those ghosts anymore. But his men would bleed themselves to death if Rikard Mazrem asks."

Castor looked as though he wanted to say something. A vein pulsed in the general's temple like an angry serpent. Tychon took a lingering sip of his wine. It was sultry and musky, with a hint of apple or something similarly sweet. A little young for his taste.

Tychon took the decanter from his serving girl and tossed it at Castor. The herald gasped quietly. The knight caught it deftly, spilling only a few drops onto the polished white floor.

"Not my year," Tychon said. "Have a drink, general."

After a pause, Castor nodded. He took a glass from a polished table nearby and poured.

"Pressed too late in the year. They should know better," he said after taking a sip.

The emperor set his cup aside and nodded. "You're a man of refined taste."

"I lived here in the palace before the war, when the Sun Court still served as your guard, Majesty. I learned admiration for fine things and the power needed to acquire them."

"You must miss it, General Castor."

"I do. Forgive me, Majesty, but there is a great deal to do before executing Legens Mazrem's pact. How may I serve you?"

"While we appreciate his gesture, we believe it ill-advised," Tychon said. "It has been thirty years since a major Alterran pact. Who knows what will happen? Legens Mazrem may spread the grain blight to the remaining storehouses. What then? So many un-practiced hands at blood pacts... What sort of Alterran mischief might they invite into Dormaen? Please thank Legens Mazrem for his continued heroics on behalf of the Carcaen Empire, but let him know that by imperial command, he is forbidden to make any alter-ations to the Erastrasus grain. The risk is too great."

Castor's jaw tightened. "With all respect, Majesty, there is no danger. Not to anyone except the knights–"

"Carry my decision to your legens," Tychon said.

Castor bowed deeply. The Star knights pulled the doors open for him and saluted again as the general passed. When Castor was gone, Tychon waved the herald out of the room and pulled the golden-haired girl into his lap. But even her soft skin and youthful vigor could not entirely distract Tychon from the problem at hand.

Rikard Mazrem would fight his emperor's decision. He was the hero of Carce and soon he would be their savior. Why else build up VEIL except to challenge the throne? The man had no gratitude. Tychon had given Rikard more than anyone ever dared ask.

Even if Gaius were right, that his father had no desire to rule, it wouldn't be long until even Rikard could not stop the tide of his own popularity. The people would take matters into their own hands. They would call for him... no, they would all *demand* that Rikard Mazrem take the throne. Tychon tightened his fingers in the girl's pale curls until she whimpered in pain.

This is all mine. I will not let it go easily, the emperor swore.

34

ON THE LYCEUM FLOOR

"Emperor Tychon unified the world into a single great empire and then created the Lyceum to grant a voice to each province, to their care and causes, needs and many, many complaints. After listening to so many arguments, one might ask why he bothered conquering the world in the first place."

— AFTER NJORN PASS, BY ALEXANDER FERRO

"Lord Mazrem! My lord, please wake up."

Rikard sat and rubbed the sleep-sand from his eyes. Bastil stood at the bedside and held out a folded parchment. The broken wax seal was stamped with a lion's head.

"What is it?" Rikard asked. Beside him, Laurael stirred in her nest of thick, soft blankets.

"Emperor Tychon has summoned you to answer to him before the Lyceum, Lord Mazrem. He says that you have failed to follow an imperial order," Bastil said. The aging steward's voice and thoughts were sharp with worry. "It just arrived. You're to be there at noon to present yourself."

"What is this, Rikard?" Laurael asked, propping herself up on a feather-stuffed pillow. She snatched the letter from Bastil and stepped down from the bed as she read it. "You refused an imperial command, my lord?"

"I didn't refuse it, Laura. Not exactly. I just... ignored it." Rikard looked at Bastil. "How long ago did this arrive?"

"Perhaps ten minutes, Lord Mazrem."

"Thank you, Bastil. Will you let me explain this to Laura on my own?"

"Hae, my lord. Of course," Bastil said. He inclined his head and went to the door.

"Bastil? Will you tell Thainna that I need to see her?" Rikard asked.

The steward nodded and left the bedroom. Rikard turned to his wife, who paced before the curtains. It was still early and the pale dawn leached the layered hangings of color. Laurael, too, was cast in stark blacks and white like a piece of art, a vase on a plinth fit for the imperial palace. She looked up from Tychon's letter and cocked her head at her husband.

"What does this mean?" Laurael asked.

Her questions were accusatory, but not as angry as Rikard might have expected. He was curious and tempted to reach for Laura's thoughts, but it was only two days since he had defended his absolute trust in her.

I will not make a liar of myself before Thainna.

"One of Castor's messengers rode to the Star Court late yesterday," Rikard said.

"Hae...?"

"Emperor Tychon doesn't want me to cleanse the Erastrasus grain shipment."

"Why not? Did you send him a response?"

"No," Rikard told her. "This is too important not to do. People need that wheat."

Laurael held out the letter toward Rikard. "Even as legens of VEIL, that was hardly your place. We *all* obey imperial commands. You cannot simply ignore them."

Rikard took the letter and read it over.

"Tychon's refusing to release the blighted grain to VEIL. Is that in his power?" he asked.

"Hae, more or less. Emperor Tychon leaves running his empire largely in the hands of the Lyceum. He sees only to greater issues of law and negotiation. The grain shipment falls under the control of the Lyceum consuls, but the emperor can call a vote on any issue he wishes."

"A vote, not a royal command. So I must argue my case to the Lyceum," Rikard said, nodding. "Hae? And so must he?"

"Again, after a fashion," Laurael answered. "The emperor himself sits on the Lyceum and holds fifty votes of his own that he may cast as he wishes."

"Fifty!" Rikard balled up the letter and flung it across the room. The crumpled paper bounced off the wall and rolled into a corner. "Fifty? Beside the VEIL generals, only one hundred men serve in the Lyceum!"

"A Lyceum vote rarely goes against the emperor, but it *has* been known to happen. If it did not, Tychon would have no need to fear that they might make you emperor." Laurael picked the emperor's summons up from the floor and handed the wad of parchment back to her husband. "But that is not the vote today. You must plead your case eloquently, my lord."

"Hae, Laura. I will." A small knock turned Rikard's head toward the door. "Thainna? Come in."

The foster came into the room and bowed. Thainna was getting better at it. Her long red hair was still tousled by sleep. She nodded to Laurael and smiled at Rikard.

"You wanted to see me?"

"Hae. It's time to cut out the stitches, I think."

Thainna blinked slowly and she swallowed hard.

Do you know how to do it? she wondered.

Hae, I've done it a few times on campaigns.

Like this? An image coalesced in Thainna's mind.

That's right. Just like cutting a seam.

Rikard sat down on a stool beside the curtained columns of the bedroom's open wall and hooked his hand behind his neck to keep the arm clear of Thainna's work. The skin stretched taut, but the pain was nearly gone. It barely even itched. Thainna's medicine had done its job well.

The foster dropped her satchel on the floor and fished out a short knife with a slender blade. Carefully, she worked the point under the first stitch until the thread snapped. When she picked it free, a bead of bright red blood welled up. Thainna wiped it away with a square of soft cloth and the pinprick remained clean.

"Good," Rikard told her. "It's healed solid."

"It looks like it left a scar. I'm sorry."

Rikard shrugged. A knight without scars was one who never took any chances. He could have struck a deal with Flickerdim or Jingleblack to remove them, to smooth his skin like wiping the lines from a Nahom sand garden. It was certainly easier than restoring five hundred tons of poisoned wheat, but counted for so much less. The scar would cost Rikard no mobility and wouldn't hurt once the stitches were gone.

Laurael pursed her full lips.

"I believe that I will leave such bloody pursuits in your capable hands, mana," she told Thainna. "Be sure to dress before you go to the Lyceum, my husband. I'll send Bastil to tell Gaius. He will find you there."

"Hae, Laura," Rikard said.

Laurael cinched her wrap tighter and crossed the hall to one of her frilly dressing rooms. One by one, Thainna carefully cut and removed the stitches from Rikard's side. When she finished, he stood and swung his arm in an experimental circle. The spot felt raw, but that would fade in a few hours. Rikard thanked Thainna and dressed himself in the saela folded on a chest at the end of the bed. Bastil must have brought it. Rikard hadn't even noticed. The man was astonishingly efficient.

"What's all this about the Lyceum?" asked Thainna.

"Emperor Tychon doesn't want VEIL to cleanse the Erastrasus wheat shipment."

Thainna blinked and furrowed her pale brow. "So he's fighting you, just like Gaius said that he would. Did the emperor give you a reason?"

"Only that it might be dangerous. I have to plead my case to the Lyceum in a few hours."

"The Lyceum? You're legens of VEIL. Don't you have a seat on the council?" asked Thainna.

"I don't think so," Rikard answered. "There hasn't been a legens of VEIL for more than a century and the Lyceum was formed only about thirty years ago. I don't think that there's a precedent for a legens vote."

"Are you nervous?"

Rikard finished with the buttons on his saela and pulled on his boots. He considered Thainna's question carefully.

No, I don't feel so.

He felt Thainna's curious, questing touch against his mind. She wasn't as practiced as even a young Alterran, but she was learning quickly how to reach for Rikard. He glowed warm with pride. It had taken him months of painful practice to learn the Alterran speech from Flickerdim.

You're so happy that Gaius actually agreed to bleed into your pact that you don't care about much else, Thainna thought. *You should be careful of the Lyceum.*

I can see no reason they would not want this done.

I don't know. The Lyceum is a complicated place.

"You'll come with me, won't you?" Rikard asked.

"I can't," Thainna said. "Lyceum sessions are closed. Unless I'm summoned in your letter, too, I can't go with you."

Rikard recovered the crumpled letter and then smoothed it out against the curved side of a column.

"No," he said when he had read over the entire thing twice. A third time, just to be sure. "There's no mention of you."

"Do you know what you're going to say?"

"Just the truth."

"You're going to be talking to politicians," Thainna pointed out. "It might take more than that. Tell me what you want to say to them. No, don't think it at me. It has to make sense in words."

Over a breakfast of fruit and honeyed water, Thainna convinced Rikard to rehearse what he planned to say to the Lyceum. They sat under the window, in the lengthening rectangle of orange morning light. By the time Rikard asked a hostler to bring a chariot to the gate, Thainna seemed confident that her ward would not sound like a madman in front of the most influential council in the world. She walked with him down the hill to the gate. The Lyncean guard, Karl, waved to Thainna and saluted his lord.

"Bastil says you're going to the Lyceum today, sir," Karl said. He still wore the fading bruises of their fight, Rikard saw with shame.

"Hae," Thainna answered. "Emperor Tychon's giving him some washy drip about the Erastrasus grain and now it's on the Lyceum to decide."

Karl frowned. "That sounds serious, Lord Mazrem."

"I'm sure the Lyceum consuls are reasonable men," Rikard said.

Karl didn't look convinced.

At the gate, a violet and blue-black kajja clawed restlessly in the traces of a chariot. Rikard stepped up inside and flicked the reigns. The long-legged bird leapt forward and carried his chariot out into the street. To guess by the lack of fading summer flowers and burnt incense, Bastil had finally ordered the offerings outside the gate cleaned up, but there were dozens of fresh ones. Those who had left them cheered at Rikard as he passed.

He made good time out of the Everstones and into the heart of the city. The cobbled street led Rikard in a curving arc, then joined another wider road that encircled a vast plaza like a champion's wreath.

Mazrem Square.

Rikard heard the name – *his* name – in the thoughts of a wagoneer driving nearby, again from the minds of a knot of students in white tabbae, and then from a lawyer hawking his services on the marble steps of his office. Rikard slowed his chariot with a thought to his kajja and steered closer in for a better look.

Who had named this place? The huge plaza was as round as a wagon wheel, paved in smooth white marble, and artfully strewn with stone benches shaded under the spreading branches of laurel trees. There was a theater only slightly smaller than the one in the imperial palace along one side, a stepped arch like a half moon pressed deep into the ground.

Rikard's chariot lurched to a stop. In the center of the plaza rose a tall statue, ten times life size, handsome and well-crafted.

That... that's me, he realized.

Rikard laughed and slapped his palm against the wooden antyx of the chariot. There was something unaccountably funny about staring at himself, towering over the center of Dormaen with such a munificent expression on his alabaster face, like looking in some sort of mad mirror. He didn't look at all like that!

With a final shake of his head, Rikard urged his kajja back out into the road and followed the directions Thainna had remembered for him to a starkly regal white building. A young hostler hurried out from the deep colonnade, bowed and took the kajja's reins. Rikard thanked the boy and made his way to the tall beechwood door. A dozen armored soldiers snapped to attention.

"Legens Mazrem, sir!" they said.

"Are they ready for me in there? To speak with me?" he asked.

"Not yet, sir. Not all the consuls have convened yet," answered one of the guards.

"Who are they waiting for?"

The first soldier opened his mouth to answer and then nodded. Rikard felt his son's thick, smoke-sounding presence just a moment before he heard the trilling call of his kajja and the creak of leather-covered wheels. Gaius jumped heavily down from his chariot and strode to the doors. The guards saluted again and reached for the handles, but Gaius held up his hand and they stopped.

"But they're waiting for you, Lord Mazrem," said one of them.

"They can wait a little longer. Father, let's have a few words."

Gaius pulled Rikard to the other side of a bronze-banded white column and crossed his arms over his clean black saela. Rikard smiled at his son. It was good to have Gaius by his side.

"This isn't going to be easy for you, Father," said Gaius. "Unless you can persuade about three-quarters of the Lyceum to vote with you, all of your planning isn't going to mean dust. I warned you about this."

Gaius' tone didn't match his words.

"You're... not worried," Rikard said.

"Bloody hell, why should I be? This is *your* crusade, not mine," Gaius answered cheerfully. "If the Lyceum doesn't release the Erastrasus grain to you, then no one has to make any agreements with the Alterra. I'm sure not lining up to bleed for them."

Rikard frowned. Gaius clapped him on the shoulder.

"See you inside, Father."

Gaius let one of the guards escort him into the Lyceum. A few minutes later, a pair of soldiers found Rikard and saluted.

"They're ready for you now, sir."

Rikard nodded and followed them through the doors. Beyond was a single vast room, circular with an arched ceiling made up of hexagonal tiles, each one of them carved with provincial crests and scenes of historical importance. A hundred serious-looking men perched on tiered seats around the Lyceum's edge, surrounding Rikard.

It was not unlike a pristine white arena. But here, battles were fought with words, not swords or blood.

In the center of the chamber and flanked by twenty knights in armor of midnight black, Emperor Tychon sat on his great golden throne. Whispers filled the Lyceum like an autumn wind rustling with leaves. A herald banged a tall, lion-headed staff on the stone floor. The room quieted.

"Legens Rikard Mazrem, the Lyceum of the Carcaen Empire calls you to answer allegations of His Imperial Majesty, Emperor Castum Tychon. The Erastrasus shipment will remain in the vaults until the matter reaches resolution," he announced. "Legens, please take your seat."

With his gilded staff, the herald gestured to a chair in a box just below the tier where Gaius and the VEIL generals were gathered. Rikard saluted the throne and sat. Overhead, Saul leaned forward and clapped his hand on Rikard's shoulder.

"Tychon will present his case first, but then you'll be able to answer him," he said. "Gods' luck, Rik."

Rikard thanked his friend quietly and looked up at the other VEIL knights. Gaius sat back on his tier, feet propped on the low wall that separated it from the drop to the Lyceum floor. Hern studiously avoided looking at Rikard. Castor watched the emperor closely. The Sun Court general felt eyes on him and looked down at Rikard.

We warned you about this, you treacherous ghost, he heard Castor think, as clear and sharp as a shard of glass. *You will make us all look bad. You will dishonor and discredit all of VEIL.*

Emperor Tychon stood. His ornately folded tabba was so heavy with gold thread and jeweled beads that it threatened to drag its aged master to the ground. Rikard barely suppressed a childish desire to ask Stumble to give the garment a little help. The whole thing was like some kind of twisted play, a show just like the Fiori on Tychon's stage – the emperor of Carce squabbling with his own knights over whether or not to let his people starve!

"Consuls of the Lyceum, honorable servants of the empire," Tychon intoned gravely. He was calm and commanding. In that moment, it was easy to remember the bold young king of Carce that conquered the entire world.

"As you all well know, the recently promoted Legens Mazrem has requisitioned the spoiled Erastrasus shipment. Five hundred tons of wheat and millet that you put under lock to avoid contamination of other city stores. With the blood of seven thousand other knights, he claims that he can cleanse the blight from the grain. While we thank the noble legens on behalf of the Carcaen Empire for the greatness of his heart, we yesterday commanded him to desist in this action."

Though the consuls were surely aware of Tychon's order, a fresh wave of whispered gossip rippled through the Lyceum. Emperor Tychon stepped down off the dais and walked a slow line across the polished floor. His long gold tabba fanned behind him like a gilded peacock's tail.

"The legens' gesture is too dangerous, consuls. It's been too long since VEIL has practiced with their Alterran pacts. And why should they? A price of blood and self is too high to pay in a time of peace. And we *are* at peace. Legens Mazrem knows better than most the danger of a major pact. Seven thousand knights, all with the best of intentions... But without the benefit of experience, men can make mistakes. All it takes is one."

Tychon stopped in front of his throne and raised a single finger, holding it aloft and showing it to the Lyceum, then leveled it at Rikard.

"One knight banished every fighting man and woman in Fiore," Tychon said, nodding in apparent respect at Rikard. "One man.

Imagine seven thousand such men, and what a single mistake of blood may cost. Anything could happen. Anything. Dormaen might vanish in the blink of an eye, like the Fiori army. The danger to our knights and our empire is too great.

"The blight of the Erastrasus wheat shipment is lamentable. It makes up the single greatest part of our winter stores, but we will deal with its loss in the manner of men, not Alterra. We thank Legens Mazrem for all he has done for Carce, at Njorn Pass and here in Dormaen, but this latest sacrifice is not necessary or advisable. Consuls of the Lyceum, I call upon you to vote with me. With all respects to Legens Mazrem, the Erastrasus grain will remain sealed in the vault until its destruction."

When he had finished, Tychon seated himself once more and smoothed his golden tabba. The shining color blended with that of his lavish throne until it seemed the emperor had almost fused with the royal seat. Not a man anymore, but a regal construct. A statue, Rikard thought, just like the one in Mazrem Square.

The herald boomed his staff against the Lyceum floor.

"Legens Rikard Mazrem, do you have anything to say before the Lyceum votes on the issue?" he asked.

"Hae, I do." Rikard raised his voice to be sure that it carried, but some clever architect designed the Lyceum better than that and his voice echoed unpleasantly back on itself. Rikard stood and turned to face as many of the consuls as he could. He cleared his throat.

"Consuls, I've met many of you before, when you came to visit me. You thanked me for... for what you call my sacrifice. I traded my Terran lifetime for victory in Fiore. A victory, they say, that was instrumental in creating the empire. But it wasn't a sacrifice, not in the sense you mean. I entered into my pact with full understanding of the risks. It was a glad trade, a willing one, and it won more for Carce than I ever dared hope."

Most of the consuls regarded Rikard with frank curiosity. They didn't understand how any of this related to the matter at hand.

Their confusion was disorienting and Rikard wished Thainna were there with him.

"I am one knight of VEIL," he said. "I was a captain of a small company in the smallest court. There were thousands like me, just men. Brothers to the Alterrans and servants of Carce. But in the decades since I saw them last, VEIL has... changed."

The Lyceum murmured.

"I'm certain it's impolite to say, or taboo, but I have been gone from your world for a long time. VEIL has grown soft. They have abused the strength of their swords and feared the strength of their blood.

"No longer. Now they remember! The knights of VEIL are eager to do this, to give of their blood and themselves for you, for Dormaen and all Carce. They know what is asked of them. Their sacrifice will keep thousands from going hungry this winter. Please, give them this chance! Let VEIL prove that this can be done, that we haven't forgotten that we are servants, not masters. By this pact, we will prove our renewed vow to ourselves and to the people of Carce. Please, give us the Erastrasus grain."

Rikard bowed his head to indicate that he was done speaking, but didn't retake his seat. He sensed a storm cloud of questions about to open up and rain down on him.

A dozen consuls stood and the herald pointed to one of them with the golden lion head of his staff – a small, wiry Nianese man wrapped in the unadorned gray cloak of his homeland. He wore the deep hood pulled back in deference to the other consuls.

"Senior consul Liam Io of Nian," announced the herald.

"Legens Mazrem, if you would address the emperor's concerns for the safety of the city and its people...?" Liam asked.

Rikard recognized him as one of the first visitors Laurael had allowed him to see.

"Hae. I ask you to have faith," Rikard answered.

"Faith, legens? In what, precisely?"

"In my knights and in the Alterra. It's been so long since any real pacts that much has been forgotten. Intentions matter, consul. The Alterra are our brothers, not street-side merchants trying to cheat us of our money," Rikard said. He drew his capped right forefinger through the air. "Dormaen will not vanish because I don't want that. Because none of our knights do. Those of the Uprising need us as we need them. Have faith, Consul Io."

Satisfied with Rikard's answer – if not swayed by it – the Nianese consul nodded and sat. The herald pointed to another consul. This one was a tall, fat Yorallian in a crisp white tabba. He rumbled in the back of his throat before speaking.

"We hear and consider your assurances, Legens Mazrem," he said in a deep voice. "However, for the safety of the city and her inhabitants, will you consider clarifying the grain shipment outside the city? On the far shore of the Mazren River, perhaps?"

"No," Rikard replied promptly. "VEIL knights have threatened and struck civilians here in Dormaen. When Sir Gallard found me unconscious outside the Rows, he believed me drunk, that I had passed out from a night of excess. He was not surprised and neither was anyone else! It alarmed no one to see a VEIL knight drooling in the street. No, we must do this where all Dormaen may see. We owe it to Carce to make our renewal vows in their sight."

"Where, then?"

"I believe that... that Mazrem Square would be a suitable location." Rikard felt ridiculous even suggesting it.

The Yorallian consul leaned forward, frowning deeply. "Under the watchful eye of your own countenance?"

"It's in the center of the city," Rikard replied quickly. His face felt hot. "The plaza is large enough to hold seven thousand knights and five hundred tons of wheat. The... the scenery is beside the point. The city has grown a great deal since I knew it best, consul. Perhaps you can suggest a better place?"

"Unless you'll consent to move outside the city, no."

"I cannot. This must be public. It must be seen," Rikard said with all the finality he could muster.

The round Yorallian pursed his lips and sat. With their questions asked by others and apparently answered, most of the other consuls sat. Only one remained standing, waiting for his chance to speak. The herald pointed at General Darius. Saul grinned at Rikard and winked.

"So when are we doing this, Rik?" he asked.

"Tomorrow, if the Lyceum will allow me."

The herald glared at Saul and then rapped his staff three times. The sharp sound echoed through the chamber. "This session of the Lyceum will break for an hour recess that you may consider the matter at hand. All consuls and invested parties must reconvene at the hour's close."

The crowd of consuls drew into tight groups like water droplets on a waxboard. The other VEIL knights gathered around Rikard.

"Well said, Rik. You'll have the vote, I'm sure," Saul assured him.

"Not everyone is as easily swayed as you are, Darius." Castor said. He looked at Hern. "What's the vote look like?"

The Moon Court general shrugged. "I don't know yet. If you'll excuse me, I'll ask around. Rikard, you should have agreed to do it outside the city. You probably lost a dozen votes on that alone."

"Go gauge the vote, Nikas," Gaius said.

General Hern gave the younger knight a mild look. Rikard felt Nikas' annoyance at the dismissal, but none of it reached the Moon Court general's face. Hern made his way across the Lyceum to speak to the other consuls. Castor was no more pleased with Gaius' tone and stood to one side, arms crossed over his chest and ignoring his fellows. Saul smiled sheepishly and spread his hands in a helpless gesture.

"Not much to do now except wait," he said.

Rikard turned to Gaius, but his son was already deep in his own thoughts, watching Nikas Hern move through the grouped consuls.

Emperor Tychon waited on his lavish throne, tapping his fingers on the gem-encrusted arm and occasionally murmuring to his guards.

Most of the interminably long hour had passed before Hern returned. The Moon Court general gave Rikard a pointed look.

"Insisting that the pact ritual take place in Dormaen lost you a lot of votes," he reported. "It will be close, but you're going to lose."

"What?" Rikard protested. "But the cleansing poses no risk to anyone!"

Saul scuffed his boot on the floor and muttered an oath. "Are you sure about it, Nikas?"

"Including the VEIL vote, which is outside the consul hundred," he explained for Rikard's benefit, "that's about seventy in favor. But with the emperor's vote, something like eighty against."

"They can't do this," Rikard said. "Can't they see that we all need this? We'll feed Dormaen and restore the people's faith in VEIL!"

"You won in principle," Saul assured him with a lopsided smile. "More than half of the consuls are voting with you. It's just Emperor Tychon's vote that's the problem. The Lyceum believes in you, in us. That's something, isn't it?"

"We serve all Carce, not just her leaders! A philosophical victory won't feed people starving in the Rows!"

Saul puffed out his cheeks and let out a slow, hissing breath. He shook his head, not sure what to say. Gaius still watched the rest of the Lyceum. With a thrust of his jaw, he indicated Liam Io.

"What's his vote?" Gaius asked.

"Against," General Hern said. "Munnan, Uthaille and Forcellus are voting with him, naturally."

"Naturally?" asked Rikard. *Politics. I have no head for this game!*

"Liam's an investor. Nian is a small province and doesn't produce much worth trading. A few metalworks, but mostly they deal in money. They hold it, invest it and they're very good at it," Gaius explained. Rikard was the only one in the whole huge room who didn't already know this. "Munnan and Forcellus are from Corvo.

They invest their provincial products with Liam and usually make a tidy profit doing it. Uthaille's the junior Fiori delegate. It's never been a rich nation. Everything they have is banked in Nian. All three will follow his lead, but Liam's typical Nianese. He plays everything very close, very safe."

"Nian didn't survive seventeen Lyncean invasions by taking unnecessary risks," Castor noted. "Liam Io won't gamble on us."

"That's because he's thinking with his head, not his wallet," said Gaius.

Just then, the herald banged his staff and called the Lyceum back to order. Rikard slumped in his seat. All he wanted was to help VEIL, to help Terra and Alterra heal! He never guessed that someone might truly want to stop him.

Gaius and Castor warned me that the emperor would fight me, but I didn't think anyone would actually side with him!

Still, Rikard had convinced the majority of the Lyceum. Saul was right. It had to count for something... But the consolation was insubstantial as mist. Rikard put his face in his hands and felt Emperor Tychon's glowing gloat of victory like a bright, hot flame.

"Consuls of the Lyceum, unless you have any further questions for the involved parties, it is now time to cast your vote," the herald announced.

Rikard heard a rustle behind him and turned to see Gaius raise his hand. The herald gestured and Rikard's son stood.

"A few final words before we vote. I believe in all that my noble father's trying to accomplish. Letting our knights feel good about themselves, feeding the city and earning back their trust. All of that. But the legens has been out of the world for a while. There's another issue at stake that he didn't discuss," Gaius said. He paused significantly and looked up at Liam Io. "Money. Even before the entire shipment was blighted, no one planned to give that wheat away. The Erastrasus shipment was bound for sale and had a number of investors."

The Nianese consul sat forward, listening carefully. Beside and behind him, his allies glanced at each other, curious.

"A lot of investors lost a great deal of money when the shipment went sour," Gaius went on. "However, if Legens Mazrem and our knights can restore the grain... Well, come winter, people will want to eat and they'll pay good money to do so. All we need to do is make sure they have something to buy, hae?"

Gaius sat. Emperor Tychon stared after the VEIL captain, fury in his eyes. The herald saw his emperor's anger, too, and hesitated.

"Do you have any additional response, Majesty?" he stammered.

Tychon shot him a venomous look and said nothing.

Reluctantly, the herald called the vote. "All in favor of granting VEIL, under the leadership and at the command of Legens Rikard Mazrem, access to the Erastrasus wheat, please rise. Those in opposition, remain seated."

One after another, consuls rose to their feet, including Liam Io. A pair of clerks, one seated at a desk on either side of the Lyceum, counted out those standing and recorded their numbers on waxboards. After they compared their numbers, one of the clerks wrote the final count on a scroll of paper and delivered it to the herald, who glanced nervously at the smoldering Emperor Tychon again.

"The... the final count is seventy-eight for, twenty-six and the imperial vote against, for a total of seventy-six. The measure is carried in favor. Legens Mazrem, the Lyceum releases the full five hundred tons of Erastrasus grain to VEIL. A courier will deliver the storehouse key to the Star Court archouse by the day's end."

Rikard was stunned. He stood on legs that felt like water-filled sacks. His mouth was dry, but he managed to speak. "Thank you, noble consuls. We will repay the faith you have shown in us!"

A chorus of praise, suggestions, condemnations and answering thanks were indecipherable as the consuls shouted over one another. They died away in an instant, replaced by tense silence as Emperor Tychon separated himself from his gold throne and stood.

Tychon stared intently at Rikard, saying nothing. Then the emperor spun on his heels and stalked away, out of the Lyceum. His guards hurried to follow.

"He's not going to forget that anytime soon," said Gaius.

Rikard had to agree.

Everyone had questions. A handful of the consuls hurried from the Lyceum, chasing after the emperor, but most remained to speak with Rikard and the other VEIL knights. Did they truly mean to act so soon as tomorrow? How did VEIL plan to distribute the grain when it was cleaned? How would legens coordinate seven thousand blood pacts? Would Rikard scribe his blood, too? Did their act require the actual presence of the Erastrasus shipment, or would it remain in the Lyceum storehouse until it was cleansed?

"Intentions matter, as I said," Rikard explained. "Alterrans don't eat as we do. They have little understanding of what healthy wheat should be, just as they would if we were healing a person. Without our guidance, they could turn that wheat into sand. Hae, we will need to cart the blighted grain into Mazrem Square so that the knights entering into this pact will be able to see it, to... to understand it for the Alterra."

"So with the appropriate guidance, Alterrans could turn wheat into gold, hae?" Liam asked.

"They could, but how long until that entirely ruined the value of your gold, consul?" Gaius said.

The Nianese representative surrendered the point with a nod and then took Gaius aside to work out the details of hauling the grain. After all, Liam pointed out, as an investor, he had an interest in making sure the shipment arrived safely in Mazrem Square. Rikard watched Gaius with growing pride. His son was a clever man. Without his help, Rikard would have never wrested an agreement from the Lyceum.

A chilly presence jerked Rikard's attention back up out of this own thoughts. Castor stood at his elbow.

Rikard nodded. "Thank you for your vote today, Castor."

"Honor demanded that we put forth a unified front," the Sun Court general said quietly. "You are my ranking officer and this is what you have commanded us to do. It would undermine your efforts if I voted differently."

"Do you believe in what we do, Castor?"

"I want the Sun Court restored to a position of honor, legens. We were the guardians of the imperial person. There is no higher calling."

Rikard didn't think so, but now didn't seem the time to argue.

"I will follow my orders," Castor said. "I'll be there tomorrow and I'll bleed."

"Thank you, General Castor. It will be an honor," said Rikard gravely.

Castor pressed his lips into a thin, bloodless line and pushed his way through the crowd, out of the Lyceum. Nikas Hern waited not far away and actually smiled at Rikard for the first time since he first woke up in the Moon Court archouse.

"Well, even Castor's agreed to this pact," he said. "His sense of honor is just as unbending as yours, I suppose. I think it broke his hard old heart when you stole the Lyceum vote from Emperor Tychon."

"I stole nothing," said Rikard stiffly.

Nikas' smile deepened until it looked like the white crescent of his court. "Figuratively only. It was close. Anyway, I suppose it was Gaius who did the stealing. I trust you won't be offended when I say that you never would have thought of the financial angle."

"Hae, you're right."

"I confess that I'm surprised that Gaius argued on your behalf. Your family is a rich one and Gaius certainly wouldn't have been facing an empty plate at year's end."

"He surprised me, too," Rikard admitted. "Earlier, he said that he wouldn't mind losing the vote."

Nikas arched an eyebrow and glanced back at Gaius, who was arguing with Liam about some detail of tomorrow's shipment. "You must have said something good to make him change his mind."

"I said nothing. The decision was his own."

Nikas glanced at Gaius again, and then shrugged. "I could not have predicted it, but I think you've had a good effect on your son, Rik. I'll see you in the square tomorrow."

"Will you bleed on the pact, then?" Rikard asked the general, surprised. "Will you actually commit to our road?"

"Hae," Nikas said as though there had never been the slightest doubt. *You won today, beat Tychon at his own game. I was wrong. Maybe you actually* can *change things, Rik.*

"I can," Rikard told him. "We can fix everything."

Nikas stiffened. "You heard that, then?"

"I don't mean to, but some thoughts are very summer... loud, I mean," Rikard apologized. Nikas had never given him permission or trusted him so closely as Thainna did.

"It's alright," Nikas said, reassuring himself as much as anyone else. "You can't help what you are now and you became that way in service to the empire. Tomorrow, Rikard. I'll notify the Moon Court. Then I'll go home and pour myself a stiff drink. An Alterran pact. Hae, I never thought I'd make another one of those."

"It's not a frightening thing, Nikas. We used to do it all the time."

"Maybe we will again. One step at a time, Rikard. Some of us are old men and we can't move as quickly as you."

"I'm as old as you are, Nikas!"

The Moon Court general laughed quietly. "No, you're not. You're really not. But enjoy it."

Rikard looked back at Gaius. "It's so strange sometimes."

"Hae, I can only imagine. Until tomorrow, my friend."

Nikas embraced him firmly and then retreated. Rikard rejoined Gaius, feeling as though he was walking on clouds, something he hadn't done since leaving Alterra. Gaius looked up at his father's approach and nodded to the Nianese consul. Liam Io inclined his head to Rikard.

"Legens, the wheat will be delivered to Mazrem Square early tomorrow. It will be ready for your ritual an hour or so after noon. There's a great deal of it to move and we can't divert all of the street traffic on such short notice."

"I didn't argue the point too strenuously," Gaius added with a smirk. "You want people to see what we're up to. Keeping the roads clear might rather undermine your purpose."

"I'm curious to see this done," Liam admitted. "I'll be in Mazrem Square tomorrow. My men and I will take care of distributing the grain when it's palatable again."

"You mean sell it."

"We *were* the original investors, legens."

"Don't worry your noble heart, Father," said Gaius. "The price of wheat was set three months ago when the Erastrasus first counted their harvest. Liam's not going to cheat anyone. You've saved him considerable embarrassment and inconvenience, in fact."

"Just so. I look forward to your ritual tomorrow, Legens Mazrem. Thank you for your time, captain," Liam said to Gaius. "If you will excuse me, I have wagons to hire."

When the consul was gone, Gaius turned back to Rikard.

"Think we've done enough damage here?" he asked. "Maybe we should collect Saul and get back to the Star Court. Seven thousand is a lot of knights to organize."

"Hae, it is. Let's go, then."

They found Saul waiting outside, sitting at the base of a striped column and chewing on the stem of a pipe. He watched the people passing in the street outside the Lyceum. Saul took a few more puffs before tapping out the tobacco against the column's plinth and then tucking his pipe away. He stood with a grunt, pressing his hands to the base of his spine.

"Got everything we needed, then?" he asked.

"Down to the last acorn," Gaius confirmed. "Liam didn't even try to talk up the price of the wheat. He's amazingly eager to please, really. He's only charging twenty-three willows for each wagon and drive team."

"I wouldn't know if that's a good rate or not. I'll take your word for it," Saul said. He grinned. "You two won the day. All I had to do was vote. I'll head on back to the Star Court and spread the word that you got us the grain. We'll be ready tomorrow, Rikard. Why don't you two drive home? I've got this in hand."

"Thank you, Saul. Thainna will be so happy to hear of our victory," Rikard said.

Saul laughed, saluted and headed for the stables to retrieve his chariot. Rikard and Gaius followed more slowly.

A thin film of clouds covered the sky, sunlit in brilliant and shining white like a bridal veil. Overhead, a ragged V of geese flew and honked raucously to each other as they made their southern journey. Rikard stopped Gaius outside the stables.

"What? I thought you were in a hurry to get back to your little foster," Gaius said. He was just as sharp and sarcastic as ever, but Rikard felt no malice in his words.

"I couldn't have gotten the wheat shipment without your help," Rikard said. "You saved everything. Thank you. I would never have even considered the investors."

The smile that lit up Gaius' round face was like the sun rising.

"I know," he said. "You're far too straight-backed and honorable. It makes for great stories and statues, but it's not at all practical."

"It's good that I have you, then."

"Hae, lucky for you."

35

THE MIRROR

"We write our own destiny. A man is lord of his fate, not its slave."

— RIKARD MAZREM

LAUREL PAGED through the papers Bastil left that morning. Bills and invoices, for the most part, that needed her signature before the steward could pay. There was more than enough money, of course, but Laurael pursed her lips to keep the line-forming frown at bay.

Gaius spent too much money. On himself, on food and clothes for his women. The boy had no restraint. Well, he would learn that in time. It was the nature of young men to enjoy their pleasures and it was a mother's privilege to provide them. She plucked her pen from the crystal inkwell and signed her name in a swooping script.

"Mother?"

She looked up from the pile of papers and nodded to her son. Smiles created as many lines as frowns.

"Hae, Gaius. Come sit," she said.

He hooked a chair from against the ornately paneled wall and pulled it up to the other side of his mother's desk. Gaius sat down and propped his round chin on one hand, elbow balanced on the seat's slender arm.

"Well, I won the Lyceum vote for Father."

His deliberately casual tone was not lost on Laurael. Gaius thought himself quite clever. Perhaps he was, but she had given him life, raised him and taught him all he knew. Gaius had no secrets from his mother.

"Tell me what happened that makes you so proud," she said.

Gaius hurried through the story to what he obviously considered the good part.

"There was no way those dry old bastards were going to give Rikard the vote unless I gave them something more than honor to think about. It was Liam, of course, holding up the whole thing. But then I reminded him that if he could sell the wheat, he could recover everything he lost when the shipment went bad. So then he voted with us."

"He would have made enemies," Laurael said. "Now he'll seem a hero to all those who wouldn't have eaten this winter."

"Liam and his investors won't seem half the heroes that we'll be tomorrow. Or that I was today. No one else could have managed it, not even Father," Gaius said, grinning. "He's insisting on doing this pact right in the middle of Mazrem Square."

"I'd not have expected such hubris from him."

"You are as snide as any consul, Mother," Gaius said. "Mazrem Square is the only open place in the city large enough. Unless you plan on volunteering our home. Tychon certainly won't offer the palace."

Another frown pulled at Laurael's lips, as insistent as Rikard on his most amorous nights. Gaius was actually defending his father. The man was a threat to her son, not an ally, but Rikard had always inspired that sort of blind, idiot loyalty. Perhaps it wasn't wise to make Gaius spend so much time with Rikard. It had clearly taken a toll on the impressionable young knight.

"You will be the hero of the day," Laurael told him sternly. "Not Liam. Not your father. Without you, Rikard would have nothing tomorrow for his grand gesture."

"Hae. I don't think I've ever seen him struck speechless quite like that."

"Your father challenged Emperor Tychon on the Lyceum floor today and won. It was a devastating blow to Tychon," Laurael said. She set aside the stack of papers she had been working on and hooked her finger at Gaius. "You did supremely well today, my son. Tomorrow night, I shall give you a present. Now thank me and go."

"A present? Gods, I hope you're not thinking of throwing some sort of party. Father and I have a lot of work to do tomorrow."

"Trust me, Gaius."

"Not likely. You're a poisonous woman, Mother."

Gaius stood and gave his mother a kiss, then left her office. Laurael rubbed her chin thoughtfully until her finger came away with a white sheen from her powder. She wiped it lightly on a soft cloth she kept on her desk and examined her perfectly buffed nails. They would stay clean, of course. She would not do the deed herself, though it might have been simpler.

I am mother to the next emperor of Carce, not some House assassin.

The moment had finally arrived. Rikard had faced Emperor Tychon as an enemy and won an important victory. All eyes were on her husband and that would only sharpen Tychon's paranoid terror of the young hero. Rikard's death would certainly be tragic, but not entirely a surprise. Everyone would suspect Tychon, so publicly shamed before the Lyceum today. The consuls would remove the emperor, perhaps even demand his execution or exile, and then all Carce would turn to Gaius.

Laurael checked her makeup in an ornate silver mirror before she left the office. It was time to set the future into motion.

He will bring them back to us, Stumble repeated. He was thinking to himself, daydreaming. *He'll bring them—*

He craned his stone-feathered head skyward. A musical crash of thunder interrupted the young curiosity, like a harp dropped from a great height. Flickerdim stirred, as heavy as lead. His stars were dimmer than ever now, little more than silver-gray pinpricks like a dusting of dull pewter. In fact, Flickerdim seemed more metal than night. The Alterrans cast about, searching for the source of the thunder.

Was it the sky? Stumble asked.

Hae. The Shatter have taken the high ground, Flickerdim considered slowly.

He has to hurry... How much time is left?

Very little.

Flickerdim tasted the air with a tongue like a wisp of smoke. All around them, the tips of the tree-tower's branches curled and blackened as though burned. At the extreme edges of vision, shuddering, shimmering shapes moved through the peeling color, tugging at it with insubstantial claws. Flickerdim closed his failing eyes and pondered. Lacking the old wisdom's introspective sense, Stumble hopped from branch to branch, closer to the trunk of the tree and then higher.

The branches here were like the blind, pale sponges that lived in the dark and secretive Terran seas. The leaves were different, too. Tiny ashen worms chewed away at the peacock-bright fronds with frightening speed. Stumble stretched out a stony green claw and shook the branch with a sharp decision, but only a few of the little gray worms fell off. The rest clung tightly to the Uprising. Stumble hopped along the branch, tugging at the worms with his beak. They were cold and tough.

They're Shattering decisions up here! he cried.

Stop! Flickerdim alarmed. *Stumble, come back! They're too close! They are pulling at the Uprising itself!*

The branch shook beneath Stumble. The curiosity beat his malachite wings, but his stone feathers were suddenly heavy and difficult to move. Stumble opened his banded beak to shout, but it grated and ground like a Terran's teeth in the grip of a nightmare. He couldn't move.

Something beneath the Uprising thundered again and Stumble scrabbled at the rotting wood, but it was as flimsy as excuses. It crumbled under his stony talons and then he was falling down through the frigid air.

With a hiss like escaping steam, Flickerdim lunged out from his perch lower in the tower. He sank suddenly substantial fangs into Stumble's shoulder. Larger, longer tendrils – each as colorless and bland as the worms gnawing at the Uprising – lashed out at Flickerdim. When the star-serpent pulled Stumble back into the relative safety of his own branch, darkness oozed from a dozen shallow wounds along his midnight sides.

Why am I heavy? What happened? Stumble asked when he had shaken his feathers back into place.

Flickerdim curled into a tight coil once more, blinking rapidly. Even the gray of his eyes was gone now... *They've broken the last lines of the song. Even his faith in us will not slow them much longer.*

What do they want? What can we do?

Nothing. Flickerdim's empty eyes drooped heavily and another star went out. *We are all that remains, Stumble. They are here for the tower. For us and we have nothing left with which to fight. Only the blood and sacrifice of VEIL can keep the Uprising from falling. The pact tomorrow must succeed.*

Cadmus Castor had to recount the story of the Lyceum's vote seven times before he left the Sun Court, then twice more over dinner when his wife and his oldest son asked. Afterward, Castor remained in the darkened triclinium while his wife put the children to bed. The servants came to clean up, but he waved them off.

He was exhausted. There were orders to give, schedules to make and infuriatingly smug men to listen to. Castor had served in the Sun Court his entire life and had never been called upon to make a single pact with the Alterra. There were some who remembered the old ways and were all too happy to teach. Castor had traced and written the glyphic pact symbols into a waxboard so many times that afternoon that they seemed burned inside his eyelids. Tomorrow, seven thousand knights would fill Mazrem Square with blood and, perhaps, palatable wheat.

Castor pressed his fingertips against his eyelids until the darkness turned as red as embers. The triclinium still smelled of the roast duck he had for dinner. For all his impassioned speeches, Rikard Mazrem gave his men no idea what the Alterra would take in return tomorrow. Did anyone ask? Castor doubted it. VEIL was caught up in the fever of Rikard's renewed vows of honor. Every knight wanted to prove themselves to the great hero.

It was growing late and tomorrow would be a long, dangerous day. Castor pushed himself up off the couch. The house seemed to sense his weariness, empty and draped in heavy gray shadows.

Someone had already extinguished most of the lamps, turning every hallway into a dark terrestrium. Only the hard marble floor under Castor's bare feet betrayed the illusion.

He found himself holding his breath as he listened for any other sound of life besides the soft padding of his own steps. Wood creaked and stone settled with grating sighs. Outside, Dormaen slept as restlessly as a child the night before his birthday.

The living sounds of his home and his city should have soothed Castor, but they didn't. Rikard's plan... it had honor and purpose, Castor supposed. VEIL was a military organization and it was easy to forget that they knew how to do anything more than fight. Rikard had reminded them. The legens didn't even carry his sword.

As far as Castor knew, the blade still hung on his son's wall, no more than a show piece.

Fury rose in Castor's throat, tasting thin and acidic on the back of his tongue. He shoved his way through the bedroom door harder than he should have, startling his wife. She gasped and dropped the shoulders of the tabba she had just been removing, leaving her naked to the waist. But Castor's anger would not abate.

"Sorry," he said.

Without waiting for an answer, Castor stalked off into the adjoining chamber. Beads of water from the bath his wife must have taken earlier dotted the floor like dew. Castor contemplated the tub. It no longer steamed, but it was probably warm enough to soothe the tightness in his shoulders.

Hae. Just take a bath and relax. Forget this.

But Castor didn't want to forget. What did Rikard Mazrem know of honor? True honor? He was only a boy, or close enough. What made him a hero? One desperate act in the icy Fiore mountains? Honor was not desperate. It wasn't sweaty and bloody. Honor was deliberate, a path that a man chose with careful forethought. He didn't just fall down a slope and find himself upon it.

Yet the honorable path Castor had chosen, a life of dedication to his king and emperor, was thirty years gone. Ever since riders had first carried news of Njorn Pass into Dormaen, he found himself sliding down that slope that had led Rikard to honor and Castor away from it.

A man must choose honor, he thought.

Castor heaved a sigh and unbuttoned the throat of his red saela. He caught his reflection in the mirror and sighed again. The man in the silvered glass looked old, beaten and tired. Perhaps Rikard's path *was* the way. The only way. Was Rikard's road the only one left to him now?

Castor thumbed open his bloodcap. Red welled up from the cannula like a blooming rose. He closed his eyes and touched the cannula to his brow. The gold was hard against his skin and slick with blood. With slow, deliberate care, he drew the circle. Castor opened his eyes and stared at his own blood. A salute, Rikard said, to VEIL and the Alterra.

The blood... moved.

For a moment, he wondered if it was some trick of the waving light filtering in from the bedroom. But he felt it on his skin, dripping upward, out and then angling unnaturally. Castor gaped at his reflection in the mirror. The blood *was* moving, rearranging itself on his forehead. It prickled with heat, as though he sweated molten metal.

Castor stared. Words.

The blood was writing out words across his skin.

Your path.

What...? Castor closed his eyes, but when he looked again, the words stubbornly remained. He scrubbed at the blood with his forearm and gasped. His arm was smeared in red, but still the words stood out against his pale, bloodless skin.

No... they had changed.

Our path.

Castor swiped his hand across his brow again, but the letters would not move. Something buzzed in the back of his skull like an angry insect, making his head ache. Castor pulled away from the glass. Even when he moved, the bloody words dripped down the mirror.

Curious and horrified, the general gingerly touched his fingers to them. There was nothing there! Nothing but cold, smooth glass. Castor grabbed the mirror from its stand and flung it across the room, intent on smashing the glass against the opposite wall. The silver disk spun through the air, but seemed to impact something else long before the wall. Something invisible, impossible. The glass rebounded and went still, floating in the center of the room as though held by invisible hands.

Slowly, the mirror spun toward Castor, facing him. Following him.

The general backed quickly away. Terror burned both hot and cold through Castor's body. What was this? What in the bloody hell was going on? If he could get out of the bathing room, he could get to his sword... The Sun Court general took another few quick, darting steps backward. His progress was awkward, but he didn't dare turn his back on the mirror. Castor risked a quick glance back over his shoulder. How far away was escape?

Something covered the wall, something like spider webs, but stretched out to unnaturally vast proportions. Each strand was as thick as a man's finger. Even so, the fibrous barrier was hard to see. It shone like ice or glass, as absolutely transparent and nearly invisible. Castor heard his wife calling to him, asking if something was wrong. He wanted to shout back to her, but some deeper instinct silenced him. This was the work of nothing natural, nothing of this world.

The Alterra... What did they want? The damned dream-eaters had never come unbidden to a VEIL knight...

There was a silver slice of motion and Castor found himself face to face with the mirror. Blood dripped down over its surface, obscuring the reflection beneath. Castor searched for his own features in the glass, but through the dripping gore, he saw only an endless roiling, cloudy grayness that should have been unimpressive, but that somehow filled him with a deep, chill dread. Icy sweat dripped down the back of Castor's neck.

The blood cinched together, flowing into the mirror's center against all natural law. And then it stretched out again like something living.

We are, it wrote.

We are who we are not.

Are. Are not.

Alterra. We are SHATTER.

The air was stiflingly cold. Every breath stung and the pain in the back of Castor's head turned into blades of ice. This was nothing like what Rikard had described.

Rikard Mazrem... The legens' name bubbled and slithered in blood. Angry, smug. The deep, endlessly flat grayness was everywhere. Still contained within the mirror, but its... taste... seemed to fill the room, painted all the world in bleak. The blood flowed again, the only point of color in all existence.

Our path. Your path.

We want what you want.

Rikard Mazrem must fail.

Cut the ties that bind. Worlds flow apart.

We will give you the knife.

Break him. Destroy Rikard Mazrem.

Shatter's enemy. Your enemy.

Bleed to us.

No pact. We want nothing in return.

Nothing.

Castor remembered the Shatter, remembered Rikard Mazrem cursing their empty name. Enemies of the Uprising. Empty ghosts that wanted each world for itself, to sever all ties.

You want the old world.

So do we.

Old, old, old.

Before Rikard Mazrem.

Before Terrans.

Undo what has been done.

Everything just as it was... before Rikard Mazrem. Before he took the Sun Court away from their emperor, before he made Castor vote against his right and honorable master...

Castor opened his cannula again. Blood spattered onto the tiled floor with every sluggish beat of his heart. Drip, drip, drip... like the rhythmic ratcheting of gears somewhere in the void.

Castor's blood swirled at his feet, a vortex of inky black in the pale light, a wordless agreement. Cold understanding flowed into him, numbing him. His wife called to Castor, but he was no longer listening. Everything was gray. Perfectly empty, perfectly ordered. The nothingness sighed breathlessly.

We will show you the way.

The way to everything you want.

To break everything he has built.

To SHATTER.

The bloody mirror cracked, shattering with a sharp retort, and fell to the floor in a hundred glittering pieces.

36

UNDER THE SUN

"A single moment can change history. It can build the future or shatter the past."

— OUR RED HISTORY, BY AVILLA SALLUSI

THAINNA WOKE AT DAWN. She was too excited to sleep any longer. After a brief visit to the bathhouse, she dressed in the nicest tabba that Narissa had sent and braided her damp hair. Did the pale blue tabba clash with the red? Thainna checked her reflection and decided that they looked fine.

Even at this early hour, the entire Mazrem house was in an uproar. Knights in full armor of every color – most carrying some report or list for their superior's inspection – pushed through the halls with swift, purposeful strides. Servants hauling food and clothes and more papers wound their way past. More than a few stopped as one of the knights asked for directions or had to be guided to the other end of the large house.

The entire Lyceum seemed to be in attendance, as well, along with all of their aides and attendants. A gray-cloaked Nianese man stood just inside the atrium, listening to a pair of Sun Court knights who kept interrupting one another in excitement.

"Thainna!"

She turned to find Bastil chasing after her, scowling. The old steward grabbed her elbow and towed her back outside.

"There you are," he said. "I've been looking for you for hours."

Bastil was probably exaggerating, but Thainna dutifully followed him down the crowded drive.

"What's wrong?" she asked.

"Legens Mazrem is already on his way to the Star Court and you're to join him at once," Bastil told Thainna without looking back. "I'm sending you down into the city with some of the other knights."

"Did Gaius leave already? Is he with Rikard?"

"Young Lord Mazrem left with his father, hae," Bastil answered with a nod.

Thainna smiled so wide that it felt her face would split open. Bastil scowled at her utter failure to treat this day with the gravity it so clearly deserved. But it was just too exciting! Thainna had never seen an Alterran pact made before and no one had ever witnessed one so vast.

Everything seemed so bright and clear and inexplicably more real today. The grass thrust up from the rich brown soil like an army of tiny emerald swords. White clouds raced across a sky the same color and soft, rippling richness as her tabba.

"Thainna!" Bastil called. "I don't have all day to shepherd you. I have Lady Mazrem's tasks to look after, too."

Thainna had fallen behind again and raced to close the distance. She let Bastil usher her into the care of a Moon Court knight who looked familiar. The man sat astride a dappled gray horse that pawed restlessly at the ground. Both horse and rider were eager to be off. The knight was about Gaius' age, but with a boyish glimmer of excitement in his brown eyes that reminded her more of Rikard.

He held out his hand to help Thainna into the saddle behind him.

"Mana Vahn," the knight greeted her. He turned awkwardly in the saddle and gave her a respectful nod.

"Forgive me, you look familiar, but I can't..." she admitted.

"Marus Gallard," the knight told her. "I came to visit Legens Mazrem shortly after his return."

"You were the one who found Rikard."

"That's me, mana."

"Just Thainna, please."

"Thainna, then," Marus answered with a grin not unlike the one she had seen in her own mirror earlier that morning. "Thank you, Thainna."

"Me? For what?"

"I might have brought the legens' body back to VEIL, but they say you're the one who saved his spirit. You've been with him at every step."

Thainna bit her lip and felt the blood hot in her cheeks. A VEIL captain in Sun Court red handed a covered waxboard up to Marus who tucked it into a saddlebag and then looked at Thainna.

"Are you ready?" he asked.

"Hae!"

Marus urged the horse out into the street, swore and reined out of the way of a chariot. He steered around a pair of litters carrying gossiping noblewomen and out into the crowded street center. Thainna clung tightly to Marus as he rode quickly through Dormaen. The roads were full of people, even this early in the day.

But what a day!

Everyone wanted to get to Mazrem Square early to claim a good view of the blood pact. Marus had to jump his horse over a heavy sedan chair and its heavier occupant, deposited in the middle of the street by its panting, sweating bearers. Nearby traffic shouted to remove the obstacle, but it would be a few minutes until the men recovered their breath enough. The fat nobleman enthroned in the middle of the road flushed and apologized to everyone with upraised hands.

The packed throng thinned a bit as Marus and Thainna turned away from Mazrem Square and toward the Star Court archouse, but they traveled against the flow of traffic. So Marus turned off the main road and onto a tiny, narrow street that was little more than a long alleyway. When she asked how he knew it, Marus explained that it led to one of the back gates of the court.

"For when knights want to return late and unnoticed to the archouse," he said. "Not that we will have much use for things like this anymore. Praise the gods."

"We're using it," Thainna pointed out.

"Well, this is for a good cause, isn't it?" Marus chuckled. "We're avoiding traffic, not attention."

At the back gate, a templar took their names and then waved Thainna and Marus through.

"The legens is in the main yard," she said.

"Thank you, tes," said Marus. "Let's get you to Legens Mazrem, Thainna."

Marus dismounted and helped Thainna scramble down from the saddle. A young squire in a black saela took the reins and led the spotted horse away. Marus took Thainna through the archouse and out into the courtyard. The lawn wasn't as crowded as the day Rikard had called for volunteers, but it was still packed and as busy as a beehive. The people gathered here weren't just listening to a speech today. Every one of them had something to do, some report to deliver or order to carry out, and each believed his or her task was of paramount importance.

Taller than Thainna by more than a head, Marus was the one who found Rikard. He was, naturally, in the center of the thickest knot of people. Marus pointed her in the right direction.

"Thainna, can you manage alright?" he asked.

When she told him that she would, the Moon Court knight let himself be pulled aside by an Erastrasan man asking after the reports he had brought.

With no small effort, Thainna pushed, shoved and ducked her way through the crowd to Rikard. When he felt her nearby, his eyes lit up and he searched the sea of faces until he found her. Thainna slipped past a short templar and took Rikard's offered hand. He embraced her briefly.

I missed you this morning, he thought to her. *I'm sorry I couldn't wait for you at the house.*

It's fine, Thainna reassured him. *You've got more history to make today. Bastil found me and sent me here with Marus Gallard. Do you remember him?*

Hae. He is a good man. Did you–? Rikard thought, but the short templar was trying to get his attention. The woman waved her arms until Rikard turned to look at her.

"Legens, Consul Liam sent a runner," she told him. "One of the wagons broke an axle. It was carrying a ton of the millet. It's being transferred to a new wagon, but it will take some time to arrive."

"Will it run us late?" Rikard asked.

She shrugged. "I'm sorry, legens. He didn't say."

"If the runner's not too badly winded, send him back to get an estimate on the delay. Give him a horse, if he can ride."

"Hae, legens."

The templar made her way back through the crowd, and Rikard looked down at Thainna again. *When we return home, I will thank Bastil for finding you. I want you to be here today.*

I wouldn't miss it for anything. Do you know what you'll promise the Alterrans in the pact today?

No. This is not a standard pact. This is much larger and much more complicated. I will ask the Uprising what they need, and we will give it.

Hae. Thainna knew he would and hoped that the rest of VEIL would follow their legens' lead. *Where are Gaius and Lady Laurael?*

My wife is at home... resting, I believe. She was out late last night. Doing something for Gaius, she said.

What was it?

I don't know. I left her the surprise. Gaius is at the square already, setting up a perimeter and overseeing the grain delivery.

You must be so—

"Legens Mazrem! Legens!"

Rikard reluctantly withdrew his attention from Thainna to receive a lengthy, detailed update on the wagons that had arrived in Mazrem Square. Thainna listened, too, but she lacked her father's knack for numbers. Some of the grain was still missing, she gathered, and more than one broken wagon. Rikard gestured another knight forward to compare their reports and find out where the numbers had gone awry.

A light touch at her elbow made Thainna jump. She whirled to find Caelin cringing and clutching the hem of his tabba.

"Caelin?" Thainna sighed. "Bloody hell, man, you scared me. What are you doing here?"

The older Talon held out the satchel that held her bandages and salves. Thainna took it uncertainly. She hadn't used any of it in days. What was Caelin playing at? He slid in closer until he could whisper right into Thainna's ear.

"Arliss was looking for you. Got a message from the House, so I told Bastil that you might need your things. He let me ride in with one of the knights. I had nothing else to do," Caelin told Thainna. "Master Gaius hasn't been touching his drams of late and Lady Mazrem's busy with the other house servants. She's going out again today."

Caelin's breath tickled Thainna's ear uncomfortably, but it was nothing beside the sudden, terrible sinking in her stomach.

"Wait. A message from the House? Gods, what is it?"

"You're to go report to the Crest. At once."

"The Crest? Now?"

Thainna barely kept herself from shouting. With an effort, she quashed her fear. She didn't want to get Rikard's attention. Not now.

"Arliss said to... to remind you of Thain," Caelin told her apologetically. "You have to go."

"Where?"

"*There.* To him, to the temple district. Do you want to tell Lord Mazrem?"

Thainna fought to maintain her composure. She felt sick. "No, I... I can't. He'll know something's wrong. I have to leave before he notices."

"Do you want me to tell him?"

"No, he could get the answer from you just as easily. Stay away until this is all over. Come on, we have to go."

Thainna looked back at Rikard once to make sure that he was still busy, then took Caelin's hand and towed him out of the Star courtyard. It was much easier to get away from Rikard than it was to get close.

"Get back to the Mazrem house," she instructed Caelin tightly. "Or anywhere else in the city. Just stay away from Rikard until tomorrow, hae? I... I don't want him to know."

"I'm sorry, Thainna."

"It's not your fault. We all come running when the Crest calls."

"Hae," Caelin agreed darkly.

When she had made certain that the old Talon was on his way out of the Star Court, Thainna contemplated taking Marus' horse. She was in a hurry, but didn't want to steal anything that might be missed or that might invite questions.

Thainna struck out across Dormaen at a brisk walk. Whether she lived in the Rows or the Everstones, when the Crest called, she had to crawl across the city to him.

Rikard had no time to dwell on Thainna's painful absence. He stood atop a hastily constructed stage in the middle of Mazrem Square, self-conscious in the shadow of his own monument. In the center of the plaza, four hundred carts of the Erastrasus grain shipment were arranged in rows, all draped in weighted sailcloth. One corner had been turned up on every wagon to reveal the sickly blue-black bruise of blighted wheat and millet inside.

Seven thousand knights formed up in tight ranks around them, filling Mazrem Square with flashing metal and creaking leather. Past them and separated by a triple guard of enlisted soldiers, half of Dormaen had turned out to watch. Rich noblemen and women in tall sedan chairs, merchants and their wives on litters, thousands standing and jostling each other for a better view, children sitting on their parents' shoulders and waving. The sound of the crowd was not unlike the ocean Rikard had seen once as a boy... a rustling roar that rose and fell, inarticulate and somehow smooth.

He couldn't afford to dwell on Thainna's absence, but Rikard felt it. Where *was* she?

"Are we ready? Rik? Rik, what's wrong?"

"Nothing." Rikard waved off Saul's concern. There were more important things right now. He turned to Gaius. "Is everyone here?"

"Near as I can tell. All of the captains have reported in. If anyone is missing, it's on their head, not mine."

"All that remains is to do this."

This came from General Castor. The oldest of the VEIL generals stood a little apart from the others, as though their presence might somehow taint him. He polished his bloodcap against a leather strip in the skirt of his armor. Castor wore no sword. No one did. By Rikard's order, this was a demonstration of peace and no arms were to be worn.

Something followed Castor, trailing behind him and wafting all around him like a lingering smell. Like ashes and old iron and cold stone. What was it?

If he didn't have time to find Thainna, Rikard thought unhappily, then he certainly didn't have time to wonder about Castor. The Sun Court general had sworn himself to the pact. There would be time to deal with the rest later. For now, the city and the empire needed her knights.

"Hae," Rikard agreed. "Are you ready for this?"

The other men nodded. It was a lie, of course. None of them were ready. Dealing with Alterra always had a price, but it was a price they paid gladly.

Rikard stepped up to the edge of the stage. He raised his hands and the crowd roared, calling out his name. The knights hammered their fists against their breastplates in a single deafening crash. Rikard waited until the noise died away before he spoke, but he still had to shout to make himself heard across even a fraction of the vast throng.

"What has been can never be again," Rikard said in as loud a voice as he could. "I cannot make the Verita et Illumina Lansinos what they were in the days before Carce became an empire. Nor would I! We are no longer nations at war. The only war that remains is within our own borders, against the beasts of our own nature, the philosopher's dragons!"

A murmur rose from the crowd as his words rippled through them, repeated for those who couldn't hear Rikard. He felt their taut nerves, thrumming inside him with every drumbeat of his own pounding heart. Blood rushed in his ears, making it almost impossible to hear his own voice. Only the breathless press in his lungs reassured Rikard he was speaking at all.

"When a man succumbs to his dragons, he doesn't suffer alone. All around him suffer and VEIL gave in to our dragons. Not every knight, nor every knight equally, but our crime is no less. We are all brothers together before you, and together we swear ourselves to a new and higher road! We are promised protectors to Terra and to

Alterra. Our pacts, our oaths to ourselves and our allies, are the lifeblood of worlds!"

Rikard knew that most of the crowd didn't care much about the Alterra, but that was the very heart of the problem. Without Terran dreams and ideas, the spark of fierce changeability and imagination that was so uniquely *human*, all Alterra would fade away.

"To every man and woman of Carce, to every question and answer of the Uprising, we give of ourselves. To Terra, we return the summer harvest of Erastrasus. To Alterra, we give our blood, our pact. Knights of VEIL, stand to attention!" Rikard called.

"Hae, legens!" they answered together.

Seven thousand knights snapped to attention. Backs straight, heads held high and proud. Rikard had been wrong. They *were* ready for this. Every one of them! He thumbed open the cap of his finger and raised his right hand. Behind Rikard, his son and generals did the same. The knights raised their cannulas, filling the plaza with gold like a field of wheat under the sun. The crowd applauded thunderously and roared their praise.

Flickerdim, I remember now! This, this is why I returned to Terra. Even if we somehow managed to defeat the Shatter, none of it would have mattered if we forgot you, if VEIL left you in silence. I remember, my friends. I bleed for you now, for my people and for yours!

Rikard knelt and traced a circle of his blood on the stage. Gaius stepped forward.

"You know what to do!" he told the knights. "Keep your head and keep your focus. We're not the VEIL he knew thirty years ago. We're even better than that! Let's show Legens Mazrem what *we* can do."

Grunting a little, Gaius knelt beside his father and winked. Rikard felt more than saw it as his blood flowed onto the wooden platform and his senses began to spread. In thousands, the knights of VEIL sank to their knees on the cobblestones and filled the swirling autumn air with the sea-salt tang of blood. Rikard reached and felt their minds open, ready and waiting. Willing. Whatever their Alterran brothers needed, they would be honored to give. The generals knelt behind Rikard, scribing their own crimson circles and joining the pact.

Slowly at first, and then with rising confidence, thousands of fingers traced the pact glyphs. A call to the Alterra to seek out the memories, the understanding of the wheat and millet, how to re-write this blighted, useless chaff into what it was meant to be.

Dormaen watched with breathless anticipation. Through slitted eyes, Rikard felt the air shimmer as though summer-hot, but the curling breeze remained cool. The crowd murmured. What was happening? Rikard reached inward instead of out, questing for Flickerdim's dusky-bright presence. Where was the wisdom? Rikard searched, spreading his senses out cumulusly.

Flickerdim...! I've brought them, my brave knights. We are ready. Reach out to me and seal our pact!

But something was terribly wrong. Cold, colorless fire licked at the base of the tree-tower, smothering it in cracked ice. Flickerdim reached back through the veil toward Rikard, but he moved so slowly, too uncertainly for a wisdom. Something was wrong with the great serpent's eyes. They were pale and hazy, clouds over the full moon... He was blind!

Stumble called from somewhere in the infinite distance. No, not infinite... It snapped in an instant into a hard, finite shape that was too far away. The Uprising was under siege. Stumble flew toward the bright VEIL blood on the glassy gray ground, but the frozen air held the young curiosity at bay.

No!

Rikard reached desperately for Flickerdim and Stumble, but his Terran senses screamed at him. The freezing fire was not confined to Alterra. It was pushing *through*. Rikard wrenched his eyes and stared. The air over the covered grain wagons shimmered like a mirage, but seethed more violently than any desert air. And cold... Not even the deepest Fiore winter was that cold.

This was wrong. Rikard's fear rippled out through the ranks of VEIL knights. A collective shiver became a frightened tremble. All except one spot of icy certainty, the cold iron spike that held everything in frozen stillness. Rikard flung his curiosity in every direction, seeking out the terrible, glacial lynchpin of the attack.

"Father! Damn it, Rikard! What's happening?"

At his son's panicked cry, Rikard surged to his feet. Gaius wasn't the only one screaming. The knights closest to the grain wagons were on their feet and staggering back, but they were packed too closely and the ground was slippery with blood. The civilians were too far away to make out the details and pressed curiously forward.

Rikard shouted for them to get back, but no one heard him over the frightened knights. He reached desperately through the veil. *Flickerdim, Stumble... I need you! We can't let this happen!*

For one stuttering heartbeat, Rikard felt their thoughts touch against his, as tenuous as a secret. If Flickerdim could just reach him, Rikard would regain control of the pact.

The cold stretched into eternity, twisted and snapped with a terrible sound. Shattering and breaking.

Pain, suffering that crushes hopes. Loss to take away even the will to fight.

It was so hard to focus, to hold on to that whisper-thin link to the Uprising. The Shattering cold pressed in on Rikard with the weight of mountains. He cast all of his old armors up around him, memories of his brother knights–

Cowards.

The Shatter sank hooked, icy talons into the thought and tore it away.

Home– Rikard countered.

Has changed. This is not the world you knew.

My family! My son, my wife!

The memories of Laurael that had shielded him for thirty years were as weak now as wet paper before the Shatter. The empty Alterra howled silently, deafeningly.

Love. I am loved... Rikard thought desperately. He wept with the effort and clung to himself.

The Shatter seized upon the flagging resolve. *Love. She left you alone in the cold,* the ice cracked. *She left you to burn and fall. She's lying to you.*

...Thainna.

She left.

You're alone.

Rikard could hold on no longer.

The fragile bond snapped and the Uprising was swallowed by broken distance. In Terra, the seething air over the lines of wagons broke. White-hot flames erupted all across wood and moldering wheat. The inferno exploded outward, filling the Mazrem Square with fire.

A hundred frightened cries became more as the VEIL knights recoiled. The wagons' canvas covers blackened and curled, burning away within seconds. A blazing wind hurled flaming wheat into the rapidly darkening sky. Thick black smoke poured out across Mazrem Square, cloying and choking. The crowd broke apart like a dropped glass, thousands of people shrieking and trampling each other, beating savagely at their own clothes as embers set them aflame.

The fire was spreading quickly, leaping from cart to cart and scorching the stone beneath. The stage was burning, too, creaking and popping as the supports caught and began to buckle. Rikard stood rooted to the spot, gaping in horror as his worlds burned. Gaius shouted at him and Saul tugged at his arm.

"Rik! Come on, we've got to get back," Saul called.

"Leave him!" shouted Nikas Hern. "He did this! Let the bastard burn!"

Swearing loudly, Gaius punched Hern in the gut. "You bloodless coward! This isn't his fault!"

"This whole thing was his idea," Hern wheezed, doubled over and clutching his stomach. "He hates VEIL and wants to burn us out like an infection!"

"Don't be an idiot!"

"This isn't the time to argue!" Saul shouted. "Get down before we fall down!"

This can't be happening... Rikard let his friend and son pull him down from the stage and out into the quickly emptying plaza. The smoky air was full of tolling bells. The alarm, a fire in the heart of Dormaen. Hot smoke seared his throat.

"Where's Castor?" asked Hern through a fit of coughing.

"He was the first one down," Gaius rasped. "He's got even fewer guts than you, Nikas!"

"Not now, damn you all. Keep going! We're not doing anyone any good dead. We need to get out before anything else," Saul said.

The entire world was charred black and blazing red. Everything was ash. Rikard reached for Flickerdim and Stumble... Surely they could extinguish the flames that the other Alterra had lit. But Rikard felt only a hot-cold emptiness and silence.

Cut away, a world alone. They won... The Shatter. They have Shattered our faith.

Spurred to animal panic by Rikard's own fear, most of the other knights had fled Mazrem Square, but a few remained, led by the blue shape of Marus Gallard. The Moon Court knight waved to Rikard and his three companions. They gathered to Rikard like iron to a magnet and he wanted to scream at them.

I did this! It's my fault! I couldn't hold on, I couldn't hold the pact together...

"We have to get moving, sirs!" Marus shouted.

Gaius grabbed his father's arm and they ran, fleeing the leaping, spreading flames. Everything in front of them was black on black, silhouettes in the smoke, and then a nightmare of cruelly twisting, crackling red as another building caught flame.

Turning down a third street, the air was finally clear enough to slow down. Rikard sagged bonelessly against the door of a studio. The sun shone red through the smoke, reduced to a smoldering spot of blood hanging high in the sky. Burning, blighted wheat was everywhere, smoking and filling the air with flying embers. The alarm bells drowned out all other sound until Rikard's head rang with the noise.

"Saerus is going to glut his damned self today if we can't get that fire under control," Gaius said.

Marus shook his head. "Everyone was in Mazrem Square. It's going to take too long for anyone to answer the alarm bells."

"What's that?" Hern asked suddenly.

He pointed down the street and Rikard squinted through the unnatural gloom. For a wild moment, he thought that the embers had coalesced into men and they marched now through Dormaen, claiming the city as their own.

No, Rikard realized – the silhouettes were knights in red Sun Court armor, escorting a cask-shaped water wagon pulled by a pair of massive draft horses. One of the knights sat in the driver's seat, whipping at the horses' heaving, sweating flanks. Hern and a few of the others that had followed Rikard cheered weakly as the Sun Court knights rushed past.

"How could they be here already?" Saul asked, bewildered. "No one could have gotten the water wagons rolling so quickly!"

"It doesn't matter now," Rikard said. "We will follow them and lend what help we can."

The Sun Court knights had been ready for the fire. They had expected this... but there was no time and no point in casting blame now. Dormaen was burning. Rikard pushed himself upright and ran on feet that felt like lead to catch up with the Sun Court wagon. Spitting oaths and ashes, the other knights followed.

37

THE CROOKED TOWER

— LIAM IO

ONCE THAINNA LEFT the bustle of Mazrem Square and the VEIL archouses, Dormaen was eerily quiet. Most of the shops were closed and the streets empty of people. If there weren't so many other things to think about, Thainna would have seized the unparalleled opportunities for thievery. But the Crest was waiting for her.

Thainna fought the urge to run. Thain needed her to hurry and terrible images of what the Crest might do to her twin chased each other through Thainna's head, each worse than the last, but she knew better than to run. She would only exhaust herself and lose any time gained as she recovered her breath.

All the wisdom and restraint in the worlds couldn't chase away the gnawing sensation inside her. The worry seemed as though it might eat away until there was nothing left of her but an empty skin slouching through the barren city.

Why did the Crest want to see Thainna?

Control over Rikard Mazrem meant nothing if never used, she supposed. Did the Crest want something from him? Thainna wiped her sleeve across her eyes. The blue tabba was soft against her skin, then warm and heavy as sweat soaked into the cloth. At some point, the Crest would want more than just control over Rikard. Money. Favors. A life or a death.

And I'll have to be the one to make it happen. That's my job, after all.

I don't want to. I don't want to hurt Rikard.

Thainna hated herself for even thinking it. The Crest held her brother captive to ensure that Thainna did as she was told. Now she doubted the job. And for what?

For whom?

Thain. Gods help me, I'll slit Rikard's throat myself to get Thain back. I will... Hae?

Rikard had offered Thainna a real life. She laced her fingers over her fluttering stomach. He helped her feel like a whole person, not a House Talon or a muddy street urchin. It was strange to think about. Until the Crest sent her here, Thainna had never considered another life besides that of a thief. Even if she won the Auction and put Thain on the Jade Throne, she would serve him as a faithful Talon of his House.

Now Thainna wondered about that plan. She wanted Thain to have a good life, but what would that life be? Crest of the House of Five Dragons or a guest in the house of Rikard Mazrem?

But it's about more than that, isn't it? It's about Caelin and his wife, too, and everyone else like them. Like me. Most of us live in the Rows, no better than rats. We need Thain, just like VEIL needs Rikard.

Thainna might daydream about staying with Rikard, but she could never do it. The House of Five Dragons needed Thain and Thain needed his twin sister. There was something sweet about the regret of a life she would never have, perfectly crystallized as a rock-sugar candy. It was nice to think about, to savor, but it wouldn't keep her fed through the winter or heal her sick brother.

Thainna guessed it was nearing noon when she turned a quiet corner into the temple district. Rikard would begin his pact soon. Thainna wished she could have been with him, but there was no other choice. Close now, she let herself break into a run and bolted across the blue-tiled mosaic court in front of Merra's temple. The doors, styled like driftwood and framed in carved jade seaweed, stood shut. Even the temples were closed today. Thainna ran past Suzukarri's shrine, where the air smelled like burnt cinnamon and salt. A dozen other ever-smaller shrines blurred past until she had bolted down the last empty street.

There. The crooked tower of the House of Five Dragons stood in a dark, secretive corner of the temple district. If it had ever been a true temple, raised to some old Carcaen god, no one remembered his name. The tower squatted in the shadow of the other shrines, dark and shaggy with crawling vines that never flowered.

Age or maybe poor design had taken its toll on the tower. Half of the foundation had collapsed long before Thainna's birth and knocked the tower askew. It leaned alarmingly, hunched and deceptively weak, like an aged knight. Rain and years stained the sloped conical roof, but there were no holes. The dark, open doorway and worm-bore windows lied. This place was not dead and it wasn't empty.

Thainna pushed the vines out of her way and ducked through the door. In her short lifetime in service to the House of Five Dragons, she had never been summoned to the Crest's tower. The point of something cold and sharp pressed against her back. Thainna froze in an uncomfortable half-crouch.

"Slowly," hissed the man behind her. "Put your hands out and turn around."

When Thainna turned, she could make out little more than she had with her back turned to the man. He was dressed and masked in dark clothes that blended in all too well with the shadows. Even the crossbow he held was finished in a flat, unreflecting black.

Thainna couldn't stop herself from staring. Crossbows were expensive weapons, imported all the way from Erastrasus. She had never seen one this close before. But she was too frightened to be able to admire it very much.

"Thainna Vahn," said the man behind the loaded crossbow. "He is waiting for you. I'll take you up."

The Talon – who still had not given his name – insisted on walking behind her. Did he think Thainna would run? Perhaps he did, because the crossbow remained pointed at her. However fast she might move, his bolt would be faster. Pointing with his weapon, the Talon directed Thainna along a staircase that coiled up through the crooked tower.

The close darkness forced Thainna to move slowly and gave her time to examine her surroundings. The dark, she quickly discovered, was much more than a simple lack of light. Everything was dark. Drapes and bunting covered the basalt blocks of the curving wall that ran along the staircase, all in twilight blue and violet. There were lanterns, too, dangling from the distant ceiling on long black chains and shielded by smoky glass. These stairs were covered in something thick and soft. They made no sound under Thainna's feet as she climbed.

The floor below vanished quickly into the artificial shadows. After what seemed like an endless hike, the stairs leveled out into a half-moon landing. The stone walls here were finished in gleaming black enamel and painted in intricately looping designs that made Thainna dizzy to look at. Or maybe it wasn't the painting – she could no longer see the off-kilter tilt of the tower, but she felt it with every step. The floor was never quite where it was supposed to be and Thainna couldn't seem to catch her balance.

"Keep moving. Take the door on your left."

There were more rooms, all steeped in lightless murk. Thainna caught glimmers of treasures shining in the dark – paintings and sculptures, tables heaped with things she couldn't see. Other things hung from the ceiling, rattling as they swung in even the faint breeze generated by their passage. One room was close and narrow, and the air was bright with the sharp copper scent of blood.

Thainna held her breath and hurried through. Was Thain somewhere here? Bound in the stifling, oppressive darkness?

Following the instructions of the Talon on her heels, Thainna tugged open a heavy ebony door and found another flight of stairs. She climbed on sore, weary legs through the shadows. There were windows up here, mostly covered in vines that allowed only thin, blade-edge rays of sunlight through. They slashed white-gold wounds across the dark stairwell but did nothing to illuminate the greater blackness.

Passing close to one of the windows, Thainna tried to look out into the city. What was Rikard doing right now? Maybe they were high enough to see Mazrem Square. But the sun only blinded her and made Thainna trip over the next step. Another cold, unfriendly prick against her spine forced her up again.

The bright spots in her vision had faded to silvery smears when Thainna reached the next stout door. There was something carved into the wood, but she had to squint to make out the design. A dragon? A dragon with five heads. Thainna put her shoulder against the door and pushed. It swung open much easier than she expected, moving smoothly on well-oiled hinges. Thainna gasped.

Nothing in the tower below had prepared her for the opulence that awaited her at its crown. She was in a large, circular room supported by an inner ring of columns, all decorated with more intricately carved dragons. They watched Thainna reel between them with glittering gemstone eyes.

Tapestries in bright colors and braided strands of crystal beads covered the walls, draped across the ceiling like jeweled cobwebs. The floor shone brilliantly, covered in a layer of burnished copper polished to a mirror sheen. Flower petals floated in colorful glass bowls and filled the air with a delicate, exotic scent.

A dozen couches filled the circular chamber, so wide and lavish that they looked more like beds, each adorned with its own slender, naked occupant, chained in shining silver. Men, women... as beautiful and silent as statues. They all watched Thainna being ushered through their midst with no more curiosity in their dead eyes than those of the stone dragons.

"Turn right."

Thainna's course led her uncomfortably close to one of the beds. None of the occupants of the room were Fiori, but Thainna couldn't shake the thought of Thain chained up here like some kind of animal, a toy. It was even worse than the dark, blood-stinking rooms below, somehow. These were slaves, men and women not just controlled, but *owned* by the Crest.

The next doorway plunged Thainna once more into darkness and then they were climbing again. Would it ever end? She was dizzy and tired. The stairs felt different under her sandals. It was not until she realized that the rhythmic sound in her ears was not her own terrified heartbeat that Thainna understood she was listening to her own footsteps for the first time since entering the crooked tower. The stairs were bare stone, barely finished and almost crude in construction.

"Where are we going?" Thainna asked over her shoulder.

"I should think that was obvious. To see the Crest, our master."

"Where is he?"

"Not far now. It will seem much further on the way back."

Thainna turned back to the stairs and nearly smashed her face into the last door. It creaked ominously when she pushed it open. Thainna could see nothing beyond but shadows, a depthless black like an infinite inkwell. What if the emptiness stretched all the way back down to the bottom of the tower?

Her guide shoved her roughly and Thainna fell through. She shrieked and braced herself for a fall, but her heels only jolted painfully against the floor a few inches down. Thainna gasped and turned to shout at the Talon for his unnecessary push, but he paid no attention. Shouldering his crossbow, he lit a single lamp from an emberbox, then pulled on a chain and hoisted it up into warped and splintered rafters. The wavering spot of light illuminated a vast chair of translucent green stone. The Jade Throne, the seat of the Crest of the House of Five Dragons.

The throne was obviously well cared for, polished and dusted frequently, cushions often laundered and replaced. Still, there was no cleaning away the immutable sense of age. The Jade Throne was as cold and remote as a distant mountaintop.

"You'll wait here."

The man in black left before Thainna could answer him. She faltered in the crooked darkness. She could see nothing outside the spotlight above the empty throne. It was hard to believe it was the middle of the afternoon on a bright day outside.

A soft rustle in the shadows made Thainna freeze like a mouse in a field, listening. Was there someone else here?

"Hae?" she called. Her voice cracked.

A piece of the darkness cut itself free and stepped into the blurry circle of lamplight. He was as indistinct as one of the shadows. Like the one who had brought her, he was covered from head to foot. Over a flowing tabba of black silk, the man wore a cloak of midnight blue with a hood so deep the face inside was invisible. Even the long-fingered hands were gloved in soft, dark gray doeskin. The shrouded figure turned its hooded gaze on Thainna. She shivered.

"Do you not know your master, Talon?" he asked.

The Crest. Thainna fell to her knees and bowed her head to the slanted floor. Her throat was cinched shut as tightly as a miser's purse. She couldn't breathe, could not speak. The Crest seated himself gracefully on the hard Jade Throne.

"You were set a singular task, Thainna. Of all my Talons, Rikard Mazrem was entrusted to *you*. I gave you every chance, every tool and resource to bring him under your control," the Crest said. His tone was easy and conversational. Civilized. Was there something familiar about that voice? But Thainna could barely hear at all over the thundering staccato of her own racing heart. "You used none of it. In fact, you helped Rikard Mazrem to hunt and drive us out of VEIL. What have you done, Thainna?"

"You took my brother!" The fury returned Thainna's voice. "You threatened him! I was just a thief. I have no business in this sort of work in the first place!"

The Crest lifted his chin to peer down his nose at Thainna. Or she thought that was what he was doing... it was impossible to tell in the darkness under his hood.

"You belong to me, Talon. So does your brother," the Crest said. His voice was suddenly all ice and sharp edges. "You were chosen for this task and you may not refuse. I trusted no other, Thainna, and you disappointed me. You let Rikard Mazrem chase every single one of our agents from VEIL. You even let him procure the Erastrasus grain."

Thainna shook her head, lost and bewildered. "What? How can you blame me for that? You only gave me one order! And what do you care if he fixes the wheat? It's your Talons who were going to starve!"

"Poisoning that shipment was an extremely delicate matter."

"You... you did that?" Thainna could not believe what she was hearing. "Why? Just to drive up wheat prices this winter?"

"The Nianese consul had a great deal invested in the shipment. Nian is trusted with the wealth of a great many powerful men and their interests. Liam Io would have been responsible for repaying that deficit."

"You were going to give him the money, weren't you? Or at least loan it to him. Either way, he's in your pocket."

Thainna knew she should stop talking. The Crest already said that he was going to punish her. If Thainna pushed him too hard, how much of that punishment would fall to Thain? But even on her knees before the Crest, she was furious and could no more silence her words than she could her hammering pulse.

"You would let half of the Rows starve to death just to get control over one consul?" she asked.

"And his three pets," the Crest added. His tone was lighter again now, but had not quite lost its glacial edge. "They would have been the first links in the chain by which I would rein in the whole Lyceum. You lost me a great deal, Thainna. My hold on VEIL and on Liam Io. Your control over Rikard Mazrem had better be more secure."

"Why? What do you want from him?"

The Crest sat forward on his wide throne. "What does it matter to you, Talon? Do you fear I might ask something... difficult of him? That I might hurt him? My little Thainna, are you fond of the great legens?"

"Rikard's a good man and he's got real steel in him! Money or girls or drams won't let you control him. You don't know Rikard. He'd rather die than do the things that you want him to!"

"Do you think so, Thainna? Truly? How unfortunate for you. You see, your beloved Rikard has made a terrible mess of my plans. I need him to leave well enough alone, to be otherwise occupied, while I figure out whether or not the situation can be salvaged."

"You want me to... to leave him alone?" Thainna asked uncertainly. The idea struck her hard as a physical blow.

"No, Thainna. I want you to return to him. The man likes you, doesn't he? He took a blade for you in the Sun Court yard. Let us put that considerable affection to the test. I don't want Rikard Mazrem worrying about anything but you for the next few days."

"I don't understand..."

Thainna trailed off as a pair of stocky, rough-faced men stepped out into the light. Scars crisscrossed both faces, and one of them was missing an eye. The other cracked his knuckles ominously.

Thainna lurched away across the slanted floor, searching wildly for the door, but the Crest's easy voice stopped her dead.

"Stay, Thainna. If you run now, I will kill your brother. He is useless to me except to ensure your obedience."

Thainna turned back. Her tears turned the room into a puddle of oily black and greasy gold. She fell to her knees. They scraped painfully on the stone floor, but Thainna didn't think that would matter for much longer. She bowed her head.

Thain. Thain, I love you. None of this will matter after winter comes. I'll buy that throne for you, Thain. And you'll fix everything.

The Crest flicked his finger at his Talons. "Begin."

He said it the same way another man might tell his son to show him something he had learned in class. One of the Talons hauled Thainna up by her hair and held her. Thainna swore that she wouldn't scream, but she did not keep that promise long. She was no warrior and her body broke easily under their fists and a stout cudgel. The wood was soon stained red. When her legs would hold Thainna no longer, they let her fall and continued their work. Only when a kick cracked one of her ribs with a wet crunch did the Crest stop them.

"Narissa," he called.

The priestess came forward from the darkness. She looked like she might be ill, but she curtsied gracefully to the Crest.

"Hae?" Narissa asked.

"Will she live?"

Narissa stepped gingerly over a puddle of blood and crouched at Thainna's side. She touched her fingers against the side of Thainna's throat, eliciting a raw moan of pain. After a few minutes inspection, Narissa nodded.

"She will live for a while, at least. The injuries to her head and ribs are extensive. They may kill her, in time."

The Crest was a black blur against a sea of red that sparkled like blood on moonlit snow. "Hae, then."

"We'll drop her somewhere that Mazrem's people will find her," Narissa said.

"No. Let her walk. Thainna, get up."

She willed her limbs to move. They felt like skins of water, each bloated and boneless.

"I can't," she whispered.

"Go to Rikard and see if he will care for you, if his affection for you is any kind of hold at all." The Crest stepped down from his throne and came to stand beside Thainna. His voice dropped to a whisper. "Crawl, Thainna. Crawl back to Rikard Mazrem and break his heart. If you die before you reach him, I will kill your brother. Be strong, Thainna. For Thain."

Thainna wept with the effort, but heaved herself to her feet. She fell, screamed and stood again. The room was gone. Narissa, the Talons who had beaten her, even the Crest. Thainna's world was full of exploding colors. She staggered, found the door and tumbled through.

The nameless Talon at the door was right – the journey down the crooked tower was far longer. An hour, a day, a week. Thainna didn't know. She walked, crawled, staggered and fell down the endless flights of softened stone stairs until the starburst haze lightened. Out, back in the streets of the temple district. The air tasted strange in her mouth, stuffy and salty. Bloody and smoky. Everything smelled like hot metal.

Home. I've got to get home... to Rikard... Is that home...?

Thainna knew that she wasn't thinking clearly, but she could do no more about it than she could change the color of the sky. All she could do was walk.

Home.

She walked. A man in Saeran black bumped into Thainna. He tried to take her arm, shouting something. He was going the wrong direction. Home was the other way, but Thainna couldn't make him understand. Finally, he released her and ran, screaming and crying.

Other people shoved past as Thainna walked, all dressed in their best. Like flowers, she thought. Frightened flowers with wide eyes. A whole garden of them.

Bells. I hear bells.

The sky... the sky over Dormaen was the wrong color. Someone *could* change the sky and had turned it black. Why? The sun was just another swimming speck of red. Thainna staggered on.

Home.

38

THE FIRE AND THE FLOWER

"It was the first night of the new world."

— OUR RED HISTORY, BY AVILLA SALLUSI

UNDER THE LEADERSHIP of General Cadmus Castor and his knights, the fires were finally contained. They claimed most of the inner district before Sun Court water wagons could beat back the flames. Armed with axes and sledgehammers, VEIL knights led laymen and soldiers out into the surrounding temples and market streets to smash down and remove anything that would burn. The hurried firebreaks caused almost as much damage as the fire itself.

Castor ordered sails soaked in the river and then hoisted on high posts around Mazrem Square to catch the flying grain embers. Burning wheat sizzled against the wet cloth and darkened like dying fireflies.

With the Sun Court in charge of containing and putting out the fires, it fell to the other courts to restore peace. Most of Dormaen's people thought only to flee the flames, but all too many had found opportunities in the smoke: looting, robbery, even rape and murder.

With Marus' help, General Hern collected the knights of the Moon Court. They spread across the city in teams of three knights and ten soldiers.

As blackened, charred buildings collapsed, there were more deaths. Rikard set his own Star knights sifting through the ashes and collecting the bodies. It seemed almost pointless... They would burn in the fires here or else in the cremation kilns. What did it matter anymore?

Two thousand knights failed to return to duty that day, either dead or fled. Gaius loudly expected the latter. Rikard didn't think about it. Thirty-seven more died combating the fire, caught in collapsing houses or locked in battle with the rioting crowds. The civilian body count was imprecise, but at least a few reports seemed to agree on a number of two hundred sixty-two dead, some four thousand injured. Burned, beaten, bones cracked when the crowd broke and ran.

The shortage of manpower meant that no one stood idle in Dormaen. Nikas Hern patrolled the city with his knights. General Castor stood astride one of his water wagons and held the oiled leather hose in his own hands. Rikard, Saul and Gaius dug through the charred ruins of the inner city until their hands burned and blistered.

No one asked the Alterra for help.

When the sun finally set on the Day of Bells, lanterns remained unlit. The work stopped and would not resume until morning. There were no stars and the moon cowered behind a thick shroud of smoke. Dormaen lay still and silent under a thick gray blanket of grit and ash.

Even after Rikard could no longer see well enough to dig, he remained kneeling in the blackened remains of a school hall. Gaius prodded at his father's thigh with the burnt toe of his boot.

"We have to get home and close the gates. Things are going to get a lot worse tonight."

"Worse?" Rikard asked. A dry, cracked laugh boiled up inside him. "How could anything in the worlds be any worse?"

"The people had something to do today. They were shocked and then they had to put out the fires, save their families and shops. But tonight, they'll have time to think. Time to lay blame."

"Blame me."

"Blame all of us," Gaius said. "Saul's gone off to give final orders to the city soldiers. They'll keep the peace as best they can until morning."

"We can't run now!" Rikard rasped. Everything tasted like ash. "VEIL will watch over the city."

"No one is going to listen to that order. The knights know what's coming, even if you don't. And who do you think you're helping, Rikard? The only thing holding this city together is panic and their hatred for every knight in VEIL. Let them stew in it, if that makes them feel better. Maybe even throw a few stones through the arc-house windows. But if you leave VEIL knights out there on the streets tonight, all you're going to do is get them killed. Civilians, too, when our men fight back. Let them go home. Let's get ourselves home, too. I found a wagon and a mule. I'm not walking all the way to the Everstones on these blisters."

Rikard had no strength to argue. He stood slowly and followed Gaius to an ash-covered flatwagon. The mule before it brayed un-happily at them and flicked its long ears.

"Who do they belong to?" Rikard asked.

Gaius snorted. "Who cares? If he's not dead, then I doubt he's worrying himself much over a wagon. We can return it tomorrow, if you want."

They drove back through charred and empty streets in silence. As Gaius drove up the hill of the Everstones, Rikard stared out across Dormaen. The glow of the last flames lit an artificial sunset to the south. Ashes sifted down from the roiling black sky. In the distance, even the elegant vastness of the white imperial palace loomed and brooded like a great dragon charred by its own flames. Lights moved through the city streets, but they were small and painfully few. Dormaen lay dead beneath him. The wagon lurched to a sudden stop.

"Bloody hell," swore Gaius. "It's me, you idiot! Let us in!"

Rikard looked up. They were home, but the house gates were closed and a knot of guards and soldiers hid behind them. Every one of them was terrified. A knight in Star Court dress stood at the gate, one of those who had not volunteered his blood for the cleansing and so had been assigned other duties for the day. He gripped his gladius tightly and his knuckles were as white as though they had been daubed with paint. Karl shoved the terrified knight out of the way and peered out into the street.

"It's Lord Mazrem!" he called back. "Open up! Open the bloody gates!"

The gates swung open and Gaius drove through. They were pulled shut quickly behind Rikard and his son. Guards and knights shouted over one another, full of terrified questions. They had little idea what was going on in the city outside. When the bells had sounded, they closed and barred the gates, fearing a riot. There were no orders and everything was in chaos.

Rikard closed his eyes against the immediate blade of pain in his skull and shoved his way through. They were all so frightened and it hurt.

"Calm bloody well down!" Gaius shouted. "I swear that I will personally punch the next man who speaks over me or anyone else. Unless you feel like being so honored, calm down! If you shut up, I'll explain..."

Rikard did not feel like lingering to tell stories or share news.

"Karl, with me," he said.

The Lyncean guard jogged to his lord's side and followed Rikard on the long trudge up the hill to the house.

"Where is everyone?" Rikard asked. "There should be twice as many guards on the gate."

"They went with Lady Mazrem, my lord."

"Where is she?" asked Rikard. "Is she alright?"

"I think so, sir. She left in the morning. I… I thought you knew! Lady Mazrem took most of the house guard with her to stay with one of the consuls. My lord, weren't those your orders? Lady Mazrem said that… that you wanted no distractions from the preparations today. We weren't to expect her return until tomorrow."

"I gave no such order," Rikard said. But he couldn't be angry. Maybe Laurael had said something like that and he had forgotten. The past few days felt even longer than the thirty war-torn years before them. "Send someone immediately to make sure my wife is safe. Not one of the knights. One of the guardsmen. No, four. Tell them to wear no family mark and to go armed. Dormaen is dangerous tonight."

"Hae, Lord Mazrem." Karl bowed and ran back down the hill.

The sprawling house was dark and very nearly empty. A maid haltingly informed Rikard that Laurael had taken most of the staff with her into Dormaen. He went to the kitchens, startling the lone remaining cook, and took a plate of bread and cheese back to the atrium. In the starless darkness, the lush garden seemed more like a menacing Jumaari jungle.

Rikard sat. His mouth was as dry as sand. A few bites of bread came right back up, curdled in stomach acid and swallowed ash. Rikard flung the plate away with a ragged cry. It shattered against a stone planter and clattered to the atrium floor. He wiped his mouth and stared at the soot smeared over his skin, caked in the clasp of his cannula.

The bathhouse was dark and empty, too. Rikard stripped and stood waist-deep in the cold water. Shivering, he scrubbed his skin clean and washed away a day of sweat and worse. After he dried and combed his black hair, Rikard went to his room and sat naked on the bed. He stared down at his toes, the beads of water on his skin. Someone had thought to light a small, shielded lamp in here. The flower-bright drapes fluttered in the dry, smoky wind.

Rikard didn't want to think. What was there to think, anyway? None of it mattered anymore. Rikard closed his eyes. He fell back into the blasphemously, unfairly soft sheets and wished he had never returned to Terra.

He didn't know how long he lay in bed feeling sorry for himself when he heard shouting outside and then someone pounded on the bedroom door. Rikard barely had time to snatch up one of Laurael's sleeping sarongs from beside the bed and tie it around his waist before Karl kicked open the door, not waiting for permission to enter.

"Lord Mazrem!" Karl shouted. "Thainna's at the gate and... and she's covered in blood!"

Thainna? Rikard sprinted for the open face of the bedroom, swatting the hangings out of his way as he went. Karl ran after him, still talking.

"I tried to convince the others to open the gate for her, but Lord Mazrem – your son, I mean – told them about what happened in the city today and they're not opening the gates for anyone. Gods, if only Lady Mazrem hadn't taken Bastil with her! He would never stand for this nonsense!"

Rikard ran barefoot down the hill on the ash-encrusted grass. The moon and stars were hidden behind smoke and the only light came from the fire that still smoldered in Dormaen, down below the Everstones. Just as Karl said, the guards and knights were clustered together in the dim red light, staring through the closed gates at the road beyond.

"Open the gates!" Rikard roared.

The guards turned to gape at him.

"But she's been fighting, Lord Mazrem," one of them argued. "Look! She's bleeding!"

Rikard shoved the man out of his way. The others hastily pulled the gates open and let the legens past. A dark, bloodstained shape lay curled in the street.

Thainna.

Rikard screamed in wordless fury, a primal howl of agony. The Fiori girl lay in the road like a broken doll, blood and ash smearing every inch of her pale skin. Her face was distorted and puffy, eyes swollen shut. It was a wonder Karl even recognized her. Her bright red hair was black with soot and blood leaked from the corner of her mouth. It bubbled up from her lips with each rattling, rasping breath.

Thainna's eyes flickered beneath their bruised lids. The whites were crimson with blood leaking from broken veins. She smiled weakly up at him.

Rikard. I came home.

Gently, Rikard scooped Thainna into his arms and carried her up to the house. Karl called for the other guards to close and bar the gates again, and then chased after Rikard. Once more skipping the formality of the doors, Rikard carried Thainna between the columns of the bedroom's southern face and laid her gently on the bed. She whimpered, clutching at his bare chest and trying to say something. He leaned close, but could make out none of the words. Reaching yielded little more. Thainna was terribly wounded and fading fast.

Karl stood over the bed, wringing his hands. "What happened? How is she?"

"Bad," Rikard whispered. He couldn't catch his breath. His heart filled his chest painfully and seemed to be tearing itself apart. "I think she's bleeding inside her head and maybe her stomach or lungs."

"I'll get a foster." Karl bolted for the door.

"The temples were evacuated this afternoon," Rikard said. He didn't take his eyes off Thainna. "Go to the Lyceum. It's been set up as an emergency fostral. Remember, no insignia. Ride quickly and take your sword."

"Hae, Lord Mazrem!"

Rikard stroked Thainna's dirty hair back from her face. Fury boiled inside him, but Rikard kept his touch gentle. He probed Thainna's scalp gingerly and felt warm blood. The flesh beneath was swollen, soft beneath that. Cracked. Rikard pulled his hand back and stared at the blood.

His sight blurred with tears. Thainna had a concussion and was bleeding inside. Rikard had been a soldier long enough to know that the wounds were fatal. Not immediately. No, she would survive to see the foster Karl brought, perhaps even to have her skull drilled to relieve the pressure. Long enough for the wound in her brain to choke out every cherished memory. But in the end, she would die.

Please don't leave me. Don't leave me alone in this world, Thainna!

Rikard pulled the girl into his arms with a broken sob. Tears ran down his nose and splashed on her shattered cheek. His hands trembled so hard that he almost couldn't make them obey his simplest command, but Rikard fumbled his cannula open. Blood welled up on the gold tip.

Rikard stared at it. What if he made things worse? Maybe the other knights had been right all along. They feared Alterrans and their pacts. What had loyalty to those forgotten bonds and rusty old honor ever won Rikard? Thirty years gone from his world, his family. Dormaen in flames. VEIL forever disgraced. Hundreds dead and thousands wounded because he – the great hero of the empire! – could not leave well enough alone.

Don't leave me, Thainna...

The red bead of blood grew too heavy to sustain itself and dripped down the side of Rikard's finger. What made him think it would work, anyway? Something was wrong, horribly wrong in Alterra. Would anyone even answer his call? Was it too painful to hope?

Rikard stared down at Thainna's battered body and heard a ragged sob from his own throat.

No, *nothing* could hurt more than this.

Gently, Rikard cleared a spot in the center of Thainna's forehead with his thumb. There was more than enough of her blood, but it was important that he mark her with his, or else the Alterra might mistake her for any one of the all too many wounded in Dormaen. He touched his finger between her eyes and drew the circle there, then quartered it with a pair of lines.

Flickerdim, my oldest friend, can you hear me? Please see my blood on this girl. Please help her!

Silence. Rikard held Thainna to his chest. Her breath fluttered against his bare shoulder, as delicate and fragile as the beat of butterfly wings. He kissed her ash-matted red hair and choked on the fetid smoky smell. It wasn't fair, it wasn't right! Thainna deserved better than this.

I wanted to give her better. The thought was startlingly intense. *I wanted to give her a life... with me.*

You burn for this girl.

Rikard felt Flickerdim's unmistakable presence in his mind, as cool and steady as stone, but weak. It must have been exhausting to push his thoughts through the veil. It rebelled against all things.

Stumble says you've bled for her. I cannot see it — my wounds are too great — but I feel your need.

Your wounds? Rikard wondered. *The attack on the tower. I saw it when we tried... when the fires started.*

The Shatter are here and the leaves are breaking. I have little time and no eyes, Flickerdim thought. The old wisdom's granite presence, so long full of hard truths and sharp clarity, was now cracked in places. He was wounded almost as badly as Thainna. *I feel your need, Rikard. You need the girl restored, like the wheat that burned. I'm too weak to mend the grain any longer, but one human girl...? This I may be able to do. I will.*

Relief and joy flooded through Rikard, so deep and profound that words would surely break under it. But Flickerdim needed no words. He felt it with Rikard.

What is the price of your pact, Flickerdim? Rikard asked. No payment could be too high. *Anything!*

Remember that we do not take out of spite, my young friend. But our need is great, too. There's little time and I must be swift. The Uprising is falling even now. Lend me your fear. You know how sharply it cuts, Flickerdim slithered. *And I have felt how you fear for this woman in your arms.*

Rikard nodded. *Take it.*

The sharp bile-bite flame of fear vanished from Rikard's mind, doused as though by water. Flickerdim's unseen – but nevertheless still tenuously tangible – presence bristled with cold starfire. It was a brittle thing, as fragile as glass, and thrice as sharp.

If we die tonight, Flickerdim mused, *it will not be silently and it will not be easily.*

Will it be enough? Rikard asked.

No, but it would be unwise to refuse any advantage at this late stage of the game. Better to pass in battle than in silent regret. Time is gone. Our enemies are here. They have brought all the ghosts of Mask and more against us. Now show me the girl as she was. I will restore what I can.

Rikard remembered Thainna as he had seen her that morning, in the Star Court yard. A lifetime ago. She had smiled, full of joy. She thought him too busy, but he had seen Thainna, if only for a moment. Hair like barely contained fire, skin like fine white satin but for the sprinkling of freckles across her cheeks and nose. Wide green eyes, as hard as jade or soft as spring grass. Her long, slim legs... Rikard blushed to think of the rest, but Flickerdim needed to know. The graceful curve of Thainna's lower back, the gentle swell of her breasts beneath her blue tabba...

Enough. Flickerdim sifted through his memory with a veteran's expert eye. *I understand.*

The mark of blood on Thainna's forehead shone with an inner fire, the scarlet intensifying until it was almost unbearable to look at. Nothing in the world was so red. It was something else entirely – a pure idea of blood, the red river of life. The blood on the hero's sword as he battled the dragon in a child's bedside story. The blood of a princess who pricks her finger on a magic needle. The blood that thundered through Rikard's heart when Thainna was close.

And then it was gone. Thainna took a deep, shuddering breath and opened clear, bright green eyes. The dirt, the bruises and broken bones had vanished. Thainna was just as she had been that morning. With a wordless cry of joy, Rikard held her close and wept grateful tears into her copper hair.

Thank you, Flickerdim! Thank you, thank you.

Be gentle with her. There are wounds to places with which you are unfamiliar that I could not heal. And be careful. You are without fear until I return it to you. By your own vow, your life still belongs to us... if we somehow survive the night.

With his comfortless caution now delivered, Flickerdim's presence vanished. He had his own war to wage and Rikard had armed him as best he could.

Who was that...? Thainna wondered. *He felt so sky...*

That was Flickerdim, a very old friend. He helped you, Thainna. How do you feel? Rikard asked.

"I'm... fine, I think," she answered slowly. "I don't understand how, though."

Thainna flexed her fingers and toes experimentally, but Rikard's tight embrace made it impossible to test further. Reluctantly, he released her. Thainna sat up on the edge of the bed and kicked her legs.

"All of the blood's gone, too, and no scars. The Alterra I heard, Flickerdim... He did this?"

"Hae."

"What... what did it cost you?"

"My fear. The Uprising is under attack and Flickerdim needs weapons. I gave him the sharpest one I know."

"How long did he take it for?" Thainna asked. "Forever?"

"I don't know," he said. *I didn't ask and I don't care. I just need you, Thainna.*

Thainna looked down at her clean, so-strangely intact tabba. "Don't say that. And don't think it," she added before Rikard could correct her. "Please don't. You shouldn't have... You should have left me outside the gates. Even if it only cost you a grain of sand, it still would be too much."

Her pain was palpable, even without the deepening bond they shared. Thainna would not raise her eyes and she hunched, pulling inward. Away. Rikard took her shoulders gently, mindful of Flickerdim's warning, and turned Thainna to face him.

"Who did this to you?" Rikard asked. "You're ashamed, I see that much. But... why?"

Thainna pulled away and stood, wrapping her arms around herself as though she were cold.

"It doesn't matter anymore, does it? I'm alright now," she said.

"Of course it matters! Was it...?" Rikard's already hoarse voice cracked. "Did someone in the city streets do it? The riots... Is this my doing, too?"

No! Thainna crackled fiercely. "How could this be your fault?"

A soft brush of curiosity against his hard indignation surprised Rikard. Thainna had no idea what had happened in Mazrem Square. Thainna followed his curious touch back and into his own memories of the day. Hopes burned in spreading fire and inspiration reduced to ash. Thainna's eyes widened and she started, dropping her hands to her sides and clenching them into tight fists. A moment later, she shook her head in weary horror.

"Gods, Rikard," she breathed. "What went wrong?"

I don't know... The attack on the Uprising, I expect. Flickerdim and Stumble lacked the strength to seal such a large pact. Maybe the Shatter interceded, turned it, perverted it. I don't know. But it has been chaos, violence in the city. Please, who hurt you?

"No one," Thainna said shortly.

Tell me who would do this to you, please. Did I do it? One of those angry men stalking the streets... I made them today.

Thainna sat down slowly on the edge of the bed, close beside Rikard. She curled her fingers into the coverlets nervously and slid them up over her thighs, wiping sweaty palms on her tabba. A sudden change in the wind tugged the curtained wall, filling the room with a soft rustling that punctuated her silence and made it all the heavier.

But Rikard felt Thainna's indecision like a great gray distance between them. Was her pain of his doing? Because of his ridiculous, endless need to mend VEIL and his beloved Carce? None of it was worth anything, not if it hurt Thainna. Not if it could have killed her today.

It wasn't you. It was a man.

Thainna's thoughts lingered on an indistinct shape, a shrouded figure sitting on a green throne. Rikard fixed on the seat, one he had only seen once before, when he swore himself, along with a hundred other raw young squires, to VEIL before the old king, Emperor Tychon's father.

That's the Jade Throne! Who is that upon it? Rikard wondered. *Why did he hurt you?*

Thainna's lower lip trembled and tears fell unchecked down her pale cheeks. She brought up her fear, the sharp-thorned barrier that shielded her most private thoughts since the night they met in the Rows, but now it cracked and crumpled before the greater need to comfort Rikard.

It's not your fault. It's not. I'm sorry. Rikard, I'm sorry.

I don't understand. He wasn't sure he wanted to. A heavy, spiteful ball of anguish bubbled to the surface of Thainna's thoughts, too tangled to immediately make sense of.

Slowly, Thainna!

"I... I'm not a foster. I'm a Talon of the House of Five Dragons, Rikard," she said in a choked voice. "I'm a thief for them. When you first saw me out in the Rows, I was going to pick your pocket. I thought you were drunk."

"What?" Rikard asked in a flat whisper.

"After I ran away from you, the Crest – my master – ordered me to come to your house and pretend to be a foster."

"You lied? Why? To what end?"

"To control you. They gave me drams and told me to... to seduce you to my bed, if I needed to. If I could. Blackmail you, if I could find a way. The Crest wants to control you, Rikard. I was supposed to do that for him."

The entire world contracted to Thainna's tear-filled olive eyes. If what she said was true – and he sensed no deception – then why did it pain her so much?

"Speak on," Rikard said shortly.

"I couldn't split you on drams. I tried bluering once, but Gaius drank it instead. You... I wasn't doing the job well enough, so the Crest summoned me. He was the one who poisoned the Erastrasus grain in the first place, to get leverage against the Nianese consul when he lost his investment."

"To control him, hae," Rikard said, nodding. It made a sick sort of sense.

Thainna spoke so quickly now that her words threatened to become as tangled as her thoughts.

"The Crest is angry with what you did. What you tried to do. With VEIL, with the wheat shipment. He wants you distracted for a while, until he figures out what to do next. So he ordered two of the other Talons to... to... And then he sent me home."

"He thought I would care for you," Rikard said. "Mourn for you when you died. How did you get here?"

"I walked."

I crawled.

All the way across Dormaen? Rikard was horrified and livid, but helplessly proud of Thainna's determination and strength.

"What does your Crest want the time to do?" he asked.

"Figure out if you're a good investment. I think he wants you to be the next emperor, unless you prove too hard to control. Then I think he'll kill you and use Gaius. I know he's been trying to get Gaius split on a couple of different drams."

Rikard jumped to his feet and only barely fought down the urge to grab Thainna and shake her. Hard.

"My son?" he snarled.

"Hae. I know it doesn't mean anything now, but... but I'm sorry."

Rikard couldn't look at Thainna.

"Why?" he asked. "You didn't know me before, except perhaps as some name from before you were born. Or the rabid animal that tried to strangle you. But since then... No one has meant more to me than you! Yet you said nothing of this?"

Thainna said the only thing that could make the whole twisted world make sense.

"The Crest has Thain."

Rikard was furious, of course. But all Thainna wanted – all she had ever wanted – was to keep her brother safe. Would Rikard have done any differently for those he loved? Rikard glared longingly at Thainna.

"And he... this Crest... had you beaten to get to me?" he asked. "Just to keep me busy for a little while?"

"Hae."

"And he would have let thousands starve just to control the Lyceum. Gods! Why do you work for such a man?" Rikard asked. She did not seem at all the type for such heartlessness.

"I was born in the Rows. My father keeps ledgers for the House. I couldn't go to school... and there was Thain to consider. What else was I to do?" Thainna asked.

Another shadow flitted through her thought, a guilty thorn in a prickly rose hedge of regrets.

"I... I stole from you, too," she admitted.

"From me?" Rikard asked. There were images of a number of trivial baubles in her thoughts. "Why? You have everything here, Thainna."

"There's an Auction held every five years. The highest bidder becomes Crest of the House of Five Dragons until the next Auction. I'm trying to win the bid." *Not for me. For Thain. He'll fix everything. Like... like you'll fix VEIL.*

Rikard sucked in a pained breath. *Not likely now.*

"Don't, please," Thainna said. *Don't say that. Nothing's beyond fixing, is it?*

The question hung in the air between them. Thainna sat up straight and lifted her chin. She was waiting for Rikard to answer, wondering. Would he hate her? Pity her? That was even worse... if he forgave her because she was no more than a hungry dog that couldn't be faulted for snapping at his fingers.

Rikard shook his head. *No.*

He knelt and cupped Thainna's face in his hands. His thoughts brushed over hers and felt the reflexive fear that so often kept him at bay. But where was there to hide now? Thainna let out a soft sigh and leaned into Rikard's touch, into his thoughts. She was so soft but so strong against him.

I've seen where you live, Rikard thought. *The filth, the misery. You never lived in the Surmaen temple. Thain did, but not you. You've taken money enough to live a better life, but you saved it all. Even when it meant you went hungry. For Thain, for the other agents of the House, all of those abused by the Crest... like Caelin. Never for you.*

Rikard was so proud of Thainna. Furious, too. She had badly violated his trust, even if he couldn't fault her reasons. Thainna put her hands over his, held his fingers against her cheeks, and closed her eyes. She was proud of him, as well, for what he had tried to do.

Even in the face of his dreadful failure, she kept her faith. She understood the desire, the need as driving as breath, to mend something terribly broken. Though it had all fallen apart, she *understood*.

I'm so proud, Thainna told him.

And beautiful.

Thainna's eyes flew open at his thought. *I didn't want to hurt you, Rikard. I love you. But I love Thain, too, and he's not as strong as you are.*

Rikard's heart raced and his whole body seemed made of heat and golden-thick honey. Anything, everything else seemed unimportant. The world could vanish in fire and still Rikard would be there on the floor, grinning like a fool. Thainna loved him. Slowly, she leaned in and pressed her lips to his, soft and warm and perfect.

I do love you, Rikard. Gods, let it be enough. I have nothing else to give. Everything else belongs to my brother.

It is enough. Rikard tasted her deeply, the smooth-grass scent of her. *It's all I want in the worlds.*

Rikard rose, lips still locked with Thainna's, and they tumbled together into the bed. They tugged at one another's clothes with trembling fingers until those barriers could be thrown aside, forgotten. The smoky warmth of the evening paled beside the sweet-searing heat where their bodies touched.

Thainna desired Rikard with a raw red lust that startled them both with its intensity. She reveled in the rich contrast of her soft skin over the knight's stark, masculine hardness, so very different than her own body. Through their mingling, interlaced minds, even that was new. She had never considered herself a great beauty, but through her new lover's eyes, Thainna beheld a goddess.

Rikard guided her at first, but her wild abandon quickly turned the tide. Lovemaking with Thainna was no stately dance, with steps learned and memorized and practiced until perfected. It was untamed, unbridled as the wild sea. Rikard had never known anything like it and quickly found himself willingly drowning in the storm of sensation.

Thainna didn't coax pleasure from Rikard with Laurael's seductress skill. They explored and climbed together into the dizzying rise of passion. Intertwined, Rikard and Thainna felt one another's peaks of pleasure, urging each other ever onward, ever further and higher and more.

When their bodies could no longer endure the rigors of their fervor, Rikard and Thainna lay in each other's arms, thoughts still intimately entangled. One body, one mind. Not forever, but for now, in one pristinely perfect moment. Rikard held Thainna to him and felt her heart flutter against his sweat-slicked chest. The heart that loved him, as delicate and full of song as a nightingale. The heart torn, that turned her traitor against Rikard for love of her brother. Thainna stroked Rikard's tangled hair. She loved so much, so intensely that it seemed it might set them both on fire.

I love you, Rikard knew.

Thainna felt it, strong and certain. A truth solid enough to build nations upon. He loved her. All of her.

I love you.

Rikard laced his fingers through Thainna's and then kissed her, tasting sea-salt tears on his lips. It no longer seemed to matter who they belonged to. Enfolded in each other's arms, they fell at last into deep sleep and shared dreams.

39

THE STORM

"When we blame fate, we are truly blaming ourselves."

— UTORA MAESUS

IT WAS LONG PAST MIDNIGHT. General Castor's boots rang on the polished marble floors of the broad hallway. The day had been long and the triumphs were hard-won, but were many and grand. The fires were contained. Tomorrow, they would be smothered entirely. The Shatter had promised it. Such prompt and diligent service impressed Emperor Tychon.

Castor was tired to the bone, but nothing short of death would have kept him from these great halls. He stopped before a pair of great pillars, striped in black and gold like bees. Between them, a dozen VEIL knights in bright red armor stood at attention outside closed doors. A high, whistling snore could just be heard beyond.

"Does the emperor sleep peacefully?" Castor asked.

"Hae, general," answered a knight wearing a captain's insignia.

"It's good to be home," Castor said, half to himself.

The captain leaned in to catch the words. "Hae, General Castor. I thank you for the opportunity. After Legens Mazrem dismissed us, I never thought I'd have the chance again."

"After what happened today, I need fresh men to safeguard Emperor Tychon. What court did you serve before, captain…?"

"Jaesun, sir," the knight answered. "I used to serve in the Star Court, but it's an even greater honor to join you now."

Castor nodded and waited for the knights to salute him before finally turning away and finishing his circuit of the imperial palace. It was good to be home.

Gaius couldn't sleep. It wasn't the empty bed that kept him awake. Gaius enjoyed his trysts well enough, but there had certainly been plenty of nights alone.

Was it the reek of smoke, perhaps? No. Try though he might, Gaius could smell no trace of the fires. Unlike his mother, who so loved to look out over Dormaen, his bed chambers were closed off from the grounds. Gaius sat on the edge of his bed, holding his face in his hands. His wet hair dripped water down his back. It itched and tickled its way down his spine.

The plan had seemed like a good one. Get the Erastrasus wheat, restore it. Restore faith in VEIL. What could go wrong? Rikard Mazrem knew more than any man alive about Alterran blood pacts. Gaius rubbed his face until his skin tingled.

His father seemed to break when the cleansing ritual went awry. That should have pleased Gaius, but somehow, it only frightened him. Rikard had been so certain, so confident in their path. To see him shaken like that was a violation of the natural order.

What would happen to VEIL now? That depended upon public reaction to the fires, Gaius supposed. Would the knighthood be disbanded?

Probably not. One day was not enough to undo the building of the Carcaen Empire. But the Mazrems and the Star Court would certainly fall out of favor. Of the two thousand knights who failed to report back, how many lay dead at the feet of those they tried to help? How many would turn to lives of banditry? Or worse? How many would join criminal rings like the infamous House of Five Dragons?

A knock on the door startled Gaius up from his thoughts.

"Hae?" he called.

The door swung open to reveal an earnest-looking young blond man. He wore a plain brown cape over his guardsman's armor. A short Carcaen woman in an ash-stained blue fostral tabba stood at his side. The pale-haired guard bowed and swept his cape back over one shoulder.

"Forgive my intrusion, Lord Mazrem, but I'm not sure what I'm to do," he said. "Your father sent me to get a foster."

Gaius frowned at that. "Why? Isn't Thainna with him? I swear those two are tied at the ankles."

The other man's expression darkened. A yellowed bruise stood out on his jaw and Gaius finally recognized him as the guard Rikard had attacked in the terrestrium weeks before.

"Thainna's been hurt. Badly, my lord," said Karl.

"Then what are you babbling at me for? Get on to her," Gaius barked. He didn't want to consider what Thainna's loss would do to Rikard, especially after today's events.

"I... I tried, my lord. We went to Lord Mazrem's rooms, but there were... voices inside. Ah... impassioned voices," Karl explained with a blush.

"So? My father's bound to be a little tight-wound after today."

The guardsman's jaw tightened and his cheeks went redder. "Lady Mazrem is in the city, my lord. She left before noon today to stay with one of the consuls."

"Has she returned?"

"Not that I know of. The guards at the gates reported no one coming or going other than me. And I... I think the other voice was Thainna's."

Gaius blinked. "What?"

"Should we... interrupt them?"

"No. I don't think so. If Thainna's well enough to bed my father, then she doesn't need a foster. She can take care of herself. Let them be. Tomorrow will be hell enough for all."

"Hae, my lord."

Karl gave a short bow and left. The foster followed behind, flapping her arms in exasperation. When they were gone, Gaius fell back across his bed and waited for morning to come, but even in the face of the crumbling worlds, dawn could not be hastened.

Rikard and Thainna. Now the worlds truly had run mad. Gaius always thought his father far too honorable to be unfaithful to his wife. Not that Gaius blamed him. Laurael hated Rikard, whether the man knew it or not. Surely he felt her coldness. And Rikard and Thainna complimented one another so well that Gaius was almost surprised it hadn't happened earlier. Perhaps all they lacked was the opportunity – an emotional night and an empty bed.

Gaius pursed his lips. Where *was* his mother?

Karl said she left before noon. Laurael Mazrem had always been a prudent woman. When the cleansing went sour, she might have fled the house, away from anyone searching out her husband. But at noon? That was before the pact had even begun, before the fires.

What about the gift she promised me yesterday...?

Folding his arms up behind his head, Gaius stared up at the painted ceiling of his bedroom. He had rarely wasted attention on it, but was sure many of his conquests had studied it quite closely. The fresco depicted an artist's best guess at his father's mythic sacrifice at Njorn Pass. It really was hardly the most romantic scene, Gaius supposed, but the choice had been his mother's, to serve as a constant reminder of the man he was supposed to emulate.

The myth, not the man, Gaius corrected. Laurael despised the real Rikard Mazrem. *How much am I really like my father, anyway?*

Even after today, there was no one better to succeed Tychon as emperor than Gaius, but how long would that last? Castor had proved himself today and already been rewarded. The Sun Court general had his own family, his own children. What if Castor's son came into Tychon's favor? No one seemed to know what had started the fires today – not even Rikard – or if it might happen again.

How low would Rikard drag his family in the name of VEIL's honor? And Carce's, Gaius supposed. His father's plan was not just for VEIL, but for the rest of the empire. His best intentions had led them all to destruction. Burning Dormaen helped no one.

Gaius held his thumb up to the ceiling, blotting out his father's face and imagining his own in its place. Maybe Rikard's time was over, after all. What place in the real world was there for legends, anyway? Stories and myths lived in books, to be closed and put away when their time was done.

Aelos Vahn stalked through the darkened, deserted streets of the temple district. The wind alternately blazed with heat and went icy cold with the promise of the coming winter. In the empty doorway of the leaning tower, Aelos side-stepped the dagger and scowled dangerously at the wiry young guardian.

"Get out of my way," Aelos hissed furiously. "I'm going up."

He mounted the stairs as fast as his creaking old joints allowed, taking the deeply carpeted steps two at a time. Twenty hidden guards watched him pass, clinging silently to the shadows like cobwebs. Aelos paused in the doriclinium. The pretty slaves were all asleep in their chains.

Aelos squinted through the shadows and then shook his head and moved on, up the tower. Kicking open the final door, he strode into the bare stone room at the top. A slender figure reclined in the Jade Throne, draped in a long robe of black silk. The Crest looked at Aelos.

"It's late. What do you want?" he asked.

"What did you do to Thainna?" Aelos shouted.

"You heard, then."

"No thanks to you! A dozen people recognized her staggering through the streets. They did nothing to help her for fear of you!"

"Watch your tone," the Crest told him coldly. "I made use of Thainna's friendship with Rikard Mazrem. The bond she forged on *my* orders."

"She's your sister!"

Thain stretched languidly. The thin smile that curled his lips would have been far more natural on a snake than a man. Even through the loose-fitted robe, Aelos could see that his son remained slender as a willow switch. Good food and lavish comforts served as treatment for his sick body, but not a cure. And Thain's power only fed his sickened mind. Aelos curled his hands into fists.

"It's bad enough that you hide your rank from her, Thain," he said. "You make her live in squalor while you feast and bed slaves! Thainna visited you most every day. She saves every acorn to make you Crest in the next Auction! She thinks you can save the House. She adores you, Thain, and you... you beat her!"

"You're very brave today, Pata," said Thain. He examined his nails, and then raised his too-bright eyes to his father's. "It was well enough to let her buy my next term, since you've made it so clear that *you* won't do it again. But now I need something more important from my sweet sister."

"You could have killed her," Aelos shouted at his son. "She may be dying, even now!"

Thain laughed. The sound sent a shudder up Aelos' spine.

"Then at least I wouldn't have to return to the fostral," said the Crest. "It's dreadfully boring there."

"You can't do this anymore, Thain. House agents aren't good people, but even they don't deserve what you do to them! And Thainna... Your sister is a good girl. Please, you have to stop this!"

"No, Pata. I am Crest of the House of Five Dragons and I don't *have* to do anything."

Aelos drew himself up, summoning all of the paternal authority he could muster. His dirty tabba smelled of smoke and trash. "You *will* stop, Thain. You're only sitting on that throne because I put you there. I embezzled the laurels, I altered the ledgers. Your reign is a lie!"

"A stirring reminder, Pata," Thain sighed. He yawned theatrically. "I have more important things to consider than your whimpering. Do hurry to the point, if you have one."

"You're clever, Thain. Brilliant. I thought you would be a good Crest. Gods, what an idiot I was. You were fourteen years old! Just a boy... I should have known better. You wield your authority like a child with his father's sword. I've held my silence on it, even from your sister."

Aelos took a long step closer to the Crest's throne. The single lamp overhead swayed in an invisible draft.

"Step down, Thain, or I'll tell the entire House how you became their Crest. You have few friends. You rule through fear and you've made many enemies. They'll tear you apart."

Now Thain sat up, but Aelos noted with a sinking sensation that his son retained his smile.

"You *are* brave tonight," Thain said. "Why? Because I bloodied Thainna a little?"

"If you're asking, you'll never understand. I love my daughter."

Thain sat forward on the edge of his throne. Now his smile was gone and his serpentine eyes glittered dangerously. "Don't you love me, Pata?"

"I love my son. You've become a monster. But you don't have to be, Thain. Give up the Jade Throne. Step down, please!"

The Crest stood up and lifted his sharp chin imperiously. He reached into the close darkness that surrounded his throne like a fortress and pulled. Somewhere in the inky recesses of the high ceiling, a bell toned. Aelos started. The door behind him banged open. Strong arms caught Aelos, yanked him back and then down to his knees. Thain strode forward, composed and confident as a king. Something sharp and heavy came to rest against the back of Aelos' neck. He twisted to look up at the Talon who held the sword.

"No, wait! Listen to me, the Crest–" Aelos said.

"Enough, Pata," said Thain. "Do you think you can break my hold so easily? These men are loyal to me, to the House. They belong to me. You all belong to me. I still have a purpose for Thainna, but you're just a useless old man."

The sword lifted and then whistled down through the air. Aelos had only a moment to wonder if Thainna would ever know. Could she ever forgive her foolish old father?

There was a strange, flat metallic pain and then Aelos fell into an endless well of starless night.

I will fight.

No, Flickerdim! Stumble shrilled. *Don't leave me here!*

The ground under the tree-tower cracked and the whole Uprising listed to the side, threatening to tumble over into the cold emptiness. Another greasy, smeary suspicion lurched and then fell, plunging into the fraying foundation of the Uprising. Where the Shatter impacted, the granite rippled and tore like paper. The colorful, ever-seething roots of the tree-tower suddenly silenced as a filmy white raced out from the crater, freezing everything in its path and covered it in viscous blankness. Flickerdim tasted the air and dipped his long, narrow head. His blind gray eyes gleamed.

They have overtaken the Uprising, he said calmly. As though a wisdom could be anything but coolly collected. *Hide here, my young friend. I will fight for as much time as I can.*

Flickerdim, no! Don't die for nothing! What good is time if he's failed? The fires... VEIL will never make another pact with us!

Perhaps, Flickerdim thought sagely. *But Rikard believes in us. We must believe in him. We must fight for every moment.*

The starry midnight serpent reared back his head and opened his mouth, screaming forth all of Rikard's anguished fear in a long, sharp wail. Obsidian fangs sprang up in his mouth like a crop of glassy swords. Flickerdim's body lengthened, thickened until it was ten times as long as the tallest Terran man and as broad as the branches of the tree-tower. His starlight took on a harder silver sheen, etching a thousand black scales in sterling luminescence. Spines rose from his back like mountain spires, stretched and flexed with a steely slither. Four strong legs grew from his side with feet ending in hooked claws, razor shards of the crescent moon. Deep shadows of terror came together into great webbed wings, like those of a vast bat. Flickerdim's low keening became a thunderous roar that made all of Alterra recoil in fear.

The great black dragon tensed himself and then swooped down, bellowing tongues of terrible crimson flames. There were embers of burning wheat in those flames, and the red of Fiori hair. So much color was painfully, beautifully bright against the surging blankness tearing at the Uprising. Flickerdim roared and rose higher.

The sky tore open high above and hundreds of formless Shatter fell from the cracks, shooting out at the great black dragon with tangles of icy gray tendrils. Stumble hopped from one foot to the other in distress.

Watch out!

Flickerdim banked into a sharp curve and snared two dozen of the lackluster Shatter in his claws, tearing them free of the others.

They shrieked in his grasp as the old wisdom crushed the Shatter into sooty ash that sifted down like dirty snow.

Go, Flicker! Stumble crackled.

The Shatter filled the cold air with brittle silence and flung themselves at Flickerdim by the thousands. More. Flat gray worms, spears of glass that roiled with mist, seething pools of whipping mirages, faceless man-shapes that marched across the emptiness toward the shuddering Uprising.

The black dragon lashed out at them all, tearing the Shatter into dusty, fluttering rags. Flickerdim's bright, roiling fear-fire filled them with Rikard's terror. The colorless, biting things darkened into night, filling the silence with their screams. Starlight seared them and the dragon's roar shook the tree-tower down to its great roots. Stumble clung to the Uprising's splintered branches and wondered if it would be enough.

Tens of thousands of Shatter feared and fell before Flickerdim. But there were millions more. The nothing filled with more nothing. They dropped from the torn sky and rose from the empty earth. Flickerdim beat his vast wings, churning the air into screams, and vaulted out of the closing army of broken things. But others were quicker. The formless Shatter needed no wings to fly and whipped out after the black dragon, hooking countless barbs of boredom and disinterest into his vast wings. Flickerdim snarled and snapped at them with teeth like ranks of obsidian swords, but the Shatter raced up from the graying, flattening Uprising in uncounted numbers, too many and too fast.

They dragged Flickerdim down, inexorably down. Where the Shatter's featureless fibers held the black dragon, the scales dulled, losing their polished midnight sheen. They cracked and fell away. Moonglow shone silver through Flickerdim's wounds, but it was bleeding away. His wings beat, struggling against the alien pull of gravity. An idle comment slashed at the wisdom's wing, opening a long rent that rippled in the frozen wind.

Flickerdim! Stumble wailed.

The great black dragon looked up at him once, and crashed thunderously to the broken ground.

40

THE CROWN

"A great man died that night and the river of his blood would bear
Carce to its destiny."

— OUR RED HISTORY, BY AVILLA SALLUSI

THAINNA DRIFTED up from the depths of sleep. She and Rikard had
been dreaming about a garden of songs and crystal. Their thoughts
remained mingled, even as the details quickly faded.

Something had woken Thainna. The sound came again, quiet
but still audible. Footsteps... The slow footfalls of someone trying
to be silent and very nearly succeeding. Only a lifetime in the back
alleys of the Rows alerted Thainna to the danger and her stomach
flipped in sudden terror. The sound had stirred Rikard, too – a
campaign soldier's ears were as good as those of any House thief's –
but without fear, he only pulled Thainna sleepily against him.

She sat up. The single lamp smoldered dimly and but for the
low ember light of Dormaen below, the sky outside was still dark,
smoky-starless and flat black as an assassin's blade. Thainna stared
into the shadow, tense and still. But she could see nothing strange.

Maybe it had been just a breeze after all. Rikard tugged at her waist. He was strong and warm and inviting. Thainna lay back once more.

There! Something flickered against the wall, a man in a dark gray cloak.

"Rikard!" Thainna screamed.

The knight was on his feet in an instant, searching the bedroom with narrowed eyes. The cloaked figure sprang from the concealing shadows and covered the distance between them in a handful of sprinting strides. A short sword flashed from beneath his gray cape. He swung the blade in a deadly arc.

Rikard hurled himself back, narrowly avoiding the sword, and came down into a wide crouch. When the assassin pulled back to swing again, Rikard darted in. He blocked the blow at the wrist, grabbed and twisted until the sword came free. It fell and clanged on the floor. Thainna leapt from the bed, snatched up the sword and then jumped back out of reach.

The assassin slithered around and slammed his knee up into Rikard's groin, making him and Thainna gasped in shared pain. She clutched her stomach, unaccustomed to the horrid, sick agony, but Rikard kept his head. He gritted his teeth and pulled back on the other man's arm until it buckled. The assassin grunted and turned in toward Rikard, trying to regain mobility enough to resume his attack. Rikard hooked his right arm across the man's throat. His metal-tipped forefinger quested for the telltale throb of his pulse and pressed. The other man writhed and struggled, but Rikard held fast. The beat faltered, weakened and then faded to a monotone buzz. Rikard let the suddenly limp body thump down to the floor.

Thainna approached warily. She felt quickly through Rikard's senses for injury, but other than the fading cramp between his legs, found nothing. Still holding the sword as though it were a live snake, Thainna knelt beside the fallen assassin and pulled back his hood.

It was a small Nianese man, one she didn't recognize. He was dressed in distinctly un-Carcaen tunic and leggings, all of the same unremarkable gray weave as his cloak. Thainna stared up at Rikard, who was reaching out with his strange otherworldly senses for any other attackers.

"Do you know him?" she asked.

Rikard looked down at the man and his narrow face for a long moment.

"No," he said at last. *Is he a House assassin? Has your Crest decided that he wants me dead?*

Thainna carried the sword over to the lamp beside the bed and examined it closely. Curious, Rikard followed her.

Whoever this man works for, it's not the House of Five Dragons, she decided. "I've known a lot of Talons and a few Flames. House assassins always use poison. Insurance, just in case the wound alone isn't fatal."

Rikard's brow furrowed and he shook his head. *If not the House of Five Dragons, then who?*

The door banged open, making Thainna jump. With his fear still in Flickerdim's care, Rikard looked up, wary but not scared. Another man stood silhouetted for a moment in the doorway and then stepped inside. Thainna snatched up a blanket and wrapped herself, blushing.

It was Gaius, but Thainna almost failed to recognize him. The younger Mazrem stood tall and proud. Purposeful. He wore his black VEIL armor, still dusted with colorless ash, and carried his father's sword in his hand.

Gaius stopped at the foot of the dais and looked down at the fallen assassin. The man's chest still rose and fell in a slow, steady rhythm.

"It seems I've joined the party a little late," Gaius said. "You should have killed him, Father. Still, it won't matter much longer. This will all be over by dawn."

"What?" Thainna brought the sword up awkwardly at Gaius, still holding the blanket with her other hand. "What are you talking about?"

Rikard put a hand on her shoulder. *Don't.*

"Full of fire, as ever," Gaius said with a smirk. "I see why you like her, Father. Put down the sword, my feisty little Fiori. I'm only here to deliver a warning, late though it seems to be. My mother sent this man. She intends to kill you, Father."

Rikard stared. "No, she would never...! Laura... she..."

He couldn't finish the thought. Nothing in the worlds made sense anymore. Gaius leveled a hard look at his father.

"She doesn't love you, Rikard. She never loved you. You must know that. While you were away at war in Fiore, Mother was abed with Emperor Tychon. She's always been an ambitious woman and now she wants you out of the way. So did I. You can't imagine how happy I was when she told me about her plan."

"Why?" asked Rikard. "Out of the way of what?"

"Of my ascension to the imperial throne. Mother meant to kill you and let the people blame Emperor Tychon. The Lyceum would demand his removal and with you dead, I would have been the natural choice to become emperor of Carce."

Could that be true? Rikard reached into his son's thoughts, but found only truth. Honest, brutal, and spoken with love.

"I think that she was relying on your all too public clashes with Tychon to damn him," said Gaius. "Everyone would have assumed that he ordered your death. It wasn't a bad plan, really."

Guards poured through the door with Karl at their head. Every weapon was drawn. The young Lyncean bolted forward to stand over the fallen assassin, his sword held ready.

"Lord Mazrem, we heard a cry! What happened?"

"This man tried to kill Rikard," Thainna answered. "Tie him!"

One of the guards ran to find rope and Karl eyed his still undressed master with an uncomfortable expression.

"Are you... are you alright, my lord?" he asked.

"Hae." Rikard looked at Thainna. *So long as I have you by my side, hae.* Aloud, he said, "Do you trust these men, Karl?"

The young guardsman looked shocked. He glanced around at the others, divided between household guards and Star Court knights.

"Hae, my lord, I think so," Karl said. "They've been watching the gate with me all night, most without sleep."

"Take them with you and accompany my son to the imperial palace to speak to Emperor Tychon. We must tell him of my wife's plan."

Gaius smiled almost sadly and sheathed the sword. "No, Father. You do it. Go warn him in good faith and heal the breach between you."

"But Laurael..."

"I'll deal with Mother," Gaius said firmly. Rikard began to protest, but Gaius raised his hand. "No, Father. You don't even know her. You never did."

Rikard nodded curtly, tears in his eyes. He dressed hurriedly in a saela, laid out to wear the following day. Thainna, too, found her discarded tabba and pulled it on as quickly as she could. She frowned at Gaius.

"You knew about this, but you never said anything. Why do it now?" she asked. "Why did you come to warn us?"

"It was hardly selfless, Thainna," said Gaius. "Nothing I do ever is."

"Why, then?"

"Mother always tried to make me like him, like my father. Act like him, look like him. I hated it." Gaius had removed his sword belt and ran his fingers over the weapon's worn hilt. He didn't look up as he spoke. "Now, I actually *want* to be like him. Really like him, not just in looks. Even if it means Tychon executes me, too. I'd rather die like my father than live like my mother."

Thainna nodded slowly, biting her lip. She understood. Rikard returned a moment later, fully dressed now. Gaius held the sword belt out to his father.

"Take this," he said. "It's yours, after all, and I don't think that I'll need it now. I came here expecting to stop an assassin, but... Well, as usual, you beat me to the point. Dormaen is still dangerous and I can't have you dying before you reach Tychon."

Rikard took his old sword and cinched the belt around his waist. After so long, the weight of it felt strange. He nodded to Gaius.

"Go safely and with my love," he said in a thick voice.

"Thainna, keep an eye on the old man for me," Gaius said. His mask was as hard and bright-polished as ever, but Rikard felt the deep reserve of respect and love beneath. *Go quickly, Father, and under the watchful eye of your Alterra.*

Rikard hugged Gaius close and kissed his son's cheek. Gaius turned away before anyone could see tears in his eyes and strode from the room.

Thainna thrust the Nianese sword through the hastily-tied sash of her tabba. She might need it later. Her hands shook with fury, but not with the man on the floor. There was no point in being angry with the assassin. Thainna knew all too well how easy it was to take a job without thinking about the target. Maybe this man had children back home to feed.

But the one who hired him, Rikard's own wife...

Why? How could she hate Rikard so much?

Karl stood stiffly at attention. "We're ready, Lord Mazrem. I have ordered the fastest horses left in the stables saddled and brought to the gates."

"We go at once," Rikard announced.

Even under his orders, only nine men proved willing to venture out into Dormaen's smoky, dangerous streets. Of Rikard's house guard, only Karl and two others volunteered. Six knights and three guards reined their horses into a protective ring around their lord.

Rikard pulled Thainna up into the saddle behind him. She wound her arms around his waist as the horses thundered down the hill and out the gates.

On the desolate roads, it was simple enough to avoid the noisy, roaming crowds calling for VEIL blood. A pack of men, streaked with soot and maddened by rage, prowled toward the Everstones. Rikard felt their approach and whistled sharply to Karl. As the men rounded the corner, Rikard and his guard spurred their horses into a run, scattering them like a handful of sand thrown into the wind. Angry cries chased Rikard through the night like vengeful ghosts.

They hate me, he mourned.

You're their hero, Rikard. They'll remember that, in time.

Dawn stained the eastern horizon with bloody red light as they rode into the city's heart. The gates of the vast imperial palace were sealed, but ten minutes' argument with the guards finally won them entrance.

Rikard pulled his horse to a halt beside a lion-headed fountain and leapt down from his saddle. Thainna landed behind him and together, they ran up the white marble stairs to the arched doors of Emperor Tychon's palace. Knights in red armor stepped into their path and drew their swords.

"What's your business in the palace at this hour?" one of them demanded.

"I have an urgent warning for the emperor," Rikard said. "There is treachery in Dormaen tonight! Who are you? What are knights of the Sun Court doing on imperial grounds?"

The others raced in behind him, hands on hilts of swords. They were jumpy, nervous. The red-clad knights shifted uncomfortably, eyeing Rikard's Star Court companions.

"Emperor Tychon set the Sun Court in charge of his guard, sir."

"What? When was this?"

"Earlier this evening. He's not to be disturbed," the Sun knight answered.

He didn't seem sure which man was more dangerous to upset, Emperor Tychon or Legens Mazrem.

"I'm sorry, sir," the knight said.

"I have no time for your politics!" Rikard snarled.

He shoved past the Sun knights and through the wide doors. A pair of them broke off and trailed behind them, shouting protests. Thainna had to jog to keep up with Rikard's longer strides. Karl and the Star Court knights marched behind in tight formation.

Do you know where we're going? Thainna asked.

Tychon's bed chambers.

Rikard shared the snatch of thought from one of the guardian Sun knights following them. Thainna nodded. Unwittingly guided by the men trying to stop them, they strode swiftly through the imperial palace.

Thainna struggled to keep up. Rikard moved quickly and there was so much to look at, far more than she could have taken in even if she spent the entire day making the journey. There were galleries and portrait-lined halls, sitting rooms and parlors. They passed a library filled by more books, scrolls and parchments than Thainna thought could ever have been written in the whole history of the two worlds. An audience chamber only slightly smaller than the entire Lyceum echoed with their pounding footsteps.

Turning the final corner, more knights came into view, all in identical red-dyed leather. Eleven of them, Thainna counted. Just like those outside, they started nervously and drew their broad-bladed swords. They stood forward and kept themselves between Rikard and the lavish doors they guarded.

"Out of my way! I must see Emperor Tychon at once," Rikard said. Did every man in this place exist simply to keep him from protecting the emperor?

"His Imperial Majesty is sleeping, Legens Mazrem," answered a knight with a deep scowl on his round, freckled face. "You can see him in the morning."

"My business will not wait." Rikard looked between the knights, taking in the marks of rank on their saela collars. "Where is your captain?"

"Captain Jaesun was just in to check on the emperor, and then he left on an errand."

"Jaesun?" Rikard tore his sword from the scabbard. "I banished that man from VEIL on the first day! Get out of my way!"

"But, legens–"

The guards tried to argue, but the Star Court knights mimicked their legens and drew their weapons in a chorus of steely hisses. The Sun knights scattered and then fell away like dandelion puffs. Rikard kicked the doors open and charged through, sprinting to the emperor's bedside.

Gods of the worlds...

Rikard fell to his knees and his gladius tumbled from suddenly numb fingers. Emperor Tychon lay still in his bed, covered in so much blood that it seemed he wore a tabba of liquid red. A gaping slit opened his throat like a sickly, monstrous smile and a naked young concubine lay contorted beside him, her body also slick with blood. The hilt of a slender dagger jutted up between her breasts, the fingers of one hand curled loosely around it and slack in death.

"Murder! The emperor's been murdered! She's killed Emperor Tychon!" cried one of the knights at the door. He and several of the other red-armored men fled into the palace, shouted their terrible news.

"Lord Mazrem!" Karl called from the door, where the remaining guards had reformed their line and now barricaded the door. "Lord Mazrem, what are your orders?"

Rikard stared down at the dead emperor. The whole world spun wrong, wobbly and off-axis like a great broken wheel. Rikard put his hand to Tychon's brow, but his flesh was cold.

"Laurael, did you do this?" he breathed.

Thainna stood on the other side of the bed. She pointed to the gash under Tychon's jaw.

No, this was a House assassination. Look.

With an effort that turned his stomach, Rikard did as Thainna asked. Barely visible under the sheet of blood, the sliced edges of the emperor's skin were an unnatural violet color.

Poison? Rikard asked.

Hae. Just like the House always uses. I told you that the Crest wants to place a new emperor... Wincing, Thainna slid the dagger from the concubine's chest and held it up to the nearest lamp. She turned it this way and that, making the flame's reflection jump and twist like a dancer over the smooth steel, and then delicately sniffed it. *There's no poison on this. We're meant to think this was what killed him, but I'd bet you a thousand laurels that Jaesun is still carrying the real murder weapon. He's probably on his way back to the crooked tower to report to the Crest.*

Rikard snatched up his sword again and slid it back into the sheath. A crowd had gathered at the door and was growing by the moment. More guards and a dozen servants, all brought running by the cries, standing on their toes or peering between bodies to catch a glimpse, to see if the terrible rumor was true. The gathered VEIL knights, both Suns and Stars, stood unified in their efforts to hold them back.

Things could easily turn ugly, Thainna worried as she followed Rikard from the royal bedroom. He pulled the doors shut behind him and turned to the nearest Sun Court knight, the freckled one he had been arguing with before.

"Did the emperor call for Jaesun when he went inside?" Rikard snarled furiously at the Sun Court knight, almost feral in his rage.

"No, legens. I don't know how the Star Court did business here, but... but we're attentive to His Imperial Majesty. We don't wait to be asked to serve!"

"How long ago?"

"I... I don't know. An hour, perhaps?"

"So you let a man that I cast out of VEIL go unasked and alone into the emperor's chambers, before dawn?" Rikard roared at him. The knight shrank back. "And then you let him leave on some vague errand? Do you know where he went? When he will return?"

"No, Legens Mazrem."

"Your captain killed Emperor Tychon right under your nose!"

"Rikard!" Thainna cried. She grabbed his arm. "Stop! Jaesun is the one who killed the emperor. And we know where he's going..."

She felt his rage like the hot blaze of a bonfire, but Rikard met Thainna's eye and nodded. He snapped his fingers at the Sun Court knights.

"You! Gather your brothers," Rikard said. "Not those I dismissed from VEIL, only those loyal to us. Go wake the Lyceum consuls and tell them to convene an emergency session. They must know what's happened. Go to the court generals, too, and tell them to hurry to the Lyceum. The temptation will be great, but they must not put Dormaen under martial law."

"Why not, sir?"

"The people of Dormaen are angry and they are frightened. If we violate their trust now, we will never win it back."

"Hae, legens!" answered several of the knights, and rushed to carry out their orders.

"You three," Rikard said, indicating a Star knight and two of his house guard. "Stay here. Keep these doors closed and sealed until the Lyceum can make their own investigation. Men and ladies of the imperial house, remain inside. News will spread soon enough and the city is restless. Karl and you five, with me. We ride to the tower of the House of Five Dragons. There, we'll find the emperor's assassin and his master."

"Hae, Legens Mazrem!"

Rikard and his remaining knights raced back the way they had come, leaping back into saddles not yet cooled from their last ride.

The dark autumn morning was cold, warmed only when the wind shifted and carried the ashes from Mazrem Square. Rikard swung Thainna up to sit in front of him. She twisted around in the saddle to look back at Rikard.

But Thain... If I take you to the House, the Crest will kill Thain for my betrayal!

Rikard kissed her fiery hair. *I will not let anyone hurt your brother, beloved. We will take Jaesun and the Crest to face justice, and Thain will be free. I swear it.*

Thainna's face and thoughts lit up with joy. She kissed Rikard and then stood in his stirrups and whistled to the other men.

"Ride for the temple district," she told them. "The House of Five Dragons is there. Hae!"

Together, they wheeled their horses and galloped back out into Dormaen.

41

A WORLD OF GLASS

"Nighttime belongs to the wolves. Only the dawn will send them back to their dens."

— LIAM IO

MARUS SLEPT FITFULLY and woke early into a dark, cold morning. The night before had been spent uneasily as everyone in the archouse wondered what morning would bring. Disbandment? Riots? No one knew, though everyone guessed.

And they understood the cause of it all even less. What started the terrible fires? When Marus finally tired of guessing with the other knights and templars and went in search of his bed, smoke and flame plagued his dreams.

Now Marus sat up in his narrow bed, grunting in pain. Every inch of his body protested its abuse and his lungs felt scrubbed raw by coarse ash. There had been other things in his dreams, obscured by smoke, but still recognizable... a great black dragon fighting the strangely empty silence and a little stone bird calling to him.

It was going to be a long day.

Marus went to the washbasin and splashed his face. The water was as cold as fresh icemelt. Strange, he thought, when fire still smoldered in the heart of Dormaen. There were some hours yet until the city would rouse itself.

What then? Just contemplating the coming day was exhausting. Marus wanted to crawl back into bed, but there was too much to do. Even contained, the fires were dangerous. How many more people would lose their homes and fortunes to the flames today? Well, that was in the hands of General Castor and his Sun knights, Marus supposed.

Who would be tasked with investigating the fires' source? No one seemed to be asking about that. Everyone simply assumed that the mistake was Rikard Mazrem's. An innocent one, some claimed. Others remembered Rikard's words in the Lyceum, that intentions mattered. What if the great hero was displeased with the world he found upon his return? If he always planned to burn it to cinders and raise an empire that better fit his vision?

It couldn't have been Rikard. Intentions *did* matter. So did hearts and Marus had never met a man with a purer one than Rikard Mazrem. So what *did* happen? Pretty much everyone in Dormaen witnessed the broken pact and still no one knew for certain. What about the Alterra? Did they know more...?

Marus leaned in close to the mirror and thumbed open his cannula. Carefully, he drew the circle of blood just above his eyes.

Alterra, allies and brothers, can you see this? Can you hear me?

Marus wasn't sure what he expected to see, but he was still disappointed. Nothing happened. No flashes of bright light or mysterious songs. Nothing. Marus sighed at his reflection. If there were answers to be found, surely they were meant for better men than Marus Gallard. Alterrans probably only answered to important men, like Rikard Mazrem and the court generals.

Marus turned away from the mirror. Men like him just followed orders.

He stopped and turned back. Had the blood on Marus' forehead just... moved?

He leaned closer to the polished surface. It had to be a trick of the light. But no, the blood *had* moved! It had drawn together in a sort of lopsided cross shape. Not a star, but the three-toed print like a bird's foot.

What was happening? The blood moved again, slithering across Marus' skin like a tiny crimson snake. He stared, fascinated. It was forming words, backward and difficult to read in the mirror. The writing was wobbly and childish.

Show you.

"Show me? Show me what?" Marus asked. He felt a little silly talking to the empty air. "Who are you? Are you Alterran?"

The blood flowed back on itself, tangled in confusion. Marus suddenly felt even more ridiculous. If the other one was Alterran, it couldn't hear him. He lacked Rikard Mazrem's strange gifts to commune through the veil. Only blood shone through.

Marus searched his room until he found an unused waxboard and sat on the corner of his bed. The sheets still smelled of sweat and ash. Marus thought for a moment, then touched his cannula to the smooth surface and began to write.

Who are you?

A long pause, and then the blood beaded into red gems and rearranged themselves on the wax.

Stumble. Help?

Marus frowned, but not at the strange name written in blood on the waxboard. Anyone who spent any time in their studies at the VEIL archouses – though those were few enough these days – knew that all Alterrans were called such things. But this one was asking for help.

And he said that he wants to show me something, too, Marus remembered.

What do you need? he wrote. *I will do what I can.*

Stumble's childish scrawl answered almost before Marus had finished. *I know who made Terra burn.*

A sudden chill ran up the knight's spine.

Who?

Another lingering pause. Marus' blood moved slowly across the waxboard as though uncertain.

I don't know the name. The Shatter reached into him and he bleeds for them now.

The Shatter? That was the other faction of Alterrans, the ones that Rikard had spent the last thirty years fighting. The Shatter wanted to dissolve Alterra into blank, primeval nothingness and sever all ties to the Terran world. Who would ally themselves with such a terribly destructive force?

Rikard saw him, but did not think much about him, Stumble wrote. *When he made the fires, he was close to Rikard on the high place. He wore red armor and is oak-ice stiff with honor.*

The... high place? Stumble must have meant the stage where Rikard and the other leaders of VEIL led their men in the cleansing ritual. Red armor? Marus read over Stumble's words a second time. General Castor? It didn't seem possible.

Are you certain? Marus wrote with a shaking finger.

Hae, Stumble confirmed. *To take the Uprising, the Shatter wanted Rikard to fall. Who is he?*

The knight stood and the board tumbled from his lap, clattering loudly on the floor. Castor had made a deal with the Shatter to sabotage the cleansing! Everyone knew that the Sun Court general had no love for Rikard Mazrem, but... but this?

"Traitor!" Marus shouted. He picked up the waxboard again. *General Castor of the Sun Court.*

Stop him, Stumble wrote. *Please. He is empty. He makes the Shatter strong. They are killing Flickerdim!*

Marus had no idea who Flickerdim was, but he had no intention of letting Castor harm anyone else, Terran or Alterran.

He snatched his sheathed gladius from a hook in the wall and belted it on around his waist. The weight was a welcome anchor against the hot, whirling feeling in his head.

I'll stop him, he wrote to Stumble.

Now?

Hae.

I go with you, Stumble replied.

Marus wasn't quite sure what that meant, but he was glad for the company, invisible though it might be. He ran out of the arc-house, heading for the stables. Marus would need a fast horse to reach Castor's manor before the general left for the Sun Court.

Gaius stepped down from the chariot and juggled the small, heavy bundle into his other hand so that he could toss the kajjas' reins to a sleepy-eyed boy. After a brief introduction, a pair of guards let Gaius inside and directed him to the room where his mother was staying. The consul's house was nice, but a considerable step down for Laurael Mazrem. Gaius let himself in without knocking.

"Hello, Mother," he said.

Laurael sat in a deeply cushioned chair beside a window overlooking the distant pewter shine of the Mazren River. She looked up at her son with elaborately kohl-lined eyes. Beneath her make-up, she looked tired and drawn. News of the fires must have upset her plans badly. Rikard wasn't as popular as he was supposed to be at the time of his death.

"Good morning, Gaius. How did you know where to find me? I told no one the details," she said. "It seemed safer that way."

"You've spent your life on ambition, Mother," Gaius answered. He closed and locked the door behind him. He didn't want to be disturbed. "You have few actual friends, especially ones willing to protect you now that the rest of Dormaen is so furious with Father. Why did you leave at all?"

"I had no desire to place myself in the crossfire of my husband's assassination. And now I have an alibi that removes me from suspicion. Is it done, then?"

"Hae, Mother. It's done." Gaius tossed the package onto the bed. It was slender, wrapped in a sheet of blank white parchment.

"I should have acted sooner," said Laurael. Her gaze lingered on the locked door. "But the matter is not unmanageable. You will go before the Lyceum today and honor your father's memory. Praise his accomplishments and swear to amend his mistakes. Don't be the first to lay blame on the emperor. Let one of the other consuls do it."

"No, Mother."

She snapped her eyes up to Gaius. "No? You must. If you're the first, you will seem too vengeful. Patience, my son."

"No. I'm not going to accuse anyone," he said. "I'm not doing it at all. Father's not dead. Your assassin failed. And Rikard knows about you. He's on his way to warn the emperor now, to tell him of your treachery."

"What?" His mother rose to her feet, graceful even now. "How? How does he know?"

"I told him."

Laurael's mouth dropped open. "You...?"

"Hae, Mother. Rikard's a good man. A little naïve, but what he's trying to do is more important than your twisted ambitions."

Laurael held out her arms to Gaius. "Everything I have done was for you, Gaius, to give you the life and station you deserve! Your father doesn't even know you. He doesn't love you as I do."

"Enough, Mother!" Gaius said. "I'm not a child. I don't need you to take care of me anymore."

"Gaius..." Laurael implored.

He opened the door and didn't look back at her.

"No," Gaius told her. "It's done. I'm done. I'm done with you and your scheming. You would drown the world in blood just to give it to me."

"Of course I would! I'm your mother. I love you!"

"They will take you before the Lyceum," Gaius said. "Everyone will know what you've done… what *we* tried to do. It will be humiliating. You never wanted that. In your own dark way, you actually wanted what was best for me and for our family. I left something for you on the bed."

Gaius finally let himself look back at Laurael one last time.

"Goodbye, Mother."

Before she could answer him, Gaius closed the door and left his mother alone.

The horses' hooves beat out a rapid staccato through the deserted streets of the temple district, galloping through deep violet shadows that stretched out from the houses of the gods like mourning veils. A layer of ash covered everything and muffled the sound of hooves as Thainna guided the knights through ever-narrowing avenues, forcing them to slow. At the end of an empty, winding road, the crooked tower thrust up into the slowly lightening sky like a broken sword.

Rikard stopped them some distance off from the tower, between the empty husks of two ancient shrines. When his men had dismounted and thrown their reins over the cracked stone, Rikard gathered them in close and spoke in a low voice.

"Thainna's only been inside once, but hers is the only information we have. Jaesun will probably be in the Crest's throne room at the top of the tower, making his report. We will pass through three stairs, four halls and adjoining rooms, one mezzanine and then a doriclinium. Much of the tower is dark and the floor is uneven, so be cautious and watch your footing. We have no exact count of the House agents inside, but expect resistance."

Karl looked nervous and out of place among the knights, but he didn't ask to be released from this strange and dangerous pre-dawn duty. Thainna shared a long look with Rikard.

Do you think they saw us coming? she asked.

I don't know. I sense a watchful violence from within, but that doesn't tell me much. I can feel nothing more exact. Rikard squeezed Thainna's hand briefly in his. *If we are to put an end to this before the Crest can harm Thain, then we must go quickly.*

Hae.

Rikard crept along the wall of the shrine and peered out into the road. He held up three fingers, shook his hand, and then three fingers again. *Thainna, stay close to me.*

At his low whistle, the knights all moved out of the narrow alley and into two lines. Together, they ran in a low crouch. Rikard stopped at the gaping door and motioned the first trio through. Their boots crunched on grit and ash as they charged in. Thainna could see nothing past their armored backs.

"Four inside. Move!" Rikard called.

He tore his sword free and stepped through the door. The knights had fanned out into a shallow arc inside the door, swords pointed outward, but there was no sign of the four men that Rikard had sensed. It was Thainna who saw the black-gloved hand emerge from behind one of the thick wall-hangings, tugging on a barely visible length of wire. But by the time she opened her mouth to shout a warning, it was far too late. With a metallic scrape, shutters grated down over the lanterns and plunged the room into sudden and complete darkness. The knights cried out and drew together as the darkness closed in on them.

Someone flung himself at Rikard. He fell back, pushing the other man to the ground gently in case it was one of his own. But no – Rikard felt thick cloth under his fingers and gloves with bladed fingertips questing for his vulnerable throat. Rikard put his knee into what seemed to be the inside of the man's elbow and thrust his sword between his ribs.

Thainna gripped the hilt of her Nianese sword so tightly that her fingers ached, but she was blind. What if she hit one of the knights? What if she hit Rikard? She heard Karl grunt and then a coach of metal and something heavy hitting the floor.

Rikard kicked another unseen attacker back and thumbed open his cannula, spraying an arc of blood into the inky blackness.

Burn, he commanded, like he had back in the Star Court yard. *Burn bright as a prayer!*

His blood vanished into the dark, splashing into oblivion. But nothing happened. Rikard staggered and almost fell. What? Why wasn't Flickerdim answering his call?

Flickerdim...? But the ancient Alterran was silent.

What's wrong? Thainna asked, full of razor-sharp panic.

Flickerdim isn't answering me at all! Something's terribly wrong.

Thainna felt along the curving wall and closed her eyes. There was nothing to see, anyway, and it helped her to concentrate, to remember. Where were the stairs? There were lamps hanging from the landing, she recalled. A sword clanged against the wall nearby.

No time, no time.

The steps were closer than she remembered and Thainna almost tripped over them, but recovered her balance and sprinted upward. She stumbled when the stairs leveled out and fell to her knees. Someone below screamed.

Rikard!

Find the light. Hurry!

Thainna crawled along the edge of the landing, feeling out the chains of lanterns she only barely remembered. It was agonizing work. With every cry, every crash, she imagined the knights lying dead below. After what seemed like hours, there was something harder and smoother than wood planks beneath her fingertips –

the metal loops, bolted to the landing where the lamps were anchored into place. Thainna yanked on the chain and pulled hand over hand as fast as she could until she felt the lantern at the end. The metal was searing-hot and Thainna shrieked in pain, nearly dropping the lamp.

"Thainna!" Rikard shouted.

Burned. Just a burn. A moment longer...!

Thainna's fingers throbbed and stung. Wincing, she felt along the bulbous lantern until she found the wire. Thainna tugged and the little tin door snapped open. The sudden flare of light was just blinding and then darkness. Thainna threw the lamp back over the edge. It clattered and then dropped to the end of its chain.

The illumination of the single lamp was as thin as starlight, but it was enough. One of the knights was already down, bled to death from a knife jammed under his arm, where his armor could not protect. Rikard caught his first sight of his own opponent, a wiry Suvestri in dark clothes, already bleeding from several deep cuts.

Robbed of their advantage, the Talons died quickly. The last bolted back toward the stairs, but Rikard caught him in a few long strides and yanked him from the steps. The Talon fell past Rikard, down to the tower floor, where two of the Star knights made short work of him.

Thainna hurried back down the stairs. If other House agents appeared from further up the tower, she didn't want to be caught alone on the mezzanine. Rikard stopped her at the bottom of the stairs.

"Are you alright?" he asked.

"Just some burned fingers," Thainna answered.

It hardly seemed fair to dwell on it when one of Rikard's men lay dead. Another limped heavily. Thainna couldn't see the wound under his armor, but Rikard caught his attention.

"Hold this level," he ordered.

"Hae, sir."

The knight's jaw set unhappily. He didn't like being held back, but he could clearly see the wisdom of Rikard's decision. A man with a wounded leg would be of little use in scaling a tower. Rikard went to Karl. The side of the Lyncean's face was covered in blood. Thainna gasped.

"Do you need to stay, too?" Rikard asked. Quietly, so no one else could hear.

"No, sir," Karl stammered. He seemed to finally notice the blood and touched his fingers to his face. Disbelieving, as though it was a mask worn for the first time. "It's his blood, not mine. I... One of them came at me with a knife and... No, sir. I'm fine."

"Move in, then," Rikard said. He raised his voice, making it just loud enough to carry to the knights. "We're going up."

There were other skirmishes, each as hard-won as the first. Karl and the three knights were able fighters, but in this time of peace, they had known little more than practice combats or short, one-sided tussles with soldiers and civilians. Only those Talons and Flames tested and hardened by the worst of Dormaen's underworld were entrusted with positions in the Crest's tower. The short, ugly battles claimed two more of Rikard's knights. One tumbled backward with a crossbow bolt stuck in his throat before they even spotted his attacker. When they did, another Star knight rushed the Talon and they fell together over the tilted railing for the tower stair, still locked in deadly combat. Even Thainna, who did her best to stay well back from the fighting, sported bloody gashes that made her singed fingers seem unimportant.

"Even the rats must have heard us coming now," panted the remaining knight as they reached the dragon-marked door of the Crest's lavish doriclinium. He slapped Karl's shoulder, who trudged wearily up the stairs beside him.

"As long as they're the only things left to chase after us, I don't care," Karl wheezed.

"They're not," Rikard said. "Behind you!"

The knight was laughing at Karl's joke as a shadow rose up from some hidden passage behind them. The Talon wrapped his arm around the knight's neck and drew his blade across the vulnerable flesh. Karl leapt forward with a shout and thrust with his gladius. Blood fountained from the Talon's mouth and he tottered back, pulling himself off Karl's blade and tumbling back down the steps into the darkness. The knight crumpled where he had stood and didn't move.

A cold, heavy weight settled into Rikard's stomach. He looked back at Thainna. Tears streaked her cheeks in silver by the pale light leaking in through the narrow tower windows. Rikard touched her mind gently.

How much further? Are we close?

Hae, Thainna thought with a small nod. *Through here is the doriclinium. If Jaesun and the Crest aren't in there, then they'll be at the top. Just one more stair.*

"Karl, we need to keep moving," Rikard said. "Are you going to be alright?"

The Lyncean guard nodded heavily. He knelt and closed the dead knight's eyes, then turned back to his lord.

"Hae, sir. I'm ready."

Together, Rikard and Karl kicked open the door and stormed through. The naked slaves chained to their beds inside screamed and hid as best they could. Thainna waved her arms and called for silence. Most obeyed, though they continued to whine softly like beaten dogs. That wasn't far from the truth, Rikard supposed. Only her fire kept Thainna from being like these young men and women, the defiant spirit that gave her the will to crawl, beaten and bloody, across Dormaen and back to Rikard.

It wasn't defiance, she told him. *It was you and Thain. I wasn't ready to leave you.*

Fire doesn't burn without fuel, my love. You are stronger than you will ever know.

Rikard and Karl swept through the room, searching for hidden attackers and finding none. But nor was there any sign of Jaesun or the Crest. At the far door, Rikard stopped Karl.

"I don't know what awaits us at the top," he said. "I want you to get these people out of here. Be mindful. They're peaceful enough now, but that may change. Get them to the bottom of the tower. Look for us there. If we're not done within ten minutes, take everyone back to the Star Court."

Karl nodded. "Ten minutes, Lord Mazrem."

Rikard pulled Karl into a short, tight embrace. They clapped each other on the shoulder once and then parted. While Karl went to find a way to unlock or cut the slave's chains, Rikard turned to Thainna.

Just you and me, the way we've begun so many things. Are you ready for this?

Hae.

Rikard and Thainna climbed the dark, steep final stairs to the top of the crooked tower.

At first, Marus cursed himself for forgetting to put on his armor, but before long, he was grateful for the small mercy. He had to move quietly and keep his sword from clanking against tables and walls. Silencing his creaking armor, as well, would have been impossible.

Marus pressed himself into a shadowed niche and waited for a sleepy-looking maid to pass. The basket heaped with freshly laundered towels swayed precariously in her arms. If the girl dropped them and had to stop, she would surely notice the knight hiding just a few feet away.

But the gods continued to smile on Marus. With a yawn, the maid rebalanced her burden and went on her way. Marus slid back out into the hallway and continued his search for General Castor.

He had tried the gate, but the Sun general used his own knights to guard his home, several of whom Marus recognized as men Rikard Mazrem had banished from VEIL. They turned Marus away without even asking his business. After pacing the street for several tense minutes, Marus found a quiet, unguarded section of fence and laboriously climbed over. He prided himself on being a lawful man and hoped that bringing General Castor to justice would outweigh his trespassing.

Inside Castor's large house, it grew increasingly difficult to avoid detection. Empty halls and darkened rooms would only conceal Marus for so long. After another close call and several quick retreats, he found himself pressed against a wall outside the kitchen door. He could just make out the cook – a big man with a face as red as his oven fires – swinging a huge ladle like a club and smacked it smartly across a young page's rear. The boy rubbed at his insulted backside and swore at the cook, who brandished his ladle again.

"Get moving! Lord Castor's waiting," he bellowed at the boy, who made an obscene gesture and took a covered platter from the nearby table.

The page hurried out of the kitchen. Marus jumped back and his sword scraped against the wall. The boy looked up, but was not immediately alarmed. He took in the knight's blue uniform and frowned.

"If you're looking for breakfast, you won't find it here. You're supposed to go to your archouse," he said disapprovingly.

Marus put on his best apologetic face. It was difficult with his heart thudding away like a blacksmith's hammer. "Sorry, no. I'm not looking for food. I have a message for General Castor. I'm afraid I've gotten rather lost. You're on your way to see him, right?"

"Hae. But he's just up. I doubt he wants to deal with business yet."

"It's very important."

That much was true, at least. Marus didn't like lying, so he kept as closely to the truth as he dared.

The page shrugged. "It'll be on your head, sir."

None of the servants paid the slightest mind to Marus as he followed the boy, each assuming he had some legitimate business in the house. They passed through a gallery lined in proud, carved marble faces and then into the hall that ran to General Castor's rooms. A pair of Sun knights stood vigil outside the closed door, armed and armored. If things turned ugly, Marus didn't want the page caught in the middle. He took the boy's arm and yanked him back into the empty gallery.

"Sorry," Marus said. "You know, I don't think General Castor's going to like what I need to tell him. Why don't you give me his breakfast? Why don't I take it in?"

The page looked torn between distrust and a youthful satisfaction at avoiding his chore. After a moment, he nodded.

"Don't eat anything. If Lord Castor complains, I'll make sure that Thestor knows it wasn't my fault."

"Hae, that's fair," said Marus gravely.

The page shoved the platter into Marus' hands and ran off. Not back toward the kitchen, Marus suspected. As soon as the boy had gone, vanished through one of the gallery doors, Marus carefully set the general's breakfast down on the polished floor and pushed it away.

Beams of early dawn light shone in through a series of small, round windows around the top of the room, warming from silver to gold. Marus crouched next to one of the pools of light and tapped the bloodcap against his chin, thinking. The two men at the door would wonder about a Moon knight in the general's house. After a moment's consideration, he thumbed open his cannula and began writing. It had been a few years since Marus last made a blood pact. Besides the one in Mazrem Square... Gods, had it really been only yesterday?

I really hope you're here, Stumble, Marus thought. *And that you read better than you write.*

Carefully, he drew his pact out on the gallery floor and marked two targets. Marus checked over what he had written, and then paused again. What could he offer Stumble in trade that might serve the young Alterran? He was embroiled in a bitter war against an enemy Marus could barely understand, let alone fight. The knight drew a graceful spiral mark, the sign for a memory.

Young Marus standing at the mouth of a dark street. A man lay just yards away, discarded like an empty sack. That's what he was, it seemed to the little boy. Knifed for his small purse and left to bleed out in a back alley. With his blood and money gone, there was only this mute monument left to mark the violence that had claimed his life.

Marus' father pulled him away quickly. It wasn't their concern, he told the boy. As soon as he was old enough, Marus would leave home and join VEIL. He always remembered that moment, the sour copper tang of blood on the air and his solemn oath to himself that he would never turn away again.

Almost before Marus finished the pact, the blood twisted in the gesture of acceptance.

Nine days keep. Go now, said the new glyphs.

Marus felt Stumble's clumsy, youthful presence in his long-treasured memory, holding it in a child's inquisitive, exploratory grasp. Resolve, certainty. Bravery, too. The twilit alley and the dead man faded like a dream, recognizable but half-remembered, like a story he had heard from someone else long, long ago.

Nine days? Well, if Castor kills me, I guess Stumble gets to keep that memory.

If either of them failed, what did that mean for the other? Even with the infusion of Marus' resolute memories, would the young Alterran survive the war that raged even now across the Uprising? What happened if the Alterran died with Marus' memory still clutched in his claws?

But if Marus couldn't arrest Castor, if he never answered to Dormaen for the fires, there would be no undoing the damage he had done to VEIL and Carce's trust in the knights. What then for the Alterra of the Uprising? Death, Marus supposed sadly.

There wasn't time to dwell on their shared doom. Marus had sacrificed the memory. If he had a prayer of capturing Castor, it had to be now, before he went to the Sun Court, filled with thousands of men who would defend their general. Marus held his breath and crept back into the hallway.

What had Marus' memory bought him? Nothing, as far as he could tell. The two red-armored knights stood on either side of the closed door. They leaned against the walls, waiting to escort Castor to their archouse. Marus simply had to trust that Stumble had kept his half of their bargain. Brothers in blood.

Marus picked up Castor's breakfast again. Might as well have some reason to go inside. He held his breath and walked down the hall. It seemed to stretch on forever. Every creak of his boots, every clatter of his gladius in its sheath made his heart skip a beat, but the Sun knights made no move to stop him. When Marus reached the door, one of them nodded absently. The other stared blankly ahead.

They're not curious about me at all. About anything...

Marus turned the handle on the door and stepped through. A handsome gray-haired woman sat in the canopied bed behind Castor. She gasped and pulled the sheets under her arms, though she still wore her sleeping sarong. General Castor looked up from buttoning his saela. He took in Marus' uniform and the sword on his hip.

"You're not here to deliver breakfast." It was not a question.

Marus shook his head and set the covered platter down on a nearby table. "No, sir. I'm here about the fires."

Castor looked at his wife. "Go take your tea in the triclinium, Aera. Take the guards with you."

"Cadmus, what's going on...?" she asked in a frightened voice. "What's wrong?"

"Nothing, just some business. Wait for me in the triclinium."

She looked back and forth between the two men, then fled the bedroom. Marus tensed. What if she raised an alarm? All the more reason for him to move quickly. Castor reached slowly for his gladius, leaning against the wall. Marus' hand flew to the hilt of his own blade.

"Don't do that, sir," he said quickly. "I'm here to arrest you for treason against VEIL and the empire. Please come peacefully to the Lyceum for trial."

Castor's eyes narrowed.

"Treason?" he repeated.

Marus tightened his grasp on his sword.

"I know what you did, the deal you made with the Shatter. You set those fires yesterday to break VEIL's bond with Alterra," he said. "One of them, one of ours, showed me the whole thing. You would throw our world and theirs to the wolves. And for what? A soft job in the emperor's palace?"

Castor snatched up his sword and stared woodenly at Marus.

"Rikard Mazrem would have us swear our lives, our hearts and minds... our very *souls* away to those dream-eaters for his own glory. We owe them nothing!"

"We're bound by our pacts, by the bonds and sacrifices we all volunteered for, general. We gave our word! To Dormaen, to the Alterra. Doesn't that mean anything to you?"

"How *dare* you!"

"What did you swear away to the Shatter, general? Your honor?"

Castor's face went as white as marble. He tore his sword from its scabbard and leapt at Marus.

Thainna stopped Rikard at the top of the old tower. The narrow, slotted windows looked out over temple rooftops too distant to be more than a jumbled mosaic. The winding stairs below were lost in shadows. The entire world seemed far away, as distant and unreal as Alterra.

I don't know what's waiting for us in there, Thainna thought. She stood on the last step, above Rikard and almost eye-to-eye with the tall knight. *Just... if something... I love you. Be careful, hae?*

And you, my love. I couldn't bear losing you now. You have brought a light to my life that I never dreamed. Now we must be swift, if we are to end this and free Thain.

They shared an urgent, lingering kiss that tasted of Thainna's frightened tears. Finally, she stood back. Rikard climbed the final step and kicked open the throne room door. For a moment, he eclipsed Thainna's entire view. His sword flashed red with blood in the light of the single lantern, and then fell from suddenly nerveless fingers. It clattered to the floor in a crash of steel.

Thainna ran through the door toward him.

Rikard! What's wrong? I...

She stumbled to a stop beside Rikard, staring out at the great green Jade Throne. Jaesun lay at the foot of the dais, in a spreading pool of his own blood. Sitting on the throne was a tall, slender figure with shockingly red hair and eyes of the same bright green as the jade. He balanced a bloody dagger in long white fingers, tossing it and catching the lavishly jeweled handle with idle ease.

Thain looked up at his twin and smiled.

"I'm so glad you could join us, sister. You're looking well. I'm sorry, you just missed Pata. Jaesun, too," Thain said. He rose and spread his arms in a gesture of welcome. "And you must be the great Rikard Mazrem. Thainna delivered you right to me."

42

IN THE HOUSE OF FIVE DRAGONS

"Our dragons consume us from within, until all that remains is a burning husk that shines with a warning fire. *Do not come to me, it says. I will burn you away until you are ashes, just like me.*"

— UTORA MAESUS

LAURAEL MAZREM STARED at the door long after her son had gone. After Gaius left her alone.

After all she had done for the boy! A lifetime of maneuvering to give him anything and everything he ever wanted, to put him on the throne of the Carcaen Empire! Gaius was spoiled, that was all. Spoiled and impressionable. It was Rikard's fault, really. If he hadn't returned, her son would have continued listening to Laurael. Gaius never would have questioned her wisdom. Rikard was just a bad influence.

It's his father's fault. Gaius loves me. He'll come back, full of apologies.

She sat next to the window, waiting, until the rising sun turned the billowing, smoky clouds a molten red-gold. Still Gaius did not return.

Laurael went to the bed to examine the package her son had left. Perhaps some symbol of his forgiveness... She peeled back the clean white paper to reveal a simple iron knife. She dropped the blade with a gasp. It clanged loudly on the intricately tiled floor. Laurael stared at the knife. It was short, heavy and pitted with age, but the edge shone brightly, as though it had just been sharpened.

A fist pounding on the door startled Laurael. She heard Bastil's voice outside.

"Lady Mazrem? My lady, knights have come from the imperial palace! The consuls ask to see you at once!"

Knights from the imperial palace... here to arrest her. Laurael imagined Rikard sitting with Emperor Tychon, all of their animosity forgotten as they plotted her fate. She would be disgraced just for trying to give her son the best life that she could.

Laurael picked up the dagger. It was cold and heavy in her hand. There was nothing left for her but shame. They would drag her in chains before the emperor and the Lyceum. Gaius would speak against her. Her own son.

"Lady Mazrem?" Bastil called out. "My lady? Can you hear me?"

She seated herself in front of the window again, cradling the knife in steady fingers. It was Gaius' one gift to her, the only escape from the dishonor that awaited her. Laurael pulled back the sleeves of her tabba. It would not do to dirty them now. When they found Lady Mazrem, she would be regal. Like a queen, mother to an emperor.

It was surprisingly easy. Laurael drew the sharp iron knife along the length of each wrist in a single swift cut. The keen edge sliced easily, almost painlessly, through her skin. Red blood welled up and ran down her arms. Laurael sat back and let her arms rest at her sides. Slow cold crept up from her fingertips. Laurael's blood spread in a vibrant pool. Every drop of bright, colorful warmth leaked away and left her a statue of ice. No, something more enduring than ice... Stone, like one of the great monuments to the heroes of Carce.

Bastil pounded on the closed door. "Lady Mazrem? My lady, please answer! They're saying that the emperor is dead! Please, my lady. The Lyceum begs for your counsel!"

Dead? Castum Tychon was dead? Laurael was too cold to be surprised. There was only a dim, remote sort of regret. So someone had gotten to Tychon first, removed him just as Laurael herself had so carefully planned to do to her husband. The emperor knew nothing damning, or else had taken those secrets to his pyre. No one was here to arrest her, after all.

So it was all for nothing. I've died for nothing.

She could almost appreciate the irony. She had lived for nothing, for political gains dwarfed in an instant by those of her foolish young husband, to buy the throne that Gaius no longer wanted. All for nothing.

Laurael Mazrem closed her eyes and quietly died.

Thainna started toward her brother, but Thain hooked his finger and a ring of men stepped into the lamplight. She stopped and shook her head, trying to banish the sight of Thain before the Jade Throne. He wore a long robe of exquisitely shimmering silk, tied at the waist with a sash of deep red. Thain looked slender and pale, but handsome in his expensive clothes.

He stepped casually over Jaesun's body, closer to his bewildered twin, but still well outside the protective circle of his men. Wiping off the blood on a Talon's offered sleeve, Thain thrust his gilded dagger back into a gold sheath tucked in his belt.

"What... what happened to Jaesun?" Thainna asked.

"You're looking well, sister," Thain said. "It seems Rikard took even better care of you than I thought. And you brought a sword, too. Nianese?"

Thain toed Jaesun's limp body.

"He was useful in his own way, but I couldn't risk him regretting his decision," he told them. "The men of VEIL can have such... unpredictable loyalties, don't you think? Well, now the emperor's dead and I can replace him with one of my choosing."

"You... you killed a Flame?" Thainna gasped. "You can't! The Crest will..."

Thain grinned and raised an eyebrow at his sister.

"Hae?" he said.

"You... you're the Crest? But how? You should be in the fostral. You're sick!"

It sounded ridiculous as soon as Thainna said it, but the whole world had gone mad. Nothing made sense anymore. Was she still asleep? Thainna watched her twin through the cage of imprisoning Talons.

"You weren't the first to think I would become a great leader," Thain said, spreading his pale, delicate hands. "Pata did, too. With a little help. What stories I told him! You should know, dear sister. I told them to you, too. How I would change the House, how I would protect the poor Talons of the Rows, the great things I would do with my power. So Pata bought me the throne. The youngest Crest ever to lead the House of Five Dragons!"

He's lying! Rikard warned Thainna silently. *At least in part. Your father changed the books to make it look like an impressive bid. I see it in his thoughts. Thain killed Aelos... He fears nothing!*

Rikard grabbed for Thainna's arm to pull her back, but the stubborn little Fiori just wriggled away. She wasn't listening to him at all.

"And I did. I changed the House," Thain said. "I turned a rat's nest of cheats and petty thieves into a true power. I infiltrated the Lyceum and VEIL. Even the imperial palace. I killed the emperor in his own bed, surrounded by his own guards! The House of Five Dragons controls all Dormaen, and soon the rest of the empire. I raised this House up from the mud!"

He sat once more on the vast Jade Throne, the monument to his power. Rikard stepped close to Thainna again, and gently put his hands on her shoulders. He frowned at Thain.

"Boasting is the sport of boys," said Rikard. "You've proved only that you are no more than a child, weak and sick, who wished to be strong. You have suffered, Thain, and so you made others suffer more. You toy with those who cannot fight because you cannot face the dragons inside yourself. Your victories are hollow."

Thain shot him an irritated look and Rikard felt a sharper blade of real anger. The Crest shared his twin's fierce spirit. "Hae, the great hero speaks against me. I'm still considering putting you on the throne of Carce, hero. You should speak better to me."

"But what about Pata?" Thainna asked softly, little more than a wounded whisper that made Rikard's heart ache. "Why didn't he tell me?"

"I told him not to," Thain answered simply.

"And you killed him? You killed our father?"

Thainna looked up at Thain through her long red hair. Tears blurred her vision. She and her father had never been close, but... *We never spoke much and now we never will.*

"You let him live in filth while you had all... all this? You beat me," Thainna said. "You lied to me at every turn. Why? Why didn't you tell me that you were the Crest? I would have been your ally, your most loyal Talon. I... You were going to fix the House, Thain! You were supposed to save us from the Crest... but it *was* you! You turned us into murderers and assassins and worse. You tortured and killed us when we resisted. Even when we didn't! I would have done anything for you, Thain!"

Now he did look angry. Thain narrowed his bright green eyes to glowering slits, thin cracks in the ceiling of hell. "For me? Thainna, you did this *to* me!"

She choked and the tears burned in her eyes. "Me? I would never hurt you!"

"Mother was too weak after giving birth to you. You killed her, Thainna. You! I was born from a dead woman! Born sick," Thain said. He held up a slender, bone-white hand and then pointed at Rikard. "Now look at him! A hero by chance, by a single desperate choice. I have fought every day for this! And you whimper and moan about the secrets I have kept, Thainna? Sitting at my bedside and telling me what you will give me. You thought yourself so strong, so brave. A hero, just like the great Rikard Mazrem!"

"At the fostral... That was an act."

"You were never quick, Thainna, but you get there in the end. Sweet, self-righteous little Thainna taking care of her sick brother." Thain lounged back in the deep cushions of the huge Jade Throne. "As you can see, I don't need your charity."

"It wasn't charity!" Thainna cried. Rikard tightened his hand on her shoulders. If she flung herself at the circle of House warriors, they would kill her. "I love you! I believed in you... I was going to buy you the throne!"

"At least you served one useful purpose," he said and smiled coldly at Rikard. "I would have trusted no other with him, my loving and devoted sister."

"You let Thainna starve in the Rows," Rikard snarled. "You hurt her and you made her an orphan!"

"And what do you care, great hero? Thainna betrayed you. She called you a friend and used you on my behalf. She stole from you, did you know? To buy my throne back for me."

"I know," Rikard said. "She told me. I don't care. I love her."

Thain laughed. It was a sharp, ugly sound.

"Love her?" the Crest said. "Why Thainna, you little minx! I never truly counted you for a seductress, but you continue to surprise me. Then perhaps you should thank me, Rikard, for sending her to you."

"You used her, used her love for you!" Rikard said. "I will never be grateful for what you've done."

"Never?" Thain cupped his sharp chin in one hand. "Well then you've just made your own fate. Thainna was right about you, it seems. If you can't be controlled, then you're of no use to me. Gaius will be considerably easier to influence. Congratulations, your son will be emperor of Carce."

"You'll never get near Gaius!" Rikard snarled.

"I already have, hero. Well, we had best get on with it, hae? I have worlds to conquer," Thain said. He gestured to the black-clad Talons. "Kill them."

"Thain, no!" Thainna cried, but her twin brother only smiled a predator's humorless grin and sat back to watch.

Castor charged at Marus, gladius held high. The younger knight jumped back and grabbed for his own sword. He unsheathed the blade barely in time to turn aside Castor's thrust.

"You know nothing of honor," the general growled. "You would follow Rikard Mazrem wherever he leads. You have never chosen your own way!"

Castor swung his sword with more anger than precision, but his furious strength drove Marus back into the wall. Marus lurched to one side, scrambling for distance, but not enough. Castor's blade slid along his leg and opened a long, bloody gash on Marus' thigh.

"Where would *you* have led us, general?" he said with a pained grunt. "How many have died for your pride?"

Castor aimed a short slash at his head, but Marus slipped beneath it. The blade shattered a flower vase instead, spraying both men with water and shards of pottery. Marus recovered his balance and drove forward again. VEIL had certainly gone soft since Njorn Pass. He guessed that it had been a long time since Castor has used his sword, even in practice. It may as well have been a ceremonial object.

But fueled by his self-righteous rage, Castor would have been dangerous wielding no more than a stick.

Marus circled, trying to force Castor back into a corner. He parried aside another swift slice and returned with an angled cut to the general's legs. Castor spun away and slashed his sword in a high arc. Marus flung himself back down just in time to watch the polished steel flicker overhead. The gladius bit into the wooden bedpost and stuck there. Marus slammed one boot hard into the other man's chest and Castor fell, losing his grip on the hilt of his sword.

"General Castor, you are under arrest," Marus panted, standing over the Sun Court general. "Come peacefully and with whatever dignity you have left."

Castor paid no attention, but seemed instead to be busy with something underneath him. Was he going for a dagger to open his wrists? He wouldn't be the first nobleman to choose suicide over the disgrace of a public trial. But if Castor took his own life, then the blame for yesterday's fires would remain squarely on VEIL and Rikard Mazrem. Marus wedged his toe under Castor's shoulder and shoved him onto his back.

Where the general had lain was no dagger, but a sloppy circle of blood, divided by lines and curved glyphs. Marus recognized a call for fire, but there was something wrong with it, in the broken lines at the pact-circle's heart. Castor was calling on the Shatter.

He reached over with his open cannula and added the last dripping line. A sudden flash of heat sizzled against Marus' skin as the bed went up in flames. Twisting arms of fire unfolded from the blaze, lashing out at Marus and encircling him. Castor grabbed his sword from the charring bedpost and turned his back, striding from the burning bedroom.

Marus searched hurriedly, but there was no escape from the constricting circle of fire. Flames surrounded him on every side. He knelt and tried to ignore the roaring flames.

Castor wasn't the only one with allies on the other side of the veil. Sweat ran down the back of Marus' neck.

Focus! He traced his own circle of blood and crossed it in an arrow marked with the symbols for speed. *Escape, I need to escape. And to catch up to Castor.* A triangle with a spiral glyph at the apex.

Marus hesitated. What could he offer Stumble? With the flames cracking like demon whips all around, it was hard to think at all. The air sizzled and his hair singed, raising a thick stench. A blind panic rose inside him, choking out all reason. Suddenly he understood very well how, suddenly in command of a losing army, his men dying around him, howling Fiori charging at them, Rikard could have begged for Alterran help with no thought for the cost.

A drop of hot sweat rolled down Marus' nose and spattered in the blood steaming on the floor. *You're welcome to this heat, Stumble.* Squinting against the smoke he added the wave-mark of sensation. Perhaps the young curiosity could do more with the burning pain all across Marus' skin and in his lungs...

Suddenly the heat of the blaze was gone, as quickly as the sun disappearing behind a cloud. Was it the heat that was gone or was the fire? Marus opened his eyes, curious in spite of himself to see flames without heat, but they were gone. The whole burning room was gone.

Thank the gods for you, Stumble!

Marus found himself in a hallway, still close to the bedroom. He still smelled the strong, acrid reek of smoke. At the end of the hall, where it opened into the gallery, Castor shouted for his servants. He held his blackened sword loosely in one hand.

"General!" Marus shouted. "You're under arrest!"

Castor turned toward the cry, eyes widening, and then dashed into the gallery. Marus swore and leapt after him. He slashed at the general as he closed, but Castor yanked his sword up between them and the fire-heated blades rang against one another, spitting white-hot sparks.

Marus forced Castor back, step by step. The general's back met the curving wall of the gallery and his elbow bumped the carved bust resting in the niche there, setting it rocking. Seizing upon the opportunity, Castor flung the alabaster sculpture at his attacker. Marus had to fall back to duck the flying stone, and then again as the general sprinted along the wall, hurling vases and statues.

When he had won himself some room, Castor turned toward the wall and opened his cannula, calling once again for the Shatter. He drew a faltering circle, but Marus closed on him again and the Sun general could not write and hold his sword in the same hand.

He passed his sword to his left hand just as Marus brought his gladius down once more. The impact shivered the sword in Castor's hand, but the general held fast and the blow fell short. Marus grabbed at his right wrist, spraying droplets of blood into the air from his open cannula.

Marus swung his sword around, battering away an awkward, off-handed defense and cutting deeply into Castor's left arm. The general snarled in fury and juggled his sword back into his uninjured right hand. Marus passed his blade to his left hand in mirror image and thumbed open his own bloodcap. He made a quick examination of Castor's aborted pact, then added his own marks.

Seize Castor. I call upon you, Stumble, my friend!

The Sun Court general lunged. Marus met Castor's blade with his own, stepping inside the arc of steel. The general turned and tried to bring his blade down on Marus' right hand. The younger knight jumped back with a shout of surprise. Blood sprayed from his cannula and streaked the floor in red.

"Without your Alterra, you're just a common soldier," Castor said, panting.

"But we *have* the Alterra." Marus' head hurt and the air was full of thick smoke from the burning bedroom. "They are our brothers, as much as any other knight! You can't just abandon them!"

"Is that what Rikard Mazrem said? And you truly believe it?" Castor asked.

"I do! And I believe that any man willing to ruin another for his own honor never had any in the first place!"

With an inarticulate roar of fury, Castor struck again, strong and sure. Marus brought up his gladius, but the enraged knight was beyond pain, beyond anything but silencing this challenge to his honor. Castor's sword slammed down on Marus' and drove him to his knees on the polished stone floor. The general leveled his sword at the kneeling knight's throat. Marus tried to back away, but Castor had him pinned against the wall.

"You're scattered and unfocused," Castor said. "You wasted your time learning the old forms, the old blood pacts. And what has it bought you?"

Marus felt sticky blood on the back of his neck, dripping down from the pact Castor himself had begun. Marus heaved himself to his feet and battered aside Castor's blade with his left hand.

"Justice," he answered.

With his right, Marus reached out and slashed the final line of blood across the circle, signing away his favorite song to Stumble for the next half year. Marus could no longer remember how it went anymore, but hoped that Stumble was enjoying the haunting melody. Singing it through the embattled Uprising, maybe...

Thick, clumsily-made iron chains rattled up from the floor and encircled Castor. The heavy links snaked around his arms and chest, cinching tight. Castor took a few steps away, overbalanced and fell, chains ringing against the gallery floor. Marus stood over him, sword and cannula held ready.

"For the last time, General Castor," Marus said, "you are under arrest."

Six Talons surrounded Rikard and Thainna, but it would not take six to kill them. The two closest men raised crossbows, drawn taut and loaded with black-fletched bolts.

Get down!

Rikard's command was urgent and Thainna threw herself to the uneven floor. Here at the top of the tower, the slope was more pronounced. The sword slid from her sash and spun away down across the room, vanishing uselessly into the darkness.

Rikard half leapt, half fell toward the leaning bottom of the room, seizing the nearest Talon as he sailed past. The man beside him turned to swing a short sword and suddenly reeled as Rikard unleashed his fury in a single sharp jab of pain. The Talon howled in agony and slapped at his face, trying and failing to reach the buzzing, blinding thing clawing at his mind. Rikard smashed the first man to the ground, yanked the crossbow from his hands and pulled the trigger. The other Talon slumped down to the ground, clutching at the black bolt suddenly quivering in the center of his chest. Neither of them moved again.

The crossbow was useless to Rikard now. He flung it as hard as he could at another huge, dark-clothed Talon charging toward him. Thain's guard slipped aside and the crossbow clattered off across the slanted floor. Rikard grabbed for his fallen sword and kept his back to the wall as the remaining Talons closed in on him.

Thainna pulled herself to her knees and grabbed the weapon in trembling hands. Now what? The crossbow's mechanism seemed simple enough, but she needed to load it.

Rikard fought uphill now, against four opponents who better knew the terrain. He changed his sword to a left-handed grip and thumbed open his cannula, holding the shining gold bloodcap up high. Flickerdim could not answer any pact – the Uprising was locked in terrible combat with the Shatter, fighting a similarly uphill battle – but these men didn't know that. The Talons pulled back as if the knight's blood were deadly venom. Rikard jumped forward, smashing his fist into one man's face and ramming his gladius into the belly of another as they recoiled.

Thainna felt around the bodies on the floor, searching, and darted another quick glance over her shoulder. She would know if Rikard were wounded as soon as he did, but she couldn't stop herself from staring in horror. Her heart pounded and blood rushed in her ears. She tried to calm herself, knowing that Rikard would feel her panic like a knife wound.

Her questing fingers brushed against the stiff bristles of fletching. Thainna grabbed the bolt and yanked back on the crossbow's oiled string, but to no effect. It was too stiff, the wood too hard to move. Thainna found a stirrup at the front of the weapon and slid her foot into it. She clenched the bolt in her teeth, biting marks into the dark wood as she pulled back on the string with both hands. At last, she heard a *click*. When Thainna let go, the bow remained flexed, straining to release its deadly tension.

Rikard now held the painstakingly won high ground against the three remaining Talons. He charged before they could spread out, before the one in the center made room to use his crossbow. When the first Talon brought up his arms to keep Rikard away, he seized the man's wrist with his free hand and held it helplessly in place. Rikard's sword sliced into flesh and he levered the knife away before letting the limp body tumble down the inclined floor. He held the knife and his gladius ready, parrying with one and striking with the other.

The fight surged closer to the Jade Throne in a violent, bloody tide. Thain was no longer sitting regally, presiding over an execution. The Crest shrank back into the velvet cushions. His sharp green eyes darted this way and that, searching for something that could reverse this sudden loss of control and finding nothing.

When the last of his Talons clung to the foot of the Jade Throne, cradling the stump of one arm in white-faced shock, Thain leapt from his throne and ran for the door. Thainna dropped the arrow carefully into the slot on top of the crossbow, felt for the trigger and found it. She swung the crossbow to point at her twin's fleeing back.

"Stop!" Thainna shouted.

Thain stopped one white hand against the frame of the door. He straightened and looked back. "You're my sister. You said you would do anything for me, Thainna. You won't shoot me."

He took a half step forward, through the door.

"Thain! Don't move!" Thainna shouted. Her hands shook and the crossbow rattled in her grip. "You... you killed Pata, Thain! And you would have killed me. You've had your own people tortured and murdered."

"I'm still your brother," Thain said.

He turned so she could see his face more clearly, so much like her own, like looking into a mirror. His tone softened, becoming the small, worried little-boy voice she remembered so well.

"Please don't hurt me, Thainna. Let's go. We'll leave Dormaen. Just... run away."

"Run away?" Thainna asked. Her throat went achingly tight, as if to stop her from uttering the uselessly hopeful words.

"Just you and me, Thainna. I hid money. We'll leave and forget all of this. I... I need you, Thainna... I never meant to hurt you..."

Rikard stopped behind Thainna, standing tall over the twins. *He's lying.*

"I can't..." Her voice cracked as it fought to be heard, but then came out stronger. "Even if you meant it, Thain, I can't run. You betrayed the House, all of Dormaen. You would have let half of the city starve just to secure more power, just to sink your fangs a little deeper. There's a lot of damage to be fixed, a lot of people who are lost and hurt."

"Oh, Thainna," Thain said. The sweet, pleading tone bled away, leaving his voice cold. "Did you forget that you're not really a foster? You can't heal them. You can't help them. You're a thief and a liar. I only feed the dragons. In them. In you."

Thainna nodded. "I know."

But she didn't lower the loaded crossbow as Rikard grabbed her brother's thin arm.

"Everyone has their dragons," Thainna said. "That's true. But some of us fight them. Every day."

Thain's eyes narrowed, but he didn't have strength enough to struggle as Rikard grabbed him. Without his Talons, Thain was little more than a weak, sickly boy. Rikard marched him down the steps of the crooked tower.

Outside, the temple plaza was already full of people as they led the sullen Crest from the bottom of the tower. Word had reached the Lyceum and they sent VEIL reinforcements to cordon off the crooked tower. Rumors were already flying about the assassination of the emperor, about a clash between VEIL and the equally fearsome House of Five Dragons.

Thainna was relieved. Soon Thain would be locked safely away. She would ask Rikard to make sure that he was kept secure in the fostral maybe, as he should have been from the beginning. A place Thain could rest and be well and perhaps even heal... Thainna heard her name and looked up. Someone was waving at her from outside the ring of knights, trying to catch her attention.

"I know him," Thainna said. "That's Caelin. Thain has his wife somewhere. Let him through."

Rikard waved wearily to the guards. They parted to let the gaunt House Talon through. He trotted their direction, his face pale and drawn. Thainna took a step toward Caelin, ready to embrace the old man, to reassure him that everything would be alright, but he brushed past her. Thainna frowned, confused.

"Caelin?" she called, but he ignored her.

Rikard was looking in the opposite direction, toward Karl as the Lyncean shouted something about Marus Gallard and General Castor. Rikard heard Thainna's shout and turned toward Caelin, but too late.

Caelin grabbed Thain and the young Crest's proud, angry face went suddenly slack. Rikard tore the boy away, shouting for help. A pair of Moon Court knights tackled Caelin and the bloodied knife fell from his hand, clattering into the road.

Thainna ran to her brother's side as Rikard lowered him to the ground. Thain's hands were folded over his belly and his fingers were already red with blood.

"I'm sorry," Rikard was saying. "I'm sorry... I didn't reach him in time, I..."

Thainna pulled Thain to her chest and brushed his matching red hair back from his face. His fading green eyes fixed on hers and he opened his mouth. He tried to speak, but blood just poured from between his pale lips, choking away his last breath and then his eyes went blank. Empty.

Thainna held Thain and cried for him to come back to her.

43

DESTINY

"For every dragon, there stands a knight ready to face him."

— THAINNA MAZREM

"WE COULD REBUILD IT," Thainna suggested.

They stood together in the charred remains of Mazrem Square, regarding the tumbled statue. Rikard looked down at his own face, broken and shattered and twisted by fire. The rest of Mazrem Square had fared no better. Blackened ruins lay everywhere, charred beyond recognition. Even months after the Day of Bells, the smell of smoke remained. The inferno's intense heat had cracked the once-white stones down to their foundation.

But even here, life was returning to Dormaen. Bright green blades of early spring grass thrust up between the broken masonry, reaching for the sun. A thick, soft moss spread along the steps of the amphitheater where deep pools of water remained, left over and forgotten after the Sun Court battled the fires. Children chased each other around the edge of the pond, laughing and splashing one another. Offended by the noisy intrusion, a black-masked swan honked indignantly and took wing, flying off to find some more peaceful swimming spot.

Rikard kicked the fragment of statue away. "No one needs more monuments to me. Too many people lost their lives here to Castor's ambition. This place should belong to them."

"Hae," Thainna agreed after a moment's thought. "The Lyceum's going to fight you, you know. They won't want to spend the money."

"We'll convince them. It won't be hard. They lost friends and family, too."

Thainna smiled. "I think I can get Liam to side with us, at least. He'll be eager to remind everyone what he lost and be painted the hero for it."

"You're becoming quite the politician, beloved," Rikard said.

"Someone has to. You're too honorable by half." She took his hands in hers and kissed him. *Don't you ever stop.*

They walked on in silence, listening to the sounds of the city. Dormaen was rebuilding. Slowly at first, but with increasing fervor as the new emperor invested more and more money. With the help of the VEIL knights, the work progressed quickly. Rikard pointed to a new library, an angular thrust of carved granite and slate in a wooden cocoon of scaffolding.

That one will be the tallest building in Dormaen. Or so the architects tell me. They'll use blood pacts to raise the stones to the top.

What do the knights think of that? Thainna wondered.

They're eager to volunteer. They all want their chance to shape the new worlds, Terran and Alterran alike.

Thainna took Rikard's hand and squeezed it gently. "You did it. You brought the worlds back together. The Uprising grows stronger every day."

"There are still plenty of people who are afraid. Afraid of VEIL and of the Alterra. Of me."

"Give them time. Your new world is still young."

"*Your* world," he reminded her.

Thainna turned away, biting her lip and Rikard pulled her into his arms. Her green eyes sparkled, the same color as the grass beneath their feet. Thainna clung to Rikard so fiercely that she almost toppled them both down onto the rough stone floor of the plaza. Thainna had every intention of kissing him again. Perhaps more, with no regard for who might be – and was – watching.

Rikard felt a blushing presence nearby and, with an effort, tore his attention from Thainna. The pair turned to see who had interrupted them. Marus Gallard limped across the plaza and bowed deeply.

"I'm sorry to interrupt, Emperor Mazrem," he said. "But you said that you wanted to know when the Lyceum made their decision."

"Hae, I did. It's been a long trial. Laurael would have faced the same disgrace, but Gaius spared her that. History may even forget her... mistakes." Rikard took a deep breath and lifted his chin. "And what does the Lyceum say for Castor?"

"They have declared General Castor guilty, sir."

"And their sentence?"

"Castor is a traitor to Carce and to the Alterra, my lord. He will be executed tomorrow morning," Marus told them, then glanced sidelong at Rikard. "Unless Your Imperial Majesty sees fit to grant him a reprieve. I doubt he could do very much damage out in Fiore or Jumaar."

"Too many have died already," Thainna agreed softly.

"Hae," Rikard agreed, but sighed and gazed out over the burned ruins. He shook his head at Thainna and Marus. "Castor is still a great danger. He has allies among the Shatter, and they are still strong. There is no place in Terra that he cannot reach them. You know as well as I how little distance means to Alterrans, Marus."

"But you would know, wouldn't you? The Alterra, Stumble and the rest... They would tell you if Castor started trouble again."

"I won't be here forever," Rikard told him.

"Hae, Your Majesty."

Marus saluted and turned to leave, but Rikard put a hand on the man's shoulder. "Don't go yet."

"What can I do for you, my emperor?"

"Emperor only for the moment. I'll be passing the crown on soon enough. Everything is changing, Marus. Especially VEIL. I want to dissolve the courts. We're fewer than ever now and there's no purpose in segregating our brotherhood. I need a man to lead VEIL and I'd like it to be you."

The knight's eyes widened. "But, Imperial Majesty, what about General Darius? General Hern?"

"Saul never wanted power, and by his own admission, he's not suited to leadership. My old friend will be happy to retire, I think. And General Hern... Nikas is a survivor. He'll manage. VEIL needs a man like you, Marus. Will you make this one last sacrifice for your brothers? Will you be their legens?"

"Hae, sir," answered Marus in a voice thick with emotion.

Thainna smiled at the men and turned, hooking her finger toward the guards that followed their new emperor almost everywhere. At their head stood the young Lyncean, Karl. It was unusual for anyone but a VEIL knight to protect the emperor, but Rikard had made an exception. Thainna gestured Karl forward.

"Karl, you've lied to me," she said with an impish smile.

"My lady? I don't think..." the young guard stammered.

"Be kind, Thainna," Rikard said. "You told her once that you didn't join VEIL because you were too frightened, that you couldn't make the sacrifices demanded by knighthood. You were wrong, my friend. You've proved yourself brave and strong. If you would reconsider, VEIL would be honored to have you."

"With all my heart, hae," Karl replied. "Thank you!"

Rikard looked at Marus. "Legens Gallard, you need a squire, don't you?"

"Hae, Majesty."

Liam stood, brandishing a white square of parchment that bore the lion and laurel imperial seal.

"Emperor Mazrem, this is highly irregular," the consul protested. "Tychon never convened the Lyceum so many times in a single week."

"Emperor Tychon had an empire to build, not to mend," said Rikard. "I know I'm asking much of you, consuls, but we have much to do and little time left to do it."

He stood on the tall marble dais in the center of the circular Lyceum. Days of scrubbing still hadn't entirely managed to remove the last traces of ash and blood, ground into the very pores of the stone on the Day of Bells, when it had served as a fostral. A little wear suited the otherwise starkly white chamber, Thainna thought.

"So you keep saying, Your Imperial Majesty. Why is that? The enemies of Carce lie dead," Liam said. He seemed to sense that his words were too harsh and softened them. "You and those closest to you have won great victories, Emperor Mazrem. Isn't it time for some rest?"

"Flickerdim and the leaders of the Uprising sent me back here for a purpose. I was tasked to bring the people of Terra back to them, to renew the bonds that strengthened our worlds," Rikard reminded them. He looked down at Thainna, who sat in an only slightly smaller gilded seat beside his own. "I swore my life to the Alterra in Njorn Pass. Nothing has changed that. Soon, I must return to the Uprising. Their war with the Shatter is not over yet."

A murmur rippled through the Lyceum, a whisper like a breeze waving dry grass. Some of them remembered the details of Rikard's deal with the Alterra, but many more had forgotten in the bustle of past months. Several jumped to their feet and shouted their protest.

"We made you our emperor!" one of Fiori consuls yelled. "How can you leave us now?"

"I will leave you in capable hands," Rikard said. "Thainna and Gaius will lead you well in my absence. I trust no others more. And I will not leave the most important tasks undone. You called for me to take Tychon's throne, though I never wanted it. Whatever Carce asks, I have always tried to give."

Rikard nodded to Liam and the summons the Nianese consul still held clenched in his hand.

"It is to that end that I have asked you all here today. Emperor Tychon built a great empire. I and thousands of others marched in his name to conquer Fiore. Out of fear and desire for the power that VEIL represented, Tychon won his empire. Fifty nations of the world united under the Carcaen banner. But fear and conquest are no beginning for an empire! While I... admire what Tychon accomplished, I will never admire how he did it."

Every consul fell silent and sat forward, sensing that Rikard was warming to his point. The Lyceum was breathless with anticipation. Rikard reached to Thainna for support.

She smiled up at him and nodded. *Hae, this is right.*

"I invite any province of Carce to leave this empire," Rikard announced. "All trade will be sustained and all sovereign rights will be respected. Fear cannot hold us bound. If we are to go forth together, let it be in peace and mutual prosperity. I do not ask for your answers now. Go to your homes. Speak to your governors and kings. Return in confidence of your nation's destiny as a province of Carce or as a trusted neighbor."

The Lyceum erupted into applause. One by one, and then in groups, the consuls rose to their feet and shouted Rikard's name.

When the thundering applause had faded, a knight in black armor came into the room and nodded at Narissa.

"The emperor's ready for you," he told her.

To her surprise, he unlocked the chains around her wrists and ankles. Narissa rubbed her chaffed skin. The knight gave her a long, studied look. He wasn't afraid that the Eye would run. What would be the point? There was nowhere she could go that Rikard Mazrem couldn't find her.

Trailed closely by the knight and following his instructions, Narissa passed through a door, a short hallway and then out into the Lyceum chamber. Row after row of consuls regarded her. How many of these men had the House of Five Dragons once owned? Now they stood in judgment over her.

Narissa held her head high as she strode to the center of the chamber and curtsied deeply. Emperor Mazrem sat on his throne, his fingers steepled before his stern, handsome face. Rather than the elaborate tabba of his imperial station, he still wore only a functional knight's black saela.

Narissa spared only a glance for the new emperor. Instead, she watched the traitor. Thainna Vahn was seated on her own throne, studying Narissa just as closely. The young Talon – if such titles even applied anymore – was as proud and regal as any queen. Her burnished copper hair lay in neatly combed waves over her white shoulders and pale green gown.

"I lived my whole life in the Rows and in the service of the House of Five Dragons," Thainna said in a voice that rang through the whole Lyceum. "I know the people who make up its ranks. Some of them are good men and women who have never known another life, but many more chose their crimes. Thain's death has brought an end to the worst chapter of the House's history, but we're not foolish enough to think that the House of Five Dragons is gone."

"The enemy we know is better than the one who is a mystery," Emperor Mazrem continued, smoothly picking up where Thainna left off. "There will always be corruption in Carce, but we can keep it in sight and in mind. Narissa, you will be Crest of the House of

Five Dragons. Your House is extensive, the largest criminal syndicate in the history of Carce."

"Control the streets. I know you can, Narissa," Thainna said. She sounded almost respectful. "Keep the shadows of Dormaen from their worst crimes. If they cross the line, we will come to you for answers."

"And if these crimes are committed by others?" Narissa asked.

"We will come to you," the emperor repeated. His expression was stern, as hard as stone.

"Control the brothels, the dram sales. You'll corner the market, Narissa, and you won't have to worry about VEIL," Thainna told her, then smiled a sad little smile. "You'll be taxed, of course. The rest will be up to you to monitor and you will report to me. Should any of the greater crimes be committed, VEIL will be brought in. Against you or to aid you – the choice is yours."

Behind the throne dais, a dozen knights loomed menacingly. Emperor Mazrem stood and strode forward. He narrowed his dark eyes at Narissa and she found herself shrinking back.

"You understand, hae?" he asked. Narissa swallowed hard and nodded. Rikard peered at her. "I feel no deception from you, mana. No more than one might expect, at any rate. Understand that I do not like this arrangement. This is Thainna's idea and I trust her when she says that this is necessary. Do not betray her faith."

"Hae, Majesty," Narissa stammered.

Rikard nodded once and then gestured to the knight standing behind her. He took Narissa by the elbow and guided her from the room. She looked back once. The emperor watched her intently. His eyes seemed to bore into her, to burn with a dark, sacred flame. Thainna stood beside him, bright as fire. They each had their own weaknesses... but together, they stood strong.

Marus wanted to make it a public affair, or at least invite all of VEIL to attend.

"They'll never forgive you if you just vanish again," he had argued. But Rikard was firm in his resolve.

He made his farewells in a small, private garden of the imperial palace. Saul, Marus and Karl offered firm handshakes and barely concealed tears. Then, sensing that Rikard had more private moments to share with his son and with his young lover, they quickly departed.

Gaius leaned against the trunk of a maple tree, shaded under the spreading green leaves. He waved as the other knights left and then went back to picking his nails with the point of his dagger.

Rikard took Thainna's hands. They trembled. Or was it him? It didn't matter. Thainna's eyes were bright with tears.

I love you, she thought. *Gods, Rikard, I thought I could do this, but I can't. Please! Let me go with you!*

Rikard held Thainna close. His own tears burned in his eyes and down his cheeks. They dripped from his chin into her hair and sparkled like diamonds in the sun.

I love you, too, my fierce Thainna. But you can't come with me. The Alterra of the Uprising are still so few. They can only bring one through the veil. Perhaps, in time... when they're stronger.

How long? How long until I can see you again?

I don't know, Rikard admitted. *I have another thirty years left to serve in Alterra...*

Thainna wiped her eyes with the back of her hand and looked up at Rikard. She pulled him down into a passionate kiss, tangling her fingers in his hair and ruining his neat tail.

I will think of you every day and visit the shrine every night. You'll see my blood, hae?

Hae, Rikard told her. His heart was breaking inside him. *Always, my love. Thainna, you saved me. I love you. My light, my fire... Always and forever.*

Their thoughts were no longer words, but a mingling of pain and love and sorrow, so bitter and so sweet. Thainna kissed his lips tenderly, his cheeks, his closed eyes and brow. They held each other in the slanting beams of golden sun. All too soon, Rikard wrenched himself from Thainna's arms and went to Gaius. His son looked up with a small smirk.

"So she *is* going to let go of you after all," Gaius said. He slipped the dagger back into his belt.

"We will both do what we must," Rikard answered, so choked by emotion that he could barely speak.

"I suppose this is our farewell, Father."

"Hae."

Gaius embraced his father shortly. Rikard shared one final kiss with Thainna and went to an open patch of flagstones, opening his cannula. Blood glittered at the golden tip of his finger, beautiful and frightening. Slowly, carefully, he drew the circle of red and slashed it with Flickerdim's name. *I'm coming, old friend.*

Rikard stood and inspected his work, then turned to Gaius and Thainna.

"I love you both," he told them. "Be good to one another and to Carce."

"Oh, you're not going to Alterra," Gaius said. He held out his hand to Rikard. "I am."

"What?" Thainna gasped. Rikard stared, dumbstruck.

"You didn't know? Hae, things have been busy and I guess it just slipped my mind," Gaius told them, grinning. He was enjoying their astonishment. "Flickerdim and I worked it out about a month ago. I'm going to finish your time in Alterra."

"You can't!" Rikard cried, finally finding his voice. "You can't go! You're going to be emperor! You and Thainna are supposed to stay here... Safe and happy."

"Emperor?" Gaius asked, still smiling. "Emperor of what? You've invited all of the provinces to leave the empire, you fool."

"None of them have chosen to leave..." Rikard answered, dazed. "You can't go, Gaius! Alterra is still at war!"

Gaius' smile faded and he put his hand on Rikard's shoulder. "You've fought enough for two lifetimes, Father. Stay here in Terra. Marry your pretty little Fiori. I'm going to go make my own destiny, for once. Stay here with yours."

Rikard let Gaius pull him from the ring of blood. Gaius stepped carefully into the circle and opened his own cannula to make the final mark on the summoning pact, changing his father's name into his own. When Gaius was done, the blood at his feet began to glow with ruby radiance that grew brighter with each passing moment.

"Look for me in thirty more years. Sixty years in all, a good lifetime for any man. Any more than that is just greedy," Gaius said from inside the circle.

If he squinted through the glow, Rikard could see his son's grin.

"Be a little greedy, Father," Gaius said. "I want to see you again. Take care of him, Thainna."

The light flared into blinding brilliance. Rikard and Thainna closed their eyes and clung to one another. When they could see again, Gaius was gone. Rikard fell to his knees on the stone where his son had been.

My son...

There was pain in the thought, but there was more joy. Thainna put her arms around Rikard and they stood together in the garden until the last sunlight faded from the sky.

EPILOGUE
ALL ROADS

"All stories must have an end, but that is only literary artifice. In truth, the worlds turn ever onward, unto a new dawn and a new chapter in the endless tale."

—AFTER NJORN PASS, BY ALEXANDER FERRO

Ssssh.

Sssssh.

Sssssh.

The long summer turned the grass into blades of gold. The warm breeze tickled Gaius' cheek. He trailed his fingers through the tall yellow grass as he walked. It was soft against his hand.

Gaius grinned. How long since he had used his fingers to feel? Even after thirty years, Stumble still didn't understand, but the little curiosity never tired of asking.

Sssssh.

Sssssh.

Clank.

The road. Gaius took a moment to remember how to use his neck – strange half-stiff, half-wobbly thing that it was – and inspected the road. It was in good repair, the interlocking stones varied in color and texture by frequent replacement. Gaius trailed his fingers over them, so very different from the soft-saw sense of the grass.

Amazing! Did I truly not notice such things before?

Terrans were a marvel. Gaius was so engrossed with his investigation of the road and his own reclaimed senses that he failed to notice the cart until its driver had pulled to a stop a few yards away. A sun-browned Carcaen man turned on the plank seat and waved.

"Hae there, sir knight!" the driver called out. "What blood-business brings you so far from the city?"

"Just wrapping up some family affairs," Gaius answered. "Can you drive me into Dormaen?"

"Hop on in," the man said, patting the seat beside him. As Gaius climbed in, he held up the switch he had been using on the wagon's donkey. "You're probably in a rush, hae? Always worlds of work for you in VEIL."

"No hurry," Gaius chuckled. "Drive slow and tell me about the last thirty years."

The leaves of the tree-tower rippled in a breeze that smelled of poetry. No two were alike. They shone in every Terran color and still bore the names of childhood. Every texture: velvety and varied, hard and soft, bottle and bloom. They shifted through every shape, some natural but many more found only in dreams. The auroral walls of Mask rose high once more, rivaling even the great white spire of the Uprising. The long war had left its scars all across Alterra, but even those were fading as the Terrans dreamed of their new world.

A green-striped malachite nightingale sang beside the drowsy, drooping shape of the great black serpent.

He's home now, Stumble glowed contentedly. *Is he pleased with the world?*

Flickerdim sunned himself on the broad, flat branch. His blind white eyes shone like crescent moons in the swirling black night of his scales. He tasted the air with a long tongue. *It's not the one he knew. I think he will love this one better.*

This is the world he will rule, Rikard thought. Even through the veil, his love shone like starfire all through the Uprising. *My son has come home!*

Home.

For more books by
Erica Lindquist & Aron Christensen,
visit us at LLStories.com